I0760818

THE CRIMSON MOUSE

To whomever inherits this map. Do take care, and may kind Father and he Goddess Megami Ua guide and protect you.

Leaf

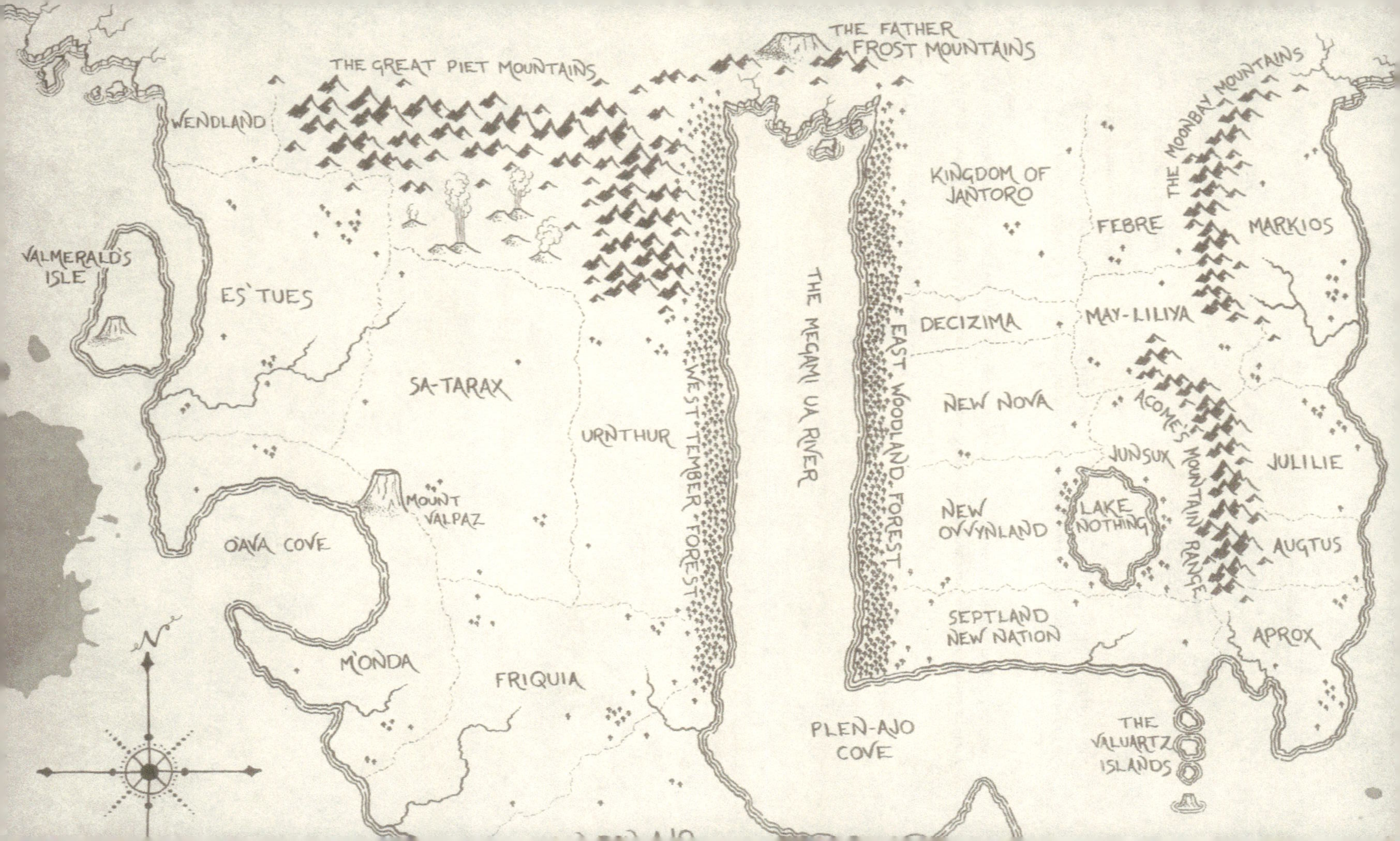

THE GREAT PIET MOUNTAINS
THE FATHER FROST MOUNTAINS
WENDLAND
VALMERALD'S ISLE
ES'TUES
SA-TARAX
URNTHUR
WEST TEMBER FOREST
THE MEGAMI UA RIVER
EAST WOODLAND FOREST
KINGDOM OF JANTORO
FEBRE
THE MOONBAY MOUNTAINS
MARKIOS
DECIZIMA
MAY-LILIYA
NEW NOVA
ACOME'S MOUNTAIN RANGE
JUNSUX
JULILIE
NEW OVVYNLAND
LAKE NOTHING
AUGTUS
SEPTLAND NEW NATION
APROX
MOUNT VALPAZ
OAVA COVE
M'ONDA
FRIQUIA
PLEN-AJO COVE
THE VALUARTZ ISLANDS
N

This book is a work of fiction. Names, characters, businesses, organizations, places, events, and incidents either are the product of the author's imagination or are used fictitiously. Any resemblance to actual persons, living or dead, events, or locales is entirely coincidental.

Cover Design by Mulan Jiang

ISBN: 978-1-962866-02-6

First Edition - 2024

10 9 8 7 6 5 4 3 2 1

Contents

This book is dedicated to every beta reader, every editor, and every friend who let me gush over my book with them. Without your support Mia and her story wouldn't be here.

Prologue

The sewer pipes rattled under the weight of dozens of tiny paws, filling the darkness with *click, click, click* sounds. The noise echoed off the damp walls as rats and mice swarmed the tunnels, gathering like flies to a corpse. With crumbs of bread in their mouths, they flooded into the deep stone pit, spiraling downward, joining their brethren who sat with their paws raised high. Thousands of squeaks filled the dank air as wet bodies crawled over one another to reach the golden cage.

Gears turned above them at the pit's mouth, causing the animals to scatter, but only for a moment. More rodents appeared from cracks and vents. They squeaked and hissed as boots splashed through puddles and voices echoed through the tunnel above. Light followed. It pierced the darkness like a jagged tooth, and the sewer dwellers scattered once more, but even this did not stop the mass.

The rats tilted their heads, some sniffing the air, and soon, the momentum picked up again in a chorus of squeaks that could be mistaken for an eerie song. They dropped their crumbs around the great cage at the feet of a most gruesome monster. All over their body were wounds that never healed, that oozed blood and pus into their matted fur, from shackles that cut down to the bone. Spit and bile drained from their muzzled mouth, dripping from their rotting teeth as they slowly lifted their head at the offering.

The rats surged, storming the cage in a rabid fever, squeaking and crawling over each other as the beast lowered their head, letting it fall back into their pool of sick. The mass of rats and mice then descended on the beast, passing through the bars and biting and nipping at mats and clumps of hardened dirt. They gnawed at the beast's face, chewing and clearing away crust.

The beast hummed, their throaty moans vibrating through the chamber. As more and more rats packed in with offerings in their mouths, eager to cure the beast's suffering. The beast opened one of their watery, pus-filled, milky-white eyes and groaned.

"If there ever was a way, I'd stand for you as you have stood for me."

The tunnel hummed as a great blue light appeared from above and stretched down like a vine. The twisted tendrils of light wormed toward the beast, and the rodents hissed and threw themselves hopelessly at the beams, biting into the hot, radiant energy until their bodies overheated and exploded. The tendrils bore into the beast's body like hookworms piercing tender flesh. The beast cried out as they felt the tendrils feed and take away their life energy. Burns appeared on its back where the tendrils latched, and the beast exhaled as it gave into its hopeless state.

The rats stormed the cage, attacking it with their teeth until they bled, biting at the shackles and attacking the tendrils that fed off the creature's body. Their cries echoed into the night as the great machinery above shot out steam and clicked and churned away. The beast, closing their eyes once more, accepting their fate.

1

Mia

Mia raced through the cobbled, litter-filled backstreets, breath even, arms and legs acting as one. Faces zipped by without a care as two, more than likely drunk, men chased her down the sidewalk. Steam ran up from the sewer holes, and Mia cut through them like a blade. It was a little too early for the creeps to be out, but it was New Year's Eve, and the city was packed with all sorts of people. Mia stole a look back, scanning the men's biceps for armbands. *Good.* At least these guys weren't runners from one of the city's many gangs.

One of the men sprinted forward, arm out and grabbing for her. Mia eyed him from her peripheral, smirked, and took a sharp turn down an alley she knew. She raced past crates of empty glass jugs and bundles of paper. And to think all this fuss because she refused to give them some play when they overheard that she worked at a brothel. Men this bold deserved a lot more than a kick to the balls. Both men stumbled behind her, and Mia chuckled, resisting the urge to taunt them. She thought she was nearly clear when she heard them curse and grunt behind her. Looks like they wanted to do this the hard way.

Up ahead, she spotted a row of trash cans right before a tall wooden lattice-style fence, providing the perfect staircase for her great escape. The men hooted and hollered behind her as she sped up and leapt onto the gray metal can. Her strong legs from years of dancing and sex work carried her with ease as she cleared the obstacle and landed perfectly on the other side. The men raced to the fence, and their fingers wiggled through the holes.

"Come on, give us a little play, baby," the drunk man slurred.

"Sorry, boys. Even if you were paying clients, I wouldn't touch you with a six-foot metal rod," Mia teased, then stuck out her tongue.

The men groaned behind her as they beat on the fence. It was annoying to have to deal with rowdy men, but that was just how life was in the city of Laurasia. She pulled her coat closer to her and buttoned it up as she carried her shopping bag. This was her last errand, she hoped, because nearly all the shops would be closing early for the holiday. This alley led to a dead end, which was a bummer, but that didn't mean it was a dead end for her. She came to the brick wall and stopped; this wouldn't be the first wall she scaled.

She tied her shopping bag around the strap of her purse and then took a few steps back, calculating how much height she would need to clear it. The ledge was about eleven or so feet up but hardly a problem. She smirked and raced at it, then did a zigzag and used one foot to push herself up, bouncing from leg to leg until her hand caught the ledge. Her fingers were like a vice, and she pulled herself up as she swung her other hand over the wall to get to the other side of the alley.

"Nice," Mia said as she hopped onto some wooden crates below.

Mia headed toward the road past large, grimy, dark gray trashcans and boxes. Clotheslines and rusted fire escapes made the alley look like a clotted artery, and it wasn't much better in the street. She stepped out onto the sidewalk. The traffic was heavy and the air dense with gray smoke booming from steam-powered cars and buggies. Mia looked up and admired a few gas models, likely from visitors from outside the city. Gas was all the rage, according to her clients. It didn't matter much to Mia; she couldn't drive, but she loved to ride.

Cars honked, and people shouted. It was much busier over here where the bars and food stands were, and it was only going to get more packed. Even with the pull of the crowd, she did notice a small airship fly overhead. Now that was a vehicle she could pass on. One day, she would love to see one up close, but that was just wishful thinking, like buying an Ao Almasi stone. Only those with money could do that. Not that it was hard to get around the city; Laurasia wasn't many things, but it was walkable.

Rats hugged the walls of shops, sneaking into alleys or down sewer drains, and Mia kept on walking unbothered by any of it. She wished she could take her time today, but she couldn't dilly-dally, with all the work that needed to be done at the brothel. Tonight was their biggest night of the year, and there was still so much to do. Street kids ran by, weaving through people as sidewalk vendors selling food and firecrackers shouted into the cold air. Thick steam fogged up the streets from Sewer Town, bringing with it the hot smell of sewage and garbage. Folks played dice and checkers on wooden crates as they laughed and drank themselves into the new year.

Mia took all of this in under the never-changing gray skies. She would for sure take her time to enjoy this after the holiday was done. Mia stretched as she came to the brothel with its dark red brick and the words 'Valkyrie House' in dim neon letters on the front. Lady Valkyrie was the madam, and she was not to be toyed with. Mia liked working for her, even if she expected a lot from the girls, but the madam also went out of her way to make sure everyone was looked after. Lady Valkyrie even had her own band of runners just in case anyone got too handsy with the girls. And even without the runners, Lady Valkyrie made sure that no one ventured out without a few tips and tricks, which meant years of intense morning parkour training. This was one of the first things she taught all the girls. The madam would be damned if one of her girls found themselves in a situation they couldn't get out of, and for the punks who they couldn't outrun, Mia was happy to introduce them to her stun gun. A new weapon powered by the very electricity that made her city run, which was way better than candlelight, in Mia's opinion.

Mia pushed open the door on the side alley and walked through the back storage area out into the halls that were filled with girls running back and forth.

"Mia!" a voice called to her. Mia turned and saw Tae'a running towards her. "Is that the extra lace?"

"As requested." Mia held up the bag as Tae'a beamed. "I picked up six extra spools."

"Oh my gosh, Mia, you're a life saver!" Tae'a bounced around. She towered over most girls at six foot one, but no one complained because she could reach just about anything and was always welcome to trade her dishwashing duties for dusting.

Mia smiled as Tae'a rushed off with the lace. It was still so early, and Mia wished she could crawl back into bed, but she knew she would regret it if the hostess found out she wasn't pulling her weight. So, Mia hurried to her room to change into more comfortable clothes.

"Okay, Mia, let's get to work." Mia pulled off her jacket and tossed it on her chair, then walked over to the dresser when she heard a thump. She jumped and looked at the wall, and it thumped again. She rolled her eyes.

"Billie, damnit! It's too early for your nonsense," she yelled, and the noise stopped.

It was nine-thirty in the morning. Did that girl ever take a break? Mia shook her head as she changed into a more comfortable pair of pants. There was still so much cleaning and decorating to do, she wondered if she would be able to get everything done in time. She stepped into some flats and checked her reflection in her mirror next to the window. The window didn't have much of a view since buildings were stacked on top of each other on this side of town, and they were mostly bars and smoke shops. On the ground, filth lined the streets, and above, the same gray skies she'd always seen. Some of her clients would ask how she could stand it, but Mia was used to it and found the glow from the many neon signs and the thud of live music radiating from the bars comforting.

A knock on her door pulled Mia from her gazing, and the door opened.

"Billie," Mia said to her best friend.

"Sorry about the noise." Billie smiled sheepishly.

"It's okay," Mia said as she walked out of her room and started down the narrow hall. "So where to today? What's left?"

"Let's see." Billie counted on her fingers. "I have some rooms to vacuum, and I think the lobby needs a sweep. Oh and the wine!"

"I thought Tae'a picked up the wine?"

"That's right."

Mia paused at the door. "I need to stock the rooms. I picked up some lubes and condoms yesterday when I went to pick up potions. Can't work without birth control."

"Shit, hold on—I'm not done my costume!"

"I thought you said you finished it last week?"

"It slipped my mind," Billie said with a sheepish grin.

"Billie," Mia scolded when she heard loud footsteps behind her. Mia turned and saw Terese steaming towards them.

"About time you lazy bums got up." Terese folded her arms, a snarl painted on her face. "Do you have any idea how much work needs to be done?"

Billie rolled her eyes. "Chill out, Terese. This holiday comes and goes without a problem every year."

Terese dismissed her with her hand. "Of course, you wouldn't care. You think shit just falls out of the sky right into place, but I actually want to get paid. Here's the list of the last-minute pickups."

"Pickups?" Billie snatched the list from her hand. "This is bullshit. I ain't picking up no catering."

"You are. Madam's orders, so quit your backtalking." Terese ignored the mini fit Billie was having and turned to Mia. "And you... Did you pick up that Diamond Ice?"

"Diamond Ice?" Billie looked at them both.

"I did, and Billie, you know Lady Valkyrie doesn't hold back. Whatever good paying customers want, they get."

"Sheesh, I know they're high rollers, but still," Billie said.

It wasn't every day that the brothel had someone from the Five Families visit. This New Year's Eve was sure to be interesting.

A smirk appeared on Terese's face as she ran her fingers through her curly blonde hair. "I wouldn't worry about it too much. You're not even on his request list." Terese grinned as Billie steamed.

"It's not too early for me to beat your ass." Billie took a step forward with her fist balled.

"Calm down." Mia stepped between them. "We're all fully booked tonight anyways, so let's just finish up and then get ready for tonight, okay?"

Billie stepped back as Terese grinned.

"If only you had been more blessed. This high roller only likes girls with big breasts, so kittens like you will have to deal with the scraps. See y'all around." Terese sneered as she spun away and marched back down the hall.

"Fat pig!" Billie shouted over the echo of Terese's laughter.

Mia chuckled as Billie fumed, but it was still a shock to hear that a member of one of the Five Families wanted to spend New Year's Eve in The Slogs and at their brothel, nonetheless. Not to disrespect Valkyrie House, which was arguably one of the best brothels in The Slogs, but it wasn't a place where high rollers from Uptown, let alone the Five Families, spent their time. In fact, there wasn't much movement in the hilly capital of Laurasia. The wealthy lived at the top, behind their great stone wall, leaving everyone else to fend for themselves. Of course, it wasn't all bad; there was always plenty of work in the mines in the countryside or in the waste and recycling centers in the sewers. But Mia knew from early on that she wasn't meant for work like that. Just the thought of her nails chipping from labor like that made her cringe.

"I can't believe someone from the Five Families is coming here," Billie said. "Wonder why Madam Valkyrie didn't tell everyone..."

"She did. You were sleeping during that meeting." Mia started walking towards the stairs.

"I was?" Billie stopped.

"Yeah, I'm pretty sure." Mia giggled.

"Well, dang, any idea who?" Billie followed Mia down the narrow spiral wooden stairs.

Mia paused, then scooted aside to let some of the other girls carrying boxes pass. "I think it's a Fort'nee."

"Think? Girl, you need to have this shit memorized," Billie said, which was rich coming from someone who forgot who was coming anyways. "You have to know who to lay it heavy on."

"I know, but it's not like the Five Families make public appearances. I don't know what they look like," Mia said.

She couldn't keep up with all of them anyways, but she did have a rough idea what most of them did. The Sapphires ran the gemstone mines out in the countryside. They mined for a precious gem called Ao Almasi, which was only found in her country, Julilie. It was a big export, one of the few things Julilie produced. She hadn't seen one in person, but it was rumored that it was magic or something. Foreigners raved about it, but since it was connected to magic, Mia didn't want anything to do with it, even if she loved gemstones. Magic wasn't something that was widely accepted; in fact, there was a heavy superstition tied to it. Only people connected to nefarious means used it, and so, it was shrouded in secrecy.

The Ruby family was in charge of the Metal Works and their foundries. They imported a ton of scrap metal that was melted down and used for buildings. At least that's what Mia guessed, but she really didn't know. The bulk of those jobs were in Sewer Town, and she rarely had clients from down there. The Fort'nees and the Hoo'naes were big into politics; they ran the country—she knew that much. Billie and some of the other girls would work their parties when they had their fundraisers in The Slogs. She wasn't quite sure what the Granites did, however. The rumors about that family were wild. Some said they were slavers, some said they were doctors, but none of it could be verified. Mia just knew they were the last family to be welcomed into the fold.

The brothel didn't open until six, but there was still a lot of work to do. Mia pushed open the door that led into the back halls. Other girls ran around cleaning and getting everything ready. Mia split from Billie and let her start on her errands so she could start her last-minute chores. She headed down the hall and checked the job board. It looked like most of the rooms would need a good once-over. Mia sighed. It would be a lot of work, but this wasn't her first room sweep. She hurried past girls, being careful of doors that were constantly being opened and shut and stopped at one of the larger storage closets. There should be extra carts in here if no one had them out, and to her relief, she opened the door to one wooden cart.

She loaded up her cart with lubes, washcloths, and bags of incense. All the rooms were on the first floor in a C-shaped layout. She started with her rooms first, which were on the right wing. When she opened the door, she was surprised to see that none of the pillows had casing, but before Mia could sigh, the door pushed open behind her, and someone carrying a fresh load of clean sheets walked in.

"Coming through," a small voice said.

Mia moved out of the way and watched as a pile of linen was carted in.

"Fresh from the laundry room."

"Thanks, Sara." Mia smiled.

"No problem!" Sara smiled back as she made quick work of the pillows.

The brothel hired no outside cleaning staff; all the cleaning was done by the girls who worked the floors or girls who retired. That was how Lady Valkyrie created stability for the women. From the kitchens to the stage, plenty of jobs for any woman to take. There was even space left for those who became too sick or ill to work so that they wouldn't wind up on the streets. Mia didn't mind this at all. As a street orphan, she didn't pick up many skills other than pickpocketing, but since she started working at the brothel, she was taught how to cook and clean and manage her finances. Best of all, she had a family to come home to and people who cared about her.

Mia refilled the baskets and made sure every nightstand and armchair was clean and tidy before spraying a few puffs of room perfume on the sheets. Then, she wheeled her cart to the next room. The hallways in the client wing were carpeted in red, and the walls a soft pink wallpaper. Each room had a queen-sized bed, a wooden nightstand, a lamp, and some had armchairs. It was a lot of work keeping the rooms clean, and she wished that there was some kind of magic that would do it for them, but magic was strictly forbidden in the lower classes. If it were possible to use it at all.

The only magic Mia ever saw was the medical necromancy used to paste parts back onto people's bodies. Like Lady Valkyrie's right arm, which was an impressive mashup of black metal scrap forged into an arm that she was never afraid to flex around unruly clients. Mia still remembered the first time she saw the arm, with fingers that looked like claws and muscles made from twisted metal rods and large joints. To a normal person, the arm would look like a metal piece of art that would go on some kind of junkyard statue, but it was more than that. The magic made it come to life somehow, like a reanimated corpse. It was a mystery to Mia how something that was never alive could be affixed to the body and work like a regular arm, and she didn't really want to know. It kind of scared her if she were being honest. Magic wasn't something that could be learned at a school down the street. It was secretive and often tied to crime. She didn't know anyone who knew how it worked, and they didn't meddle in it either.

But this medical necromancy wasn't available to everyone—that was a luxury for the rich, who could afford to replace anything that no longer worked. Mia pushed her cart from room to room as girls rushed by. The door was open, ready for her.

She hummed as the sound of vacuuming filled her ears and started to fluff the pillows and refill the baskets. This room really needed some extra care, it was so lowly stocked and musty. She opened the window to air it out and refilled the basket with condoms and lubes. Sara popped in again, looking for something.

"Do you have enough washcloths?" Sara asked.

"Yup, I think so," Mia said.

"Good." Sara turned to leave but stopped. "Um," she muttered as she pulled at her short brown hair. "N-nevermind." She scurried out.

Mia stopped what she was doing and waited, knowing Sara would be back, and as predicted, a figure inched its way back into her room.

"Ar-are you sure?" Sara asked.

"Yup. Are you low?" Mia asked.

Sara twirled the end of her shirt. "All the ones left are hanging to dry downstairs. Could I use some of yours for Lola's rooms?"

"Of course." Mia turned to her cart and picked up a few.

"Thank you so much, Mia." Sara bounced in place.

Sara ran from the room as Mia let out a chuckle. Sara was one of the newer girls. She was the daughter of the laundry room supervisor. She applied to work here when she came of age, and Lady Valkyrie welcomed her. That was another thing Mia loved about the madam; she accepted all women, even those who did not have vulvas, stating that women come in many lovely varieties and all were welcome here. That was one of the reasons why

Mia felt at home here. This was truly the only place she felt welcomed in a cold city like Laurasia. Even if the work wasn't considered respectable, it was a trade she picked up, and she was very good at it. Mia hoped Sara would have just as much success. That was, of course, if she and Billie didn't run off into the night like a pair of foolish young lovers first.

It took Mia a few more hours to finish all the rooms. She would have finished a while ago, but Terese insisted that they put out extra decorations since Mr. Richy Richy Fort'nee was coming. Mia wanted to roll her eyes so bad because she could have started getting ready already. All this talk about the Five Families was starting to get old, though. She wasn't disillusioned when it came to the wealth of the Five Families. Sure, she probably won't turn any of them away, but she'd met and fucked enough rich people to know that most of the lot were pigs, but what could anyone do about it? All of Laurasia was like this. In fact, the entire nation of Julilie was like this – poor, overcrowded, and gloomy – and it had been this way all her life. It wasn't like the city was going to up and change any time soon, and all the papers said the neighboring nations were no better. As long as Mia had Valkyrie House, she had a job and a safe place to live, and that was enough.

Mia headed to the closet to return her cart when she remembered that she never gave the accountant the receipts for the potion order she picked up from Mr. Pimshit yesterday. She loved visiting his shop. He never overcharged, and he had the best remedies. Mia put back her cart and rushed back up to her room to get the receipts. If there was one thing Miss Rivers didn't play about, it was money.

"Mia," a familiar voice squeaked from behind her.

Mia turned around and saw Sara again. She looked relieved when she saw that Mia had noticed her. Sara hurried over, holding a bundle of fabric. She looked anxious.

"Mia, I ripped my costume," Sara blurted out. "I tried to put it on, but my toe went through one of the holes and ripped the thing wide open. I-I can't dance in this, and I have clients who booked me! I can't show up in this."

Mia could hear the shakiness in her voice. "It's okay, Sara. Let me take a look," Mia said as she looked around for someplace to check out Sara's costume. The foot traffic was too heavy to even stop and have a conversation. "Hey, let's go to the back." Sara looked nervous at first, but then Mia grabbed her hand. "I can take a better look somewhere where it's not as busy."

Sara nodded, and Mia led them to the laundry room, but Sara put on the brakes. "If my mom sees that I ruined my costume, she'll be furious," Sara said.

"Of course. Shall we go to my room?"

"Could we go to mine? I'm sorry if I'm making this harder."

"It's no problem. Let's go." Mia led the way.

They passed Tae'a in the hall and waved as they headed upstairs and down the hall into a sea of open doors. Perfume wafted from every room as well as the sounds of humming and talking. Mia stopped at Sara's room so she could open the door. Sara flipped on the light, revealing her small room, and put her costume on her nicely made-up bed.

Sara's mother was not only the head of laundry, but she was also a well-known dancer and was highly requested by clients well into her mature years. The story went that Sara's mother had her with a Sewer Town worker. Some of the older women said that he was one of the nicest men they knew, and he often helped to keep the brothel's pipes working until his tragic death in an accident on the job. Widowed, Sara's mother made sure Sara knew how to take care of herself by teaching her a laundry trade, even teaching her how to read and write. But she was also strict and quick to temper when people moved too slowly or made too many mistakes.

Sara took a step back and brushed her short brown hair out of her face while Mia surveyed the costume. There was a large tear through the holes on the side of the costume. It would be hard to fix, given the material. Mia picked up the leotard, lifting it delicately. On the hips were fixings for Sara's feathered cape. She turned the light blue leotard around and saw the same fixings.

"It's ruined, right?"

"There's nothing these hands can't fix. Leave it to me, Sara."

Sara cried as she hugged Mia. "Thank you! Thank you! Thank you!"

Mia worked quickly but delicately on Sara's costume. She really didn't have time to take on a side project with only a few hours to get ready, but she liked the challenge. She scanned the garment again, then looked around the room and spotted a box of fabric scraps. She brought the garment to Sara's workbench, which had a small foot pedal sewing machine on it. Sewing the holes close would only create tension and cause more rips, but maybe she could mend it with a bit of fabric. Mia fished around the box and found a bit of silky light blue fabric. She threaded the machine and patched the holes with diamond-shaped patterns.

"Wow!" Sara gasped, but Mia wasn't done.

"It's missing something." Mia held up the costume, and a glimmer of something caught her eye. "Yes!" Mia reached into the box and smiled. "These will look great."

Mia flashed the iron-on glitter patches to Sara before she melted them on with the heat. "Perfect!"

"Oh my gosh, Mia! Thank you so much!" Sara clapped and jumped around the room.

Mia was out of breath but pleased to see that her friend avoided a crisis. "Anytime."

Sara glowed with excitement as she slipped the outfit on slowly and moved gracefully around the room. She really was graceful like a bird, just as Billie said. "Thanks again, Mia," Sara said as she carefully rolled the costume off her shoulders.

Mia said her "you're welcomes" and headed for the back office, passing girls rushing by with drapes and boxes of decorations. All the closets were open, and chatter filled the air. Mia walked carefully to avoid tripping on all the boxes and bags in her path.

"No, this simply won't do!" Mia heard from her right and turned toward the voice. It sounded like her friend Tae'a. One of the big storage closets was open, and Mia peeked in just as another girl walked out. "Ruined, absolutely ruined," Tae'a said.

"What's wrong?" Mia asked.

"What's right?" Tae'a turned around. "Mia—oh good! You're good at fabric. It's those darn rats again. They went and got into the boxes of wall decorations." Tae'a pulled up a stained piece of white lace.

"Eww." Mia walked in closer.

Tae'a made a deep sigh as she put her polished pink nails to her lips. "I could soak them in a little diluted soap, but the party is tonight, and no shops are open to make a quick run."

"Do we have any extras?" Mia bent down.

"These are the extras. I repaired the rest of them, but now all that's left are the ones with hella stains and rips, so I dug around some more, found these, and..." Tae'a sighed.

Mia frowned. This didn't look good, but maybe there was a way to save them. "You know what, maybe you can soap 'em and hang 'em in the dim rooms. With what goes on in there, no one would be able to tell the difference."

Tae'a made an O with her mouth that bloomed into a smile. "Mia, you're a genius."

"There you are!" Terese's thunderous voice boomed. Mia whipped around and sighed. "Did you finish stocking your rooms?" Terese huffed. Standing behind her, quietly and with her head down, was another one of the girls name Lola.

Lola was older than Mia but well-requested. She often followed Terese around like a shadow. They even took clients together. Mia's eyes flickered to Lola. Her normally full, curly, bubblegum pink hair was in a ponytail, which made Mia think that she was dressing down so as not to outdo her boss.

“I can’t believe everything is still a mess.” Terese folded her arms and barked before Mia could get a word out.

“Relax, hun.” Tae’a stood up, towering over Terese at six foot one. “You’ll turn us all gray with that energy.” Tae’a pointed a polished finger at her. “Mia, why don’t you go on? I’m good here.” Mia nodded, and then Tae’a turned to Terese. “And if things are such a mess, why don’t you plug your can and grab a box?”

Terese gasped, but Lola interjected, “S-she didn’t mean it.”

“You got a problem, bitch!” Terese roared.

Mia tried to hide a laugh as she inched away. She gave a quick smile to Tae’e, who returned her goodbye with a wink.

“I can make it my problem!” Mia heard Tae’e say.

Those two would probably be at it all night, but Mia had work to do. She twisted and snaked her way through the narrow halls, uttering “excuse mes” to the head cleaning girls and dance girls who didn’t take clients. A door swung open, and she skirted to a stop. One of the hostesses gasped and apologized as she pushed a heavy metal cart full of boxes past her. Mia hurried up the incline under the string lights that lit the hall.

All the back halls were a mishmash of oddly connected corridors and rooms because the brothel had been converted from a shoe factory. Sometimes, Mia could still smell the rubbery fake leather. She walked down another incline that was rough beneath her soles, then back up another that veered to the right toward the end of the hall, where there were two offices and a larger room that was part of Lady Valkyrie’s private library. Mia peeked into the first office. The sounds of feverish typing filled the space.

“Um, excuse me, Miss Rivers?” Mia’s voice was small and could not compete with the typewriters and receipt machines. “Miss Rivers?” Mia said a bit louder.

The noise stopped, and an older woman with a brown, round face and gray and black hair popped up from the side of her work easel. “Mia!” The woman moved some papers out of the way, rolled her wheelchair out from behind her desk, and opened a file cabinet on the wall. “How can I help you?”

“I forgot to give you the receipt for the potions I picked up from Mr. Pimshit.” Mia walked over and put it next to the typewriter, where every letter was worn, and most of the numbers were missing.

"Yes, yes, yes! I was looking for that! Thank you," Miss Rivers said. "We girls need our potions."

Mia nodded. Miss Rivers swore birth control was the work of magic, even though the remedy was pure science. Not that Mia knew the science behind it, but the doctors that Lady Valkyrie paid to visit the brothel said it to be so. And so, she trusted these medicine workers more than the myths and secrecy of magic.

"Mr. Pimshit doing okay?" Miss Rivers asked as she rolled back to her desk.

"Yes, ma'am," Mia said as Miss Rivers smiled with delight. "Is there anything else I can get for you?"

"I think we're good for now, though this is sure to be an interesting New Year's with a Fort'nee coming."

"I wonder why he's coming all the way down here," Mia probed.

"Don't matter to me or the madam as long as his folks treat the girls right and pay their tab. Hell if we ain't gon' recover the cost of those eight bottles of Diamond Ice."

"I hear you loud and clear" Mia said with a laugh, then left the office.

Mia turned and was on her way back out when she heard a door close toward Lady Valkyrie's private library. Mia peeked into the room filled with bookshelves that were stuffed full of vases, statues, and plates, all free of dust. On the polished dark hardwood floors were dozens of small rugs with different patterns and pictures. On some were horse-like creatures with the body of an animal and the torso of a nude human woman—those were Mia's favorite. The walls were lined with tapestries of different women in clouds or praying over temples, places that reminded Mia of the stories her clients would tell her to impress her.

Mia's head turned at the sound of voices intertwined with footsteps, and around a bookshelf walked Sara and Lady Valkyrie. The madam had her metal right arm wrapped around Sara's shoulder as she ushered her to the door. Lady Valkyrie looked so elegant as she strode through the room in a long black silky robe that matched her perfectly silk-pressed long black hair. Her sharp, dark eyes fixated on Sara with a gentleness only found in a prey bird looking over its baby. Sara smiled and thanked her as the two stopped at the edge of the library and parted ways.

"Hey, Mia," Sara greeted in passing. Mia responded with a smile as she watched her friend leave.

"Perfect, isn't she?" Lady Valkyrie's voice pulled Mia back into the room. "She doesn't have a lick of bone in that back, but she is as beautiful as a night moth's wings."

"She is, and she's a good dancer too."

"That she is," Lady Valkyrie said as she swayed around her private collection. "She just needs a bit of a push."

Mia watched Lady Valkyrie run her metal finger across the wooden shelves. She let her black silk robe drape lower on her dark brown shoulders where the flesh and metal fused into one.

"You yourself are a beauty, too, Mia."

Mia looked at Lady Valkyrie's face only to find that she was staring directly at her with those dark, expressionless eyes.

"Uh..." Mia looked away. "T-thank you." Mia heard Lady Valkyrie chuckle.

"Modest child. You already possess everything you need to conquer this world. Have I not taught you that?"

"Yes, ma'am, you have, and I am so very grateful."

Lady Valkyrie closed the distance between them, floating over to Mia like a cloud of smoke rolling down the street. "Never forget that you are powerful. Your body is your key and will conquer the heart of any man, but your mind is your blade. Use it to carve out a life of abundance."

Mia melted under her gaze. Her dark eyes, nearly as black as her silky hair, enveloped her, making it so that all Mia could do was nod. Lady Valkyrie smiled and stepped back.

"It's going to be a good New Year's, especially with the arrival of the rich pig. He's already made quite the deposit."

"T-the Fort'nee?"

Lady Valkyrie waved her hand. "Fort'nee, Sapphire, Hoo'nae—they're all the same, gender be damned. They all like good food, and they all like to fuck, but don't let their opulence fool you."

Mia ignored her nervous brain and probed. "H-have you met a lot of the members of the Five Families?"

"A lot? No, but I've met their dogs." A glint of something dark moved across her face. "But now is not the time for stories you've already heard. We must finish preparations."

"Yes, ma'am."

Mia scurried away, not wanting to bring up painful memories. Everyone in the brothel knew Lady Valkyrie's history. How she was forced to marry one of the Jakyda brothers, a well-known runner family in The Slogs that had connections to the infamous Siler Gang. Mia had never seen a Siler runner before, but she was familiar with the stories and knew to stay away from them and anyone connected to them. The Jakyda brother who married Lady Valkyrie was especially horrible towards her and violently abused her until one day, she slashed his throat and ran away.

She was later caught by the eldest brother, who was so impressed by her sudden outburst of violence that he let her go. He too felt dishonored by his brother's actions towards her and the women he kept. The rest was history. Lady Valkyrie had built quite the name for herself, and while she promised not to interfere with the Jakyda's business, the other gangs weren't so lucky. Runners and gang lords were not Mia's thing. She wasn't a fighter, but her madam's powerful underground empire built on sex work helped clear the debt of many women and offered them work and a safe place to live, and that was fine by Mia.

By three in the afternoon, Mia had finished all her chores and last-minute errands. Her stomach growled, so she headed to the kitchen to grab a bit of bread and jam before going back to her room to freshen up before the brothel opened at six. Even though it was early, the clients were probably already outside waiting. She could see through the windows that the main street was filling up, and they would probably remain busy for at least a week after the New Year, which didn't bother her at all. In fact, if this kept up, she could probably buy herself some new shoes as well, maybe even a new nail set.

When she walked into the kitchen, she wasn't expecting to find Billie fishing around the fruit basket.

"You know that's off limits," Mia said, causing Billie to jump.

Billie turned around and put her hands behind her back. "What?"

Mia laughed. "I'm kidding. What's in the basket today?" The brothel sometimes took payments in the form of exotic foods, which usually drove Miss River up the wall, but Lady Valkyrie liked to humor her most loyal clients from time to time, and none of the girls complained about fresh food.

"Nothing but nasty ol' bananas." Billie made a face.

"And here I thought you liked phallic fruit."

"It's not a fruit; it's dick-shaped mush," Billie said as she turned around and grabbed a banana anyway.

"Proving my point exactly," Mia said.

"Fuck off." Billie peeled the fruit and took a big bite. "Shit, I gotta work on my costume."

"I swear I thought you said you finished it last week?"

"I did, but the seams ripped."

"So, you rushed it."

"I did not rush it! I sewed on all the feathers by hand. It's not my fault my ass got bigger. Besides, it'll be an easy fix. I just need to find some glue."

"Glue?!" Mia shook her head. "Come to my room now, and I'll see what I can do."

Billie rolled her eyes but moved to the door. Mia let her walk out first, following behind her. It was so like Billie to half-ass things; she was a big-picture person, someone who didn't care about the details. They broke off when they exited the narrow stairs leading up to their rooms. This would be her second outfit fix of the day, a new record. Billie's room was next to Mia's, and Billie rushed inside to grab her stuff while Mia unlocked her door.

Tonight was going to be busy. She was sure clients would have her completely booked. She started to gather her good makeup to take downstairs when she caught a look outside through her light coral pink curtains. It was beautiful today. The sky was light gray, which meant there would be no rain—good for business.

On her floor were boxes filled with outfits and accessories for work. On a normal night, she would be thinking about who she would be. A shop girl next door? A naive scholar? Perhaps just the virgin new girl. Every girl had their thing at the brothel; people liked to pretend, and Mia's thing was playing the sweet little girl next door. Their clients loved to buy into innocence, but tonight was not the night for simple pretend. It was going to be tits out clits out for the guest. Even the affluent expected no less.

Billie pushed open the door with her butt; she was holding a crate with her sewing bag in her mouth. She let the door close behind her and placed her stuff on the floor, then fished through the materials and carefully pulled out her New Year's costume. The sleeveless body suit was a deep crimson red with a cut out from the navel to the chest. She pulled out some bright red thigh-highs and her masquerade mask, too.

"Did you finish your wings?" Mia asked.

"Yeah, but it was a pain in the freaking butt. Feathers are expensive," Billie said as she continued to go through the crate. "Got it!"

Billie stood and showed Mia her idea with some measurements and notes scribbled on a notepad. As Mia read, Billie held up the costume.

"Looks good, huh?" Billie grinned.

"Not bad. Your sewing skills have improved."

"Now if only I could fix the sides and attach the back cape part."

Mia stood. "Where's your dress form?"

"It's all the way downstairs at my workstation."

"Why is it all the way down there?"

"I use it to pin my accessories to."

"What did you use to make your costume?"

Billie shrugged, avoiding eye contact in the way she always did when she was doing something she wasn't supposed to.

"Billie, I swear..." Mia placed her hands on her hips. "Okay, well hurry up, put it on, and I'll help you with the cape."

"Thanks," Billie said as she stumbled to get undressed. "I'm not a big fan of the theme, but I can't wait to see Sara's costume."

"Oh? You two are more alike than you know." Mia knew how Billie felt about Sara and thought their blooming romance was adorable, even if they fucked louder than a five-person orgy.

"Yeah, she's going to look so cute, I don't know if I'll be able to control myself." Billie clasped her hands in front of her chest.

"And you've been controlling yourself so far?" Mia teased as she got to work. "Or is she the reason you were making all that noise this morning?"

"Hey, I said I was sorry," Billie huffed. "Ouch!"

"Stay still." Mia worked her fingers slowly around Billie's waist, trying to pin the cape. "It's okay. I know how you feel about her."

"She's something different, Mia. I mean, yeah, she's nineteen, a little young, and I've got three years on her, but the way she dances and talks about dancing...who knew someone could be so passionate about shaking ass?"

Mia nodded as she wove the needle into the fabric.

"I think she really has talent–enough to make it to the Landmark."

"In Uptown?" Mia chuckled. "I don't doubt her talent, but that's a reach. I mean, Uptown is a whole other world."

"It ain't, and where do you think those dancers come from?" Billie grinned. She had a point. "Only difference is that you need more talent than sucking dick to make it up there. I mean, the dancers there are like graceful birds or some shit, and the way Sara talks about dancing... I just want to see her up there, you know."

"I understand. You're in love, and you want to see her happy."

"You know, this doesn't have to be our ending place. And while I'm grateful for everything Lady Valkyrie has done for us, we're not bad dancers ourselves. We could reach higher."

Mia didn't like to think about her future like that. Sure, she could dance, but life outside of the brothel? She couldn't imagine that. When she was a child, her dreams were consumed by where her next meal was coming from and how to find safe shelter from runners and pimps. Of course, she could have moved out to the countryside, but more people moved into the city from the rural areas, and for good reason. Jobs were bad out there and hard, especially for women. Mia shuddered at the stories she'd heard from some of the girls. Then there were the mines. They offered good work, but Mia heard the labor contracts were horrible. It was even rumored that most of the labor contracts were held by local gangs. So staying at Valkyrie House and working clients sounded like a good life. She could even retire, maybe become a full-time seamstress. It wasn't grand, but it was stable and safe, just how Mia liked it.

"Billie, you're always the dreamer," Mia said to her grinning friend. "Tonight will be fun, though. I've spent hours practicing the opening."

Billie nodded. "I'm excited to see Mr. Diamond Ice. Maybe what he really needs is a little domination in his life."

"Oh, Billie, stop," Mia laughed, but Mia was curious too. Not that she was on his request list, but someone like that could really turn a girl's life around. It's not every day that someone from the Five Families mingled in The Slogs...

2
Mia

As the sky darkened, the main street came to life. Colorful lights decorated all the bars in reds and yellows to welcome the New Year. White lights illuminated the dark red of the building, making the gold garlands and lanterns shine. Every streetlight was lit, and people filled the roads. The windows on the first floor were all open with celebratory displays, and the hostess opened the door to a line of customers that wrapped around the building, all eager to get in whether they were on the guest list or not. Guests entered, flooding into the grand lobby below.

It was crunch time for Mia now. Her only saving grace was that on a whim last year, she decided to cut her thick, curly, dyed blonde hair and kept it that way, which meant a shorter styling time and more time to focus on her nails and makeup and pinning her costume to her body. Mia couldn't play around today, not on a major holiday like this.

The noise flooded in from the streets below as Mia sat at her vanity in her room, rushing to put on her foundation and setting it with a spray as Billie poked her head out of the window.

"Still no sign of 'em." Billie turned around in her beautiful crimson-red New Year's Eve outfit.

"Do you have your mask?" Mia asked as she undid her silk scarf.

"Yes, Mom," Billie teased. "We're going to make some serious cash tonight. I heard that rich guy is bringing his friends." She rubbed her hands together.

"You and everyone else are so obsessed." Mia picked up a bottle of spray gel and tidied up the edges of her neatly laid finger waves.

"Oh, please. Don't act like you aren't interested." Billie smirked. "You're just mad 'cause you weren't requested."

"I'm not mad!" Mia huffed. "Okay, maybe I do wish I was his type."

"See!"

"But only for the money and the Diamond Ice." Mia clasped her hands together. "I bet that stuff tastes like perfection."

"Still, it would be nice to be off and go to the real parties." Billie sat on Mia's bed as she continued to get ready.

"Where? You mean..." Mia pointed down.

"Oh yeah. In Sewer Town, they throw down."

"You sure love going down there. I don't get it. You can't even breathe in certain areas—some places, you have to wear a gas mask!"

Billie shrugged. "It's not so bad once you get used to it. And besides, does it smell any better up here?"

Billie had a point. "At least the rain is rain and not runoff."

"Even the rain smells like shit, Mia. We live in a horse's ass," Billie laughed.

"Forty minutes, ladies!" a voice shouted from the hall.

"Shit!" Mia said.

"Relax. You still have time." Billie got up. "Here, let me do your makeup."

Mia allowed herself to relax as Billie looked at her face like a painter would see a canvas.

"I want everything to match lavender," Mia said.

"Girl, I know your colors. Now pipe down and let your girl work."

Billie made quick work of her face, painting on eyebrows and putting mascara on Mia's lashes. Billie used a nude shade to paint Mia's lips so that all the attention would be drawn to the eyes. She added a little rouge and highlighted her face with a shimmery glitter before setting the entire thing with spray.

"Perfect," Billie said.

Mia looked into the mirror and beamed. "Thank you so much!"

"Anytime."

The hostess ran down the halls, calling the time. Mia and Billie hurried down the stairs, making their way through the narrow halls to the backstage area. They fell in with the rest of the girls, all fifty of them, in a sea of brightly colored feathered leotards and masks. Flowery perfumes filled the air along with the chatter. The noises from the ballroom confirmed that it was going to be a full house.

Mia looked around for Billie and saw her standing in place. She waved, and Billie waved back.

"Oh my gosh, I am so nervous," Tae'a said next to her as she fluffed her long, thick, curly black hair. "I haven't had to move these hips around like this in weeks."

"You look so beautiful tonight, Tae'a. You're going to do great," Mia said.

"Thanks, hun." Tae'a smiled. "I finally got these old breasts to cooperate. I'm banking on tonight so I can buy me a new pair. Have you ever been shopping in Uptown?"

"Uptown?" Mia shook her head.

"Oh hun, pinky promise me you'll go with me next time. I would love to dress you up." Tae'a held out her pinky.

"It's a deal," Mia said, closing her pinky around Tae'a's.

The hostess rang a bell, calling everyone in. All the girls lined up on each side of the stage entrances, twenty-five on each side. Mia patted down her feathers. She could feel the excitement in the air. The hostess walked by counting heads while Mia adjusted her mask and practiced her smile as the band fired up. She closed her eyes and took a deep breath, reminding herself that she wasn't some newborn; she could handle this. She wished herself and all the girls an amazing and prosperous night.

The heavy red curtains drew back, and the girls filled the stage in unison, dancing in a perfect line. The pianist hyped them up as their partners on the trombone and saxophone backed them up. Mia skipped alongside her housemates, spinning round and round as she gyrated her hips, making sure the audience was pulled into their mesmerizing and seductive dance. Each girl presented themselves as they walked past the entrance of the catwalk. When it was Mia's turn, the music swelled as she shook her rump for the crowd. Mia then locked hands with her dance partner and twirled, making her beautiful feathers dance. The pair broke apart for the next duo to follow, and Mia stepped back in line flawlessly as the audience cheered. When the number finished, all the girls lined up and walked down the catwalk, out into the middle of the ballroom, where the guests showered them with applause.

Mia smiled and bowed with the other girls, but even as she played to the whole audience, she stole glances at one booth in particular. In the back, sitting in the largest booth, was the man everyone was waiting for. Surrounded by runners in starchy black suits and guests in beautiful gowns and colorful suits was a man with dark brown skin and short, straight black hair. He had on green-tinted glasses and a green suit. He laughed loudly as the barmaids poured him drinks. In his mouth, Mia could see a sparkle that looked like gold teeth. This was a member of one of the Five Families, and he looked as rich as everyone said he was.

As Mia broke away from the group to work the room, a hostess hurried past her to gather Lola and Terese. The two girls headed to the back booth. Mia watched them melt into his arms. He ogled over them as if they were his prized dogs, squeezing and touching their breasts without shame. Mia turned away. He may have been rich, but he acted like every other client.

Mia hopped in and out of eager arms all night, pouring drinks and laughing along with guests before it was time to take private clients. Sitting around a booth of about six men, Mia made small talk as they begged her to show more, hurling cash her way. She politely giggled, playing up her sweet and innocent act, when a hostess tapped her on the shoulder. It was time to take her first client.

Mia excused herself but not before blowing kisses to her now distraught guests. In her place, another girl stepped in. That's how the night worked. Half the girls took private clients, the other half worked the room, and all the while, the dancers filled the stage, ensuring there was plenty of entertainment to go around. Mia followed the hostess to the back. Once the door closed, Mia took a breath.

"Your first client is two pairs. Couples, it looks like," the hostess read from the sheet.

"Any specific request?" Mia said as she walked alongside her.

"They mentioned something about a threesome with the women, but otherwise, it should be pretty vanilla."

"Thanks," Mia said as she broke away to her vanity in the backstage area to freshen up.

It was packed as usual, and she only had about twenty minutes to get ready. She also had a copy of her client list, but the hostess would find her when they were ready, so she wouldn't have to constantly look over her shoulder. Billie walked in just minutes after, sweat running down her face and body.

"What happened to you? Your clients take you on a run?" Mia joked.

Billie laughed hard, wiping her sweaty face with the back of her arm. "Hell no, but he did like to be tickled, and he tipped well, too."

Billie pulled a wad from her chest and stuffed it in her cash drawer. She started working on her face as she glanced up at her schedule.

"Taking another client?" Mia asked as she powdered her face.

"Not until late. I think I have a small group, but I'm working the room for now. I spotted some rich Uptown clients, and I think I'm requested."

"Requested? Fancy," Mia teased, acting as if she were jealous.

"Girl, please. Don't act like you don't get requested. How long is your client list tonight?"

"Too long." Mia touched up her lips, then spotted the hostess. "Shit, looks like it's time."

"Alright, girl, work it! We all need new linens for our beds this winter!"

Mia laughed as she headed towards the hostess and then joined her clients. The hostess was right about the double pair. Turns out the men just wanted to watch their wives get it on with another girl. They were nice enough, but Mia could tell this was their first time at a brothel.

When they were done, the hostess returned right away with the next client. This was a regular, not a wealthy man, working class, but he loved to end his year in bed with Mia. It was his thing. She freshened up and picked him up personally from the lobby. She didn't normally do this, but he was special.

"Mr. Homby." Mia waved.

"Miss Mia!" Mr. Homby opened his arms wide and hugged Mia like she was an old friend.

Mia pulled back to look him in the eyes. "Here for your yearly special?"

"Miss Mia, there is no other place I'd rather be on the last day of this glorious year."

Mia giggled. "I feel honored."

The hostess walked them to one of Mia's rooms, where Mia worked her magic. She liked working with her regulars. Mr. Homby worked downtown in The Slogs at the raw material plant. He was widowed after his wife died of green lung. He had no other family in the city, but despite all this, he was still nice. He said that Mia reminded him of his late wife, and saving up all year for the opportunity to be with her was one of the few things he had to look forward to in this gloomy city.

Mia finished her night with him by offering him a soft kiss and chocolates. She knew he liked them. It was her treat to a wonderful and caring man.

Heading back downstairs, Mia learned her schedule was mixed up a bit because of a cancellation, so she had to work the room. She didn't mind since it gave her time to recover. She headed back to the powder room just as Terese arrived.

"Fuck!" Terese plopped on her vanity, "Finally a fucking break."

Tae'a turned around. "You? Tired? No."

"Shit, if it wasn't for the money, I'd ditch this pig," Terese said as she started to fix her hair.

Mia stopped at Terese's vanity. "Is he trash?"

Terese shrugged. "He ain't polished metal, but he's *rich* rich. I mean, you would think he'd be, you know, a little classy 'cause he's a Fort'nee, but I swear he brushes his teeth with liquor and bathes in grease. But the creepiest thing is his little red eye."

"Red eye?" Tae'a gasped.

"Relax, it ain't diseased. It's mechanical or something, like Lady Valkyrie's arm. It can move on its own and everything. It's weird. I swear, it's looking through my clothes or something."

"Is it magic or something?" Mia asked.

"Witchcraft," Terese said. "Only folks dealing with the underground can afford it; its necromancy."

"Oh, please, Terese," Tae'a said. "It's just privileged taste. I would replace anything that didn't work on me, too. No need to drag a bum leg if you don't have to."

Terese huffed, but the hostess monitored her carefully, pointing to her watch.

Mia had about thirty minutes to freshen up this time, so she decided to do a quick wash-off. She redid her makeup and touched up her hair, puffing out a few pumps of perfume to end her routine.

Heading out again, Mia took a deep breath as the hostess opened the door to the ballroom. The stench of alcohol laced with perfume burned her nose but didn't dim her smile. She glided around to the music as the bass player carried the room. She waved at patrons in booths who were too drunk to tell left from right. The New Year was coming, but it might as well already have been here by the looks on everyone's faces. Up ahead, on a table, Sara danced for a crowd of people who whistled and threw money at her as if they had lost their minds.

The next hostess waved Mia over to a booth covered in cups and spilt alcohol. A man with a bright red face threw glitter in the air like it was gold while his friends laughed themselves silly. When they finally noticed Mia, they waved her closer, passing her around like drinks. Mia threw glitter with them, entertaining them like a mother would do a child, while the barmaid brought more alcohol and hauled the trash away.

Mia eyed the large, decorated clock that sat on the center stage. The New Year would be here in just under an hour, but she was far from last call. The red-faced man fell onto Mia's outfit, pulling the sleeveless part partly down. Mia was quick to stop the haltered part from showing her breast as she playfully tapped his hand away.

"Oh my," the man slurred. "Almost made an oopsy."

His bloodshot eyes stared at her chest as his grabby hands hovered in the air. Mia smiled and leaned away, falling on the shoulder of another drunk man.

"Would you be a dear and help me with my feathers?" Mia stood and faced the table and threw her head back. She lifted one leg onto the table and bent down, flashing her ass.

The group went wild. Mia smirked, then used the metal pole in the center of the table to pull herself up with her back facing the group. She did a little flick with her hips, making the feathers on her cape dance. She eyed the man who she'd asked to help her and used her pointer finger to call him up.

"I think one of my feathers is out of place. Would you be a dear?" Her voice was soft, floating into his ear.

The man melted, but before he could get a chance to touch her, the others eagerly volunteered. Mia clapped happily and returned their enthusiasm with a dance, making the men fall all over themselves. They begged for more as they rubbed her legs and hollered. Mia moaned at their touch as she ran her fingers down her stomach and in between her legs. The red-faced man pushed himself towards the front, hard cash in hand. Mia counted at least seven hundred. She turned her gaze fully on her meal ticket and bent down so that her crotch was in his face.

"Oooo! Gimme gimme!" he begged, and Mia grinned.

She played with her puss for him, showing him where he could make his deposit. He eagerly reached for the fabric covering her crotch and fingered the outside before tucking the bills behind the thin fabric, just above her clit. Mia moaned and played it up as she jumped up and continued to dance for her party. She flashed a look at the clock; it was almost time. One of the men grabbed her ass, and Mia wiggled out of his grip. She turned and wagged a finger at him as his boys laughed.

The clock in the middle of the stage activated at ten seconds to midnight. All the girls stopped their work to watch the second hand and led the crowd in a countdown.

Ten, Nine, Eight, Seven, Six, Five, Four, Three, Two, One! Happy New Year!

Gold confetti rained from the ceiling as all the girls lowered their tops, revealing pasties with the year 2042 on them. Lanterns honoring the Five Families lit up and floated into the air as the room began to sing. A hostess tapped Mia on the leg, replacing her with another girl. She doubted the men would even notice. Mia stashed her cash in a safe place and followed the hostess out to the lobby.

"Do you need to freshen up?" the hostess asked.

"What are they asking for?" Mia asked, plucking little bits of confetti from her hair.

The hostess shrugged. "There's nothing special on his form."

"Okay, give me five minutes."

The hostess nodded and let Mia slip away to one of the hidden stairwells. Near the door was a basin with fresh water and perfume. Mia's face looked a mess, and she considered redoing her makeup, but she didn't have time. She patted the sweat away and wiped her neck and arms, putting a little perfume behind her ears. This would be good enough. It was just for a single client.

She met back up with the hostess. She checked Mia over and did not look pleased.

"What? I only had five minutes."

The hostess wasted no time, pulling Mia away and touching up her face with a little eyeshadow, rouge, and lipstick. "He's not looking for much, just a quick suck and fuck, but he looks rich, so do your best," the hostess said. "Middle-aged, dark brown skin, the suit with the red flower on his breast. Howard Longfoot."

The hostess pointed, and Mia dashed over to him right away. When the man made eye contact with Mia, he looked almost as if he were surprised to see her. He was about average size, his salt and pepper hair shaved short but neat. His hands fidgeted nervously around his round stomach, picking at a gold button on his suit. From shoulder to toe, everything about his suit was ironed, lint-free, and neat. He was no doubt someone with money.

"Mr. Howard Longfoot?" Mia said, peeking up at his lowered eyes.

He jumped. "Y-yes, I'm Mr. Howard Longfoot."

Mia smiled. "Happy New Year, and welcome to Valkyrie House. Shall we proceed?"

Mr. Longfoot stared into Mia's eyes, and that was when Mia noticed the bags that hung from the bottom of his eyelids and the milky, dark brown shade of his irises. He may have come from money, but his face looked as if it were bedfellows with overwork.

Mia held out her hand, and he took it. His hands were large and rough, though gentle, but there was a tension there that seemed to prevent him from relaxing fully. He looked over his shoulder, his eyes darting around at the other faces.

"It's okay, sir," Mia said. "No one will judge you here. This is a brothel, after all. No need to be shy about why you came."

"Y-yes, of course," Mr. Longfoot blurted out. "Shall we? I don't want to put you behind schedule."

"Impossible. Every client gets a personal and warm experience here at Valkyrie House," Mia said, and Mr. Longfoot smiled, exposing the wrinkles on his face.

Mia led the way, crossing the lobby to the left. The hostess waited for them at the door and nodded to let Mia know the room was ready; she closed the door after them. Mia's room for the night was decorated in lavender-scented artificial flowers. Cloth flower pedals decorated the bed and floor, giving the room a sense of warmth often unfound in the smog-filled city.

Mia slid onto the bed, lifting one leg on top of the other. Mr. Longfoot stood before her, fidgeting with his black satin tie, looking everywhere except at Mia. She smiled and stood up. It would seem that she had to take the lead tonight, but she didn't mind.

Walking over to him, she eyed his tie and placed her fingers on his hands. He tensed, and that's when she noticed his rings. He wore three on one finger. Two were worn, thin gold bands, but in the middle was a polished rose gold ring in the shape of a crown or rook's top. There were indentions for gems, but none were embedded. Only zigzags lay in the middle of the indentions. It was plain but beautiful.

Mia looked up at the man's face and pulled him to the bed. Their bodies were so close that she felt his heavy breathing. Mia lifted his black satin tie and started to loosen the knot.

"I hope you don't mind if I get rid of this, Mr. Longfoot?" Mia asked, staring deeply into his brown eyes.

"Please, call me Earl." The man cupped Mia's chin before kissing her.

3
Aries

Water dripped from the dank sewer tunnels in a soft, beautiful morning chorus. Rats scurried past the metal bars of the vent that made Aries' window with their young sticking close to their side. Aries pulled her blanket further up her arm, tucking in her feet to conserve as much heat as possible. Sounds from The Slogs alerted her that there was still a world up there, a world that woke up with the brightened sky and not by sound or clock. Aries finally gave up and decided to get her day started early. A day after a major holiday was always the busiest. Aries pulled away the cloth covering her hole in the wall of a room and saw that tea had already been made on the gas burner. Her parents must have already left for work. Her family were pickers for the recycling plant, and it paid to start early.

"Karina, you up?" Aries shouted to the other room. When she didn't hear an answer, she walked over and tore open the curtain. "Where is that girl?"

She threw on some clothes, then left her burrow and walked outside to the guard rail, where she looked down at the slow-flowing water below. She sighed and headed to her sister's favorite hiding place. Already, half her clan was at work. The older folks liked to start early, and for good reason. They were paid by the pound, so the more waste they collected, the more they made.

"Yo, Aries," a voice called out to her.

Aries turned around and smiled at her older cousin Zopi. "Morning." Behind him were his two young children, Nyekundu and Bluu. "Someone is up early."

Zopi laughed as he wiped his nose. "You know I don't play. I'm a hard-working man."

"You heading to Auntie's?" Aries asked as she made faces at the little ones.

"Yeah," Zopi nodded. "Someone has to keep these two in line," he laughed as he playfully tugged his little one's arms.

"You heading to the plant after?" Aries asked.

"Hell naw. You know me, always looking for bigger and better. But I have to run. See ya'll later?" Zopi asked.

"Sure, you know where our burrow is," Aries said as she watched Zopi and his kids leave.

She really hoped he was staying out of trouble, but she couldn't dwell on it now. Aries climbed up the metal bars on the side of the wall and stuck her head up through the open manhole. She looked down the walkway lit by patches of light that filtered in from the garbage pile in the center of town, hopped up, and followed the path until she reached the old metal stairs that led to the platforms above the trash pile. She peeked over the metal grates and saw two large red puffs and sighed.

"I knew I would find you here," Aries stood over her younger sister.

"What? I wanted to watch the machine," Karina pointed to the burning incinerator, fed by giant metal claws.

"They do this every day."

"I know, I just think..." Karina didn't finish her sentence.

"Come on, we have work to do," Aries said.

"Do you think things will ever change?" Karina watched the workers scramble to feed the piles with bags of trash.

"It's too early to be worried about that right now," Aries pulled her sister up by her arm. "It's the day after New Year's Eve, and we have a lot of work to do. Mom and Dad have already left." Karina huffed but Aries pushed her along back to their little burrow. "Get dressed and put your boots on," Aries ordered once they got inside.

Karina dragged her feet. "It's not like the trash is going anywhere."

Aries ignored her, pouring them both a cup of tea and pulling out two slices of bread. Aries looked to the cutting board and noticed a message from Mom.

Happy New Year,

Sorry we didn't wake you. Rest easy and join us when you wake.

Love Mom & Dad

Aries smiled and left the note for Karina to read. She opened the cabinet and reached in for a jar of sowberry preserves when she heard a little squeak. Aries pulled back her hand, then reached in to grab the little pest. The rat squeaked and squirmed.

"Tink, what have I told you about getting into the food?" Aries placed the soft brown rat on her shoulder. "You want Dad to cook you up?"

Aries carried the food to the table just as Karina walked in in her dark green waders.

"You're not even dressed yourself," Karina folded her arms.

"Relax. Eat so we can leave," Aries said. "Also, Mom and Dad left us a note on the counter."

"I don't see why we gotta go out so early." Karina took a bite of her bread.

"If you want to linger and scrub vomit from the walkways, that's your choice, but if you want the good stuff, then we have to leave early."

"One day, we won't have to do stuff like this, Granny says."

"Granny says a lot of stuff," Aries bit back harder than she would have liked, and Karina slumped and put her tea down. "I'm sorry. Granny says a lot of stuff because she's a dreamer. Old people can do things like that, but we youngins can't because we have to work. And besides, you're not even practiced for most of what she goes on about anyways." Aries plucked Tink from her shoulder and placed him on top of her sister's head. "Your job is to work hard and stay out of trouble."

Karina huffed and ate quickly despite Tink's pleas for a bite. "One day the prophecy will come true and we won't have to pick up this stupid trash. We'll be able to live up top, too."

Aries stopped at the entrance of her room. "Just finish your breakfast, okay?"

Aries disappeared behind her curtain. She passed a wrinkled picture of her family as she fished around for her waders. Karina was too old to keep believing in Granny's tales. It wasn't like believing did them any good, especially their Granny, who could drop dead any day now from green lung. Aries balled her fist before letting out a short sigh. There was a time that she did believe, but that was a long time ago. Hearing about those stories now brought little comfort to their day-to-day struggles.

Fairy tales and prophecies were for children. From sewer lords to tax collectors, there was no chance Aries and her family could ever move up top. Even if they wanted to, the price was still too high. That was the trap when people moved down here. Sure, there were plenty of jobs, if anyone could call them that, but once you became a resident, you could never leave. And it wasn't like the sun ever shined in Laurasia anyways. In this dreary hell, the above world was probably no better.

4

Karina

Karina pouted as she waited for her sister to finish getting dressed. She didn't know why Aries gave up so easily when the prophecy could come to life at any time. Her older sister and the others in her clan were so lucky that they got to spend their childhoods training in the traditional ways while Karina received none of that. It wasn't fair, but really, there weren't many people left in her clan who could train her anyways. In fact, most of the elders and their rich history had been lost to time. Their uncle, who was one of the last traditional fighters, died when she was nine, and her mother refused to let her train. It was hopeless. Aries walked back into the kitchen, but Karina didn't move.

"Still mad?" Aries asked.

Karina didn't even want to honor that with a response, but when she felt a warm hand on her shoulder, she looked up.

"You can visit Granny before work." Aries handed her a cloth pouch.

Karina perked up. "Really?"

"Don't be long; you got five minutes," Aries said.

Karina jumped up and rushed out the burrow's door and down the musty walkway to their granny's burrow. She only lived a few burrows from them, and Karina loved checking up on her every day. Karina reached her door, knocked, and stepped back. She heard some noise, and then it unlocked and opened.

"Granny!" Karina hugged her grandmother.

"Child, Happy New Year," her granny said before slipping into a fit of coughs. She looked so much better than she did yesterday despite the dark bags under her eyes and her thin body.

"Granny, you should be taking it easy," Karina said as she helped her granny to a chair.

"Easy?" Her granny waved her off. "Easy ain't going to get this place cleaned up."

"I can come over and clean for you, Granny."

"It's busy season, child. You go out and make your money."

"I'll never be too busy for you, Granny," Karina said.

"That's my girl." Her granny smiled as she relaxed in her chair. "You know, one day, things are going to be better. The skies are going to clear up, and them devils that run the city are going to get flushed out."

"Because of the Crimson Mouse, right?" Karina asked.

"Because of us. It's our job as the Darkness to follow the light and flush the evil out," her granny said.

"Flush it out, huh?" Aries said.

Karina whipped around. "It's true," Karina puffed.

"And I don't doubt it, but we gotta go," Aries said as she stepped in to hug her granny. "Happy New Year, Granny."

"Thank you, child," Granny said as she started to drift to sleep.

Aries stepped back and sighed. "Help me get Granny to bed."

Karina got up, and they both took an arm and helped their grandmother into her small bed, which was nothing more than a mattress in a hole, but it was decorated with beautiful hanging chimes made from bits of glass. Aries stepped away, and Karina could hear her sister picking up dishes and putting items away. Karina looked back at her granny, but she was grinning like a rat, and then she opened one eye.

"She gone?" Granny whispered, and Karina nodded. Her granny chuckled. "It's going to happen one day, child, and I'd bet blood on that. The rats know it—I can feel it."

Karina beamed and bent down to kiss her granny on the forehead before leaving. She watched her granny close her eyes before looking at one of the pictures that sat above her granny's bed. It was a very old painting of what looked like a rat, painted in red. She remembered her granny telling her that this one was special. She could feel it. Karina believed it, too, because every time she looked at it, she could just feel its energy.

Are you watching over us, Mr. Rat? Karina said as she walked to the door. How much of her history had been lost? Forgotten? But even if the mind forgot, the heart and body did not. The proof of that was in her bright red hair and crimson eyes, which occurred naturally in her people. Her people were blessed, and their time was coming, and even if everyone was making her feel foolish for believing, she knew her day would come.

Aries locked up and led them upward to level four, where the trash sorting plant was. They lived on level six, but it wasn't hard to find a tunnel leading to the higher levels. They joined the crowd of sewer people all dressed in patched and tattered waders, big work boots, and hats. The trash sorting plant was one of the sewer's biggest employers, besides the metal recycling plant; it wasn't a traditional job like a barmaid or store clerk, but it was better than being shipped to the mines. Karina knew too many horror stories about debtors being forced into unfair labor contracts, most of which were controlled by the gangs. But trash sorting didn't require contracts; anyone could show up, grab a bag, and sort.

Karina hated the work, but it was the only consistent work in the sewers. She followed the large crowds up the ramps on level five until they reached the metal arches of the trash yard on level four. On the walls were hundreds of bucket bags. Aries pushed her way through and grabbed one for Karina and one for her. People griped and complained as Aries made a path, but at six foot tall, Aries wasn't one to easily be pushed around. Aries handed her sister a bag.

"Cheer up, okay?" Aries said. "I know it sucks to get up early, but today and tomorrow are going to make us a lot of money. Money we can use to buy things. Things you like." Aries nudged her sister until she gave in.

"Fine," Karina said, "but I don't have to enjoy it."

"No one enjoys it," Aries chuckled as she led the way into the yard.

From above, two large trash shoots dumped trash into large metal train carts, which were then moved by rail to dumpers, who moved the trash into piles to be sorted. Paper and metals were highly valued. The paper was used as fuel, and the metal was shipped out of the city to Ruby-Gyme Metal Works for recycling. Everything else was fair game and free to keep as long as the runners didn't see. Karina shuffled along in her heavy metal-toed boots. She was already sweating from the heat of the incinerator that blazed in the center of the plant. Aries led them to a fresh pile, and the duo fell into their system. Aries went for the metal, and Karina went for the paper; that way, they wouldn't waste time scavenging for the same things.

Beside her, children ran by and dug through the trash. They ripped open a bag and flung the trash everywhere. A woman, who looked to be their mother, walked over.

"Careful, Amani. Don't fling trash in the walkway," she said.

"Sorry, Mama," one boy who looked about eleven said.

"Look what I found!" the other boy, who looked to be six, said, holding two gold plastic cup-shaped objects.

Karina eyed them. She had seen that type of cup somewhere, with its way too narrow bowl and long stem, with a wide base. It finally came to her—it was a champagne flute. The mother smiled as the young boy begged to keep it. The mother gave in, and the boy jumped for joy as he put it in his little satchel. Sometimes, Aries found goodies in the trash, too, but most of the time the items down here were unusable.

Large loaders full of trash rolled by, and workers scurried to get out of the way. Karina inched closer to her pile as the machines dumped their load in nearby piles. When her bag was full, she left her sister's side to dump her load in the paper bin and collect her pay. She found her line and had just stepped in when she heard a blood-curdling scream. She jerked her head to the left and saw a man writhing in pain on the ground, grabbing his bloodied right arm; it had been ripped off above the elbow. Someone rushed to turn off the chipper and help stop the bleeding when two runners walked over. The gang members with their bright orange armbands laughed and then kicked the injured man.

"Dying already, Weaver?" one of the runners said. The workers helping him held their tongues as they tended to the man. "Can't talk? That's okay, but you know, you're worth more dead to us anyways. Those organs you got would fetch a pretty price and clear out all your debt."

Weaver inched back as the runners closed the distance. The runners laughed and faked like they were going to kick him again. This made Karina's blood boil. She clenched her teeth, reaching for a magic that wasn't there.

"Don't," Aries said beside her.

"Hey! No cutting!" an older man said behind Karina.

"Fuck off, shit head," Aries bit back. "Smoke in your eyes or something? I've got metal, I'm checking on my sister."

Karina watched the other workers hold up their hands and beg for the man's life. Someone wrapped up his arm and dragged him away as two other workers stepped in their place and turned the chipper back on. The gurgling sound it made when it started again made Karina's stomach churn. Her sister held her hand and pulled her forward so she could dump her load in exchange for the daily rate. It just wasn't right. How could any of this be right?

5
Mia

New Year's Day was the only day the brothel was closed, but it wasn't a day of rest. After a wild night of partying, there was plenty of cleaning to do. Mia started early; it was better to get it out of the way instead of waiting. Coming from one of the hidden hallways, Mia's shoes crunched on bits of glitter and paper confetti. The floors were covered in it. Mia slipped through the hallway door, closing it behind her. This was going to be a pain to clean, but all this mess wasn't for nothing. From tips alone, Mia was sure to have enough to buy new jewelry, new winter clothes, and fabrics since she made most of her clothes. Heading through the lobby, Mia went left to her room. She only had one to clean, which would be the easiest chore for today. Up early, the laundry girls were also hard at work. The door next to Mia's room opened, and out bounced a pile of laundry with legs attached to it. The pile was tossed into a cart next to the wall opposite the door. Mia barely made it out of the way.

"Oops," Sara gasped. "Sorry, Mia."

"It's okay," Mia looked into the room. There were bottles of wine everywhere. "You're up early."

"I have to be," Sara said before disappearing back into the room and then scurrying back to throw a handful of pillowcases into the cart. "All this stuff needs to be washed and dried ASAP. We nearly went through all our reserves."

"Wow," Mia said. "Let me get mine then."

"Are you sure? I can get it?" Sara said.

"It's okay, my room is right here. I came down to clean it anyway."

Mia opened the door; the room was disheveled but not a total mess. The small trashcan next to the bed fell over, and half the pillows were on the floor. Mia tugged at the fitted sheet, pulling it off and shaking it out. She rolled it into a ball, along with the tucked sheet and quilted blanket. She counted her pillows and stripped them all of their pillowcases, adding to her pile. On the dresser were hand towels and washcloths. She would come back for those. Sara had moved onto the room next to Mia's, but she smiled at Mia as Mia dumped her sheets into the cart. The room didn't smell too bad, though it could use some air. Mia half-opened both the barred windows and looked through the iron bars at the alley below. A chill came in, and Mia rubbed her arms as she returned to work. Next, she grabbed the hand towels and washcloths on the dresser; she scooped them up into a ball, dropping a few before taking them out to the cart.

"Oops," Mia said as she bent down to pick up the dropped washcloths. She paused when a shimmer of gold caught her eye from under the nightstand. "Huh? What's this?"

She reached down and picked up the object and gasped at how unnaturally warm it felt. The heat was working good down here. Upon closer inspection, she realized it was a rose gold, crown-shaped ring. She tossed it a little in her hands; it had some weight to it, too. Mia fingered the indentions and zigzags that layered between them. The edges on the top end were rougher than she expected, but on the inside, she felt something engraved. She looked closer and found strange markings, not in any language she had ever seen, along with a symbol that was square with a dot in the middle and a triangle top that looked like a little house or arched window.

She heard the cart move and she remembered she had washcloths to put in it. She pocketed the ring and went to toss the washcloths in the cart. She had a lot of clients last night. Though she remembered the ring, she couldn't quite place the name of the client. She sighed; it wasn't her problem. Per brothel policy, all lost items must be returned, and then it was a problem for Zetti, who was in charge of client relations.

She picked up stray cups, bottles, and other larger trash from the floor, trying to recall who the owner was. Maybe she could help narrow it. She fingered the shape of the ring through the cloth of her shirt pocket as she thought back through the night, but nothing was coming to her. She pulled the ring out again and eyed it. Rose gold was so rare, and the rook shape on the top must have been crafted by someone with great talent. She rolled the beautiful ring between her fingers, trying to resist the urge to put it on. She loved jewelry, but Lady Valkyrie forbade any worker from stealing from clients, even if something was left by accident. She would rather have something lost surrendered to the authorities than have the reputation of her brothel tarnished, which was a policy put on display for all guests. Mia looked at the ring closer and squinted as if the ring would just tell her who their owner was.

"Hey!" someone shouted.

Mia yelped, and the ring flew from her hands. She scrambled in midair to catch it before it hit the ground. She spun around, ready to curse out the person, and fumed when she saw Billie.

"Damnit, Billie!" Mia snapped.

Billie threw up her hands as Mia waved her fist at her. "Okay, girl, chill. What's got you all wound up?"

"Nothing," Mia huffed as she turned from Billie to finish cleaning.

"Gee, sorry." Billie stepped in and looked around. "Looks like you barely used it."

Mia ignored her and continued to straighten up the room.

"Okay, Mia, I'm sorry. Hey, let me get the cart, and we can tag team this together."

Mia stopped, then turned around. "Sure...but you're not trying to rope me into helping you clean your rooms, are you?" Mia placed a hand on her hip as Billie sheepishly looked away. "Fine, but I have to stop by Zetti's."

"Sweet! Mia, you're the best," Billie said, turning to leave the room. "Hey, do you need carpet cleaner? I'm going to grab two kits because my room is...um?"

"Huh?" Mia said, not realizing she was looking at the ring. Billie looked down at her hand, and Mia hid it behind her back.

"Whoa! Is that a solid tip?" Billie peeked over Mia's shoulder.

"N-no." Mia stumbled back.

"Don't be greedy, girl, I'm not going to take it. I just wanna see." Billie reached around Mia's back.

"It's not mine; it's a client's," Mia blurted out.

Billie froze, and her eyes darkened. "You know what that means."

"Yes." Mia lowered her head. "I have to turn it in."

"Heck no, girl, you take that bad boy to the pawn shop and see how much it's worth!"

"Billie," Mia huffed.

"I'm kidding," Billie laughed. "What is it anyways? A ring? Worth anything?"

Mia shrugged and held out her palm, opening her fingers slowly. Mia heard Billie gasp.

"Whoa!" Billie snatched the ring before Mia had time to react.

"Billie!" Mia tried to reach for it, but Billie held her at arm's length.

"Relax. I just want to look at it."

Mia folded her arms and pouted, but Billie ignored her.

"Rose gold? You don't see that every day." Billie turned to Mia who was still pouting. "Fine. Here you go, crybaby." Billie held out the ring, which Mia quickly took. "It's kind of ugly, but it ain't a cheap ring."

"I don't know, I kind of like it." Mia gazed at the ring.

"Yuck. Any idea which client dropped it?" Billie asked, and Mia shook her head. "Hmm. You may want to check in with the hostess then. We can go after we finish our rooms and then dump it off with Zetti, I'll get the cart."

Mia nodded and sat on the bed. She didn't think the ring looked ugly. It looked like a relic she would find in a glass case in Lady Valkyrie's private library. Shiny but well worn, she wondered if it were a ring at all. It would make a pretty necklace.

That's when it started to come back to her. She had a client who wore three rings. The other two were about as average as they come, but she remembered seeing this ring on his finger. She closed her eyes and tried to materialize his face, but all she could remember were bits and pieces. His clean suit and polished shoes. His rough hands and tired eyes. He could have been a million people, but she remembered his tired brown eyes.

Mia looked down at the ring, turning it vertically so that the rook end faced her fingernails, and then she aligned the hole with her left ring finger. The ring still felt warm to the touch, and she kind of liked it. The hole hovered at the tip of her finger when she heard a knock on the door and tucked the ring into her shirt pocket instead.

"Oh!" one of the hostesses gasped. "I'm sorry."

"No, it's okay. I was just waiting for Billie to get back with the cart. I'll have my room cleaned soon."

"Take your time." The hostess smiled. "I'm surveying rooms for damage. Have you noticed anything out of sorts?"

Mia shook her head, lifting herself off the bed so the hostess could do her work. When the hostess left, Mia's mind floated back to the ring. Though it wasn't her style, it would have been nice if she could keep it. She didn't know why, but it was growing on her.

Billie returned, and the duo tagged-teamed their rooms. Cleaning went much faster with two people, and Mia looked forward to getting out and doing a little shopping today.

"All done!" Billie said.

Mia nodded and walked the cart back to the closet. There was still a lot of cleaning to be done in the ballroom, but that wouldn't be open for guests tonight. Billie then led the way to Zetti's office which was on the basement level. They walked through the narrow staircase, lit by dozens of bulbs attached to black wire. The wood creaked under their feet, and at times, they had to squeeze by other girls coming up past them.

To the left were the vanities where they got dressed and to the right were a series of smaller rooms for Zetti and her girls, who handled customer complaints and problems. Already, there was a line.

Billie sighed. "Is Lema down here?"

"Not sure," Mia said as she tried to get a peek. Both Lema and Kary served as Zetti's assistants, and their tiny offices were on the left and right of Zetti's.

The line moved, and Mia peered into Lema's office. She wasn't there, and when Mia checked Kary's, she saw that she was on the phone, feverishly writing something down. They were busy, which wasn't a surprise.

"Next!" Mia jumped when she heard Zetti shout.

"Sorry to yell," Zetti said as she sat at her desk. She had a very young-looking face and petite body, even though she was pushing forty. She smiled at them both, and that's when Mia noticed her ankle was wrapped in bandages and resting on an ottoman.

"No biggie," Billie said. "What happened to you?"

"You know me, always tripping over stuff. I rushed down the stairs too quickly and arrived at the bottom sooner than I would have anticipated."

"Ouch," Billie winced.

"I'm sorry that happened to you," Mia said.

"It's not as bad as it looks," Zetti said. "How may I help you?"

"Lost item." Mia reached into her pocket to present the ring.

"Oh my." Zetti leaned in to eye it. "Another piece of jewelry—that's the fifth piece today."

"Dang," Billie said. "Folks always get wild on New Year's Eve."

"Unfortunately," Zetti said. "That's why Lema is out. She's returning some unclaimed jackets and shawls. We're really backed up."

"I don't mind helping," Mia said, closing her fingers around the ring.

"Huh?" Billie eyed her.

"Really?" Zetti perked up. The glint in her eye showed that she would not let Mia back out of this. "If it won't be any trouble..."

Mia forced a smile. "I-I still have a copy of my client list. I could probably narrow it down."

"Thanks, Mia. I could really use the help, with Kary tied up on the phone and with my ankle." Zetti smiled.

Billie shook her head, but it was too late to take it back now.

"If it's too much, take it to the precinct. They'll charge a finder's fee to the client, but as policy states, returns are usually made in person. So wear something nice," Zetti said. "And don't forget to get a claims receipt."

"Of course," Mia said.

Mia guessed that there couldn't have been a better day to go on a lost and found mission. The brothel was closed, and with a list of clients, she would have the ring returned in no time. The two of them left, squeezing past the others in line.

"Way to ruin a day off," Billie said.

"It won't be so bad," Mia said as she reached down to touch the ring again.

"You're right. And besides, there's no rule on how quickly we need to complete this." Billie grinned, and Mia picked up on what she was hinting at right away.

"Shopping trip?"

"Shopping trip!" Billie said as they giggled to themselves.

Billie stretched her arms through each of the sleeves of her black puffy jacket. She loved that jacket on Billie; it really showed off her waist because of the stretchy fabric around her mid-section. Mia wasn't planning on dressing up today, but she didn't need much convincing. With all the money they made, they might as well do a little shopping, even if they still needed to return the ring. Both of them went for the same style: cropped, puffy jackets and miniskirts with thick winter tights underneath.

Mia's puffy jacket was multi-colored chrome. She put on some thigh-high boots and a white body suit with a low square neckline. She grabbed her favorite tan scarf with pink hearts she sewed on the ends right as Billie walked into her room.

"Ankle boots or mid-calve?" Billie asked.

Mia looked over Billie's outfit. She was wearing a black tube top and black fishnets under her jacket. "The black ankle boots for the full street style aesthetic."

"Girl, yes. This is why the brothel can't live without you. You have a freaking gift for fashion."

"Girl, you know it," Mia said. Mia loved fashion, and street style was all the rage in this industrial age. Though she also loved the classic style where the ladies wore long, lovely empire dresses with printed or lace corsets. That was still very much in fashion but more for the upper class.

She ran her finger down the pages in her notebook at the list of clients she had taken the night before. She hadn't realized how many singletons she had, but at least she had names. This was going to be a lot of work; she didn't know how Zetti and the others did it all. Mia tucked her hands in her jacket pocket to make sure the ring was still there. It was probably unsafe to have it stored loosely in her pocket, but she had no other place to put it.

"So, were you able to dwindle down the list?" Billie asked as they walked downstairs towards the back alley door. Mia shook her head. "Sheesh, you have a worse memory than a drunk."

"Shut up, I do not. I just had a lot of singletons."

"Relax, I'm joking. So the client... He must have been rich right?"

"Maybe." Mia opened the first page to a list of eight names.

Billie looked over her shoulder. "We can at least knock off the regulars."

"I did already."

"Yikes," Billie said. "Oh, well. We'll figure it out on the way."

"On the way where?"

"Uptown." Billie opened the side door leading to the alley.

"Uptown? How do you know this ring belongs to a client from Uptown?"

"Rose gold. Who walks around with that? And you said you remember a crisp suit. That's money, Mia."

"Okay, but how are we going to get through the city walls to Uptown?" Mia followed Billie into the alley, but Billie headed in the opposite direction of the road.

"Easy." Billie pointed downward. "The same way everyone else does."

"Oh, no no no, I'm not going through Sewer Town. Look." Mia flapped the paper in Billie's face. "This guy, number four, owns an import shop on the nice part of town. Let's stick to places around here."

"Fine." Billie folded her arms, letting Mia lead the way. "And I hope you're not going to leave that thing in that shallow ass pocket of yours."

Mia huffed and folded her arms when she felt something wiggly and cold hit her face. She screamed and nearly fell to the ground.

Billie laughed. "Relax, it's just a chain. Keep it around your neck; we don't want this trip to be for nothing."

Mia fetched the chain from her shoulder and looked at it. It was worn but probably for the best to keep the ring on a chain. Mia reached in and pulled out the ring; it looked even prettier outside in the natural light. She strung the chain through the hole and pulled the two ends of the chain around her neck, clasping it underneath her short, tightly coiled blonde hair. She pulled her hands away, and the ring dropped and bounced around her chest.

"Looks good," Billie said from the street. "Now come on."

"Coming!" Mia ran to catch up with her.

6 Vincent

Smoke floated to the ceiling joining a thick cloud gathering above the desk of Vincent Lorne the VII. Vincent put his cigarette to his full brown lips, which he held in his hand, and drew from it slowly. He allowed his lungs to fill up with smoke before allowing it to escape from his mouth and join the cloud that hovered above his head. He moved papers on his neatly organized desk, stamping each invoice with approval. A fan on the wall filtered in light, though dim, through its slow spinning blades. Vincent was not bothered by the poor light; he could see perfectly. In fact, there were a lot of things Vincent could do perfectly, and it was because of his unique talents that he landed this cozy office job in the city's most ruthless gang, The Silers. Vincent beat the ash from his bud into a metal trash bin beside his desk and brought the cigarette to his lips again.

"You should really stop smoking, Vincent," Yrwen said.

Vincent did not look up, ignoring the disgust he heard in Yrwen's voice, and exhaled more smoke. He moved another paper from the stack and stamped it. "What does it matter, anything that is broken can be replaced," Vincent said without emotion.

"As true as that statement may be, there is a cost to everything as well," Yrwen said.

Vincent looked up, staring at the accountant in his tight black suit and black string tie, tied a little too tight around the neck like a present. Vincent smirked, but it was nothing more than a flash. Though he wasn't trying to be cool. Yrwen's group weren't normal runners like Vincent. His family were born and bred to perform sensitive task for The Siler Gang. In exchange for protection and a relatively good life, including some education, workers like Yrwen pledged their life and lineage to The Silers. Not that children born into the position had much of a choice, that decision was made long before their birth. He touched the left side of his head chasing a fathom itch where a metal plate was embedded instead of locks of hair.

"If payment is required, I am compensated well enough." Vincent sat his cigarette in a crowded glass dish and waved his hand forward.

"This is also true." Yrwen brought Vincent the paperwork.

"I trust that everything is in order?" Vincent flipped through the paperwork without a hint of emotion on his face.

"Yes, sir, the sewer lords in the north deep have become very compliant with our new terms."

"Excellent." Vincent nodded.

Vincent placed the paperwork in a file holder behind his desk, then returned to his work, picking up his cigarette again. Yrwen nodded and turned to leave when the sounds of two men shouting caught his attention. Vincent homed in on the footsteps. There were three, maybe four people approaching. Yrwen looked at the door as the voices drew near. Calmly, Yrwen stepped out of the way as if he knew exactly what was about to happen.

"Shut your freaking mouth, pig," a harsh voice snapped, silencing the wails of what sounded like two other men.

Another voice cussed loudly followed by the sound of someone hitting the wall. Vincent stamped his next paper as he kicked the ashes off his bud into his metal trash bin. A runner stormed in; a hulk of a man with eyes too small for his bloated scarred face. He dragged behind him a smaller man who Vincent recognized immediately. Another runner appeared behind them, who's face resembled a jigsaw puzzle with only the wrong pieces sewn crudely together. He held tightly in his hands another man of average height but a little rounder. Vincent sharpened his gaze as the runners who dragged the wailing men in looked at Vincent and Yrwen and bowed.

It was only then that Vincent stopped to put his reports and stamp on his desk. He waved off the runners, who nodded and dragged the old, rusted metal door closed behind them. The thud of the door made the men jump. The two men before Vincent looked at him and sucked in their breath as if they had just been submerged in water. The thinner man with the light brown skin quickly rose to his feet. He was taller, about five foot eleven, and beat the dust off his high dollar suit and straightened his tie.

"Vincent." Dr. Granite struggled to compose himself. "I am gravely sorry we have to meet under these circumstances. Surely you know of my work ethic and please know that I am just as surprised at the news as you are. As a proud and respected member of the Five Families, I can guarantee you that this issue will be resolved right away."

Vincent went to place the cigarette back on his lips, only to realize the bud was finished. He deposited it in the glass dish with the others before turning his eyes to the rounder man in the back, then at the man who spoke first. Both looked as if they would crumble with the breeze and Vincent resisted the urge to sigh. Vincent was fully aware of the situation. He didn't ignore the news buzzing throughout his gang. In fact, he checked in almost weekly to make sure every leader in every faction was doing their job to their boss' satisfaction. It was tedious at times, not that he wasn't the type to get his hands dirty, but whatever his boss' demanded, they got. And Vincent's reward for his loyalty was this job, which he liked. Even if it was nothing more than stamping invoices and reviewing reports. So, imagine his surprise when he received the news that someone under his charge had failed in their duties.

"Words mean nothing to me, Doctor Granite. You of all people should know this," Vincent said.

"Y-yes of course, Vincent, but I can prove to you—" Dr. Granite stopped when he saw Vincent's hand go up.

"A requirement of a great leader is that they know how to control their people. The actions of the people under you speak as loudly as if the actions were performed by you yourself. And yet, despite your shoe licking, we find ourselves here in this mess, three days before the ceremony no less." Vincent's eyes slanted, narrowing as if it were a noose. Dr. Granite choked and coughed, as sweat started to build on his greasy brow.

"I can fix this," Dr. Granite said. "Everything else is in place, I will send out the best men to find Earl. The Black Gate, every runner I have, anything. I'll even take care of him and the body and everything. Edward." Dr. Granite waved to his son. "Edward here will make sure everything is in order, won't you, son."

Edward stumbled forward in his suit, as stiff as a board. Sweat beading on the brow of his medium brown skin. "Y-y-yes sir, Mr. Vincent, sir." Edward rubbed together his shaky hands.

"There is no need for that." Vincent's face returned to its normal blank state. "The runners have already begun to spread. As I have said before, a requirement of a great leader is that they know how to control their people. The runners have been tracking him since he stole the item yesterday evening. And from his receipts, he seemed to be enjoying himself quite a bit."

Dr. Granite's jaw clenched as he pursed his lips into a tight smile. "Of course, I-I expect nothing less from you, Vincent. Please allow my people to join the runners. I'm sure I'll have no trouble extracting the reasons behind this mess once I have my thieving brother in custody."

Yrwen came to life at that moment. He had been standing so still that it was almost as if he had blended into the wall. He walked over to Vincent, leaned down and whispered. "The West King gang have recovered Earl's body on the west river a mile from his car."

"And the item?" Vincent asked.

"Not recovered," Yrwen said, then pulled away from Vincent's ear.

Vincent tilted his head and closed his deep brown eyes, opening them as slowly as a torturous blade drawn against tender skin. "There is no need for your men to accompany the runners," Vincent said.

Dr. Granite looked between Vincent and Yrwen. Yrwen pulled his thin black hair behind what was left of his right ear. Dr. Granite swallowed hard, eyeing his very own handy work in Yrwen's embedded earpiece.

"If you would excuse me, Vincent," Yrwen said, then flashed a respectable nod to the men.

Vincent watched Yrwen walk past the two men, pull open the heavy door, and close again. Dr. Granite jumped when it made a thud, his face now pouring with sweat and his pits soaking through his suit.

"The runners have located Earl," Vincent said.

"T-that's good," Dr. Granite said.

"He was found dead, floating in the west river, a mile from his car," Vincent said. "The item, however, was not located on his person."

Dr. Granite's light brown face sunk, going pale as a corpse.

"Doctor Granite, I do believe in stirring action to get results," Vincent said. "That is why I am placing your eldest son Edward in charge of the investigation. You have three children and in three days the ceremony will begin. For every day the item is lost your child will join your dear brother in the afterlife."

Both Dr. Granite and Edward gasped.

"I recommend you redirect all your resources into tracing your brother's final movements, because if the item is in the river then you have a lot of footwork to do," Vincent said.

Dr. Granite's legs shook as he bit his bottom lip hard enough to draw blood. Vincent slid open his desk drawer and picked up a small white box of cigarettes, drawing one out before placing the box back. He stuck the cigarette in a small thimble shaped lighter next to his glass ash tray and then put the bud to his lips. Dr. Granite clenched his fist tight and bowed.

"O-of course, we will not disappoint you." Dr. Granite turned to his terrified son, walking past him to pull open the heavy metal door.

Vincent inhaled the smoke and held it in his lungs. He felt a tinge of heat coming from the brand that gave him his magic. He moved his right hand to the back of his neck where the sigil was burned into his flesh. The last thing he needed was a babysitting job. He exhaled, but he was more than capable of knowing what to do to get the job done.

7

Mary

Mary Granite walked out of her walk-in bathroom, hooking her silky black brassiere around her chest. She reached for her pink silky house robe and wrapped it around her body as she turned her attention to the half-naked young man in her bed. She brushed a finger behind her ear, to move her straightened hair from her beautiful brown face and gave him a look. Kym, her lover, wore a seductive grin on his face, but Mary waved him off. His good looks wouldn't be enough to get him off the hook this time.

"Ouch." Kym tore the covers off his chiseled body, revealing his flawless tawny brown skin and walked over to hug Mary from behind.

Mary shrugged him off. "How is it that I am supposed to marry you when you can't keep your cock out of the Hoo'nae's?"

"Relax, my love," Kym cooed. "You want an experienced lover, do you not? I need to perfect my craft." He kissed her on the neck as he reached up to grab her breast.

Mary turned to face him. "You're toying with me. I know you want that slut."

Kym's smile did not waver. "I don't."

"It's because she's younger," Mary huffed as she pulled away. She hated those whores, all three of them. They lusted after Kym like a bunch of dogs, especially Gloria, the youngest one.

"Hardly, the girl can't keep her hands off me. It's just physical, nothing more."

"How can I trust the words of a man who can't keep his cock out of the mouth of my enemies?"

Kym closed the gap between them and wrapped his arm around Mary's waist and pulled her closer, spinning her into a dip. Mary's heart fluttered under the heir to the Sapphire's fortune. His piercing brown eyes captured her every thought as his soft short black curly hair fell perfectly around his strong jaw. He was nearly twenty-one years old and in a few months, he would be of age to marry. She had been waiting for this moment for so long, even though she was only twenty. She was sure her mother and father would give them their blessing if it were a Sapphire. Kym pulled her to his bare chest and rubbed his gentle thumb across her full lips.

"She may wet my cock, but you, my Lady Mary, have my heart." Kym closed the gap between them with a kiss, slipping his tongue into her mouth to steal away any doubt that lied there. Mary moaned from the embrace, wanting him to take her again right there, but he pulled away.

"My love, I shall return again after my morning's meeting."

Mary gasped at the sudden coldness of her skin. "R-right."

She watched Kym get dressed, paying extra attention to committing his front and backside to her memory. His chestnut-colored suit complemented his skin perfectly. He always looked so polished and princely. He left her with one last kiss, and she watched him leave, holding her breath. When the door closed she fluttered around the room. Kym was the only eligible bachelor for a woman of her status. No one else deserved even a word in their direction, but of course she wasn't the only one in line for the honor. Lady Amma Sapphire had opened her legs a little too much and cursed the world with three hideous daughters. Mary huffed just thinking about them as she got dressed at her vanity. She was sure that bitch Faith, the middle child, was finding a way to ruin her life at this very moment, but none of that mattered. Those women didn't hold a candle to her beauty. Mary finished painting her face with makeup and walked across her marble floors to her large walk-in closet to select a long-sleeved black lace empire waist dress.

She put it on in haste because she had a lot of things to do today. The ceremony was in two days, and she had a dress fitting to attend with her mother. She walked to her jewelry box when she heard her door open and in rolled one of her father's *assistants*. Mary scoffed at the dreadful, lifeless thing. It was female in the face, but had nothing below the waist, except the machinery it used to wheel itself around. At least her mother had petitioned to give the thing a skirt to cover the awful bits welded together to make its bottom half. Mary hated their milky white, dead eyes. Silent and obedient, Father said they would make the perfect servants, but Mary actually preferred the living helpers. At least they looked more aesthetically pleasing. That was the problem with this necromancy business, it produced the ugliest results. At least the only scar she bore was the brand that rested on the back of her neck. The scarring was minimal, and she wished she could have forgone the entire thing, but father insisted. *Magic is a gift, my dear Mary, we must get our blessing from the spirits in order to use it.* Blah, blah, blah, the spirits answered to them, not the other way around.

The assistant stopped at the door and turned towards Mary. "Doctor Granite request your presence in his study," it said in its singsong voice.

Mary huffed with her hands on her waist. "Can't it wait?"

"This request is urgent," it said.

"For all the glory," Mary cursed. "Fine."

The assistant bowed and rolled away. What a hassle. What could possibly be so important so close to the ceremony? She had things to do, not to mention she needed to get her legs waxed and finish up her last-minute shopping with her mother. Mary grabbed her purse and walked towards the elevator. They didn't have an operator because Father said it was a waste of resources, which Mary always scoffed at. All the other families did, but of course her family was always looked down on. Always given the scraps. It was almost embarrassing coming home to their modest mansion with just enough rooms for their thirty plus family members.

Mary stepped out of the elevator and headed to her father's private elevator where she ran into her younger brother Alvert, who was only seventeen.

"Father call you, too?" Alvert said as he walked into the elevator after his sister.

"Unfortunately," Mary said dismissively.

"Wonder what it's about."

"It's hardly important. Does he not know how busy I am?" Mary said.

"Busy? Shopping is hardly an important task."

Mary gasped. "And what would a boy like you know about that? Scratch that, it's not like you have anyone to impress."

"Ouch," Alvert said playfully. "It's the same ceremony that happens every year. All my friends and I are going to do is smoke weed and get wasted. Same as last year."

Mary rolled her eyes. What a child. As they went down the quietness of the surface level was replaced with the sound of machinery. The old gas generators hummed loudly as the lights of the small elevator flickered. The elevator grinded to a halt and Alvert pushed open the metal cage. Mary gagged at the dank smell as the sound of water rushing through rusted pipes grated against her delicate ears. Mary took the lead towards her father's study. She hated coming down here. The halls were ghastly.

When she stormed into her father's study, she found him digging through his floor to ceiling shelves. Assistants lined the walls, standing silently with their awful milky colored eyes staring into nothing. She ignored her eldest brother Eddy who stood at their father's desk.

"Father! Father!" Mary yelled as she stopped in front of his desk that was covered in dusty old spell books.

"Mary." Her father rubbed his temples as he reached for his glasses on the table.

"You know that the ceremony is in two days. Mother and I have a lot of work to do," Mary said. Her father grabbed one of the books from his desk and flipped to the table of contents. Mary inched back from the cloud of dust it produced. "Father, I demand to know what's going on!"

"Your Uncle Earl is dead. He stole the gear ring, and it's lost." Her father stopped looking through the book.

Mary's stomach dropped. Her mouth opened but she couldn't find the words.

Alvert looked between his father and sister. "Uncle Earl is dead? What happened? And why did he steal the gear ring?"

"I don't know," her father's voice fell. He placed his open palms on the desk. "I don't have time to explain to you everything right now. Mary, I need you to help your brother Edward find the ring. I've already dispatched runners to the location your uncle's body was found."

Mary tore her gaze between her father and eldest brother. He couldn't be serious. "H-help? We employ a mountain of runners and w-what about your *assistants*?" Mary used air quotes. "Wouldn't they be better suited for the job?"

"Mary, I don't have time for your mouth right now. This is a serious matter, now do as you're told," he shouted.

Mary froze at the verbal lashing. "Y-yes, Father." Mary looked down at her feet.

"Alvert." Her father looked at his youngest son and balled his fist. "I will be arranging a trip for you."

"Father!" Edward yelled.

"Silence," he said. "Alvert, you are to go to the port house and wait there until Steward comes to get you."

"But, Father," Alvert said.

"Listen to me, I need you to run some errands for me. Do not bother your mother. Now go to the port house and wait there you hear me."

Alvert looked at his brother, whose face was covered in anger. Mary eyed them both.

"Alvert, what did I say!" he snapped, which spurred Alvert into action.

Their father watched Alvert leave before sitting down. Edward watched the door with his mouth wide open, then snapped back to reality and slammed his hands on the desk. Mary jumped. What was going on here? And why was Father sending Alvert away? All this shouting was starting to make her head hurt.

"Father, why is it that you won't send me away?" Edward shrieked. "Have I not been a good son? I'm sure there are places we can all go that even Vincent cannot reach."

Vincent? What did Vincent Lorne have to do with this? Last time she checked that lowly runner worked for them, not the other way around. Their father waved off his son's comments and buried his face in his palms.

"Father," Edward whined.

"Father, what is going on?" Mary demanded.

"Silence!" Their father cut Eddy a nasty look. "Your brother is not even a man, and it is an older brother's duty to step up. Sending your brother off takes away at least one worry in my mind. Now, you will report to the location where the runners are unless you want to see your sister and brother dead."

Mary's jaw dropped as Eddy flinched. "D-dead." Mary looked to her father. "W-what are you talking about?"

Their father looked at her with a pained look in his eyes. "I am so sorry, Mary. I am, but your Uncle Earl, he stole the gear ring and without it we won't be able to perform the ceremony."

"S-so? We can make another one. You've trained dozens of necromancers. Weren't they trained to take care of things like this?" Mary pleaded, but her father's eyes looked heavy with despair. "And who is going to wind up dead? We're members of the Five Families, no one can touch us."

Eddy turned and paced around the office as their father sighed.

"I wish it was that cut and dry, my dear, I really do," her father said. "Now, please listen to me carefully. I need for you to go with your brother as I look for a backup plan."

"Backup?" Eddy stormed back to their father's desk, his eyes wild and full of panic. "There is no backup. We've been performing this ceremony the exact same way for decades."

"Don't you think I know this! Without that damned ring we're screwed! Now take your sister and go check on the child and make sure he's secured. I don't need anything else going wrong today."

Edward froze, looked back at his father, but he said nothing more. Edward clenched his fist, then turned and walked away. Mary watched the door before turning back to her father. What was the big deal? It was just a dumb ceremony that they performed every year. They had an endless supply of children, and the damned beast was practically dead. What did a stupid ring matter? It could easily be forged in one of Father's shops. Mary turned to her father.

"Father."

"Go, go quickly, Mary, please."

Mary was shaken by the level of desperation in her father's voice, but she did not want to anger him further. "Yes, Father."

Mary hurried to catch up with her brother. She wore heels today and wasn't prepared to run around these underground tunnels. She caught up with him as he stormed down the halls, pushing past his father's assistants in a fit. Mary reached out and yanked on his arm, dragging him to a stop.

"What the fuck is going on, Eddy?" she demanded.

"Don't you get it! The gear ring is missing and without it all the fucking magic that keeps this shit hole of a city running will disappear."

Mary gasped.

"For all the glory, Mary, you can't be this dumb. This is our family's legacy!" Eddy spun around and continued down the hall.

Mary knew that her family had a part in making sure the magic in their city remained stable for the Sapphire's to use for their precious gemstones. It wasn't like she didn't know how Ao Almasi was made. It was an open secret amongst the Five Families. The enhancement gems were nothing more than a trick of alchemy, scrap metal melted down and infused with the essence of the spirit beast they kept as a slave, but Father and Mother kept her in the dark about most of the details concerning more complex magic. She barely had a grasp on her own magic, being capable of only summoning a few keys. Mary shook herself out of her shock and pulled up her long black dress to catch up with her brother.

"And of course, Father favors Alvert, that little dick weed," Eddy fumed. "We could all leave right now and be safe and let the Hoo'naes deal with this. It was their bloodline that formed the pack, them and the fucking Fort'nees."

Eddy arrived at an elevator that led to where their father kept his slaves. He punched the button summoning the elevator. He paced as he ran his fingers through his high-top bushy hair. Mary's heart started to race as she watched him. This sounded serious, so very serious, and part of her wondered why father hadn't sent her away. The elevator door opened, and Eddy stormed in, and Mary shuffled in after him. The gate to the elevator closed and started with a jolt, causing Mary to lose her balance and use the wall to brace herself. When the door opened again, Eddy stormed out.

"Eddy, Eddy, slow down," Mary called after him. She hated the way it smelt down here. It was like walking into a ballroom sized toilet.

Edward approached the cages and stopped. He started to chant in the old language, the language of the old spirits from which they drew their power. A summoning key, which was a type of spell that could be used for a variety of things, appeared in the shape of a small wooden house. These little gates were where the magic was taken from the spirit realm and brought into theirs. Fully corporealizing in the air next to his head, the gate appeared with a triangle arch above a door with a sigil on it. The same object branded on the back of the necks of all magic users. The sigil glowed when Eddy finished the chant, and the door opened as a tiny blue tendril slipped out and broke away to open the lock. The door opened and the screams and yells of people filled the air. Mary winced at the noise, but quickly followed. Edward walked past the people their father used in his experiments. Most were street people or sewer dwellers from the body part trade, and others had been born and raised here. The ones who no longer served a purpose would be turned into assistants. While any woman of reproductive age was kept for the ceremony.

A woman reached out to grab Eddy, nearly causing him to trip. Mary gasped in disgust as she backed away.

"My son! Please!" she wailed.

"Bitch!" Edward yelled, about to crush her arm with his foot, when an assistant stopped him.

He growled at the zombie like figure his father called an errand boy. Their eyes an unnatural milky pale gray and their lips sewn shut. Eddy stepped back, glaring at the sobbing woman. She was of child baring age and highly valued, so it was no wonder the assistant stepped in. Eddy scoffed and headed to the back where a few stronger assistants had been posted as guards. They looked at Eddy and Mary with their pale gray eyes and it freaked her out, but Eddy didn't seem fazed at all. He summoned another key, and from the door words appeared and floated towards the guards.

Obey me, for I am your master, move.

The guards stiffened and moved to the side so Eddy could enter. Mary knew these words by heart, it was the first summoning key her father taught her. Mary followed and watched him walk through the door and into a golden metal cage where a three-year-old child sat in a sea of red velvet pillows. Why was he checking on the sacrifice child?

The assistants in the room stood and attempted to block Eddy, but these assistants were no more than preprogrammed dolls and were easily pushed away. Eddy looked down at the child and scoffed.

"He's healthy enough," Edward said, as the child tried to reach for him.

When Eddy turned to exit, Mary was on his heels again as the doors locked behind him. Dread poured into her heart at the ramifications of what her father and brother said. She couldn't hold these thoughts in her mind any longer and rushed forward to stop her brother again.

"Eddy, I-I don't understand this at all. Why the rush? I'm sure we can delay the ceremony a little?"

Eddy turned his steely gaze onto her and Mary stumbled backwards. "The ceremony cannot be moved. The binding spell is bound to a certain day and bound by blood, so unless you can find us nine caster monks to sacrifice, we're screwed."

"B-but we have tons of necromancers," Mary blurted out. "The Black Gate, there are at least ten of them and they are the strongest casters in all the land."

"That are trained in the new magic, all the old stuff has been lost! Destroyed! Those bastard's arrogance screwed us."

"W-what?" Mary wasn't following.

"The Fort'nees, the Sapphire's, the Hoo'naes, all of them. The descendants of the original spell casters. Lazy, all of them. We may be a member of the Five Families, but we are nothing more than their dogs and if I don't find the ring by midnight Vincent Lorne is going to personally send me to the afterlife and it'll be your head next on the chopping block."

Eddy turned and left Mary standing in the hall, with the backdrop of screaming slaves to torment her.

"This...this can't be happening." Mary dropped her purse.

8 Mia

The day dragged on with Mia and Billie not any closer to finding the owner of the ring. This was a lot harder than it looked. She wasn't sure how Zetti did it. Mia walked beside Billie, with her hands resting behind her head, hoping Billie wasn't mad for making her run all across town. They walked through a busy part of town, packed with people here on New Year's Day. In New Town things were nicer, mostly rich shopkeepers and their families lived up here, hoping their proximity to The Great Wall would earn them some respect. The pair walked down the cobbled streets passing store fronts selling items they had only seen on affluent clients. Mia's eye caught sight of a beautiful waterfall silver chain necklace and stopped.

"What?" Billie spun around.

"Look at this, Billie." Mia pointed a polished nail to the piece. "Isn't it beautiful?"

Billie walked beside her, making a face at the necklace. "Looks gaudy to me. I bet it weighs a ton. And look at that price! Yuck."

"Oh hush, it's not ugly." Mia's eyes wandered over all the pieces on display. She spotted a belly chain and melted, she really wanted one of those, too. "I got paid pretty good, maybe I'll come back."

"And waste your money?"

"It's not a waste." Mia put her hand on her hip.

"And seriously, how are we going to find this guy? We've been wandering around all day," Billie said. "It might be easier to dump the ugly thing off with the authorities."

"Yes, but Zetti said we have to make a house call. This client might be extremely wealthy. Lady Valkyrie would want him to come back."

Billie sighed. "You're right."

Mia looked down at the ring. Billie wasn't wrong, finding one person in a congested city like Laurasia was a near impossible task. If they ditched the ring with the cops that would start a paper trail, taking the heat off the brothel, but she also didn't want to let Zetti down. Mia was the one who agreed to take on this task and she didn't want anything negative getting back to Lady Valkyrie. Mia fingered the ridges of the ring, she liked wearing it, but she wanted to find the owner and personally return it to them. Her memory was still fuzzy, but a name was starting to materialize. Mia pulled out the list.

"Howard," Mia said suddenly.

"Who?" Billie turned around.

"Howard," Mia looked up. "I feel like this is the guy, but for some reason the name doesn't quite fit."

"Howard?" Billie walked behind Mia. "Howard Longfoot. Well, ain't that the fakest sounding name I've ever heard."

"Shut up, it's not fake. You know policy requires names to match ID cards." Mia looked down at the name, but ID cards could be faked. "Or maybe it's Aaron."

"For all the glory, Mia," Billie said. "We're getting nowhere, just ditch the thing at the local pawn so we can go shopping."

"No, Billie, I'm returning it." Mia cupped the ring in her hand.

"I'm kidding," Billie said with a laugh, "but I'm starving. Let's stop at the pastry place for lunch. Tae'a has a client that swears by it."

Mia nodded. It wasn't often that she came to New Town, so she might as well enjoy it. They probably would never find the owner at this rate, so she wasn't sure why she just didn't chuck it at the police. Record keeping was the only thing those glorified runners were good at. Mia walked down the street following Billie out of the corner of her eye. She looked at the ring, paying attention to the marks engraved on the inside. How strange and what did that symbol with the dot in the middle of it mean? It wasn't a fashion ring; it was too basic for that. Perhaps a family heirloom? A man walking quickly brushed up against Mia, knocking her off balance.

"Ow!" Mia said, looking behind her, catching a glance of the harden face of the man who bumped into her. She rubbed her shoulder, but it was odd, he didn't look like he was from around here either. His clothes were too dirty, his shoes too scuffed.

"Mia." Billie pulled at her jacket sleeve.

"Hmm?" Mia turned around.

"Stop staring at that thing and move," Billie said.

"I wasn't. This guy bumped into me," Mia snapped back.

Billie looked past Mia. "Well fuck him, let's keep going."

Mia nodded, but not before looking over her shoulder again. She guessed it didn't matter where you were, people could be in a nice area and still be rude.

9

Aries

Aries ate her lunch to the sounds of trucks rumbling above her. Dust floated in the air like snowflakes, sparkling in the yellow light of the tunnels. People walked by in their waders, carrying buckets of trash towards the processing plant, paying her and her little sister no mind. Aries hated how the day started, but that's how it was at the plant. Their parents never stopped hammering in the idea that they needed to keep their heads down.

Taking large bites of her sandwich, Aries stared up at the flaky dark brown and black ceiling, not bothered by the hot smells of burning trash that wafted through the air. She closed her eyes and leaned against the wall where she could feel the vibrations from the surface better. She imagined the people walking above in the fresh air under the gray skies. Surface people complained that the sun never shone, but anywhere was better than the musty air of the tunnels, where the sun could never reach.

Her granny once said that there was a time where the sun rose every day, and the ground was covered in vast fields of green grass. That was impossible to imagine in a city like this. Wild plants didn't even grow in the city and Aries heard the outskirts were worse. She had heard all the stories about what went on at the mines. It was ten times worse there, and yet a tiny part of Aries wanted to believe. She wanted to believe that her granny's stories were real, but hope was fleeting. Especially since her granny was sick. It wouldn't be long now, just like with their uncle. And just like her parents and many other members of her clan, she was starting to feel like it was time to move on from those silly stories. After all, how much of their history had been lost to time? How much of it was even true and not the results of a twisted game of grapevine. Embellished to keep the fading hope alive.

Aries opened her eyes and looked down at her palm. Her hands were calloused from work, but also from years of training. She closed her fingers and balled them into a strong fist when the sound of a book slamming on the ground snapped her out of her daydream. Aries went on the defense, glaring at the object that assaulted her ears. The worn embedded text on the old brown book was one that she recognized immediately. Aries quickly snatched up the book, looking up at her sister who stood next to her, who seemed too casual for this encounter.

"Karina, where did you get this?" Aries tucked the book close to her, as she glanced around at the faces walking by.

"What?" Karina shrugged.

Aries glared at her sister and stood. She packed what remained of her small lunch in her sack, along with the book.

"Hey," Karina whined.

"You shouldn't be reading this in public." Aries drew the sack closed by the string.

"It's my break I can spend it how I want."

Aries got into her sister's face. Aries was taller, she towered over her sister. Her thin frame was small but underneath hid nothing but muscle. Aries looked past her sister, a smile appeared on her face but not for Karina.

"We can talk about this later," Aries voice was just above a whisper. "Come on."

Karina groaned, and threw a little fit, but Aries had already started walking down the tunnel. So, Karina had no choice but to run to catch up. Aries walked quickly, her watchful eye checked each tunnel before crossing. The pair walked under the yellow light deeper into the sewer. Aries ignored her sister's whines as they pressed on down the dank tunnels. People started to thin the further they went, as Aries put distance between themselves and the incinerator.

Up ahead was an old brick shoot where water once traveled. Aries stopped and Karina cautiously stopped, too. Aries looked behind her, making Karina jump, but she grinned and nodded towards the shoot. Aries climbed in first, using the worn brick to climb up a few feet to the next level which was nothing more than a dead end. Aries pushed away the cobwebs and smiled. It had been a long time since she had been up here, she pulled a small flashlight from her pocket and turned it on. A family of rats squeaked and scattered, as Aries reached over them to hang the light by its end on a rusted coat hanger.

"Hush hush," Aries said to the rats, "It's just me."

One of the rats squeaked when Aries got too close to its food pile. Aries stopped, then scooped up the bit of food and placed it further into the tunnel to make room for everyone. Aries moved a bit to allow room for Karina to come up.

"It's all clear, just dusty," Aries said. When they were young, they used to come here all the time. It was the perfect place to finish their break.

"Wow, this place is a mess." Karina looked around. From the front of her waders a tiny bulge moved up from her stomach to her chest. A small brown head popped up and looked around.

"Karina, what have I told you about bringing Tink to work?" Aries scooted to the back of the sealed wall.

Karina shrugged. "Excuse me, everyone." Karina waited for the rest of the rats in the tunnel to make their decision before moving further.

The rats scattered everywhere, some exiting through holes in the brick while others resettled in the back. Karina smiled and decided to sit on the other side of the shoot and let her feet hang out. She reached for her flashlight and turned it on. The light was bright, causing her to push the light away, but when her eyes adjusted, she shoved the flashlight into a small hole in the brick. The tunnel, no bigger than a closet, was fully illuminated. Aries spotted their little handprints in faded red paint on the wall, joined together with their cousins and treasured friends who were allowed to visit and all the little doodles her younger cousin Jasmany drew for them. It had been so long since Aries got the chance to see any of them.

Aries watched Karina get lost in the nostalgia, but the reminders also brought attention to those who were no longer here. Like her twin cousins who were crushed to death during a collapse, or their grandpa who was executed by his gang's boss for stealing food to feed his family. Then there were the countless others lost to the green lung, an ugly disease that rotted the lungs and promised a slow agonizing death. But that was just how it was down here. Aries folded her legs into a pretzel, careful not to disturb the rats sleeping by her leg. All the trinkets of their childhood covered in cobwebs littered the walls. Old coins and bottle caps, broken jewelry, and papers with pictures on it. It was a wonder some street person hadn't reclaimed this place, but people weren't fighting for room down here. Holes where a plenty, finding ones without dead bodies was the real issue.

Aries looked up and saw her sister looking at her. She looked into her crimson red eyes, a feature only found in her people, who also had thick bright red hair, which was probably some kind of mutation and not the *sign* her people were given by some spirit or another, then she remembered the object of her sister's attention.

"Alright."—Aries shrugged her sack off her shoulders—"but don't let me catch you reading this thing out in the open."

Karina made grabby fingers for the book. Aries watched her sister thumb through the pages. Magic was not favored by most people and her uncle said it was because they did not understand its use. Their world was filled with it, but only a few knew how to summon the keys to use it, and the few that did used it to line their pockets.

"I don't know why you're so distant about this stuff. Granny said that the prophecy is still alive and well."

Aries rolled her eyes as she moved one of her legs upright, so she could rest her head on her knee. "I'm only giving you time to read that thing because we gathered more than enough for today."

"It's not some *thing*; this is a key book." Karina lifted the book, waving the ancient text in Aries' face.

"You know as well as I do ain't nobody in our clan is caster favored."

"So, new people are born every day. Someone could and besides I've been studying every day. I could very well be the next caster."

Aries laughed.

"What, I could!" Karina said.

When Karina was born their granny believed that Karina was soma, and she was right. Somas were traveling spirits, considered to be good luck. Even if some didn't believe Granny back then, many came to see it as Karina grew older and presented more femininely, despite being assigned male at birth. Which was one of a telltale signs of the soma. So, her name was changed to Karina, gifted by their granny, to better match her spirit. Named after one of the daughters of the beautiful flower spirit Ariel. Granny had a way with things like that, knowing things, but the prophecy was older than their grandmother. Older than everyone in her dwindling clan, but to Aries it was just some fairytale about darkness and light and how a better and brighter world was just around the corner. Aries wanted to scoff. If this legend was so deep, as she was raised to believe, why hadn't anything come of it? Her clan's numbers had dropped well under three hundred, if that, and yet when questioned about its validity all pointed to their *precious* bloodline which was the only one that produced children with red hair and red eyes. Aries wanted to roll her eyes.

Aries' name, like most in her clan, came from the stories their granny told them. She always spoke about traveling spirits and guardians of shrines with such vigor. Like the fierce Moonbay Mountain Guardian Aries, who shared her name, who was gifted a golden staff for their loyalty. There were dozens of stories like this and back then Aries was proud of her name, so devoted to the cause that she dedicated herself to training under her uncle on how to use the retracting pole. As if she were some guardian to a shrine spirit. But her uncle was dead now, like most of her clan, and soon their granny would be, too.

"Look here, this is a key that could break a chain," Karina said as she read the ancient text. "And this one was used to blast holes in walls."

Aries smirked. She used to be able to read the old books as well, now she struggled to read a sentence. "You don't say."

"It's real," Karina snapped. "I know it and one day the prophecy will come true, and the sun will return just like Granny said."

"Okay, I believe you." Aries put her hands up in defense.

There was no harm in allowing her sister to believe. It was better than the reality anyway. Aries listened to her sister read the keys aloud, correcting her in their native tongue, for which she was still fluent. Tink crawled out from Karina's shirt and scanned the pages as if he wanted to learn, too. Aries smiled and scooped him up, placing him next to her snack.

"Don't eat it all, either. Share with the others," Aries said as Tink fussed and scurried around, protecting his bread crust from the other rats who gathered.

What were they going to do when their granny passed? How would Karina take it? Was Aries even ready? The smile on her face dropped as the pain and exhaustion built over years washed over her. *There had to be a better way to live. There had to be more to this life than this.*

10
Mia

Mia plucked the last strawberry from her plate, running it through the chocolate syrup before plucking it into her mouth. Empty plates covered the round metal patio table where she sat with her best friend Billie, who leaned back and rubbed her full belly.

"I can't believe people eat like this every day," Mia said between chews.

"I can't believe the food here is so cheap! I love the holidays," Billie said. Their waitress walked over to collect their dishes. Billie and Mia thanked her and paid the amount they owed for the food. "You know what," Billie said. "We should stay in town after we find this john."

"Billie, we don't have the money for that," Mia said.

"Don't need it, I know a place we could go." Billie smirked.

"I'm not working for room and board," Mia said.

Billie shrugged. "I know this bar, they take walk-ins. We could do a little escort work, crash, and use the money to go shopping tomorrow. Think about it, that pretty little silk nighty you saw earlier could be yours."

"I am not spending all my money on a nighty." Mia leaned back. "But I could use more earrings and rings. I want to pierce my ears again. Do you think two in each ear is too much? I don't want to turn off my clients."

"Fuck them. It's your body. And besides, every girl starts off with that girl next door thing. If they like you, they'll stick around. If they don't, there will always be men who grovel for pussy."

Mia laughed. "I guess you're right."

Mia looked down at the ring as people passed the patio around them. The waitress brought back their change and Billie tipped her, chatting her up. Their conversation floated to the back of Mia's mind. She was going through all this trouble for this ring. Not to mention Billie's idea sounded good. She didn't want to work tonight, but she did want to shop, and it wasn't like she had to be to work early tomorrow. Lady Valkyrie didn't care how long they stayed out, they were free people after all. Mia lifted the ring into the air, inspecting it. She loved rose gold and admired the engravings.

"I wonder if this is some kind of family heirloom," Mia said aloud.

"Ooo, that means the guy looking for it may offer some kind of reward," Billie said, resting her head on her hands.

"You think so?" Mia's face lit up.

"Naw, it looks cheap to me. I mean rose gold or not, it doesn't even have any gems in it."

"Do you think it's a wedding band?" Mia gasped; wedding bands were something only the superrich wore.

"I wouldn't be surprised, the little cheats." Billie snickered. "A quarter of my list are claimed men, though I enjoy the men who also bring their wives. Hey, let me see that thing again." Mia nodded and removed the ring from her neck. Billie eyed it once again before returning it to Mia. "You know what, it could be a wedding band, though no one around here could afford something like this. Plus wedding bands are kind of tacky. I prefer branding."

"Billie you're too kinky for your own good. What if you and your partner break up?"

"It's till death do us part, meaning the only way someone's leaving me is through a body bag."

"Billie."

"I'm kidding, though I wouldn't mind having Sara's name tattooed under my left tit."

"You really like her, huh?" Mia smiled.

Billie sighed. "I swore I would be single to the bitter end, but Sara is different. She's like a dreamer, you know. Like I've got dreams, to make a bunch of money and find and fuck good pussy, but Sara actually dreams about something more. She stares at the stage like she can see a future."

"As a dancer?"

"Not just as a dancer, but as a star. She wants to touch people with her moves, you know, move their hearts and souls and shit. Now I can dance, shake my ass, but I'm doing it for the money. Sara wants to weave in all this storytelling shit."

"That's deep," Mia said.

"It is and the more I listen to her, the more I want to see her dream come to life. I've been to Uptown, to all the big show houses. Those people can move, but I believe the Earth would really shake if Sara was up there." Billie stood and stretched, then paused.

"Everything okay? Mia asked.

"Think so, but I could have sworn I saw someone looking at us," Billie muttered, then shrugged. "You ready?"

Mia nodded and stood as well, brushing the crumbs from her corduroy mini skirt and tights. Billie asked where to next and Mia had no idea. If this was a wedding band at least that narrowed it down a bit. There was only one wedding band maker in this part of town. So Billie led the way, content on peering through the shop windows at all the items and imports. Mia didn't think much about the future like that. Even something like marriage never crossed her mind and it wasn't like she wanted kids, but she was happy her best friend was enjoying thinking about her future.

Mia marveled at all the imports. Her country's biggest export were gems, and they only imported scrap metal for the recycling plant, but the Five Families had a taste for ancient Tyrazian art and delicacies, which made the city a good place for foreign business owners. In New Town people took their time, cleaned up, and acted at least halfway decent. Mia and Billie would be no different. After all, people watching was just as fun. Mia watched the faux affluent browse through the shops and peer into the large window displays in their thick winter furs with every hair and every piece of their outfit laid perfectly in place, as they walked the same smog filled streets as the rest of The Slogs. This playing pretend tickled Mia, but she loved how pieces of The Slogs still poked through, despite the paint and cement they caked on to hide the cracks in the old buildings. These little details to her made the city look more honest, because in reality, no matter how much these people painted their faces and dressed up their bodies, they were really no better than a sex worker, working her body for rent.

Billie stopped Mia and pointed to a shop up ahead. Mia followed her finger and saw the beautiful dresses in the shop window. They rushed over, pass a few store fronts down to the shop at the end of the block.

"Mia, look at this one." Billie pointed to the long shimmery red bodycon dress. "I've never seen a gown this beautiful."

Mia leaned closer to the window. "I like the drop waist fuchsia one in the back, with the corset, what do you think Billie?"

Mia looked up, but Billie wasn't smiling anymore. Mia furrowed her brow, but quickly saw what Billie was fixated on. Five large men approached them fast and these men didn't look like they belonged here with their worn pants and tunic style shirts and suspenders and leathered jackets. All of them had metal bands around their biceps. They looked like runners, but she had never known runners to wear metal bands on their arms. Billie pushed Mia back as the men stopped in front of them. Their eyes lowered to their chest as their grins grew wider.

"Evening, ladies." A man in the front with a jerry curl smiled. Mia cringed at his mouth full of missing and yellowed teeth. His eyes seemed to be on her specifically. "Let me be the first to wish you Happy New Year. I ain't here to cause no trouble, but I'll take off your hands that ring you got around your neck."

"Not a chance, pig," Billie snapped, only earning her snickers and grins from the runners.

"Feisty," the ringleader said.

"Take a hike," Billie said, before grabbing Mia's hand and walking off.

"Hold on, buttercup." The ringleader grabbed Mia's arm.

"Hey!" Mia yelled.

"Let go of her." Billie balled her fist and swung.

The man leaned back just in time and laughed loudly, drawing the attention of the other shoppers. The man yanked Mia towards him, pulling her close to his chest.

"Hey! Let go of me!" Mia jerked, but the man only grinned at her.

"Now play nice for me, girly," the man said.

"No way!" Mia shouted as the crowds thinned, not wanting to become involved with runners.

"I said let go of her!" Billie growled and charged for the main guy. One of his buddies stepped in front of her, but Billie elbowed him in the gut and leapt high in the air. Mia ducked as Billie kneed the ringleader in the face and landed perfectly on the ground beside him.

"You dumb bitch!" the ringleader hollered.

"Let's go!" Billie grabbed Mia's hand and took off.

"Fuck! Get 'em!" the leader shouted from behind them.

Mia looked over her shoulder. The runners were fast, but Billie weaved through the crowds, not caring who she bumped into. The men were closing the gap with ease, as the small metal ring bounced around on Mia's chest. These men were persistent and for what? A silly ring? Billie took a sharp left, pulling Mia from the crowds down a narrow alley. Commotion from the street echoed behind them as the runners ran down the alley after them.

"Shit," Billie cursed under her breath. "Hey!" Billie shouted to Mia and pointed up towards a metal fire escape.

Mia got the message and ascended the stairs, hoping to lose the runners, but they were persistent. Mia climbed up the five flights behind Billie as the stairs rocked from the weight of all the people on them. She reached the top and took off after Billie, who darted around chimneys.

The runners weren't far behind and were faster on flat surfaces. Mia looked behind her, then in front. There was nowhere else to go, and they knew the runners knew that. Billie looked back at Mia and pointed to the other side of the roof.

"Alright, ladies, there ain't nowhere else to run!" the man shouted.

Mia looked ahead and nodded. The two picked up the pace and sprinted towards the edge. They reached the ledge, below them a wide alley, and jumped. The runners sprinted to the ledge as Billie and Mia floated in the air, gliding like birds, and landed on the other side with perfect form on the slanted side of the other building.

Not losing an ounce of momentum Billie and Mia scaled the roof, much to the flurry of curses flung at them from the runners on the other building. They reached the top of the slanted roof and disappeared over the edge and slid down. They did not stop there and with perfect balance the two ran as fast as they could to the other side of the roof and jumped down onto the metal canopy of an old steam car. Mia stopped to catch her breath and check to see if the runners had followed.

"Mia, come on," Billie said.

"Shit, what was up with those runners?" Mia said.

"Don't know." Billie shrugged. "But they're bad news."

"Bad news?" Mia asked.

"They were Silers, Mia," Billie said.

"Oh shit." Mia's eyes widened. She had heard of them, but never seen one in person. "The metal armbands!" Mia gasped.

"Yeah, and they're the meanest gang in the city, they really don't give a shit about anyone or anybody, so let's go," Billie said.

Mia nodded and followed. She knew better than to stop with runners on her tail. Pimps were hard enough to deal with; being kidnapped and sold by runners was like asking for a death sentence. The ring bounced on her chest wildly. It appeared in her vision from time to time. She reached out and clumsily caught it and pulled her scarf loose to tuck it inside of her shirt where the cool metal chilled her warm sweaty skin. It was bold of runners to make a scene like that in New Town, but then again, when had runners ever cared about respectability? Still, she felt as though it was odd that they would make a scene like that over a tiny rose gold ring. Was it really worth that much? Or was it connected to something more?

11
Mary

Mary sat in the small field tent Eddy had set up for their operation near the river. It was freezing outside and yet no one could be bothered to bring them a heater. She swore this ring mess would turn her gray and how embarrassing would it be for the other members of the Five Families to find out about this little incident. Mary dreaded the look in that bitch Joy Hoo'nae's face. Joy always acted like she was better than Mary because she was five years older. That hag was old news and Mary was sure it got under her skin that she would have to compete with her younger sisters for the best bachelors. Afterall, what an embarrassment it was to be twenty-five and unmarried.

Eddy beat his brow with his handkerchief as he paced around their makeshift base. He pulled out a pocket watch and groaned. Mary hated that she could feel his worry. Even though they didn't always see eye to eye, he was still her brother. Which was why this entire operation pissed her off. Her father had all these secret organizations and ties and yet, here she and her brother were, doing the dirty work. What the fuck were those Silers doing? And what about her father's secret Black Gate? Useless. It was nearly supper time, and if Vincent was known for anything it was that he always kept his word.

Runners walked by the tent opening, talking and carrying on. It angered her that they were in this mess at all, but the gravity of it all had been made uncomfortably clear at how much trouble their family was in. Early in the evening, Mary returned home to change her clothes, and the news had already spread to the entire family. Their mother was hysterical and still their father refused to send them away, instead he put all his energy into protecting Alvert. It ate Eddy up so bad, but Alvert was just a kid. He couldn't handle something like this. It overwhelmed her just being here. So instead, Mary turned her focus to her mother. She should be helping more, but their mother was bedridden, claiming that her heart couldn't take it. So, Eddy and she were left with all the work.

Another runner walked by and still there wasn't any news. With all the street thugs and runners that moved around this city how could anyone breathe without a member of the Five Families' private guard not know? And yet they couldn't even find a stupid ring.

"My, someone's nervous," a deep but feminine voice said.

Eddy spun around and his voice caught in his throat. Mary glared at the woman before them. She turned to Eddy, but his eyes were glued to her chest like a horny teenager.

"Lady Rosemary," Mary greeted the woman coldly as she walked in.

Lady Rosemary smirked as she pushed a lock of her moss green hair from her face. "Lady Mary."

Lady Rosemary greeted her as she walked by in her gaudy tight green dress. Her large breast were practically popping out. Mary bet they were fake, knowing what the witch could do. Her wide hips rocked as she approached Eddy and wrapped her long green polished stiletto nails around Eddy's shoulders, causing him to gulp.

"My my, someone has naughty thoughts on the brain," Lady Rosemary said. "Don't you think you should be more concerned about the situation you're in?"

"I-I," Eddy stumbled over his words, which made Mary roll her eyes.

"Why are you here?" Mary bit.

Lady Rosemary slowly unwrapped her arms from around her brother's neck and sat on the edge of the desk. Her large butt tugging at the tight fabric of her long green dress exposing the tops of her high heels. "You know how Vincent is, he likes to be...thorough."

Mary clenched her teeth. If Lady Rosemary was here then that meant even Vincent had little faith in Eddy's efforts, after all she was number three only to Vincent himself.

"You have a nice set up here though. I like the smell of totally fucked in the air."

"Don't you think I know the situation I'm in," Eddy growled. "My family is the backbone to this whole operation and yet the others dare not get their hands dirty."

"Doctors and slavers, the great Granite family. I hate to burst your bubble kid, but you only had one job."

Eddy slammed his palms on the table. "It's not our fault!"

A runner with a large scar on his face appeared at the door and caught Eddy's attention right away. "I have word from a group of runners from New Town. Someone has spotted a pair of young girls with the ring."

"T-That's excellent!" Eddy said. "That's fabulous news! Gather everyone, bring those women to me."

"There is one problem, however, the runners were unable to capture them. They escaped, but it is still believed they are in New Town."

Eddy's face twisted into a scowl. "Damnit! What good are you thugs if you can't even catch a pair of women!"

Lady Rosemary stood and lightly wiped the wrinkles from her dress. "Leave this to me." She motioned to the runner, who bowed and exited the tent. She turned to Mary and smirked, but Mary only glared at her, before she turned her full attention back to Eddy. "It's clear that Lord Edward is under a lot of stress. Allow me to take this problem off your hands," she said as she tucked and straightened his tie.

"La-Lady Rose—" but she silenced him by pressing her finger to his lips.

"Let's not stress out your poor family anymore. Surely you can see that your sister wants you to end this. Isn't that right, Lady Mary? I know you've had your eye on the Young Lord Sapphire and I'm sure you still have a chance, after all wealth tops looks," Lady Rosemary said as she rolled her shoulders back which made her large breast stand out more.

Mary stood with a retort ready, blood boiling at the comment, but Eddy stepped in front of her.

"O-of course, my lady, please handle the situation as you see fit and perhaps you will put in a good word for me for my expert leadership? A-after all, this is my operation."

Lady Rosemary grinned. "Of course, Lord Edward, just have the preservation tanks ready when I return. I don't want to waste an ounce of their precious blood." A blood thirsty grin stretched across her face. "Consider it my fee."

Eddy groveled at her feet like a dog. It was disgusting. She was nothing more than a dirty blood witch who used magic to enhance her beauty. Mary couldn't stand her, but at least the search was over. Lady Rosemary would find those women, and everything would return to normal.

Mary left an hour after Lady Rosemary. She was sick to death from running around with runners in their musty cars. It was truly a task that was beneath her. Her driver drove her back to Uptown, but when they approached the Sapphire manor, she asked them to stop. The driver did as they were told and pulled around back. They got out and opened the door for Mary and she waved them off. She needed to see her Kym after the long day she had.

She walked towards the gardens and into the beautiful maze of perfectly trimmed bushes full of winter roses that only bloomed because they were enhanced with magic. They smelled so intoxicatingly good that it pulled Mary straight into her dreams with Kym wrapped around her. Oh, how she longed for him. She needed to feel his warm skin, capture his soft lips. She walked past the fountain in the center of the garden and saw the light was on in Kym's private garden study. She gathered up her dress and rushed to the door and reached for the handle, expecting to see him at his desk, but when she opened the door he wasn't there. Mary furrowed her brow. She checked the sunroom, then the bathroom, then it occurred to her that he was probably downstairs in his dungeon.

"That bastard," Mary cursed as she stormed over to the bookshelves and pulled on the gargoyle statue on the fourth shelf.

The door slowly slid open. The lights were on and that meant only one thing. Mary fumed as she walked down the stone steps as the door slid closed behind her. Before she reached the bottom she heard a loud moan. Mary gathered up her dress and stomped towards his viewing room, nearly running into Kym as he came out. Kym looked shocked to see her but captured her lips with his fingers.

"Hush, my love," Kym whispered as he let the door close behind him. He pulled Mary to one of his dark brown tufted-back leather couches, but Mary jerked away.

"Who do you have in there?" Mary hissed as she stormed to the special one-way magic window Kym had invented. "If it's Gloria, I swear—"

Mary gasped when she saw that it wasn't the youngest Hoo'nae daughter at all, but instead, Mary's biggest rival and enemy, Faith Hoo'nae. She was completely naked, hanging by her leather-bound arms on Kym's vertical table in clear view for Mary to see. Mary inched back into Kym's arms, then jerked away.

"You piece of horse shit." Mary felt sick.

"My love, when have I ever lied to you?" Kym said. Mary's face twisted into disgust, but Kym only smiled. "Take a closer look. She's such a whore, she gives her blood to me willingly."

Mary spotted the tied pieces of white cloth on Faith's brown skin. Then she noticed the chalices of bright red blood.

"You know that I am in The Yield, practicing necromancy," Kym said. "I want to impress your father, after all, and one day join The Black Gate, and blood makes the summoning's stronger."

"B-but she's naked." Mary tensed as she looked at Faith's full chest, thin waist, and flawless skin.

"She's a whore. She begged me to make her work for it, so she can earn my love. My love for you has not changed, my dear. I do this for you and only you," Kym said, but Mary only scoffed. "My love, look, I can make her do whatever I please."

"Prove it," Mary said coldly to which Kym responded with a grin.

"This is what I love about you, Mary, you're not like the other girls who are so easy to manipulate," Kym said. "And you know what, now might be the perfect time to test a new invention of mine."

Kym walked to a table and picked up a smooth, foot long, black stone that was nearly as thick as Mary's wrist. Mary eyed it with suspicion.

"This type of stone is very sensitive to magic, especially magic enhanced with blood, for which you of all people know is the fuel to a necromancer's magic. I've been working on designing the perfect enhancement stone in my laboratory at my family's factory and whose blood would be more perfect to experiment with than another member of the Five Families?" Kym held the stone in his hands. "And I think these will be *very* popular."

"Get on with it." Mary folded her arms impatiently.

"I have one inserted in our dear friend Lady Faith. Can you guess where?" Kym smirked as Mary's eyes went wide.

Kym kissed her cheek and slowly backed away. Then walked to the door leading to his playroom. Faith's face lit up immediately as Mary watched through the one-way magic window.

"Lord Kym," Faith smiled.

"Sorry for the wait, Lady Faith," Kym said. "Are you ready for more?" Faith giggled with delight and it made Mary's blood boil. "That's a good girl, but I'm going to need you to beg for it."

Faith did as she was told. Mary didn't want to see anymore, when Kym calmly turned his back on Faith and looked directly at Mary. It was like he could see her and it made Mary's heart flutter. Kym smirked as he turned back to Faith and pulled out a needle and found a vein on her arm. Faith moaned as the syringe entered her skin and soon her bright red blood flowed into a chalice. Mary watched, furious, but Kym wasn't finished. He chanted and his key gate appeared above his head. The little door creeped open and out wormed the bright blue tendrils made from pure magic. Kym continued his summoning as the tendrils wrapped around his arm, traveling to his fingers. When he dipped his fingers in her blood the tendrils turned an electrifying red, making his hand glow a hot orange. He flicked his finger upward and Faith yelped. Mary watched closely and noticed an orange glow coming from between Faith's legs. He was doing something to her, Mary gasped. Kym smiled, before flashing a quick glance to Mary.

Mary's heart raced. He was doing something to her...and she was liking it. Mary gritted her teeth. Faith the slut, she hated her so much, but part of Mary wanted to see her writhing and begging on that table. As if Kym could read her mind, he sent forth his now burning hot orange tendrils all over Faith's body. She gasped and cried out as the buzz of his magic squeezed and stung her breast. *More,* Mary's lust had taken complete control now. Kym called the glowing stone out of Faith, then forced it upward. *More!* Mary's excitement was so hard to contain. Faith moaned and gasped as Kym chanted again and dipped his other fingers once more into the chalice of blood. He summoned a second stone, and it hovered in the air towards Faith's ass. He flicked his fingers and Faith screamed with pleasure as it worked itself in. Heat pulsed through Mary's body. She wanted to see Faith torn apart. Soon, Faith's screams filled Mary's ears and the pleasure she felt was otherworldly. Mary reached for her dress and pulled it up, touching herself as Kym penetrated her rival like a pin cushion.

"Oh, Kym," Mary moaned his name. He always knew how to make her feel good on her bad days.

12

Aries

The day ended early for Aries. Her family had earned more than enough for the day, the spoils of the post-holiday season. At least for today their family would eat good. Aries set out to town to grab something for dinner. She wasn't sure if she was in the mood for fresh carrots and turnips, which were very expensive or if she should spend her money on uyoga, which were a large hardy type of mushroom that tasted like meat that grew down here. Aries took her sister along, who loved to go to the markets.

They both walked down the old metal stairs that creaked beneath their feet. The markets were still open, which Aries was very grateful for. Maybe she could get both on a deal close to closing. Aries long crimson red hair bounced behind her back as she descended. Tied in two calf length long braids, this was the only way she could manage the beast. She didn't know why her hair grew so long or so fast, but she didn't mind it in the winter, when all the tunnels were drafty and cold. Her sister on the other hand kept her hair in two large puff balls. Though she was a young woman, Karina didn't care about her looks that much, or flirt with suiters. They were alike in that regard, and it wasn't like suiters weren't interested. Relationships were just hard and complicated, borderline annoying to Aries. She was twenty-six and had turned down too many to count. She just didn't see the point of laying up with someone in a burrow, when they lived in Ozama's personal hell.

Aries reached the path leading into the outskirts of Heathera, a small settlement and marketplace next to Gomi City on the ground floor. She waited for her sister to catch up before walking down the curved dirt path into town.

"What are we picking up for dinner?" Karina asked as Aries started walking again.

"Not sure," Aries said.

"We should get fish! No no, let's get king uyoga!" Karina jumped.

"Oh, you think we have big money," Aries said. "We'd be lucky if we could afford a pound of carrots."

"Yuck." Karina stuck out her tongue.

"It's not that bad. How about some uyoga then? We can make a stew," Aries said. "We haven't had that in a while."

Karina folded her arms against her flat chest.

"Fine, we'll get *king* uyoga," Aries gave in. That would be a real treat.

Karina's face lit up as she bounced around. Aries shook her head. She still acted like a child even at eighteen. Karina ran up ahead, mentioning something about a junk shop. Aries raised her hand to let her go. She was a woman now; she could take care of herself. Aries followed down the incline and noticed a group of men walking too close for Aries' liking. She picked up the pace, eyeing them as she turned around the bend with the path. Runners, but it didn't look like they were part of a faction. One snickered as they closed the gap.

"Hey, there." One reached out towards Aries.

Aries dodged and grabbed his hand, twisting it until she could hear the bone break. The man hollered as his buddies inched backwards.

"What the fuck, bitch?!" the man yelled.

Aries' blood red eyes shut him up. "Consider this your only warning." Aries sharpened her gaze

The man inched back and looked to his buddies, but none took an inch towards Aries. The guy cursed then got up and ran. She watched them disappear down a known path before moving again. She had to be careful how she interacted with street gangs, but those guys were nothing more than a bunch of punks. The outskirts were infested with wannabe street thugs.

Aries continued into town, which was nothing more than a block of shops made from large metal train carts. This part of Sewer Town used to be a large train tunnel, but trains didn't run on the ground level anymore for fear of collapse, which was always an ever-present threat down here. Aries blended in with the crowd. The air quality was better in Heathera, but some still wore their gas masks. Children zoomed by, holding colorful paper windmills in their hands. Aries smiled and moved out of their way.

The shop keepers haggled and shouted their offerings, but there was one vendor in particular Aries looked for. Aries made her way through the crowds searching, looking at booths from afar, which she could do with ease because of her height. Then she spotted a vendor she liked and squeezed over.

"Got any king uyoga today?" Aries asked an old man with wildly growing gray hair.

"Eh, ain't got no king." He struggled to open one eye, but his tone changed once he got a better look at her. "I'd know that crazy red hair from anywhere, you're one of them Rat People." The old man smiled, and he rubbed his cracked hands together.

"I wouldn't call us Rat People, but that is what the translation says." Aries smiled.

"I've known your people from back when you use to be on the other side of Sewer Town in Old Newkent."

"Old Newkent, it's been a while since I've heard of that name," Aries said. That was on level seven, but it was nearly impossible to live there now.

"I'm not surprised." The old man stood slowly and reached for his cane made of rebar. "The place up and collapsed. It was a terrible loss. I was born in Voreheaven. There used to be a bridge from Voreheaven to Old Newkent, but when the city fell..." The old man lowered his head.

Aries understood. She was born in Old Newkent and lived there until she was about three. She remembered her granny saying that it was such a humid place. The city was close to the sewer lines. It was so dank and moist that most folks weren't sure what would kill them first, the mold or the poor infrastructure, but it was safe from the worst of the gangs and crime and that's what made it home.

The old man walked to the back of the container and returned with a rare treat. It wasn't king uyoga, but a bit of chicken meat. He offered it to Aries for half the price, even threw in a few beets. Aries gladly took the deal. Animal meat was super rare down here. A nice hearty meal like this would be a change of pace from the bread and cheese they had at home.

"Thank you so much," Aries said.

The man waved, as he eased himself back onto his stool. He cracked a smile and Aries bowed to him again. Aries looked for her sister next. It didn't take her long to find her. Aries made her way to a junk vendor, where she found her sister poured over a pile of old books.

"You ready?" Aries asked.

"Ready? There are so many books here. Do you think they have some on magic?" Karina said, not paying attention to who could overhear.

"Hush, let's go." Aries looked at the vendor, a young man whose eyes seemed to be focused more on her sister's body than his merchandise.

"Aww," Karina pouted.

"Now," Aries said firmly.

Karina got up and slumped away. She could be so dramatic sometimes, but she needed to be careful how she spoke of magic. While Granny's stories may be hard to believe, the rumors about the Siler Gang's necromancers were not. The Siler Gang worked in the shadows, but there was no mistaken who ruled over Sewer Town. They were the only gang that wore metal armbands. Her uncle told her all about them. How they trafficked people for organs and forced people to work in the mines to the north and the grain fields in the south. She'd seen them from time to time and she could just feel their evil radiating off them, but the locals feared their magic the most. Evil and twisted were the kindest things said about them and in turn that fueled everyone's fear of all things magic. Which made it dangerous for people like her clan, who practiced magic, to talk about it in the open.

The pair made their way back home to their level in the sewer. The incinerator was being put to work tonight, so it was warmer than usual which made their little burrow cozy. Aries announced herself and moved out the way to allow Karina to squeeze by to get to her room.

"Aries, you're back," her mother Sasha said.

"Hi, Mom. How was work?" Aries placed the food on the table.

"Good today, made a killing," she joked.

Aries smiled and looked at her father who had already passed out drunk for the night. She guessed she knew what he spent his holiday money on. Her mother started on the food, surprised to find chicken instead of seasonings and root vegetables.

"Is this real chicken?" Sasha asked.

"Yep, the man offered it to us on a discount." Aries found a seat at the table and relaxed.

Her mother eyed her. "And you didn't ask why?"

Aries laughed. Their mother was always suspicious. "It's about to go bad, I can smell it, but we were going to cook it tonight anyways."

"You ain't doing no street work are you, Ari?" her father Kurk slurred.

"You really drunk tonight, Dad." Aries saw her father smirk.

"Hey, ain't that drunk." He leaned up, slob falling from his mouth and grinned, flashing his yellow teeth, as he rubbed his long thick red beard.

"You a fool, Kurk," Sasha said, "and wipe your mouth."

"Oh." Kurk rubbed his mouth on his forearm.

Aries leaned back and allowed herself to let her guard down for a bit. It was rare that they had family moments like these, with her parents constantly working to help their sicker relatives. Aries watched her mother clean the chicken under the sink, before laying it out on the cutting board.

"Aries I want you to keep a sharp eye out there. I've noticed a lot of runners on the prowl," Sasha warned.

"Yes, Mom." Aries straightened up.

"I'm serious. They're swarming like cockroaches. Tell her, Kurk." Sasha turned to him, but his head was buried in his arms. Sasha sucked her teeth. "I don't know what they're after, but they're up to something. I can feel it in my bones. In fact, later tonight I want you to go to your cousin Zopi's and make sure that boy is inside taking care of them babies."

"Yes, Mom." Aries did what she could not to frown.

Sasha shook her spoon in Aries direction. "I haven't seen him at the plant, so who knows how he's getting his money and paying his rent."

Her cousin Zopi had a big head and always ran with trouble. He, like their grandfather, thought the gangs would be their ticket out. Aries' mom and dad thought he had turned his life around after he married someone from outside their clan, but his bride died of green lung at the age of twenty-three. It was tragic, but she had what the elders called the Jeni, which was a kind of birth defect where babies were born with light brown eyes and dark spots on their tongue. Folks born like that were often sick as babies and died young. Aries hated that for them and the clan elders hated them even more. They admonished him for marrying someone sick, but Zopi was in love.

He wasn't like his parents, who were traditionalists. They believed that it was only safe to marry someone selected by the family, like her mother and father were forced to do. And Aries didn't blame him for not wanting to spend the rest of his life with a stranger.

Granny also disagreed with this practice, but there was little she could do against Grandpa's fist. The entire thing frustrated Aries to no end. Their clan was already so small. They had no business raising their fists against one another. Aries stood and walked to her nook to change into something more comfortable. It was warm tonight because of the incinerator, so she settled on a pair of thin pants and a baggy shirt, which she hunched over to put on because the ceiling was too low. She got dressed, then checked on her sister, who was in her usual spot in her cut out of a room, painting on her bed.

"What you working on?" Aries startled Karina on purpose, making her smudge the text she was writing on her arm.

"You're gonna make me mess up!" Karina snapped.

"Why are you writing on your arm? It's gonna wash off," Aries said as she leaned on the wall with her arms folded.

Karina pouted, but eventually gave in. "Cause the book said so, okay. I'll be able to improve my casting if I memorize the keys."

"Is that so?" Aries raised an eyebrow. "Well, when you're done come help Mom with dinner."

"Did you get king uyoga?" Karina's face lit up.

"I got chicken," Aries said from the main room.

"Yuck!"

Aries walked back into the main room, her family were still talking to each other, or rather, Sasha was talking at Kurt who wasn't normally this drunk, but it was a holiday and Mom allowed it. Aries was just about to take a seat when they heard a knock at the door. Everyone froze. Sasha and Kurk looked up, but Aries was the first to move.

"Who is it?" Aries said.

"It's your granny!"

Aries opened the door and stepped to the side as a pile of multi-colored robes pushed its way in.

"Mom?" Sasha peeked around the cabinet door.

The old woman was out of breath as she used her cane to find herself a seat at the table. She coughed and hacked but put up her hand when Sasha and Aries moved towards her. "I-I came, I came as fast as I could." Their granny flipped the robes from over her head. Her once vibrant red hair was lighter and thinner. It fell all over her face as if she couldn't be bothered to tame it.

"Mom, what's going on?"

"I had a vision!" the old woman croaked.

"Now, Glenda." Kurk started to stand.

"I ain't crazy either," Granny said. "I saw a vision! A vision of the Crimson Mouse!"

Silence covered the room. Aries stood, stunned, as if a bucket of cold water had been thrown in her face. At that very moment Karina rushed in from her room. Sasha looked over at Kurk, his face cold. He sat back down and instead reached for his bottle of rice wine and took a sip straight out of the bottle. Sasha looked to Aries then back to her mother.

"Mom," Sasha said.

"King Nezumi'Mfalme appeared before me himself!" Granny waved her finger and Karina gasped.

"The Rat King?" Karina's eyes went wider.

"Yes, child! And he showed me the great plains! The fields of grass! And the bright shining sun! It came to me just this evening as I was cooking, as serious as a heart attack I fell to my knees. I couldn't take it."

"Mom," Sasha said more firmly. "It's the New Year, how about we start in a place more grounded."

"We in the ground. How much more grounded you need us to be?" Granny snapped back.

Karina ran to her granny. "Granny!" The two hugged tight. Karina let go to take a seat next to her, while all Aries could do was watch. "Tell me about the vision. What else did the Rat King show you?"

"Grass, child, miles and miles of it," Granny paused to cough, which sounded so violent and wet, but she cleared her throat and continued. "Grass! Grass so green you'd think it was painted right off a billboard. And the sun, baby, the sun was shining so bright, and there they was."

"The great spirit?" Karina asked.

Granny nodded. "Acome."

"Mother, that's enough," Sasha said sharply, then returned to cooking. "Stop filling her head up with all those lies."

"It ain't lies." Granny tried to stand, but Karina tucked her back into her seat.

"I don't want to hear anymore," Sasha shouted, and Granny frowned. "Now you can stay and eat, but I don't want to hear another word about that."

Sasha's voice snapped Aries back to reality. It was usually like this when Granny got dramatic about her dreams, because Granny was a seer and seers were the only ones who could receive the vision for the prophecy from Acome, the spirit guardian of this lawless land. But their Granny mentioning King Nezumi'Mfalme, that was something new. It didn't matter though, nothing ever came from her Granny's visions or any of the seers before her. Aries looked to her sister; she looked hurt by their mother's words. She wondered how long Karina would hold out, how long she would keep believing.

"Aww, Mom," Karina whined.

"Listen to your mother, Karina," Kurk said, warning heavy on his voice.

Granny glared at the group. "You done lost your way a long time ago, but what's gon happen gon happen, whether you believe it or not," Granny huffed. "Now what you got cooking for dinner?"

13
Karina

Karina jumped at the idea to walk her granny home. She rushed to grab her flashlight as Aries followed behind her. Her older sister said goodbye to their mother as she tucked a switchblade into her pocket. Karina was aware of how unsafe it was to travel at night, but she didn't care because all of her wildest dreams were about to come true. The prophecy was real, and she believed her granny. Karina helped her granny along, offering to hold her hand. Heat from the ground kept them warm as the smell of burning trash rose through the air. Her grandmother was lucky to have a place near the street vents, though it could get nasty when it rained. Karina remembered that her mother said their clan had a hard time finding a new place after the collapse, but eventually they found this abandoned dug out that used to belong to a gang, and it was perfect for their needs.

"Granny, please tell me more about the prophecy and start from the beginning," Karina begged.

Her granny smiled as Aries closed the gap between them. She kept her watchful eye out for runners, but Karina wanted to hear the story. Maybe if Granny spoke about it her older sister would finally understand.

"Alright, child," she hummed. "In the beginning, the world was wild and free. Folk could move around every which a way. There were no tolls, no debts to keep you pinned. And all the land was guarded by the great Eastern Noramican Mountain spirit."

"Acome," Karina said with delight.

"That's right. The land was protected by the great mountain spirit Acome," Granny said proudly. "They made sure the sun reached our crops and looked after all the people and animals, no matter how big or how small. But folk got greedy. Rumor has it that some of the old mountain monks weren't content tending to the temple, tending to Acome. Or so they say." Granny winked. "I'm old, what do I know, but one day a great bolt of lightning lit up the night sky and on the next morning the sun didn't rise. All the people and animal folk walked up the mountain to visit Acome, but they wasn't there. And soon after, the crops stopped growing in as strong, and the rivers stopped filling up the lakes. Child, nothing wanted to grow, and folks didn't know why. They went to the monks, who said that change is the way of nature or some roach shit like that."

Granny scowled. "But our people knew the truth. The true believers knew. Acome was gone and it won't the way of nothing. So, somewhere along the line our people were chosen to seek the truth."

"The gift, right?" Karina said. "From the Rat King."

"That's right." Granny smiled and pointed to her red hair. "Proof enough up here and seers were born soon after, but only one alive at once, and the first one proclaimed, that one day a Crimson Mouse would appear and lead us to Acome, and the sun would rise again."

Karina never got tired of hearing this story. Acome was the spirit of this land, the great keeper of balance, even though their name was treated more like a curse in her household. But Karina knew better. She had read about it in all the old books and Acome wasn't the only great spirit. There were hundreds across the land. Beyond the Great Noramican Mountains were the domains of other spirits, whose strange and mysterious powers could move land and summon fire. There were even stories about sentient non-human races who had powers that rivaled that of a necromancer, that lived west beyond the great Bustani River. A river so vast that an entire city could be built in the middle of it and was protected by Megami Ua, a powerful water spirit.

All of this fascinated Karina and now the prophecy had begun. All they had to do was find the Crimson Mouse and it would lead them to Acome.

"And you think the prophecy has started?" Karina asked.

"Yes, child, I even went up to Chief Lipmist and told him myself," Granny said a matter-of-factly.

"What did he say? What did he say?" Karina bounced.

Granny grunted. "He ain't nothing but an old fool."

Aries chuckled "He didn't believe you either?"

"I don't care what he believe," Granny bit, "but what I say is true."

"Well, I believe you, Granny," Karina said.

"Thank you, child." Granny smiled.

There wasn't many members of her clan left. It seemed that each passing year more members died than were born. Her granny used to say that when someone in their clan died, they became rats. Something a normal person would find disgust in, but her people always had a way with rats. Though small, Karina knew what gentle and intelligent creatures they were. Her folks held them in high regard, earning her people the name Rat People, but in truth their clan's name translated into 'keeper of history' or 'Ratalia' in their native tongue.

"Alright, you two," Aries said as they approached Granny's burrow. "Tomorrow will be another busy day, so we've got to go to bed early."

"Aww," Karina whined as the vents blew wafts of fresh air into the tunnel, which made Karina glad Granny lived here.

"No whining," Aries said. "Alright, Granny, we're here. Feel free to stop by anytime, I'm sure Karina would love to talk more."

Karina looked at her granny, but the old woman didn't move an inch. "Granny?" She stared at the doorknob so intensely Karina started to worry.

Aries sighed. "Granny—"

Suddenly their granny reached out and grabbed Aries' arm so fast that it startled Karina. Aries gasped and as their granny held onto Aries' so tightly that she was shaking.

"G-Granny?" Aries winced.

"It has begun," Granny's voice trembled. Her crimson red eyes looked bloodshot and turned a deep shade of vermillion.

"W-what are you talking about?" Aries struggled to pull her arm away.

"The prophecy," Granny said.

"Granny, look." Aries looked to her sister then back at her grandmother.

Her granny's mouth hung open, but no words came out, until Granny forced out. "Please," Granny pleaded.

"G-Granny, I-I have work in the morning. I'm sorry, but I have to go."

"It is said that one day a Crimson Mouse will appear and lead the Darkness to the light and free our people." Granny's entire body trembled. Her forehead beaded with sweat. "I have seen her, a fiendish ring! A gold tainted by blood! A golden cage awaits!" Granny said through her teeth. "Acome has shown her to me. She is the Crimson Mouse, and you are the Darkness. You will lead our people into the light."

Aries finally pulled away. "Ah-ah, okay, Granny. H-how about we talk about this later? We really have to go."

Aries walked past their Granny, who was frozen in place, and pulled out her spare key. She opened the door and gently ushered their grandmother into her burrow. Karina followed behind, shaken by the look of terror in Granny's eyes. They couldn't leave her like this, but clearly Aries didn't feel the same. She was already removing Granny's robes and leading her to her bed. Karina rushed to her Granny's side, but Aries stopped her.

"No," Aries whispered. "She's got herself all worked up. See, she's lost in her seer vision."

Karina looked down at her granny, whose eyes were wide open, staring up at the ceiling of her bed cubby. Her mouth hung open as if she were caught mid-scream. Her entire face looked like it was connected to a machine that had stretched it out wide. Karina wanted to break down and cry, but Aries pulled her away. Her older sister made sure to tidy up before they left and turned off all the lights. In the darkness Karina shivered as if she could feel her granny's eyes on her.

"Karina," Aries whispered.

Karina jumped and scurried to the door, but not before catching her granny's blood red eyes, boring into her, illuminated by the light coming from the door.

14

Aries

Aries walked home in silence, still shaken by her granny's words. She had never outright attacked her like this. Aries rubbed her arm and tried to wipe away her unease. Their granny was sick and sometimes green lung could mess with a person's mind, but this felt like something more. She reached their burrow, and Karina went in without complaint. Their mother waited up for them in their small den and nodded so that Aries could go and check on her cousin Zopi. She had completely forgotten her mother asked her to check up on him, and she didn't feel like it after what happened, but a nice walk would help to clear her mind. Her mother packed her cousin a plate of stewed vegetables and Aries carried it out with her.

It was still early and quite a few locals were out on the paths. No one paid attention to her, and she was grateful for that. All this prophecy stuff was hurting her head. She stopped believing in that stuff a long time ago. Nothing she or anyone in her clan ever did made a difference, so why should she believe it now? Life was far from perfect down here, but it was livable and Aries was ready to accept that. She just hoped that her granny would find some peace.

Aries walked up a metal grate towards Zopi's burrow. When he married Ashnee, he moved into her burrow, which was bigger. It had two small bedrooms and a big den, which was considered prime real estate down here. Her family were welders, and she had her father to thank for the space. He built it for her and their two young children, Bluu and Nyekundu. Aries loved babysitting them. Nyekundu was five and Bluu was four, both full of energy.

Aries approached the metal stairs that led to their neighborhood. The dim yellow light led the way as rats scurried past her feet. Zopi's burrow was the fifth one down. Aries spotted it, but she slowed when she noticed the door was cracked open. She sat the plate down on the ground and palmed the switchblade in her pocket as she inched towards the door. She listened carefully for any sign of movement, but only the hum of rushing water from the pipes above reached her ears.

"Shit," Aries cursed. She didn't have time to play detective. She hoped that Zopi would come running out, laughing and carrying on like he always did.

Aries stopped at the door. It was dark inside the burrow. She took a deep breath. If there was someone in there up to no good, it was pointless to knock. She steeled her nerves and relaxed her shoulders. She would cuss her cousin out later for leaving the door open. Aries swung open the door and the stench hit her first, sharp and familiar. Blood covered every inch of the apartment floor and in the center of it all, the gutted corpse of her cousin Zopi. Aries stumbled into the doorway and fell to her knees. Tears wet her face before she could even register that she was crying.

Zopi's body lay wide open to the air. All of his organs were gone, even his eyes, with their lids slashed open. Runners, he must have run into some trouble with one of the gangs. Maybe he owed too much? What were the children going to do now, without both of their parents?

"The kids!" Aries shot to her feet.

She ran into the blood-soaked burrow and shouted their names. She searched the living area. Everything was covered in blood. The dining table was turned over and on the floor were torn open packs of charm, a popular street drug.

"Damnit, Zopi," Aries cursed.

Aries rushed to the bedroom and pulled on the string light. Aries checked under the messy bed, while calling out the children's names. She imagined Bluu's big smile and Nyekundu's playful laughter in her mind. Aries rushed to the back room, where the children slept and flung open the door. Light hit the blood that covered the bed the two children shared first. On the soaked sheets lay Nyekundu's body, eyes open, staring at nothing. She had been stabbed to death over a dozen times. She was only five. Aries' arms dropped to her side as she noticed a white piece of paper stabbed through the child's neck. Aries walked to the body emotionlessly and gently removed the knife.

She picked up the folded sheet of paper, it read: *Debt Paid.*

Aries let the paper fall to the bed, when she heard a sneeze followed by a cry. Bluu. Aries blinked away the tears that wouldn't stop falling. She searched around the room for something to cover Nyekundu's body. She pulled the pink quilt their mother made for them off the wall and laid it gently over the body, then she walked to the small air vent in the corner. The sniffling grew louder.

"Get it together Aries," she said through clenched teeth.

Aries looked around the room for something she could use as a blindfold and found a large t-shirt, probably belonging to their dad. She picked it up and bent down to the vent.

"I-it's okay, Bluu, it's me, Aries, your cousin." Aries reached for the vent cover and gently pulled it open. She pulled out her flashlight and shined it on her face for the little one to see, then shined it into the vent. Two terrified brownish-red eyes stared back at her. "It's okay, Bluu. Come on, let's go to Auntie Sasha's, okay?"

When Bluu didn't moved, Aries reached out her hand and slowly waved to him. "See, it's me. Aries." She turned the light on herself again and watched Bluu's eyes well up with tears. The four-year-old wailed as he crawled into her arms. "Hold on, hold on. Before we go, I'm going to need you to wear this like a hat. Can you do that for me?" Aries said. "It'll be just like dress up, okay?"

Bluu hesitated but then bowed his head, and Aries gently slipped the shirt over his face.

"Can you breathe?" Aries asked and the young boy nodded. "Good, let's go."

Aries scooped him into her arms and kissed him on the forehead as she hugged him close to her chest. She walked past the bleeding body of his older sister out into the den where his father lay gutted on the floor. She closed the door behind her and walked home in silence.

Morning came and Aries found herself staring at the ceiling of her nook. When she returned home last night her mother and father fretted over her. Her father was the one who let the family know. He was more experienced with things like this. Her mother took Bluu. With so many sick and poor in the family, there would be no one to look after him, so her mother volunteered. When Karina asked what happened, all Aries could remember hearing was their mother uttering something about gangs, then there was nothing. The night was lost to her, fractured into its most painful parts.

Was this all that life was? Violence and death? Surely, this couldn't be it. Aries laid on her back, crying again, but she hadn't the strength to wipe her face. Zopi, Nyekundu, her uncle Roman, how much blood did these sewer's need? How many more people needed to suffer to keep this world going? That's when her granny's words rung in her ears.

You are the Darkness.

Aries cried out and covered her mouth to smother the sound that came out. She wasn't the Darkness. There was no prophecy. No one was coming to save them and yet the echo of her granny's words rung in her mind.

"Be quiet!" Aries shouted, then sighed in frustration.

Now she was the one acting like the mold and sick was getting to her head. *Fuck,* Aries closed her eyes. She couldn't do this. She couldn't stand another moment in this pit stain.

You are the Darkness.

"No, Granny, I'm not." Aries voice came out a quiet whisper.

There was no prophecy, but if there was no prophecy, then she had nothing to lose looking into it, right? What was she saying? Now she really felt like something was wrong with her mind, but she hated sitting up in her room alone. Yes, it most certainly was a waste of time to run around and play the Darkness. But the images of Zopi and Nyekundu...

Aries clenched her fist. She wasn't going to look into this, but she was going out for some air. If the path helped ease her granny's mind, so be it, but Aries was not the Darkness.

"Get it together, Aries," Aries said as she pushed herself to get up.

Aries packed herself a day bag and sighed. The prophecy... This was nothing more than a waste of time, a ghost from the past trying to convince her of something she already knew wasn't real, but her heart ached too much to stay put. It had begun, according to Granny, this big prophecy she had grown up hearing about. The prophecy everyone believed in.

But with it came the pain, the weight of the knowledge that so many people had died and wouldn't see this day.

Aries balled her fist. This really was a waste of time. She should be doing something more productive like everyone else, but her body still moved to pack. Her granny's words muddied everything in her mind, and Aries had little strength to resist. This was just for her granny's peace of mind and to help Aries clear her head. Doing this for Granny would ease her pain and make her last days more comfortable. She found her heaviest jacket and nicest slacks and boots. She was going to the surface, runners be damned. Aries turned to leave, nearly forgetting the most important item, and with it came the sting of memory. Aries tensed but took a shaky breath. She went to her drawer, which was nothing more than a slanted crate with a few boxes stacked on top of each other.

She pulled out the box on the bottom, which released a cloud of dust in the air. Aries fanned the dust away. The box was plastic, faded blue, with a little gold clasp barely hanging on. Aries sat down and laid the box on her lap. She stopped opening this box years ago, there was no reason to pack this item, but she did not place the box back. She flipped the clasp, which finally took its last breath and broke away, landing on the floor. She opened the box and inside were her magic items, gifts from her Uncle Roman who trained her.

There was a fake ruby stone on a fragile black cord, some rolled up papers with summoning keys she knew she would never cast, and on the bottom was the silver retracting pole. It stared back at her with such pride, she almost felt unworthy to carry it. What would her uncle think of her now? She was practically a nonbeliever. She felt hollow, like she was just going through the motions. The pole rolled around in the box, hitting the side with a thud. Prophecy or not, a weapon was a weapon.

Aries took a deep breath. She was doing this for Granny, if for nothing more but to calm her granny's nerves. At least that's what she told herself. She grabbed the pole and tucked it into her holster. Then she stood and took a deep breath. She guessed this was it. She grabbed her bag. She would be back soon, maybe by the end of the day.

Aries walked quickly down the tunnels leading to the surface paths. There weren't many unguarded paths to the surface and since she had never been she could only rely on the rumors. Most of the paths that led to the surface were guarded by runners that demanded high bribes for safe passage. The threat increased if you were female, as traffickers were always on the lookout. The pain of her cousin' gutted body reminded her that there were worse fates than slavery around here, but she pushed away that thought.

Aries stopped at a stairwell she had overheard her friends talk about. It led to the first of three floors that came before the surface. She would need to cross all of these to get up top. Aries took a deep breath and wiggled her arms to calm her nerves. This was crazy and she knew it, but she couldn't turn back now. Her head was in too much turmoil to focus on anything else. This is for Granny. she repeated, as images of her dead cousins tried to force their way up like bile on an upset stomach. Aries ascended the stairs. Halfway up she caught a glimpse of red bouncing towards her.

"What are you doing?" Karina said with her arms folded.

Aries froze. Karina was the last person she wanted to see. "I, um, wait, why aren't you at work?"

"The same reason you aren't?" Karina said, but Aries only glared. "I took Bluu to Miss Neenee's, okay? She agreed to watch him during the day, and I thought it would be nice for him to be around kids his age and then I came back and you were gone."

Aries couldn't shake the image of Nyekundu's lifeless, pale brown eyes from her mind and the last thing she wanted to do was deal with Karina's pro-prophecy nonsense, despite the fact that she was only here because of said prophecy nonsense. "This doesn't concern you. Go back down."

"Not a chance," Karina huffed. "You're going to the surface, aren't you."

"What, no." Aries saw a group of people walking towards the stairs and jumped off. She pulled her sister to the side and forced a smile at the group who started their ascent. Aries turned back to her sister, lowering her voice, her grip tight. "I'm not."

"Ow, ow, ow, if you're not heading up, then why are you at one of the surface access points?" Karina winced and Aries let her go.

"Why do you know this?" Aries snapped, but Karina only pouted, poking out her lip. "Look, Karina, I'm not going to the surface alright. I just, I just have some errands to run for Mom."

"Bullshit. We live in the same burrow. When did she ask you to run errands?" Karina folded her arms. Aries did not have time for this. Her patience was on the ground level, and she didn't want anyone around her right now, but Karina was not backing off. "Look, I know you just came back from seeing something messed up."

"Karina," Aries warned.

"I know. You don't want to talk about it and that's okay, but I also know that you're not going on a harmless walk. I know this has something to do with Granny. Aries, you're the Darkness."

"I'm not!" Aries said a lot louder than she had intended. "I'm not, okay. Now go back. Mom and Dad need you at work."

"Mom and Dad need us both, but they'll be fine, I promise. Just listen to me Aries. I've been reading about this my entire life," Karina said as she started to take off her backpack. "This is it, I know it."

Aries impatiently looked around as others walked by going up and down the stairs. Her sister pulled out a book and flipped through pages as if they weren't in the middle of a public area.

"Karina," Aries said more firmly this time.

"Hush, look," Karina held up the small spell book. "It says it on the very first page, that the seer will have a vision of days long past. This world, it has all the signs. Look."

"Karina I don't want to hear it, now let me be." Aries turned from her sister and started towards the stairs. This was so stupid and she knew it and yet why was she putting up this much of a fight? Why was she so focused on something she knew wasn't going to bring Zopi or Nyekundu back?

Karina stomped her foot. "Fine! Go without me, but good luck getting to the surface. The routes have long since changed since I've been and trust me it can get bad." Karina gasped and clasped her hands over her mouth. Aries stopped dead in her tracks and whipped around.

"What did you say?" Aries stormed over to her sister and lifted her by the shirt, leaving her legs almost dangling.

"I-I," Karina squirmed.

"Spill it," Aries hissed.

"It-it was just a few times." Karina winced when her sister lifted her higher. "Okay three, it was just three times, and I didn't go anywhere, I promise. I just wanted to see."

"Are you insane? It's dangerous heading up to the surface." Aries let her sister down. "You could have been hurt or worse."

"I know, but things are different now. There are safer routes."

"Bullshit," Aries said.

"There are, I promise and I-I know the way. Aries please, just allow me to help you get to the surface and I promise to go back down. I promise."

Karina's face was sunken, but Aries was in a tight predicament. On one hand she needed to get to the surface, but she wasn't exactly sure how to get there; on the other hand, if she allowed her sister to lead what would happen if they ran into trouble? No,

Aries knew what would happen if they got caught, but what did it matter? Her little sister could easily get snatched on the way to work or at the market. Runners weren't picky and those were just the organized threats. It was a miracle that her sister made it this far.

Aries looked down at her little sister. She didn't like the idea of putting her into any kind of danger. At least if Karina went with her, Aries could protect her. Keep her safe from harm, even if it were just for a little while. Aries sighed and looked behind her, then back at her sister again. Both Mom and Dad knew they weren't at work today and this should only take them a couple of hours tops. Aries closed her eyes, but she could only see Nyekundu's playful smile beaming with so much life. Aries pushed away those painful memories that soaked her mind. She was hurting. She could at least be honest about that, but maybe, selfishly, she wouldn't have to bear it alone if she had a little company.

"Alright," Aries finally gave in.

"Yay!" Karina jumped up and down, but Aries stepped into her space.

"But when I go up, you are to go straight back down to Mom and Dad. Is that clear?"

"O-okay," Karina said. Aries relaxed. She couldn't believe she was doing this. "So, about the prophecy—"

"And that's another thing. There will be no talk of the prophecy," Aries said.

"Aww," Karina pouted.

"I mean it." Aries started to walk up the ladder. The last thing Aries needed was for some wandering ear to overhear them talking about prophecies and magic. That was asking for trouble.

The pair climbed the two flights to the third floor with ease. The space was tight, but not well traveled. The route Karina took them proved to be a good access point, but they weren't in the clear yet. Aries heard voices down the well-lit corridors. There were so many ways to go, it was impossible to pick. She looked to her left then to her right. There was a long, tiled tunnel that stretched both ways, then in front of her were three brick tunnels. She couldn't remember which way to go and she was sure it showed in her body language.

"You know," Karina said. "It's not the third and first floors that you have to worry about. Those are easy."

"Huh?" Aries said.

"Take either of the brick tunnels, they all go the same way. I think they were meant to be sewer lines."

"What about the tiled paths?" Aries asked.

"Those just wrap around, you'll just end up where you started," Karina said. "Take one of the brick ones." Her sister pointed.

If she had only been up here three times, how could she be sure? So much could have changed, but what other option did Aries have? "So, what's this about the first level not being hard?" Aries said as she walked down the middle brick path.

"Yeah, turns out lots of street people live on the first floor. It's practically overrun and many of them are only night dwellers, so the gangs don't care. It's when you get to the second floor that it gets tricky."

"Why?"

"Because that's where all the industries are. Or rather, that's where their meet-up places are. They still use the old rail system to bring goods up and down and where there are goods, there is crime."

"So what about this level, what's up here?"

Karina shrugged. "Street people? Drunks? I heard a lot of people just come up here to get to different parts of Sewer Town. It's easier than walking all the way up and all the way down several times on the stairs, and we all know how many dead ends there are down there. From up here you can take the blue or green tiled paths to other parts of Sewer Town."

"That's convenient."

"Yeah, it can be if you're heading to certain parts."

"So, how do we get to the second level?"

Karina stopped; her shoulders stiffened as she slowly turned to face her sister. "So don't be mad..."

"Karina," Aries' eyes slanted into a glare.

"It's not that bad and this way you can get from level three to level one super easy." Karina made a nervous smile, "but to get through you have to go through the tunnels under the train rails."

"The train rails, you mean we have to go through manholes where trains are coming in and out? Karina that's dangerous."

"I said don't be mad, it's not as bad as it sounds."

Aries squeezed the bridge of her nose. Of course, she would say that. "I can't believe you went that way. Who told you this?"

Karina looked away as innocently as she could, which meant that Aries wasn't going to get an answer. Aries sighed and looked down at her sister. Her red eyes were so determined.

Why hadn't the prophecy picked her? Aries pushed that thought from her mind, even if her sister was a little bit too gullible to lead a wild rat chase like this, it was also very dangerous. That thought alone should have deterred Aries from starting, but if her sister was already traveling to the surface, what would stop her from running off on her own? Aries sighed and kept moving.

The brick tunnel opened into a large room that looked like it was once a train station people used to board trains. Her Uncle Roman told her about them. Long ago back when Ruby-Gyme really used to employ people, folks would take trains to work. Her uncle said it stopped when the company discovered it was easier to shift the recycling sector to day workers and cheaper to run when they didn't have to maintain expensive railing infrastructure.

Dimly lit, street people and sewer folks drunk or high lounged around on the yellow chipped walls. Aries spotted a few runners from big time sewer gangs smoking in the corner and watched them out of the corner of her eye. She looked back and saw the other two brick tunnels, and guessed her sister was right.

"Come on," Karina whispered.

Aries followed behind her sister who headed to a tunnel on the left side of the room. No one paid much attention to them, which was good. They entered the tunnel, which buzzed from the flickering lights above. Trash lined the floor and the air smelled of fresh pee. People eyed them as they walked by, some grinned with their toothy smiles, but Aries cut them a nasty look, which quickly caused most to avert their eyes.

The further they walked the more the dim yellow lights that lit the tunnel flickered or were broken all together. The walls also looked worse for wear. Large cracks streaked the broken tile, like webbed fingers and piles of concrete joined the trash. She wondered if all this damage was caused by a collapse. Around a bend she got her answer, but it wasn't what she expected. In the ceiling there was a great big hole that looked man made. Concrete, rusted bent pipes, rebar, and tile, all sat in a pile leading up. Karina approached the pile; it was sloped low enough to climb and it appeared well used. Aries looked above the pile into the darkness that seemed to stretch for ever.

"What's that way?" Aries asked.

Karina stopped her ascent and shrugged. "Not sure."

"What? How do you know someone isn't hiding right there waiting to attack you?"

It looked like Karina wanted to roll her eyes, but she slid back down the pile of rubble and pulled out her flashlight. Illuminated by light, Aries saw the tunnel only went on for another ten feet or so before hitting a wall. There appeared to be a door down there but it was boarded up. Karina turned off her light and started to climb again, which only ground Aries' nerves more. She couldn't believe Karina had wandered through places like this. How could she be so careless and then Aries remembered how sheltered she was. Sure, Karina saw her fair share of grim things, but the worst of it was always placed on Aries' shoulder. Afterall, that was the job of a big sister, a job that sometimes felt too heavy to bare. Aries started forward, but her breath was shaky.

"Nyekundu, don't climb on that," Aries called out.

"I'm not, Bluu's toy is up there." Nyekundu pointed.

Aries followed her little cousin's finger and spotted Bluu's wooden airship on top of their auntie's stack of vegetable crates. Aries smiled and walked past her. "Here, let me get that for you." Nyekundu pouted and folded her arms. "What?"

"I wanted to get it," Nyekundu said and Aries bent down and handed the airship to her.

"Hey, it's okay to get some help from time to time, but one day you will grow up and be an amazing big sister." Aries smiled and Nyekundu's tantrum melted away.

"Aries?" Karina called back.

"Uh-coming," Aries said with a shaky voice.

She balled her fingers into a fist to stop herself from crying and shook the tension from her body. She needed to hurry this up before their parents really started to worry. Aries followed behind her sister and immediately noticed the heat coming off the ceiling. The ceiling was also very low, they would have to walk bending down to get through.

"Be careful. There's a lot a junk up here," Karina warned as she turned on her flashlight.

In the crawl space, bricks, tile, and trash littered the place. In the darkness Aries made out bottles and old sleeping pads next to piles of dusty needles. The further they went the more humid it got and the stronger the vibrations from the trains got. It rained dust and cobwebs onto their heads, which made her skin itch. Aries wiped the dirt from her face as she kept a careful eye around the space.

"Ow!" Karina yelped.

"What is it?" Aries moved beside her.

"Stubbed my toe." Aries flashed the light on a bit of exposed rebar.

"Be careful," Aries said.

Another train rumbled by, shaking the place so much Aries thought it would collapse. She held onto a brick pillar as tiny pebbles danced around their feet. Sand rained on them as Aries cut Karina a dirty look.

"We're almost there, I promise," Karina whispered.

Karina flashed her light on a manhole on the ceiling up ahead. Gray light lit the surrounding area and as they moved closer, Aries heard the sounds of voices. They continued towards the manhole and stopped when the shouting became more audible.

"Hurry up and get the load out!" a man shouted from above.

Karina stopped and listened, then she started walking again.

"We're not using this one?" Aries said, standing under the light.

"Shush, get out of the light." Karina waved. "We have to use the manhole in the train tunnel.

Aries stepped back into the shadows. Perhaps her sister was more aware than she gave her credit for. There was no way to tell who those people were up there and with no money or valuables to bargain with they could easily risk getting captured. Karina covered her light only illuminating enough of the room to navigate around the brick pillars. The crawl space rumbled once more, but Aries kept walking. She had no idea how Karina could find her way around here, it all looked the same to her. It was all darkness mixed with small burst of gray dusty light that filtered in from the manholes above. Karina slowed and pointed her light ahead of them. There was another manhole, but little light came from above. Karina walked towards it and turned off her light.

"This is it," Karina said.

"How do you know?"

"It's uncovered. Above us is one of the train tunnels. One just went by so we may be able to get across to the metal ladder on the wall."

"Ladder? Won't we be spotted if we start climbing in plain sight?"

"No, there aren't any people over here, just trains. But we have to be fast. There are like five or six tracks we have to cross and some of the old trains don't have lights."

Aries didn't like the sound of this. Trains could be very dangerous; trains she couldn't see, sounded even worse. Karina stood up to her full height, slowly inching her head above the surface through the uncovered manhole.

"Karina, be careful." Aries watched, she could barely make out her sister's face.

"Hush," Karina said. "Okay okay, it's clear." Karina waved Aries over.

Aries moved closer to her sister as Karina hopped up to the next level. Aries followed with ease and was stunned at how dark it was. Light filtered in from grated manholes high above, but barely enough for them to see. The two of them stood between what looked like two rows of tracks, on the right were about three tracks and Aries saw a train stopped on one of them. To her left were about four, but it was impossible to say for sure. Karina pointed to the other side and Aries squinted as she followed her sister's finger to a metal bar ladder on the wall. It wasn't far off, but suddenly the ground started to shake.

"We have to hurry!" Karina said.

The thunderous sound of a train radiated in the darkness, much more powerful than she had ever felt before. Karina and Aries took off towards the wall as they ran across the tracks. They made it to the other side, and there was barely enough space for them to stand between the wall and the tracks. Aries let her sister start up the ladder first, when the train that was dead on the tracks blared to life.

The horn screamed as the wheels ground against the metal tracks. Aries watched the train slowly pick up speed as the ground rumbled below her. The train from before was still coming and it didn't feel like it was going to stop. Aries looked up at her sister then looked to her left and right, it was impossible to tell which direction the other train was coming from. Aries laid flat against the wall, hoping the train that was coming wouldn't be on the track closest to her.

"Come on, Karina," Aries muttered to herself, but the ladder had to be at least four flights up. Karina screamed and Aries snapped her head up. "Karina!"

"I'm okay, my foot just slipped," Karina shouted from above.

Aries clenched her teeth, she did not like this one bit and the fact that her sister had come back this way alone made her feel even worse. Light illuminated the tunnel from Aries' right, growing so intense that it blinded her. She couldn't see a thing. She could only feel something charging towards her through her boots. Metal on metal screeched in her ears from the train that had just come to life a few tracks over, making it impossible to tell where the other train was. Aries slapped her hands over her ears as the vibration caused her to stumble.

"Aries, watch out!" Karina screamed.

Aries' head jerked up, then she slammed her body against the wall just as a gust of hot air blew in her face from a train that sped by only feet away from her face. Aries gasped and turned her head away from the heat as the force of the train blew through her body like a steam vent. Sparks popped at her feet, but she dug her heels into the gravel and pushed her back into the wall as hard as she could.

The train passed, and Aries let out a breath. She panted hard as she followed the disappearing light. The smell from the sparks lingered from the beast that could only be described as a carrier to the afterlife.

"Aries!" Karina shouted. "Aries, are you okay?"

Aries took a deep breath and looked up at her sister; she was about three quarters of the way up. "I'm fine. I'm heading up now." Aries started her ascent.

She could still feel the rumble of the train in her bones. It was so close she felt like it could tear her skin off and steal her soul. It reminded her of the stories her granny told her, the ones about powerful scaley demons that lurked in the shadows of the sewers. But she didn't want to think about that right now, when she was climbing who knew how far up from the ground.

Aries made it a good ways up when she noticed another train coming in. Its light a dull yellow and when it passed, it looked like its carts were filled with ash. She wondered if that was from the incinerator and if so where was it going? Aries continued to climb. Her sister had already made it to the top where she paused. Aries couldn't make out what she was looking at, but she could see the outline of something jagged.

"Watch your fingers," Karina said.

Karina went first. She carefully climbed through the manhole and disappeared. Aries wasn't far behind. She poked her head up from the tunnels, careful not to cut her fingers on the metal mesh of a gate, where she was welcomed by more off-white tile walls that were a dingy yellow on the bottom. Aries pulled herself completely up and looked around. Were they in a bathroom? It looked like the corner of something. On the walls were the outline of three wooden rectangular boxes with wires hanging out. Trash littered the floors but on the other side she could hear voices around a seven-foot wall.

"Are we on the first floor?" Aries asked.

Karina nodded. Laughter echoed from far away as the familiar rumble in the floor added to the background noise of the room. This was where they would part. Aries looked at her sister, but she wasn't looking at her. The light of a train passing below caught Aries' eye, then disappeared back into the belly of the tunnel.

"All you have to do is go out from here and head towards the turnstiles. Then go left through the black iron gates and that'll take you to midtown," Karina said with her head lowered.

Aries looked behind her, then back at her sister. She knew what she wanted, but it was not something Aries was willing to risk. "Thank you." Aries hesitated for a moment, before turning around to leave. When she didn't hear her sister's footsteps she stopped, with her back facing her. "Head back now, okay, and be safe."

Karina didn't say anything, but when Aries heard the sound of footsteps she started to relax. Then a pair of arms wrapped around her waist.

"I-I..." Karina hugged her sister tight.

Aries tensed at first. She already knew what her sister was going to ask, but she couldn't risk putting her sister in anymore danger. Karina wasn't trained like her. She was still young and Mom and Dad could use all the help they could get, especially now that their little cousin would be staying with them. Not to mention the shock her parents would be in if anything happened to the both of them. Karina rested her head on her sister's back.

"Karina..." Aries said.

Karina broke away, which replaced her warm embrace with cold. "It's okay, I understand."

Aries turned around this time. Her sister met her eyes. She looked much more mature in that moment, like she wasn't the naive child Aries always thought of her as.

"I'll go back down," Karina said. "I know you're the one, the one who will lift the darkness from this world. I believe in you, Mistress of the Darkness."

Aries was taken back by her sister's response, hearing this from her sister broke something inside of her. Karina believed in this so much, and here Aries was, using her granny's visions as a means to escape her own trauma. Why had the stupid prophecy chosen her? Why did the damned thing have to take so long to awaken? Why wasn't her Uncle Roman and her cousin Zopi here to see this day? Aries choked as a single tear ran down her cheek. And Nyekundu, why did a five-year-old have to pay a debt with her life? It was all so much to bear, too much to bear, so much so, that Aries wasn't sure if she even wanted to live in this awful place anymore.

Karina smiled one last time before she headed back down the tunnel and Aries watched her leave. This prophecy was bullshit, but even shit had a purpose. If this thing even had a one percent chance of being true and could fertilize the land and make it a better place than it was worth it. Aries took a deep breath. What she was about to do was a stupid idea. Karina's head disappeared down the manhole and Aries balled her fist.

"Hey," Aries said. "You can come with me."

Karina gasped and her head popped up. A great big smile bloomed on her face as she climbed back up. "Good, because I have to be honest with you I was totally going to follow you."

"Karina!" Aries glared.

"I'm sorry" —Karina looked away— "but I can't let you do this alone. What if you need back up? I've been practicing my summoning keys and I kind of lied a bit from before. I come to the first level a lot."

"Karina!" Aries snatched her sister up by her shirt again. "What have I told you about coming up here?"

"I'm sorry." Karina pouted as squeaks came from her shirt. Aries let her go and from Karina's stomach a small budge worked its way up her chest. "Oops."

"You bought Tink as well?" Aries rubbed her temples, as her sister sheepishly shrugged. "I cannot believe you."

"So, what's the plan," Karina asked as if it were nothing. "How do we find the Crimson Mouse?"

Aries sighed, but why was Aries surprised? Honestly, she didn't know herself, but this was it. This was the big chance they were waiting for, but she had no clue where to begin.

"Right," Aries said.

Their granny said the Crimson Mouse would be a person of light. One that would lead them to Acome, but the city was huge and finding a single person, with no idea what they looked like outside of gender, would be near impossible. Aries looked back at her sister and thought. If there were truly something big going on, then there had to be foot soldiers. That was something she learned from her cousin Zopi, who always had an eye for reading people, and if there were any truth to the stories she grew up with, then all she had to do was be still and listen.

"Shit will always pop off when there is tension." Zopi grinned as he played with his lighter. "All you gotta do is watch and listen."

Aries exhaled and opened her eyes. Zopi's smile dissipated from her memory and she never knew she could miss someone so much. He was only twenty-seven years old, they practically grew up together. Aries looked away from her sister before turning back to her. "While you've been up here, have you noticed any places that runners like to hang out?"

Karina nodded vigorously.

"Show me."

15
Mary

Mary took a shaky breath as she applied powder to her nose at her vanity. It was currently thirty minutes to midnight and that stupid witch hadn't made any progress in helping Eddy at all. Honestly, she didn't understand why her family used these people at all. That witch was nothing more than an overpaid whore. Where was her father's Black Gate? Her family's necromancers where way better than the Fort'nee's Siler scum. Mary sneezed and wasted her foundation powder on her blue lace dress.

"Shit." Mary reached for a wet cloth and patted herself clean.

This entire situation was ridiculous. Who was Vincent Lorne to boss them around? Didn't he know who her father was? Didn't he know what her father was capable of? Mary was so angry she shook. Vincent Lorne wouldn't even be alive without her father's remedies. He practically perfected medical necromancy. In fact, every member of the Five Families should be serving under them. Her family's magic was the strongest and yet, they had the nerve to look down on them for doing all of their dirty work. Especially the Hoo'naes. They barely even taught magic to their three daughters and yet, everyone hung on Joy, the eldest, words, the hag. Mary huffed. She was tired of thinking about this. She could barely think over the sound of her heart. She sighed, poor Eddy.

Mary got up from her vanity and walked to her window to gaze up at the cloudy sky. She wondered if Kym were looking at the sky at this very moment. She missed him so much. If this stupid drama wasn't going on, she would be in his arms right now. Mary heard a knock at the door and turned. A milky eyed assistant was here to fetch her. Mary glared at the disgusting thing as it rolled forward.

Luckly for them, her father and mother weren't going to let a dirty bottom dweller like Vincent terrorize them. Her mother was fully prepared to give him a mouthful and if that didn't work, they were sure their money would. Mary patted down her fly away hairs and straightened out her dress as she followed the assistant to her father's study in the main house. Another assistant waited for them at the door and stepped aside to let them in. When Mary walked in, everyone was standing. Mary held her breath and she reframed from asking why Alvert wasn't here. The lucky bastard.

"Mary." Her mother Amber ran to her and hugged her. "My dear, I was worried you would be too traumatized to come." Her mother swayed as she hugged her, before pulling away.

Eddy scoffed as he rolled his eyes. He looked terrible with bags under his puffy eyes. His once clean, pressed suit looked wrinkled, and the pant legs were stained with dirt.

Mary crossed the room to her father. "Father, please, let's stop this," she pleaded, but her father only looked away.

The pain in his eyes hurt Mary. He was normally such a cheerful happy man. Her mother rushed to Eddy's side, but he pushed her away.

"My Eddy." Her mother reached out.

"Be calm, Amber," her father said, but this only seemed to put Eddy in an even more sour mood.

"Calm? Calm! How can any of you stand here and say *be calm*? When Vincent fucking Lorne is on his way to kill me at this very moment," Eddy spat.

"Eddy." Her mother reached out.

"No." Eddy paced. "I don't want to hear it."

Mary winced. "Eddy, Mother and Father aren't going to let him do it. Vincent is bluffing."

"Yes, my dear," their mother said. "He won't dare lay a finger on my precious baby's head. We are his boss, after all. Right, dear?"

"That's right," her father said.

Their mother grabbed Eddy's hand and cupped it in hers. "I'm going to personally put an end to this myself."

Eddy seemed to relax from their mother's words, until the big grandfather clock struck midnight. Everyone turned and watched the second hand run from the hour and minute hand as if it were in a race against Ozama himself. Mary felt a pinch in her chest as she nervously stared between the door and the clock. Time was running out and nothing had happened. Mary watched the clock add a minute and a smile reached her face.

"See, it was bluff—" Mary was cut off by the sound of the study door opening.

She turned and saw Vincent Lorne walk in along with four other metal banned Siler members. Vincent looked at his wristwatch, with a cigarette draped from his lips.

"Doctor Granite, Lady Amber," Vincent greeted them respectfully, before he withdrew a long black pistol and pulled the trigger, blasting a hole through her brother's head.

Brain matter sprayed the bookshelf behind him and Mary screamed as her mother fainted in her father's arms. Eddy's body hit the ground with a thud, landing in a pool of his own blood.

"Forgive me for being late," Vincent said, before he walked to Mary. "Lady Mary, I believe your watch starts now." Vincent said with no emotion as he nodded to her father and walked out the door.

"M-m-my watch." Mary shook to her knees. She could not shake the image of her dead brother from her mind and vomited all over her dress and floor. "M-m-my watch? F-father! Father, do something damnit! Father, do something!" Mary wailed.

16
Mia

Mia turned over in bed, wrapping the covers around her body. She hadn't intended on staying in town after what happen with the runners, but Billie found a consignment store and the rest was history. She opened her eyes to a beautiful room with soft peach walls that smelled of rose and honey. She did do a little work last night, but nothing serious. Billie knew the owner of a bar in town and the pair played nice for a group of foreigners from out of town. So, with a belly full of food and wine, she slept like a queen.

She turned over in bed and saw Billie's dark purple braids sticking out from under the covers. It was still early, so there was no point in waking her up, but there was still the matter of returning the ring. Mia looked at the wooden nightstand that sat between their beds. The ring sat on a bed of chains, still as beautiful as it was yesterday. It was a nice ring, but the odds of finding the owner were too low. She should just carry it to the authorities like Zetti told her to do. Afterall, she and Billie had stopped by a wedding band store yesterday and the jeweler said it wasn't one of theirs.

So that was it. When Billie got up she would tell her that they would be ditching the ring. It wasn't worth the trouble anymore. She would just have to let Zetti know and give her the proper paperwork. Mia pulled the covers over her shoulders and closed her eyes again. She laid there for a few minutes, but it was too late, her body had fully awakened now. She looked at the ring again, nestled in the chains, and reached for it. It was cold to the touch from being away from a warm body for so long, but she would fix that. She brought it to her face and fingered the engravings on the ring. This ring was really starting to grow on her. She had other rings that would go perfectly with this one, even a few bracelets too. She hovered the mouth of the crown shaped ring over her ring finger, letting the tip of her nail slide through.

"Wanna keep it?"

Mia yanked her hand back as Billie laughed at her.

"Chill," Billie yawned. "I know you wouldn't steal that ugly thing."

"Shut up, it's not ugly." Mia made a face.

Billie shrugged and looked at the time, it was a little after noon. "So, you wanna play detective again with the *you know what*?" Billie eyed the ring.

Mia pulled the ring from under the covers and gazed at her fuzzy reflection. "Nah, it's pointless, Let's just turn it in."

"Good idea, it'll be someone else's problem. Besides I know Terese is running her mouth since we've been gone. Good thing we already cleaned our rooms."

"Right." Mia sat up. "I'm going to shower."

"Okay, save me some good soap," Billie said as she rolled over back to sleep.

Mia smirked and placed the ring back on the nightstand. Billie was right, it was time to make this thing someone else's problem. Mia pulled the top blanket from her bed and wrapped it around her body as she slid off the bed towards the window. The streets were packed, and the sky was a light gray. She could see the lighter gray clouds moving in front of the darker ones. It was beautiful. She looked around their room and admired the paintings on the walls that were mostly of the countryside, big fields of golden grain, the other a forest of trees. Did trees still grow? If so, she'd never seen one.

When she was a kid, she used to read about trees and grass and stuff, but stuff like that didn't grow in the city. In fact, nothing really grew in the city, even window plants wilted fast. Fresh flowers were the most expensive, she heard it was even a luxury for people in Uptown. Mia slid her feet on the inn's soft baby blue carpet, looking forward to having a fresh shower in a fancy bathroom.

Growing up, she was also told it wasn't much better outside of the city, even outside of Julilie. The throughline for the city was always "*It won't be any better than this*," and yet, most of the foreigners talked about how good life was outside of Julilie. It must be because of their money—money made everything better—and if they were traveling that meant they were rich.

Mia turned on the lukewarm water and allowed the bathroom to steam up a bit before entering. Stepping into the shower, Mia exhaled as she reached for a clean cloth and soap. Showering in fresh lukewarm water, this was a life she could get used to.

When Mia came out of the bathroom Billie was sitting on the bed topless with her clothes ready. Mia ran her fingers through her damp hair.

"You sick?" Mia asked, standing in her bra and panties.

"Nah, just thinking if I should get my nipples pierced."

Mia cringed. Billie already had a few piercings in her ears and one in her belly button. "You're braver than I." Mia touched her ears. "Though I wouldn't mind going with you if you did. I'd like another set in my ears."

Billie got up. "Go for it, be out in a bit."

Mia nodded and looked around for her clothes. She put on the same ones from yesterday, starting with her white bodysuit, then her tights and mini skirt. She packed up the new clothes she had bought the day before in her little backpack she had bought yesterday as well. Perhaps she would do a little more shopping before heading back to the brothel. She could use another pair of thigh high boots. The ones she was wearing were so worn down or at least they could get some lunch somewhere nice. Billie finished her shower and got dressed quickly. Then the pair headed to the front desk and checked out of the lovely inn.

"I wouldn't mind taking Sara here," Billie said as she pushed open the door.

"I bet she would like that," Mia said.

"Or we could do a little escorting on the side." Billie winked. "I know a bar that takes business travelers only. They're always looking for girls."

"You're always looking for a hustle," Mia said as she stood on the sidewalk, taking in the fresh air.

"Always, girl," Billie laughed. "Want to grab something to eat?"

"Sure," Mia said.

Billie led the way. Behind them, a dozen or so blocks away, Mia could see the great concrete wall that separated New Town in The Slogs from Uptown. From here she couldn't see the doors, but she noticed the birds flying overhead. She hadn't been there before, but Billie had. Billie traveled a lot, but Mia liked to stick close to home. She'd done enough exploring as a street kid and it wasn't like she would be welcomed. She used to be afraid to even look towards the wall. They said only the holy walked there. That only the purest and smartest would have the honor to walk the same streets as the Five Families. But when she met Lady Valkyrie that all changed, she knew better now.

"Looky." Billie pointed. "This café sells little sandwiches. What do you think?"

Mia looked through the large glass window and could see a few tables and chairs. They had a few tables outside too, some filled with chatting patrons. Mia spotted a middle-aged couple on one side and two tired looking men, dressed in neatly pressed suits, with cigarettes hanging on their lips on the other. The men looked up when Billie and Mia walked by, curious but didn't say anything. Billie pushed open the door and a woman at the counter said that she would seat them.

"So?" Billie asked.

"Huh?" Mia said.

"Is this place okay with you?" Billie asked just as the waitress appeared carrying two menus.

"Yeah, of course." Mia said.

"Would you like to sit inside or outside?" the waitress asked.

"Outside is fine," Billie said.

It was mid-winter, but it wasn't too cold today, so Mia didn't mind. The waitress led them outside and sat them on the side with the middle-aged couple, close to the door. She left the menus and walked back inside.

"Nice, they have mushroom soup here." Billie scanned the menu. "And it comes in a bowl made from bread."

"What?" Mia looked down at her own menu. "That's fancy."

"So, after this you want to hit another shop or what?" Billie asked.

"Maybe just one," Mia said as she pulled away her scarf to reach into her shirt to pull out the ring. "But first we have to return this."

Billie eyed the ring for a second before rolling her eyes. "Are we still doing this? Let's just ditch the thing."

Billie was right and Mia knew it, but she just couldn't part with it. Whenever she wore it, it felt like it belonged there. It was weird to admit, but she just didn't have the heart to part with it. "It's so weird, I wonder what its story is?"

"Who cares." Billie sounded bored.

Mia wanted to roll her eyes, but she also didn't want to waste Billie's day. "If we keep searching, we can keep shopping."

A grin bloomed on Billie's face, earning Mia the reaction she was looking for. Billie looked at her menu as Mia turned her attention back to the ring. The rook top design of the ring almost looked like clock gears or an old fashion crown. She was sure it had to have had some kind of story, even if it was something mundane like an exchange between a wealthy gentleman and their lover. Rose gold was also rare, it had to have been specially crafted. She wished she could keep it. She wanted to so bad. The waitress returned with their water. Mia hid the ring in her hand and the pair placed their order, then the waitress walked away.

"Still though, I'm sure that guy must have been using a fake name," Mia said.

"Told you," Billie said. "What was it again?"

"Howard something, but he kept telling me to call him Earl," Mia said.

"Weird," Billie said. "But money talks. I'm sure he could produce a fake ID easy, not like Lady Valkyrie would ride his ass as long as he paid up."

Mia chuckled as she overheard the waitress talking behind them. The woman thanked the two men Mia noticed earlier, before hearing their chairs scoot back on the stone sidewalk. The men walked past Billie and Mia. One of the men nodded to Mia and she noticed that he had a thin polished copper band on his arm. Was this man a Siler? She knew they wore metal armbands, but this band was copper and looked more like a piece of jewelry than a clunky armband, plus he was dressed way too nicely to be a runner. She smiled politely back as the men passed, then turned her attention to Billie.

"You're right. We should ditch this, but I'm going to miss this old thing," Mia said.

17 Mary

Mary rode in silence in the back of one of Vincent's runner's cars. She sat with her hands balled tightly into a fist to stop them from shaking. She couldn't get the violent sight of her dead brother out of her mind and the fear that she would be next made her want to jump off a bridge. Last night was utter chaos. Her lip quivered as she sucked in anxious breaths. She still couldn't believe what happened. Her father was a frantic mess and refused to hear her out. All he talked about was his stupid plan and The Black Gate, like that had made any difference for Eddy. He should have just sent them away and carried the consequences himself. It was clear Vincent had no need for them.

With two days until the ceremony everyone was getting antsy. Already two of her family members had run away. Why was this happening? What was Uncle Earl thinking? All he had to do was breed those filthy children. It was easy enough; the breeders did all the work anyways. Mary clenched her fist. With all the money they paid their uncle, he should have had nothing to complain about.

The driver turned onto the cobble stone road, which made the car rock. Mary grabbed the arm of the door and tried not to let her motion sickness take over. She felt disgusting and dirty from having to spend so much time in The Slogs. She couldn't stand looking outside at all the old ugly buildings. She hated this part of town. She stared at the people in disgust as they walked around. They were so filthy, and shouldn't they be working or something? The driver turned down a narrow alley, the car rocked wildly from the potholes that littered the road.

"Ugh," Mary groaned. "Can't you go any slower in this dreadful thing?"

"I'm sorry, Lady Mary." The driver slowed down.

"I swear I will see that this place is torn down," Mary said as she grabbed her stomach.

"We are here, ma'am." The driver parked and got out at once.

He ran to Mary's door and opened it for her. Mary nearly gagged at the smell. That was another thing she hated about being here. She swung her leg out over the uneven cobblestone and nearly tripped.

"Curse this wretched place!" Mary yelled as the driver caught her from falling. "Take your filthy hands off me."

The driver nodded and gave her room.

"Lady Mary," a woman's voice said from the backdoor of one of the shops.

Mary turned around and immediately anger boiled up from her stomach. "You!" Mary stormed over to Lady Rosemary. "You were supposed to be helping Eddy and he's dead now. You better have a damn fine excuse for showing your ugly face around me, hag."

Lady Rosemary frowned, then bowed. "My deepest apologies, Lady Mary. I've been working tirelessly through the night. The time must have slipped pass me."

"Bullshit," Mary cursed. She may have been third to Vincent, but she was nothing more than a trick playing hag. "Move out of my way."

Lady Rosemary stepped aside, making room for her. Inside was the storage room of what looked like a small shop. The scent of cheap spices made Mary's nose itch and eyes water. She pulled out her handkerchief and dotted her nose.

"Don't mind the mess. We won't be here for long." Lady Rosemary allowed the door to close and walked gracefully towards Mary.

Mary sneezed and blew her nose as she looked around. "I don't care how long we'll be here. A-any word from the runners?" Mary struggled to assert herself as her allergies flared.

"Nothing yet, but we still have time. Oops, I'm sorry," Lady Rosemary covered her mouth.

Mary glared at her. She wanted to kill that woman with her bare hands. "I'm surprised Vincent can take such pride in such useless workers. It's been two days already." Mary walked from the storage room out into a narrow hall.

Lady Rosemary shrugged. "It's a big city."

"Then order your runners to work faster! And what about you? What's your plan then?" Mary asked. "Surely you have some purpose for bringing me out here."

Lady Rosemary smirked. "I do. A jeweler said he thought he saw someone come in with a ring of similar design."

Mary gasped. "And he let it get away?"

"He wasn't the master jeweler but a junior apprentice, and he only caught a glimpse. But he said for sure that the band was made of rose gold."

Mary balled her fist, her eyes still burned from the spices. Lady Rosemary walked past her and opened a door to a small office.

"Good thing Vincent ordered all the runners to check jewelry and pawn shops first." Lady Rosemary circled around the small cluttered wooden desk. "So, it shouldn't be long now. Here, have a seat. This shop is owned by a good friend of the Hoo'nae family."

Mary cringed at the name. Of all the people who should be handling this mess it should be them. Their family were the ones who helped form the original binding key. It was absolutely ludicrous that the ceremony could be completely derailed by such a small insignificant item. Mary looked up and saw Lady Rosemary smirking at her. She found it hard to hide her anger. She rather spend the night in a sewer than to spend another second with her.

"Well surely you don't think you can sit around here all day," Mary spat. This was still her operation and she would put the hag to work.

"Of course not," Lady Rosemary said. "But I am curious about one thing. What will we do without the item? You would think they'd had a backup." She shrugged.

Mary rolled her eyes. Of course she would know so little about the ring. "It's not some cheap trinket you can buy in a pawn shop. The binding key requires great magic, in fact I'm sure my father's necromancers could create an even better ring than those arrogant Hoo'nae, Sapphire, and Fort'nee descendants could ever come up with."

"Interesting that you should mention that." Lady Rosemary smirked, "Because your father created quite the bloodbath behind that idea."

"What—" Mary said.

"Excuse me, Lady Rosemary." A runner startled Mary from behind.

Mary whipped around, her eyes wild and watery. The runner stepped back, with his hands in the air in defense, which only fueled her anger more. "Didn't your mother teach you any manners!" Mary used her handkerchief to wipe her burning eyes. "You've got some nerve sneaking up on me."

"I-I'm sorry, Lady Mary." The runner bowed. He was just a boy, his arm band a cheap green metal to show his new initiation.

"What is it then," Mary barked. "What do you want?"

"I-I have a message for Lady Rosemary," the boy stuttered.

Mary was spitting mad now. She wasn't going to allow that woman, or anyone else to walk in and make her the puppet of her own operation. She was put in charge of this mission, that included overseeing Lady Rosemary.

"Whatever you have to say to her, you can say to me." Mary placed her hands on her hips.

"Y-yes, ma'am." The boy bowed again. "A couple of Siler brokers spotted the ring holders."

Mary gasped, "They what? Well, did they capture them?"

"N-no, ma'am, the two suspects were in public, b-but—"

"For crying out loud! Do they think we're playing a game of cat and mouse!" Mary yelled. "Surely, even a lowly grunt such as yourself must know how much weight rest on this operation?"

"Lady Mary." Lady Rosemary stood. "Please, allow me to handle this."

Mary turned around. Her head throbbed from the smell of spice, combined with all the stress she was under. She was tired of dealing with this, tired of all this mess.

Lady Rosemary walked to the door, her long green dress flowed behind her, exposing her rich golden-brown skin. Mary gritted her teeth. She wasn't jealous of the hag because she knew what Lady Rosemary was, a witch. A wicked blood caster and no doubt she worked her magic to maintain her looks.

"And why should I trust you?" Mary hissed.

Lady Rosemary stopped at the door and smiled as she opened her hands. The runner jumped back to life and reached into his pocket and pulled out a small crystal ball. "Thank you. I assure you, Lady Mary, I will not fail you," Lady Rosemary said as she held out the ball for Mary to see, then she reached into her drawstring purse and withdrew a vial of purple liquid. She popped the cork and poured the potion over the ball and grinned. "Come."

She spoke one word and the ball deflated into a lumpy sack, like a leathery snake egg. Then something poked and pierced the shell and out came the tiny head of a crystal snake. Mary jerked back. What the heck was that? Lady Rosemary smiled, unfazed, and walked the thing towards Mary.

"Go on, show her," Lady Rosemary said softly, and the crystal snaked swirled its body around itself into the perfect flat roll.

Then reflected the image of two women walking side by side. Both looked young, one had dark purple box braids and the other a short blonde bushy hair, but in the hands of the blonde one was the gear ring. Mary gasped, then she noticed the tiny hint of crystal shining from the woman's bag. Lady Rosemary pulled her hand back.

"We're tracking them as we speak. I should have this issued resolved in a few hours."

Mary sat back in her chair and watched Lady Rosemary leave. Relief washed over her body. She had no idea what Lady Rosemary was going on about with her father and some bloodbath, but that didn't matter now. Soon, they would have the ring, and this nightmare would finally be over and then she would make everyone pay for putting her through this hell.

18
Mia

Mia walked behind Billie, letting the rose gold ring twirl around in her hand. She knew she should put it away, but they were close to the police station anyways so what harm could possibly come from one last look? The streets on this side of town weren't as busy because there weren't as many flashy shops or bars. There were a few secondhand shops and classier pawn shops around here, but the further they went the more paper pusher offices popped up. These types of businesses were usually related to the law, like bond offices, labor recruiters, and post offices.

Folks on motor bikes zipped by, along with a few gas carriages that shot their black smoke into the air. They crossed the street and passed a few dry goods shops, a medicine shop, and a small law office. The police station was a little out of the way considering where they had to go to get home, but there wasn't much they could do about it. The closer precinct was closed and this one was the next closest one. Not that cops were much help in The Slogs anyway. Most were either runners or bribe takers. Tae'a said she once sucked off a cop to let her go after she beat a man bloody because he attacked her. Which was good to know in case Mia found herself in a bind, but as far as solving crime, only folks with money got justice. As for turning in the ring, cops were good at one thing and that was paperwork. Anything they could get value off of, they made sure to charge a hefty finder's fee, so even though Lady Valkyrie couldn't give two craps about law enforcement, and she had runners of her own, they still proved useful in protecting the brothel's butt.

Mia looked on the inside of the ring again at the strange language and symbol. She wondered if it was some ancient Tyrazian language. Maybe the person who lost it wasn't local at all. Julilie shared a border with four other countries and had a rocky coastline. She didn't know too much about the countries outside of their names, but she did know a little about their history. Many of the countries on the coast were involved in violent civil wars way back in the day. Back when the Tyrazi people were enslaved and many of the natives were slaughtered. Though, now things were relatively peaceful, she never heard anything about any of them being a paradise either. Julilie's neighbors—Markios to the north, May-Liliya and Junsux to the west, and Augtus to the south—were all smaller sized and probably just as poor. The only nation travelers ever gloated about was Septland New Nation. They were famous for their imports, she knew that.

She wished she could take the ring back to the brothel and show the others. She sighed and smiled as she held up the ring on its long, worn chain. *You'll be home soon.* Mia's smile grew, not realizing Billie had stopped in the middle of the sidewalk. Mia crashed into her best friend causing her to lose her grip on the ring. It fell down her chest, caught by the chain Billie had given her.

"What gives, Billie?" Mia said as she took a few steps back. She checked the ring, then looked at her friend who appeared to be sniffing around like a rat. "What are you doing?"

"You smell that Mia?"

"What?" Mia stood there clueless.

"Seriously, something smells good." Billie sniffed around some more. She glanced at the shops ahead, none caught her eye then she pointed. "Maybe it's coming from there."

"Where?" Mia looked.

"I think it's a bakery or something," Billie said. "Let's check it out."

Mia shook her head but agreed, they would have passed it anyways. The closer they got the more Mia started to smell what Billie was smelling. The fresh smell of honey cinnamon roasted peanuts with a hint of pepper spice floated in the air overpowering the musty smell of the city. Mia couldn't believe such a combination existed. They ran the rest of the way, and their hunt was rewarded with free samples.

"Wow, these smell amazing," Billie said as she stood in front of the small spice shop. "And they're free."

"Lilly's Imports," Mia read the sign carved in wood above the door. "How nice."

Mia admired the cute green shutters that matched the door. Billie rubbed her hands together before plucking a few free samples off the plate. Mia tried a few herself. She liked them enough, but she was more pulled in by the walls of imported and local spices. There were spices in here she had never even heard of before. Mia reached out and read the labels of nutmeg, lemon grass, and allspice.

"Good evening miss. Could I interest you in a free sample? We're trying out a new flavor of roasted nuts."

Mia turned around and her breath was taken away by the absolute beauty of the woman standing before her. Her soft golden-brown skin radiated with such a glowing healthy color and her deep jade green eyes sparkled in the middle of her long locks of curly moss green hair. She was so beautiful, even in her plain white blouse and black apron. The woman smiled softly and held out the free sample tray and Mia noticed her crystal snake bracelet as well, which was just as beautiful as she was.

"My, what a beautiful ring," the clerk said.

Mia looked down only for a second, breaking eye contact with the woman as if she were resurfacing for air. "T-thanks," was all Mia could muster.

"Would you like to try a sample?" the woman asked again.

"Um, s-sure," Mia smiled and reached for the nuts when Billie called out her name. Mia looked towards her friend, who was fast approaching. The woman pulled back and performed the same friendly greeting for Billie.

"Thanks, but I've already had a ton," Billie said.

"How about you then, miss," the woman offered, holding the dish out again.

"Try some, Mia," Billie said. "They're like super good."

Mia nodded and took a handful. She thanked the woman and continued to browse. She couldn't believe such a beautiful woman worked here. She was so beautiful Mia was sure she could make a killing at any brothel. Mia watched Billie shop; she was surprised that she wasn't affected by the woman's beauty. That must be the power of love. Mia continued to browse, reading all the jars and packets. The rest of the shop was so very pleasant. The smells wrapped around her like a blanket. She tailed Billie as she stopped at each and every spice rack and shelf rambling on and on so fast Mia could barely keep up.

"Mia, look! They have something called..." Billie bent down and placed her hands on her knees. "Something called...I...I don't know."

Billie laughed so hard that it rung in Mia's ears. Mia giggled, feeling a swell of good feelings float up her chest. Billie continued on, but Mia stood back and allowed this good feeling to wash over her, leaving her in a pleasant haze. Billie's laughter mixed in with the sounds of jars clanking together, lifting the worries from her mind, and her soul from her body.

The room lightened as the spice racks started to swirl. Billie's laughter echoed through her brain as light faded from white to gray. Mia giggled at the sound of heels slowly approaching, not realizing she had found herself on the floor. Billie lay not far from her, silent, but Mia only coughed out a few more laughs, before the world faded to darkness.

Light burst into existence and Mia was falling. A pair of eyes watched her. She was a small pale pink rat that twirled deeper and deeper into the darkness. Colorful starburst of gold, silver, and copper exploded around her as she spun down down down. So bright and soft, as the cool air blew through her short fur and tail. It was marvelous and she never wanted this sensation to end.

Her pale pink fur faded to a bright electric white, she watched as the last of her soft orchid pink color leached from her in brilliant spirals as she sunk deeper deeper deeper into the cozy abyss. Just as she was about to close her eyes, a glint of dark silver popped above her and danced in her vision. The spark shifted and zigzagged until it morphed into the shimmering shape of a rat. It reached its paws out to Mia's and a flash of crimson burst before her eyes.

A wave of warmth rippled through Mia's body as the rat above her shifted from shimmering black to midnight silver. Mia gazed into its starry eyes that swirled with bands of silver and dark blue. The two spiraled down down down as the rat pulled Mia closer and nuzzled her nose.

"Wake up, little one," a voice said and from the rat's mouth a burst of vermillion and scarlet exploded around her.

Mia's eyes rolled under her eyelids as a buzzing sound grew in her ears. She slowly opened them as voices echoed around her. She could barely move her body, but she could make out the hazy purple lump beside her.

"B-Billie," Mia opened her dry mouth, then let out a laugh.

Her head was spinning so fast that all she wanted to do was go back to sleep, but something wasn't right. She didn't remember going home. Mia suddenly felt a pair of cold hands move her head to the side. The smell of honey wafted through her nose as Mia stared at the burst of green.

"My, what a shame," a woman said. "You are so beautiful, too bad you were born poor."

"W-what," Mia managed to utter.

"Hush, rest, my little butterfly," the woman's jade green eyes came into focus. "Now, before I transport you back to my apothecary, I do need a little blood. You see, that crystal key I cast ate up all my reserves. It won't take long; I just need two pints."

"W-what," Mia began to squirm. "L-let me go."

The woman hummed as she disappeared from Mia's sight. She heard the click clack of her heels on the floor as she struggled to lift her head. Mia tried to focus on moving her arms, but it was like her body wasn't paying attention. Mia felt a presence on her right side, then a cold hand on her right arm.

"Now hold still, my little butterfly. Mama doesn't have much time, so I'm going to have to make this quick."

Mia felt a sudden tight pressure on her arm that set off alarm bells in her head. She mustered all her strength to turn to her right side where she saw the very same woman from the spice shop hold what looked like a giant blood red tick. Its serrated jaw chattered as its eight legs squirmed in the air. The woman pinned down Mia's arm and lowered the thing to her flesh. It pierced the arm sending shockwaves of fiery heat throughout Mia's body. She screamed as the tick worked its jaw and head deep into her arm. She choked as a foam built in the back of her throat. Her entire body was on fire and her head throbbed with pain. Tears ran down her temples as she looked towards the woman for mercy.

The woman grinned. "Now now, doll, no need to fear. Blood harvested from the belly of a hungry garden tick yields the best kind of skin blemish treating magic and a woman must do what she can to stay young."

Mia choked and as the searing pain tore through her body. Every nerve in her body screamed.

The woman looked away, Mia could see through her blurry vision, then she looked back down at Mia. "Looks like my time is up, hun, so we gotta speed this up." The woman pulled back her hand into a fist, bright green sparks of energy popped off it. Then she punched Mia square in the gut sending a blast of bone crushing pain through Mia's body and Mia blacked out.

19
Mary

Mary rubbed her temples as she tried to get comfortable in the small room provided to her. She was just about to lay down when a sudden scream jolted her awake. What in all the glory was that? Mary gathered up her dress and ran out of the room and noticed the door to the storage room was open. Mary glared. That hag, she must be up to something. Mary hated her and her dirty blood magic so much. Mary stormed down the hall and flung open the door.

"Put a pin in it, will you!" Mary shouted. "Can't you see that some of us are trying to sleep."

"My apologies." Lady Rosemary stopped whatever she was doing. "This will only take a minute."

Mary scoffed, but not before catching sight of the thieves who had caused her so much trouble. The girls looked like a couple of cheap tricks, and probably were the ones who worked the ring off her uncle. She was so furious, she wished she could strangle them herself, but the hag had them and they deserved any fate that came with that.

Mary left before the witch could say another word. She was so very tired of this, but they finally had the ring. Frustrated, there was no point of trying to sleep. She was fully awake now and took a seat in the office. She was still haunted by the imagery of her brother's body. That monster Vincent Lorne would not get away with this. Mary would make damn sure of that and what a mess this was going to be. Eddy was her family's heir. What would the council say? They were members of the Five Families after all. Members of her family held prominent positions. What would the others think if they found out that Lord Jadan Fort'nee let his thugs do this to her family? Those Fort'nee scum were on her shit list for sure, the entire system needed to be taken down. The door creaked open, and Mary flashed a nasty look to the person who walked in.

"My my, that look doesn't suit you," Lady Rosemary said, but Mary only scoffed.

"We have the gear ring, there is no need for further conversation." Mary turned away and waited for Lady Rosemary to leave, but she didn't hear any footsteps. "Didn't you hear me?"

"I heard you." Lady Rosemary seemingly ignored her words and walked further into the room, sitting down on a chair near the wall. "But you should really lighten up."

Mary fumed, but she was tired of wasting her energy on this hag. "Do whatever you like, I don't care."

Lady Rosemary chuckled. "All this stress over a little ring. It's a real shame though. I doubt those girls were a part of an organized group. Maybe they robbed ole' Earl or maybe it was just their rotten luck to come across it."

"Like you care."

"You're right, I don't. Their bodies will do just fine for my work, but still, I can't believe all the fuss for this little ole thing." Lady Rosemary lifted her hand to look at the rose gold ring that twirled on an old, rusted gold chain.

Mary looked at her in disgust. Of course, a woman consumed by her own vanity wouldn't know the true purpose of the ring. That gear ring was the key to renewing the summoning keys that kept the factories alive in this shithole of a city. Mary knew at least that much. Without the magic they gained from the re-binding spell no one would have a future in this city. Or rather, certain families wouldn't have a future in this city. At least her father's work was universally beneficial. Medical necromancy had come a long way, and Mary was sure if her father wanted to, he could spread his medical treatments far and wide, which would surely be more sustainable over the wicked alchemy that churned the Sapphire's mines. Not that she would ever blame her Kym for his family's practices. He was the innovator; he saw the value in her father's work and as a member of The Yield, he had a bright future.

Lady Rosemary stretched her arms high, then slumped. "I've already called Vincent; he'll be on the way over soon."

Mary jerked up at the mention of his name. "In person? Why's he making house calls?" But all Lady Rosemary did was shrug. Mary clenched her fist.

She really hated that woman and after all this was said and done, she would see to it that every inch of that woman's body would be burned to dust.

20

Aries

The sound of metal slapping the ground echoed through the steamy sewer chamber. In the dim light dust rose from the place the retracting pole struck. A strong man, with deep dark brown skin and broad shoulders smiled, then clapped as he pushed himself off the wall.

"Now try it again, but this time strike as though your life depends on it, Aries."

"Yes, Uncle."

Aries squeezed the pole tight, cutting the air around her. Her heart raced as the sweat of a well-earned workout built up on her face. She charged at ghosts no one else could see, slaying them with her lightning-fast strikes.

"Good job." Her Uncle Roman smiled. "Why don't we take a break?"

Aries frowned.

"It's okay." He offered her water from his drinking jug. "Come here."

Aries pressed the button on the end of the handle, retracting the pole in one snap. She hesitated at first, but her mouth was as dry as a cobweb filled tunnel. She walked to her uncle, wiping away the sweat that built on the edges of her long, thick, curly, crimson hair.

"Do you know why I'm training you, Aries?" he asked.

"Of course, Uncle, so I can fight evil."

He laughed, his chest raising and falling with every chuckle. "Yes, but it isn't all about fighting evil. I'm training you so you can help protect the balance."

Aries drank from the jug then put it down. She wiped her mouth dry with her forearm and glanced up. "But isn't that the same thing?"

"It is not. Fighting evil is a pleasure, a past time even, but protecting the balance requires more than a strong arm. It also requires a kind heart, a quick mind, and a desire above all else to protect those who cannot protect themselves."

Aries nodded. Her uncle stood up and motioned for her to start again. She extended her thin silver pole and attacked.

Aries awoke, sitting next to her sleeping sister. They found a place to sleep for the night on the first level of the sewers. She had slept in short bouts keeping an eye on passersby. It was noisy here, but not the worse place she'd slept in. Yesterday wasn't as fruitful as she had hoped. For one, she didn't know where to start and none of the information she gathered made sense. She did however take notice of the large amount of runners in the area. She wasn't sure if this were common or not, but her mother was right. They flooded the streets like cockroaches.

Aries sat perfectly still, allowing her sister to get a few more minutes of sleep. She dreamed of her uncle last night. She hadn't had a dream like that in a long time. She didn't want to ignore her past. She just felt tired and part of her felt like she was dishonoring her elder's memories by not fully believing. Now she was out on a scavenger hunt to find a pebble amongst a thousand rocks. How was she supposed to find this Crimson Mouse?

Her granny's gift of sight could only reveal so much. From what she recalled, she knew she was looking for a woman, but the word woman could mean anything, a child even, if menstruation didn't count. She also mentioned something about a bloody ring? Or a blood covered ring. Aries rather not see that or even know how it became that way. Then there was something about a cage. It was all very confusing, and she doubt there would be any insight in the text. The seer's prophecies didn't work the way children's tales did. Tales that dealt in chosen ones and heroes destined for greatness, in stories with clear beginnings and endings. The way her granny explained it, was that prophecies were like seeds, they only needed the right conditions to sprout. Any details could change at any time, except for two things: there would aways be a Crimson Mouse and there would always be a shadow mouse who follows it to victory.

Aries sighed. It was painful to think about her granny. She couldn't shake the image of her granny trembling as she spoke about the prophecy. It made Aries feel uneasy. Her granny was known to be eccentric, but when her dark red eyes deepened, it scared her. She wished her uncle was here; heck, she even wished Zopi was here. Her cousin may have found himself in trouble from time to time, but the guy could fight, and he had good street sense, too. Aries closed her eyes. Her memories took her back to her mother's house where Zopi was trying to teach Bluu how to fight.

"Gimmie ya hand." Zopi crouched down with his palms open.

Bluu's laughter filled the room as he swung at his father's hands. Sasha laughed as she brought over a plate of cheese and bread.

"Nyekundu," Sasha called.

Aries opened her eyes and blinked a few times to suck back in all that grief. Her heart ached, and suddenly she was aware of just how tired she was. What a mess. Even if she did all this, it wouldn't bring any of them back. She could only hope her parents weren't too worried about them. Karina turned a little and awoke to the sound of people laughing that echoed off the walls. Karina pushed the thin blanket from her hips and attempted to stretch.

"Sleep okay?" Aries asked.

"Never better." Karina smirked as she slumped down to the floor and continued to stretch.

"Well, let's get a move on. We have a lot of ground to cover." Aries started to stand, taking her time to stretch as well.

"Do we have any leads?"

"No, but I'm noticing an increase in runners the further north we go."

"Why don't we just ask the rats?" Karina asked bluntly.

"Rats?" Aries eyed her. She knew her sister believed they had some special connection to rats, but perhaps the rats in the sewers were just friendlier than others, because they lived so close to humans. Not to mention that most people didn't eat rat meat for fear of illness. "Karina."

"What? I talk to Tink all the time, see." Karina lifted her shirt. "Tink, you up?" She heard a little squeak, then a bulge popped up on her stomach. Karina giggled as Tink climbed up her chest. "Hey, Tink, has any of your friends seen anything suspicious around?" Karina asked, to a confused rat who only tilted his head. Tink blinked a few times before turning his attention to Aries then back to Karina. "It's okay if you don't know, but maybe you can ask your friends?"

"Karina." Aries shook her head.

"Shush, I know he can understand me," Karina said. "Look, Tink, we're on a mission for Granny. We're looking for the Crimson Mouse. It's a girl and she's carrying a ring." Tink's ears perked up as he stood on his hind legs. He squeaked and Karina smiled. "Good, yes we need to find her, Tink, because my sister Aries is the Darkness."

Aries sighed. "Karina..."

"We need help finding the Crimson Mouse so we can restore balance to the world by helping Acome." Tink squeaked and ran up and down Karina's shirt. "Now go!" Karina commanded.

Tink looked off in the direction Karina pointed then stopped and looked back at Karina. He tilted his head as Karina pointed again. Tink sniffed the air, then moved towards Karina's legs. He dug into her pocket and came back out with a half-eaten cracker in his mouth.

"Tink," Karina frowned.

"It's okay Karina, he's still helpful in his own way. Speaking of which we better grab a bite to eat ourselves."

"Do you have any money left?"

"Not a lot, but it should be enough to buy some bread," Aries said. "There's a water fountain down the hall. Let's fill up and get moving."

"Okay!" Karina jumped to her feet.

The pair walked up the dirty, crack-ridden stairs to reach the above ground world. Aries blocked the light with her forearm, it was so much brighter up here than in the sewer. She squinted to see as her eyes struggled to adjust. The air was fresher, but the smell of sewage and trash still lingered. A light fog hugged the streets, but slowly dissipated, revealing more of the bright upper world. Karina jumped out beside her. Her eyes wide, a big smile was plastered on her face.

"Nice, huh?" Karina smiled and all Aries could do was nod.

So this was the great big world the folks in The Slogs lived in. Aries eyed the wide paved streets filled with people and shops made of brick and not rusted train cars. In the streets were dozens of different types of motorized cars. Some looked more like horseless carriages, while others were the more modern gas cars, with shiny finishes and thick rubber wheels. There were motorbikes, too, that zipped by with people on them. Aries couldn't believe so many people drove, but then again, it was mostly flat up here and not full of awkward narrow stairs and tunnels.

"Hey, look up," Karina said.

"Huh. For all the glory..." Aries ducked as an airship zipped by. "Is-is that actually—"

"An Airglider? Yup, it's still an airship, but smaller and faster, too." Karina smiled as they watched it disappear.

"A-and people actually ride..."

Karina nodded with a chuckle. "If you think that's cool, wait till you see the big balloon ones. They look like giant water jugs."

This was unreal, but with all the space and no ceilings to stop you, why not? The weather was chillier up here too, there was no vents or sewers blowing warm air and there was a light breeze, but the thing that amazed her the most was the sky. It was massive.

"You know," Karina said. "Granny said that the great big sky used to be blue and the sun came every day."

Gray or blue, just seeing the sky was overwhelming. It seemed to touch the edge of the ground all around her. She was used to the crowded narrow tunnels of her home. Out here she felt exposed. Aries took a deep breath.

"I guess we should get going," Aries said

It was Diday, so the crowds where still thin coming off the tail of the holiday weekend. A few runners walked across the street in front of them. They chatted in the cool morning air. She noticed their armbands, they were part of the Dakota gang, not a gang too common in this area but one she had seen a few times in Gomi City, the sewer's biggest city. She wasn't surprised they were up early; it was post-holiday season and a lot of runners traveled in for the money. She listened to their chatter as they passed. The group spoke enthusiastically about their conquest and betting games they played in the bars the night before, but of nothing else. Out of the corner of her eye she noticed Karina slump off her backpack and pull out her notebook.

"Okay, so we covered a lot of ground yesterday." Karina ran her fingers down the scribble of a list. "I think we should head east."

Aries peered at her list. She wasn't as familiar with the above ground world, but her sister's makeshift list was about the closest thing they had to help them narrow things down. Karina pointed to a location on her list.

"Isn't that where the markets are?" Aries eyed her sister. She might not know the specifics, but markets were easy to pinpoint due to all the noise and trash that found itself in her home below.

"N-No," Karina said, but her mouth curled up into a smile, giving her away.

"We're not up here to sight see, we have a mission." Aries felt silly saying that out loud, but at this point she might as well accept it.

"I know I know, but we worked so hard yesterday," Karina said. "Can't we take a little break?"

"No, we have no money and Mom and Dad are maintaining the household on their own and looking after Bluu, the tax lords do not care about adventure and the tax will be due soon."

Karina folded her arms, but Aries started walking anyways. She wanted to continue north. There were more runners there, perhaps they might know something. Karina dragged her feet behind her sister, with Tink sticking out of her pocket.

"You see this, Tink, Aries'll have us walking around this entire city and we won't even get to visit the best parts," Karina said to the curious rat.

Aries ignored her sister. Up ahead was a small stand that appeared to be selling goods. Aries walked towards the counter and looked inside. It was cramp like a closet and dried goods in brown cloth bags were nailed to every inch of the wall.

"Hello?" Aries called out. She could see every inch of the space except past a narrow door that was slightly ajar. "Hello?"

"I heard ya wailing!" a woman's voice rattled from the back. Aries heard the sound of sandals scraping across the floor next and soon a short elderly woman appeared in its opening. She took one look at Aries and glared. "We're closed!"

Aries glanced at her sister. "Are you sure? We have money."

"I don't want any money from a bunch of beggars. Now get outta here." The woman waved them off.

Aries glared, and she could feel her sister getting riled up. She had heard rumors of people above ground not liking sewer folks, but to be turned away even after disclosing that she had money rubbed her the wrong way.

"Fuck her," Karina said.

"Come on, let's go." Aries turned and started walking again.

"What? Aries!"

But Aries didn't stop. Karina grumbled behind her, then Aries heard the sound of glass breaking on the ground. Aries turned around and saw Karina sprinting towards her. Aries ignored the shrieks of the woman from the shop and took off after her sister. She would pretend she didn't hear that, but she guessed they would go without breakfast. They would be fine. It wouldn't be the first time they had to tough it out.

The two continued their journey, walking further and further north towards the great wall to the upper city. It was hard to focus on the mission, as Aries found her eyes darting into every building and shop. It was so clean and spacious up here. Even the people looked clean in their suits and dresses. Wouldn't it be nice to just stay up here? That thought flashed into her mind and was quickly extinguished when she realized she didn't even know what she would do for money. She was trapped in the world below and there was nothing she could do about it. As they walked they earned their fair share of stares, with some stopping to look and whisper before moving on. Perhaps they did stick out a little with their crimson hair and tattered clothes. To the people above she must look more like a street person, but below no one would spare her a passing glance. Not that they could do anything about it, but then her mind started to wonder what her younger sister would look like in one of those nice dresses. Or her mother. Their smiles created a safe place in her mind to hide.

"I still think we should have headed to the markets," Karina said, pulling Aries from her thoughts.

Aries looked across the street. There was an open bar. "For what? I already said we don't have any money."

"So, we could still look," Karina grumbled.

"Come on." Aries waved.

"Wait!" Karina struggled a bit. Tink started squeaking towards an alley beside them and Karina opened her hands for him to jump into. "What is it, Tink?"

Aries stopped and Tink jumped from Karina's hands and took off into the alley. The girls ran after him and when they did, they spooked a dozen or so rats that were already there.

"Tink!" Karina shouted as she tried to search for her friend. "Tink!"

Aries eyed Tink from across the alley. He was sitting on a wooden box next to another rat. Aries locked eyes with him and in that moment she thought she felt something. Tink stood on his hind legs, sniffed the air, then disappeared with the other rat.

"Tink!" Karina stumbled after him. Then fell to her knees.

"It's okay, Karina. He probably spotted a few of his friends. He'll be back, he always returns." Aries stood beside her sister, not sure if she believed her own words or not. It wasn't uncommon for Tink to wander off, but there was something about the way he looked at her. Then she shook the idea from her head, was she seriously thinking that her pet rat as trying to communicate something to her?

"Are-are you sure?" Karina cupped her hands to her chest as she shifted her worried gaze back to her sister.

Aries nodded with a soft smile. "He's a rat, he knows the city best. He'll be back for sure." That seemed to at least get Karina off the ground. "Come on."

The pair headed to the bar. It was dimly lit and mostly empty except for a few patrons at the bar and in the back. Karina stayed close to her sister as the bartender eyed them as they walked by. Aries took note of all the runners with armbands. There was a mix of at least four different gangs in here. She took a seat in the back that was within hearing distance from a few of them.

"Hey," Karina whispered. "This place gives me the creeps."

"It's okay, we'll only be here for a second." Aries' eyes darted to the left of her when she heard a group of runners laughing loudly behind her. "Why don't you go up to the bar and see if they sell food."

Karina looked at the bar dubiously, then back at her sister. She forgot how shy she could be sometimes. So, Aries took off her backpack and pulled out a few coins. Karina's face lit up and in an instant she was off. Aries watched the groups out of the corner of her eye. A few of the men noticed Karina walk by but went back to their conversation, much to Aries' relief.

"Shit, man," a man from the West Point gang whined. "I'm behind on dues."

"Well, that's what you get for spending your money on babes," his friend said.

Aries listened in on another group, one with a few women and men, who were playing cards. They laughed loudly, right as one of the women laid down a winning hand. No one was saying anything of interest and Aries sighed. This was starting to feel like a repeat of yesterday. Aries rubbed her temples. She was doing this for her granny, but maybe what her granny saw wasn't a prophecy vision. Maybe it was her mind playing tricks on her.

Aries looked up to find her sister. She was still at the bar, sitting a few seats from the rest of the patrons. One silver lining was at least Karina was enjoying herself. It was rare to have a nice break, she would likely never go this far into the city again, at least not this freely.

The bar door creaked opened and a group of three entered, all runners. Aries noticed their armbands, but she couldn't place the gang. The guy in front look pissed, his face was bandaged up crudely and his right eye was bruised. His buddies smirked behind his back as they took a seat in Aries' part of the bar which was darker and closer to the back on the wall.

"Shuddup," the man in front said, "and get me a beer, make it two."

His friend left but snickered under his breath.

"Dumb bitch," the man pressed his fingers to his face and winced.

"Well, at least you made it out with your life. Could have been a lot worse," his other friend said.

"I don't give a fuck! They ain't going to kill me, I'm their number five guy, those bitches just got lucky."

"Well, it's over for 'em now, got word they've been caught."

"Good and I hope they skin 'em, too." The man rested his head in his palm. "All this fuss over a damn ring. Fuck them upper class trash bags and their Siler dogs."

Aries glared but hid her intentions by pretending to read the bar specials on the table. Karina returned, blocking Aries from the men's line of sight. She locked eyes with her sister and Karina stiffened up. Karina started to look behind her, but Aries kicked her lightly on the foot. Karina stopped then leaned in.

"Got something?" Karina whispered.

Aries looked past Karina. One of the guy's buddies returned from the bar with two frothy red drinks. The bandaged guy picked up a pint and chugged, finishing it with suds still fizzing at the bottom of the glass.

"Gotta take a leak." The man slid the glass across the table into the palm of his buddy's hand.

He walked three tables away from where Aries and Karina sat. Karina glanced between him, and Aries as Aries rose. Karina reached for her sister, but when she looked up, Aries gave her a knowing look. This man knew something, and she could handle herself against one drunk runner. Aries reassured her sister with a nod and walked to the back.

Aries entered a small, dim hall with the only light coming from crudely strung up light bulbs, but there were two bathrooms at the end. One was dark and the other had its light on with the door slightly ajar. The sound of piss hitting the water, along with a grunt, echoed off the walls as she got closer. Aries tiptoed up to the room and peeked in from her position on the wall. There was nothing more than a single stall and sink. She slipped into the room and shut the door with a thud, startling the man. He turned around with his dick out and stumbled backwards, falling onto his butt.

"What the—"

"Shut it." Aries withdrew her retracting pole and swiped him across his face. He wailed and she popped him again. "I said shut it." Aries stood over him with the tip of her retracting pole at his throat. "The ring, where is it?"

Tears wet his eyes as he trembled. "W-what ring?"

Aries glared as she drove the pole deeper into the tender flesh of the knot in his throat, hard enough to leave a mark this time.

"Ow! Ow! Ow!" The man inched back until he hit the wall. "I-I don't know anything about a ring."

Aries popped him in the lip and the man yelped. Tears mixed with blood as he grabbed his face.

"Okay! Shit." The man trembled. "But I didn't steal it, it was special orders. It belongs to Vincent's people."

Aries narrowed her eyes.

"You know, the Silers? The runners with the metal armbands, shit." The man rubbed the side of his face, "but it's through now, they caught those bitches."

Aries glared at the man, her hand gripped tightly around the handle. Could this be the Crimson Mouse? And did he just say Silers? They were the most ruthless gang in the sewers. What would they want with a ring? "The ring, what did it look like?"

"Shit, I don't know." The man flinched when he saw Aries jerk her hand. "Rose gold! Rose gold. It was some kind of weird ass ring, like a fucking gear I don't know. All I know is that Vincent's people had to have it, heard his number three nabbed them."

Rose gold? What did that look like again? Aries glared at the man. "Where is this number three now?"

"Uptown? I don't know." The man trembled.

Aries delivered a few more swift blows, making the man jerk and wail.

"Near the wall! Heard they set up shop near the wall!" the man cried out.

The man was a crying mess, but she had the info she needed. She struck him behind the neck, knocking him out, but not killing him. Rose gold? She could only envision copper, but that didn't seem right. Granny said, a gold tainted by blood. Could this be the sickly pinkish gold ring her granny saw in her vision? If so, did this mean her granny was right? Aries was suddenly dizzy as a strange pressure built in her chest. She gasped. It felt like she was choking. She panted and grabbed at the lump forming in her chest.

She clutched the wall for support as the pain crept up to her jaw. Where was this feeling coming from? Was it the air? Was she exhausted from hunger? She had never felt this way before. She glanced at the man. She had only hit him hard enough for her to slip away. He would be awake soon. Aries retracted her pole and stumbled through the door as the pain intensified and spread across her chest down to her arms. She reached for the handle of the door and opened it wider, surprised to see her sister Karina standing there.

"Aries? What's wrong?" Karina tried to peek past her.

"We...need to...leave...now," Aries said between gasps as sweat rolled down her face and the darkness closed in.

21 Vincent

Vincent sat in the passenger seat of one of his Saint Henry Model cars as the driver took him and two runners to the Fort'nee manor. Normally he wouldn't take out this clunky car, but what it lacked in subtlety it made up for with luxury, the perfect gaudy vehicle for visiting his bosses. He glanced at the light gray sky as they passed the council buildings towards the manors. Each of the opulent buildings and all their grandeur were nothing more than a front for the neighboring nations. There was no great monarchy and democracy like in the other nations, only this toxic oligarchy. Julilie was one big corporation with workers populating the highest percent of the population and a council of rich spoiled leaders at the top. Not that Vincent had an option or even cared how Julilie was run. He knew his place, but he hated drama. This entire thing had put such a strain on his resources he could only imagine the paperwork that would follow. He was however glad to be through with this tiresome ordeal. Having to work so closely to his sometimes-incompetent bratty employers made him want to smoke the strong stuff. The driver turned onto his boss' street and Vincent eyed the manor.

The Fort'nee manor was by far the largest manor out of the Five Families. The compound sat atop a hill of bright green artificial grass. Five mansions were on the property, arranged like a pyramid where the entire Fort'nee family lived. At the tip of the pyramid was where the current family leaders resided, and they had the largest mansion to themselves. The driver pulled into the brick loop of their driveway where the help waited to usher him inside. He was sure Jaden would be pleased with the news. He just needed to tell him, then he could pick up the gear ring from Lady Rosemary. The driver stopped and Vincent and his runners started to get out when Vincent stopped them.

"I'll only be a minute," Vincent said to his driver and his runners.

"Understood," said the driver.

Vincent left behind his two runners and walked to the door where a housemaid waited for him. He followed her through the mansion, but this time she took him to the back garden towards another smaller, but still large, house. She opened the door to a large sunroom and continue to a wooden patio that overlooked a small pond. Vincent walked through the sliding door and found himself in the company of the head members of each of the Five Families. They all stared at him with glasses of wine and plates of nicely cut vegetables and cheeses in their hands. In the middle of the patio was a large table full of cold cuts, breads, desserts, and other imports Vincent could not even name, all arranged around large, elevated platters of wine. Vincent bowed politely.

Jaden Fort'nee was the first to approach him. He was Vincent's true boss and bank roller for the Silers. "I trust you have good news?"

Vincent met his eye. The man looked at him impatiently. "I do. Lady Rosemary has recovered the gear ring. I am on my way to pick it up now."

Nia Fort'nee, Jaden's wife, gasped with relief as Jaden smiled and turned to his guest. "Well, that settles it," Jaden said.

Henry Sapphire, head of the Ao Almasi company grunted as he took a large swig of his wine. "We wouldn't be in this predicament if someone had done their jobs." He flashed a look towards Dr. Granite and his wife. Henry's husband Porter snickered behind his drink.

Jaden laughed to beat off the tension. "What does it matter? The deed is done."

Amma Hoo'nae, whose family were the descendants of one of the monks who cast the binding spell, scoffed. "I don't think they should get off that easily."

Jaden forced a tight smile in her direction, while the others talked about Dr. Granite and his family like he wasn't standing three feet away from them.

Nia rolled her eyes as a housemaid filled her cup. "You're one to talk, Amma. Was it not your family that was responsible for the binding?"

Amma gasped as if someone had slapped her across the face. Her husband, Lor'es Hoo'nae, turned and snarled at Jaden. "Jaden, control your wife."

Nia scoffed, but Amma cut her off. "I'll have you know we did our part, the cage is perfectly designed. Our business with the Granite's is strictly regulated to the supply of sacrifices and nothing more." Amma shot a look to Dr. Granite. "And surely breeding out a few dozen slaves can't be that complicated with all the funding we pour into your operation."

All the eyes were on Dr. Granite now. Shame and anger colored his face as his wife gripped tightly to his shoulder.

Amber, Dr. Granite's wife, finally stood. "My husband works hard. We're the ones that do all the heavy lifting while you lay idly in your manors," Amber bit.

Nia laughed. "Idly? We are more than capable of handling our business, unlike your reckless fool of a husband who sacrificed his entire precious Black Gate for the mess our Siler's cleaned up for you."

"Enough!" Jaden shouted. "I am tired of the bickering. We all know that Jadi-Alan Hoo'nae was a lazy old fool, but he struck the deal, so we are stuck with the Granites and their...sometimes subpar work." Jaden glared at Amber, who lowered her head and sat back down next to her husband. "But I also recognize their usefulness. Now unless the Hoo'naes want to pick up the slack again, I don't want to hear another thing about it."

No one said a word, in what quite honestly had been the most entertaining exchange Vincent had ever seen. Jaden finally noticed that Vincent still stood near the door. Jaden flashed one of his fake smiles and opened his arm to usher Vincent out. Vincent bowed to the family heads and walked back into the sunroom. The housemaid closed the door behind them. Once out of view of the rest of the family heads, Jaden's fake smile disappeared.

"I want you to keep an eye on the Granites. Do whatever necessary to prevent this from happening again."

"Yes, sir," Vincent said.

Jaden straightened his suit and relaxed just as a door opened next to them. Jaden flashed a smile. "Gladie, I hope you are feeling better."

Vincent bowed to Gladie Ruby, matriarch of the Ruby family and chief executive to Ruby-Gyme Metal works. Gladie ignored Jaden with a wave before she turned to Vincent.

"Vincent Lorne, right?" Gladie slurred.

"Yes, ma'am."

"You don't need to be polite with me, dear, not with all these pocket cocks swimming around," Gladie said.

Jaden let out a frustrated sigh. "Seriously, Gladie, can you not act normal for one second?"

"Normal?" Gladie let out a loud laugh. "There's nothing normal about any of this. You about to kill a baby tomorrow and normal is the adjective you choose?"

Jaden seethed now. He straightened out his cuffs and pursed his lips into a smile. "It happens every year, Gladie," he said through gritted teeth.

"And every year is another mark on the devil's ledger. You're all going to burn in Ozama's hell, and I'll be right there beside ya, laughing my big black ass off." Gladie stared wildly at him, then she burst into a fit of laughter. "You take care Vincent honey."

Gladie walked towards the sliding door and the housemaid opened the door for her.

"That bitter, zealot bitch," Jaden cursed under his breath, but Vincent acted like he didn't hear. "Alright, Vincent, I have a ceremony to plan. Deliver the gear ring and prepare the men. I want the security to be tight."

"Yes, sir." Vincent bowed, then turned to leave.

This was an amusing evening. It was always a treat to see Gladie. She was the most eccentric and unpredictable of the Five Family leaders, but she was also the only one who didn't skirt around her complacency in the gruesome task. Maybe it was because she lost her husband in her prime or because her son died tragically when he was six, but she wasn't as conceited as the rest.

Vincent pulled out a cigarette as one of his runners opened the passenger side door for him. He stepped in and the door was closed after him. He pulled out his lighter as the driver pulled away, feeling amused. Gladie may be somewhat of a zealot, but sometimes it really felt like Ozama's flames cooked right beneath the city. Vincent blew smoke from his nose, but even with a creature bound by their magic, Vincent knew there was no greater power other than the unstoppable strength concentrated in this city.

22

Aries

The world spun as Aries struggled to keep herself up. She sensed that her sister was hauling her somewhere, but Aries felt so dizzy she couldn't make out up or down. Suddenly they stopped and Karina lowered her to the ground. In her daze she saw the red brick wall of an alley and a large gray object to her right. The smell of trash soured in her nose, making her think she was near a dumpster. Aries felt her sister shaking her and calling her name, but she couldn't find the strength to utter a word. Aries' vision started to fade. Her heart raced and her body felt like it was on fire. What was wrong with her? Aries dipped in and out of consciousness. She struggled to keep her eyes open then Karina's voice and all the sounds around her went mute as Aries fell into the darkness again.

"It's okay, child, come to me."

A voice called from the void. Aries winced. Who was speaking to her? Was she dying? Was this the voice of the souls of the afterlife?

"Come to me, child."

The voice sounded clearer now, soft yet familiar. Aries was afraid, but she still fought back. How could she be called away when there was so much work to do? Who would look after her sister in this strange city and what about her parents and family? Aries still felt the ground beneath her fingers, and she rushed towards that feeling. She ran, sending the signal to her body to move. She shouted it in her mind, but she couldn't shake this sleep paralysis.

Her heart raced and her breathing increased, but then there was a current of warmth. It started on the small of her lower back, then grew up her spine and over her shoulders and down her arms. It felt so good, like someone was hugging her. She wanted to lean into it, but her heart still resisted. She wasn't ready to go, not yet.

"It's okay, child, I've got you."

Clear as day a face appeared matching the voice. It was her granny. The darkness enclosed around Aries' mind, then lightened to a foggy gray plain. Aries looked around, she could see nothing through the fog.

"You are as strong as I expected you to be." Her granny chuckled as the rest of her materialized out of nowhere.

Aries blinked several times. "G-Granny?" The elderly woman nodded. She looked regal dressed in gold robes. Her face clear of worry and hair neatly tucked in place. "W-where are we?"

"I am where you are," her granny said, *"and it appears that Karina is having quite the fit. So, I will not keep you."*

"H-how?" Aries said. "Is this a part of your sight?"

Her granny smiled softly. *"It is a part of your sight now."*

"I-I don't understand?"

"Aries, I'm sorry I can't be with you right now. I know how hard it must be to shoulder the weight you're carrying, but my time has come, and I am choosing to use the last of my strength to speak to you."

"Granny," Aries' lip trembled. Her granny held her hand up in the way she always did to calm her family.

"Do not worry about me, I am in good hands, but you, the world still has plans for you,. Aries, I would like you to meet Acome."

"What?" Aries took a step back as a strong wind came from behind her grandmother. "I-I don't understand."

A powerful wind passed through her granny's body, nearly knocking Aries over, followed by a light so intense it blinded her. Aries covered her eyes with her forearm as she struggled to see her granny. The pale white light of this strange plain faded to a pale blue light as a wall of warm air washed over her. Tears brimmed her eyes as she struggled to keep them open, but the light and wind were so intense that it knocked her over.

Aries fell onto her back, but there was no pain. When she opened her eyes, a great shadow blocked her view. She gasped and leaned up and saw a beastly blue figure with the head of a dog but the body of a wild bear. It turned its starry black eyes onto her, then hundreds of rats charged toward her. Aries screamed as she braced for the animals to attack her, but they stampeded around her. She watched them run by, there had to be thousands of them. Then she gazed back at the creature; it was still looking at her but somehow, she could feel it. She felt its desperation and sadness. It was hard to bear. It was in pain. It was so intense that it clutched Aries' heart like a vice.

"There is still time to change this world," her granny said as a pale blue light radiated from her. The light grew stronger and more intense until it deepened into an electrifying purple, before it intensified into a powerful bright red. *"You are the Darkness. You will lead our people into the light with the help of the Crimson Mouse."*

Her granny's voice doubled and behind her appeared dozens of red-haired people. All of which looked like they belonged to her clan. Their crimson red eyes glowed as their red auras radiated upward into the shape of a giant red rat.

"This we can assure you. You will also have our strength, my strength..."

That voice was not her granny's voice. It came from the shape of the giant red rat that flared before her and a memory unlocked. Aries felt a burning on her palms and yelped. When she took a look she saw an angry red mark in the shape of a rat.

"It is my strength that burns through your veins," the flaming rat spoke. *"My gift that grants you access to my keys."*

Aries covered her face to block the flames, but somehow Aries wasn't burned. "W-who, who are you?" was all she could muster.

The flames that made the rat's fur flared and its mouth turned upwards into a grin. *"I am your blood's binder and champion. I am the one who brokered the deal between your ancestors. Your clan bares my mark and my blessing, but you may refer to me as friend to you and Acome. I am The Rat King Nezumi'Mfalme."*

A wave of warmth blew through Aries. She absorbed it as its soothing wind calmed her. She felt so connected to her people, all the ones who had lived and passed before her time, all gathering before her. Her granny appeared again, but she started to fade.

"G-Granny wait!" Aries cried out as she stumbled to reach her. "I-I don't know what I'm supposed to do!"

In a final gesture, her granny gracefully lifted her arm to Aries' chest. She rested her palm over Aries' heart and smiled. *"Everything you need to succeed rest here..."*

Aries rested her hand over her granny's.

"The deals behind this have been made long before my time and we have all gathered to lend you our strength. Trust in this heart of yours and we will help you with the rest."

Aries gasped as tears welled in her eyes. She didn't understand. She didn't want to understand. She only wanted more time with her granny. Her legs refused to move as she reached for her granny one last time as she faded into the light. King Nezumi'Mfalme's flames flared, surrounding her entire family and Granny in flames. The heat created a hazy wave as thousands of rats appeared.

"Now go, my the Darkness, honor our binding." King Nezumi'Mfalme opened his palm and sent her away. Aries cried out as the rats closed in around her and swept her into the darkness.

"Aries!" a loud voice echoed through her head. "Aries, please wake up, please!"

Aries took a full breath of air then coughed. She opened her eyes to the daylight, and it burned. She took a few more shaky breaths as her eyes adjusted. Voices of people and the rumble of cars flooded in along with her sister's pleas. Her vision cleared to the image of cracked black asphalt and trash bens. She felt hands on her shoulder that shook her.

"Aries," the voice trembled.

"K-Karina?" Aries looked up and saw her sister's bright red eyes, that started to water.

"Oh my gosh, Aries. you scared me so much." Karina hugged her big sister. "I thought that runner did something to you."

Aries relaxed as her senses slowly came back to her. Karina kept talking, but Aries' thoughts were elsewhere. What the heck did she just go through? And had something really happened to their granny? It felt so real that she still felt the tingle on her skin where the flames and rats had touched her. Then she thought about the creature her granny showed her. What kind of animal was that? Nobody knew what Acome looked like, was that truly them or was she poisoned by sewer gas? And what of the rat king and his pack? There was so much she didn't know, so much about her clan that was lost to time that she couldn't parse through what was real or fiction. Aries heard something to her left, a squeaking sound that almost sounded like a high-pitched kid's voice. She turned and saw her little friend.

"Tink?" Aries muttered.

"Huh?" Karina followed her eyes. "Tink! There you are!"

Karina reached down to pick him up. Aries blinked a few times as she watched Karina cuddle their friend. She swore she heard something that sounded like words. Aries leaned forward. She was sitting up right now and was feeling better. She watched Tink and her sister and smiled.

"Best be getting a move on then."

Aries froze. Whose voice was that? Aries looked around, until her eyes fell back on her sister and Tink. Tink was looking directly at her, then he nodded towards the back of the alley.

"Not much time left. They'll be here for the ring soon."

Aries' jaw dropped.

"What's wrong?" Karina asked.

Aries didn't even want to say it out loud, it was clear that she must have hit her head at some point during the day. "N-Nothing, but we have to get moving." Aries struggled to get up.

"Hold on! Hold on!" Karina helped her up. "You just went through who knows what, maybe we should take it easy."

"We can't. That guy back at the bar said the girl in Granny's vision has been captured, which means the bad guys have the ring."

Karina gasped. She stared down at the ground, biting her lip. "I-I don't care. Aries there's something wrong with you, you're sick. We should head back and see a doctor."

Aries was surprised at Karina's response. Who was this mature girl? Aries smiled warmly and placed a hand on her sister's shoulder. "I'm going to be fine. We have a mission to complete, remember. So, let's get moving."

"But..." Karina looked worried.

"I appreciate your concern, but I'm fine, really."

Karina eyed her, but she eventually came around. Tink jumped from Karina's shoulder to Aries' shoulder. "Okay, but how are we going to find her?"

"That way."

Aries heard Tink squeak. "D-don't worry, leave it to me," she said, trying to sound more confident than she was.

Karina was quiet for a second, "Okay."

Aries led the way, following the little squeaks from Tink. She had no idea what was going on or if she was really hearing Tink's voice, but suddenly all those stories she heard growing up started to feel real. Something was growing inside of her, maybe it was hope, maybe it was the green lung, but whatever coursed through her veins fueled her in her pursuit of finding the truth. Could the world really be made better because of a ring? Was there really a sun and fields of bright green grass and powerful spirits like her granny spoke about? It seemed all too good to be true, but she was certain of one thing, she wanted to find out the truth.

23
Karina

Karina followed behind her sister as they crossed the street. She still wasn't over what she just went through a few moments ago. Back at the bar she had this weird feeling, like someone was turning up the dial on her nerves. It was weird and it made her feel anxious. Did she eat something strange? But the tightness in her chest was different from a normal stomachache. The pain sat higher, then it moved to her gut. It was so overwhelming that she felt like she was going to puke, and it got worse when she thought about her sister. That's why she had to check on her. And she was glad she did, because something had happened to Aries. She wanted so badly to go back to the bar and beat the snot out of that guy. She knew he did something to her, but Aries probably wouldn't talk about it. She often guarded her emotions.

Now they were back in the thick of it, searching for the Crimson Mouse and for the first time since they started, Karina questioned whether it was worth it, because she didn't want to lose her sister. Aries ran down the street, crossing three blocks. Karina had no idea where they were going, but her sister seemed sure.

"We're not far now," Aries said as they drew closer to a row of three shops.

"O-okay, is the Crimson Mouse, is she near?" Karina asked as Aries slowed to a stop.

"I think so, but I think Tin-I mean, I think there's going to be a lot of runners, so we need to come up with a plan to distract them."

Runners? She didn't like the sound of that. "Um, good idea. I've been practicing my magic." Karina held out her hands.

"Not that." Aries cut her off. "We need a real plan."

Karina stuck out her lip. So what if she wasn't a caster, that didn't mean she shouldn't try. Tink squeaked on Aries' shoulder like he wanted to get in on the action, too. Aries looked around and pointed to a rusted fire escape on the side of the building.

"There's my in, I'll take the runners," Aries said. "You stay here."

"No way! I'm not letting you go alone. What if you start feeling unwell again?"

Aries sighed, but she really did look out of sorts with sweat still beading around the edges of her face and her eyes looked darker. "Fine, but no talking and stay low."

"Okay," Karina said, but felt relief at her little win.

Aries led the way and they both walked cautiously across the street towards the alley next to a row of shops. Aries stopped at the metal fire escape and tugged at it to test its strength. It was rusty, but well secured in the brick wall. Aries started up first, up the two flights to the roof, with Karina not far behind. Karina reached the top, which was littered with trash, as Aries navigated around chimneys that released thick gray smoke. They kept their bodies low to the ground as they made their way to a metal box when Aries grabbed her head and winced.

"Aries, you okay?" Karina whispered.

"I'm fine," Aries said through clenched teeth, but Karina knew that was a lie.

"Aries, I'm serious." Karina reached out to stop her from getting up. "I don't want you to jump into something when you're not feeling well."

Aries took a deep breath. "I'm going to be okay, alright. Just trust me."

Karina poked out her lip. "Bullshit." but Aries only smiled. "I don't like this. I don't like this one bit."

"I know, but trust me, I'm going to be fine." Aries meet Karina's eyes and there was nothing but calmness there.

Karina still didn't like this, but at least it seemed like Aries was all in at least. Aries smiled as she started walking again. They moved across the roof and climbed up the slanted siding of another building towards the next roof. The wind blew and Karina knew it was chilly because she saw her breath, but she didn't feel cold at all, quite the opposite. She felt warm as she moved. Karina heard Tink chirp and Aries got low as she crawled to the edge of the roof. Aries turned to Karina and waved her down, before she took a quick look over the edge.

"What did you see?" Karina whispered.

"Runners, a long black car, and a woman," Aries said.

"A woman? The Crimson Mouse?"

"I don't think so," Aries said. "She looks too overdressed."

"Maybe the Crimson Mouse is fashionable? How many people are down there?"

"Huh?" Aries turned to Tink.

"Huh?" Karina said. "I asked how many people are down there?"

"I-I'm not sure, maybe six or seven."

"Okay, so that's not too many."

"Wait, what?" Aries said. "We don't know if they're armed or if the Crimson Mouse is even down there."

"That's okay, because we are armed." Karina smirked. "You've got your pole and I've got my books. I can whack them on the head."

"No," Aries said flatly, and Karina frowned, "but we do have the element of surprise. Here's what we're going to do. We're two stories up, there's a car down there, we can jump on it, take out the runners and find the Crimson Mouse and the ring." Tink squeaked in agreement as if he could understand.

"Got it," Karina said, but Aries didn't move. "Everything okay?"

"Huh, oh, okay," Aries said as Tink squeaked. He was very chatty today.

"I'm ready when you are," Karina said, but Aries only sighed. "You are not going to convince me to stay up here," Karina whispered harshly, but her sister looked like she was struggling to comprehend something. "What is it?" Karina asked, but Aries only put up a finger to quiet her. Karina folded her arms. Why was her sister acting so weird? Then she heard her sister sigh again.

"Karina, I need you to be quiet for a bit," Aries said. "I-I need to talk to someone."

Karina furrowed her brow. Who did she need to talk to, they were the only ones up here? "What are you—" but Aries cut her off with her finger again and turned to Tink.

"Tink, do you know where the Crimson Mouse is? Is she inside?"

Tink nodded and Karina looked on with wide eyes.

"You can talk to Tink?"

"Shush shush." Aries quieted her sister, then pointed downward.

Karina had no idea what she meant, until she heard the voices below.

"Are you sure you want to wait out here?" a woman said.

"I'd rather stand in this disgusting alley than spend another minute in that rat infested hell hole," another woman said.

"Suit yourself," the first woman said.

"Lady Rosemary," a man's voice said. "Vincent will be here soon."

Karina looked at Aries as Tink squeaked and ran up Aries' braid and jumped onto the ledge.

"Tink, do you see anything?" Aries whispered.

Karina watched as her friend peered over the edge, just like a person would do. Granny didn't mention anything about this. Of course, she always felt a special bond with rats, but speaking to them? That was cool. Karina listened to Tink chirp as she tried to ignore how hot she felt. She hoped the runners couldn't smell her pits because she knew she was sweating. Karina tried to ignore the building heat, but it was starting to make her feel dizzy.

"Thanks, Tink," Aries said, then turned to Karina. "Tink says that the Crimson Mouse is close."

"Is it one of the women? And who is Vincent?"

"I'm not sure, but there's two women down there and the one with the green hair is called Lady Rosemary. There's also about seven runners, maybe more and I believe they'll be leaving soon," Aries said.

Leaving? If that was the case, they needed to go now. Karina checked to make sure the strap on her bag was secure. "Okay, let's go."

"Tink, are we clear?" Aries asked. Tink nodded. "Alright, on my count." Aries held up three fingers, then reached for her pole. Tink jumped from the ledge back onto Aries' shoulders. "One...two...three..." Aries mouthed as they both got close to the ledge.

On three Karina looked down. It wasn't that far and suddenly she felt super pumped. They jumped up over the edge and landed on top of the car. The thud startled everyone in the alley. To Karina's right were two women. The one in the nice black dress screamed, while the other woman with beautiful long moss green hair glared at them. Aries moved at once and extended her pole and struck the woman Tink said was Lady Rosemary on the arm. The woman jerked her hand away from her bag and wailed as five runners charged them.

Karina kicked a man in the head and swung her heavy bag around, striking another one. Her sister struck a runner that reached for Aries' foot, popping him in the head, before using his face as a step, and landing perfectly on the ground. Karina watched her sister take them out one by one and cheered, when suddenly someone grabbed Karina's ankle and dragged her down the front of the car. Karina screamed as she slid down the car, then turned on her back and kicked the runner in the cock, then in the head. The runner fell next to the nicely dressed woman who screamed again and backed up into the wall as two more runners ran towards them.

Was that nicely dressed woman the Crimson Mouse? Karina jerked away from a runner, then Aries turned and finished them off with several intense blows to the back and head. Karina ran around the car and swung her bag at a runner that charged her sister, hitting them in the gut. They went down and Karina knocked them out with her bag, and grinned, when she felt someone grab onto her arm and yank her backwards. Karina yelped and Aries tore around as Karina struggled to break free. She flashed a look to her sister and saw Tink, who hissed and ran down Aries' pole and jumped directly onto the woman's face.

"Eww! Get off me, you filthy rat!" Lady Rosemary swatted at him as Karina rushed away, but into the arms of the other runner.

He grabbed her, but Karina head butted him in the chin, causing him to bite his tongue. The man wailed as he grabbed his mouth that quickly filled with blood. Karina took a step towards him and swung her knapsack filled with books wildly across the face, knocking him out cold. The man fell as she panted, but there were no more runners left. Aries turned to the woman on the wall.

"Are you the Crimson Mouse?" Aries asked.

"The what?" the woman shrieked.

"Where's the pinkish gold ring?" Aries demanded.

"Thieves! Thieves! I won't tell you a thing!" the woman screamed.

Aries slammed the woman against the wall. "Where's the ring!" Aries retracted her pole, making it short enough to slap the tip right next to the woman's face. The woman whimpered, but didn't say a word.

"Gotcha!" Lady Rosemary shouted.

Karina turned around. The woman had Tink by the neck. "Hey!" Karina shouted, then searched the ground and found a glass bottle and threw it at her.

Lady Rosemary hollered and flung Tink in the air. Tink glided through the air, then fell onto the woman's sack and wiggled himself inside. Karina gasped and ran to help him and punched the woman in her large breast, knocking her off her heels. Karina grabbed the sack, but the woman swatted at her hand, and the sack fell to the ground.

"Crap!" Karina said as she scrambled for the sack as black sand trickled out along with Tink.

Tink shook the sand from his fur, then start digging feverously with his nose at the sand, until something in the shape of a ring was pushed to the surface.

"A ring!" Karina grabbed the object and wiped it off on her shirt and gasped. It felt so warm. Holding it made her fingers tingle, but she quickly pocketed it, then turned to her sister who walked toward her.

"Aries, look out!" Karina shouted.

The woman Aries pinned to the wall got behind Aries with a bucket in hand. Aries spun around and punched the woman square in the chest. The woman hit the ground and started to cry. Then Aries popped her in the butt with her pole and that sent her running down the alley.

"Good job, Tink," Karina said as the rat squeaked, "but where's the Crimson Mouse?"

Tink's head jerked up and then he ran down Karina's leg towards the trunk of the car.

"There." Aries ran to the trunk and lifted the latch.

Karina rushed to her sister's side and gasped when she saw two unconscious women with their arms and legs bound and a cloth wrapped around their mouths.

"Hey! Do you hear me!" Aries shouted.

Karina hoped they weren't dead. Aries reached down to shake them when Karina felt a presence behind her. Before she could react, a strong hand found its way around her throat and sent a shooting pain through her entire body. Karina screamed as she was dragged backwards.

"Not so fast!" Lady Rosemary said as she gripped Karina's throat harder.

Karina gasped and tried to claw at the woman's hand, but her body jerked and twitched from whatever was shocking her. Karina cried out as she noticed a green glow that sparked around the woman's hand.

"Karina!" Aries growled.

Lady Rosemary sent another pulse of electricity threw Karina's body; this time so hard that it made Karina feel like something was going to explode from her chest. The pain radiated outward all the way down to her hands and feet. Karina felt weak, but also overheated, like she was being cooked in an oven.

"That's right." Lady Rosemary clenched her fingers tighter around Karina's throat. "Now why don't you scurry off and I'll let your little friend go."

"A-Aries d-don't worry about me," Karina struggled, as she gasped.

"Can it. bitch, or I'll kill you."

A flash of green burst next to Karina's face, then a sharp pain shot up her spine. Karina screamed and saw spots of black in her vision, but she could see that her sister was pissed. This woman was clearly an experienced key master, who could kill her and her sister with ease. Karina heard voices from the inside. It could be more runners; they were way in over their heads.

"Go!" Karina squirmed. "Go! Get out of here now!"

"I'm not leaving without you or the ring!" Aries growled.

Tears welled up in her eyes. The heat and pain coursing through her body made her head spin. This woman's magic was too much.

"Stupid woman," Lady Rosemary cackled. "Listen to the girl. Save yourself, unless you want to become the plaything to a necromancer."

Karina strained against Lady Rosemary's grip. The woman pressed her long fingernails into Karina's throat and Karina cried out. There was so much pressure building in her body. Her head throbbed and her stomach felt tight with bloat. Suddenly Aries eyes went wide and Karina wasn't sure why, but she just wanted her sister to go. She wanted her to run away, run as fast as she could from here. Karina's vision went red as the pain and heat reached a breaking point. Karina gasped and pulled at Lady Rosemary's arm.

"What the!" Lady Rosemary growled as a burst of red electricity went off around them.

The two of them stumbled to the ground and Tink jumped from the car onto Lady Rosemary's face and clawed at her eyes. The woman screamed and Karina gasped as she crawled away. What the heck was that red light? Lady Rosemary swatted Tink, but the little rat would not cease. Karina had never seen Tink so enraged. He bit and scratched at Lady Rosemary's face, causing her to trip over her own heels and fall to the ground. Aries closed the gap in between them and kicked the woman in the face, knocking her out cold. Tink ran back to Karina and snuggled her.

"My friend," Karina said between breaths. She was so tired. So very tired.

"Karina, are you okay?" Aries leaned down beside her sister as she retracted her pole.

Karina nodded as her sister helped her up. Karina stumbled a bit, but she regained her footing as her sister led her to the trunk.

"Can you walk?" Aries asked. Karina nodded as she slowly started to get her bearings. "Okay, help me carry them."

Karina bent down and felt dizzy. She grabbed the side of the trunk, and her sister caught her.

"Karina," her sister sounded so worried.

"I-I got this." Karina took a deep breath, then reached into her bag for some water. She drank the entire thing and gasped. "So good." Karina sighed with delight.

Aries smiled. "Okay, I'll grab the blonde one okay?"

Karina nodded as she went for the woman with the purple hair.

"Ow!" Aries yanked her hand back.

"What?" Karina looked at her sister.

"I-I'm not sure." Aries looked at her fingers. Karina hoped her sister hadn't got hurt, but then Tink started squeaking. "Runners! More on the way."

Karina nodded as Aries shook off the pain and grabbed the blonde woman and tossed her over her shoulder. Karina did the same with the woman with the purple braids. She was heavy, but nothing an experienced picker like Karina couldn't handle. Karina readjusted the weight, like she had done a dozen times at work. Aries waited for Karina to catch her balance and when she did, they were off.

24 Vincent

Vincent leaned his arm on the door and gazed out the window as his driver took him and two other Silers to the meet-up point. He pulled out a dull silver case from the inside of his coat pocket and pulled out a cigarette. He placed the cigarette on his lips and lit it. What an eventful day. His boss' were throwing quite the fit, but that's how they always were, bitter and afraid of their own shadows, despite the fact that they ruled the entire city.

Vincent rolled the window down far enough to let the smoke escape. He never liked all this running around. He preferred the comfort of his office or the bar, but every once in a while he'd take a stroll down the streets he used to run. Before this life of paperwork and gangs, he was nothing but a simple-minded street boy. Growing up with nothing, he dreamed of this life. He guessed he got what he wished for. Vincent pulled the cigarette from his lips, as he watched people huddle together across the street.

The driver crossed into New Town, where most of the shops and businesses were open. People walked casually down the streets without a care in the world as Vincent drew from his cigarette again, taking his time to enjoy it this time. The car turned down a bumpy alley where the street people pitched their tents and huddled around trash fires. The contrast was like night and day, New Town was nothing more than a pretty blanket that rested over a maggot filled corpse. The smoke was getting to his head, making him feel good, as Vincent mulled over the idea of buying something stronger when he got back. The driver pulled out of the alley and turned left and stopped in front of a closed business.

"I'll be back," Vincent said to the driver.

The two runners followed him as he walked into the business. Six runners shot up and bowed and Vincent acknowledged them with a nod as he reached into his coat pocket again to retrieve another cigarette. He looked to one of the runners standing in the room and glanced briefly at his green metal armband. He was just a kid, who looked no older than sixteen. The runner lifted a shaky finger to the back, pointing to where Vincent needed to go. Vincent lit his cigarette and walked to the back into a smaller room with a desk and a few chairs. Mary was the first to get up. She looked as if she had gotten into a fight, which surprised Vincent.

"Good evening, Lady Mary," Vincent said, with his cigarette between his fingers.

"Vi-Vincent, it's so good to see you," Mary's voice shook.

"Likewise, where is Lady Rosemary?" Vincent asked.

"Sh-she's outside, in the alley."

Vincent nodded and made his way outside. There were a few more runners outside, all of which moved quickly out of his way. Lady Rosemary was screaming at someone through her telepathy power. Mary rushed out behind him and stopped at the door.

"I don't care what you have to do, just do it!" Lady Rosemary shouted. She ended her connection and turned. She froze when she saw Vincent.

"Good evening, Lady Rosemary," Vincent said, tapping the ash off his cigarette.

"Vincent," Lady Rosemary said with great enthusiasm. She brushed some hair from her bruised face and went to him at once.

Vincent took a look at the black car and all the injured runners who stood around it. "I trust that you have the ring?"

Lady Rosemary froze, but then worked up a smile. "I-I don't have it, but it's not my fault. We were ambushed by these girls, they attacked us out of nowhere and took the ring. I don't know which faction they're from, but I have my people on it."

Vincent put out his cigarette with his fingers and flicked it to the ground. "So, what you're saying is that you failed?"

Lady Rosemary choked on her words. "Failed? N-No, Vincent I have the situation under control. I have my people on it."

Vincent looked away and adjusted his cuffs, before he reached for his gun on his waist and planted a bullet between Lady Rosemary's eyes. Blood, brains, and skull fragments painted the wall and splattered across the black car. Mary screamed as the runners gasped and backed away as Lady Rosemary's body ignited into bright green flames and fell to the ground.

The flames reduced her corpse to a pile of ash. Vincent sighed and pulled out another cigarette from his case and lit it with his gun still in hand. He put away his lighter, unphased by the look of pure terror in Mary's eyes. He turned to Mary and laid his gun hand over Mary's shoulder. His employers were not going to like this. Mary jumped when the gun clanked against the brick. Tears flooded from her eyes.

"Alright, Lady Mary," Vincent said. "You got until midnight to get this cleared up. You fail I kill you, and your brother Alvert will be put in charge next. And don't think I didn't notice your father trying to hide him away. That understood?"

Mary hiccupped sobs, but not a word came out. Her entire body shook as she nodded.

"Good." Vincent walked past her.

He noticed the runners in the room, none of them met his eye. They probably didn't know anything about what happened. Either way his boss was not going to be happy about this. He took a drag from his cigarette and reflected on Lady Rosemary's words. They were ambushed, but by who? A foolish gang looking to ransom the ring? Were there any gangs stupid enough to do that? All the gangs in the city answered to the Silers. Or was this someone working on their own? Vincent turned his attention to a runner with a bruise on their face, who sat in a chair leaning against the wall, his expression pained.

"Hey, kid." Vincent stopped before him.

The runner jumped up, "Yes, sir."

"You know anything about the ambush?"

"I um-um, I-I don't know," the runner tripped over his words.

Vincent sighed. "Were the chicks from a local gang?"

"N-No sir, they didn't look like they were from a gang at all, just a pair of sewer girls. Both had red hair, but the chick with the long red hair had some kind of pole. She could really fight."

"They ask for anything?" Vincent asked.

"N-no, sir." The runner shook his head. "They just came out of nowhere and took the two chicks Lady Rosemary bagged and ran."

"I see." Vincent turned and left. He went back to his car with his two runners and nodded for the driver to return to base.

Sewer girls with red hair. Where had he heard that description before? Vincent leaned back in his chair, kicking the ash off his bud. Red hair wasn't all that common, but they were running out of time. Vincent put the cigarette out in the ash tray, then placed his hand on his left mangled ear, where his hearing implant was embedded. He closed his eye and uttered the summoning key to get the mechanism going. The magic shocked him a little, but he continued his chant and pulled the keys to the spell from the air with every syllable. His gate appeared next to his head and glowed as a connection was made. The device clicked, and at first there was static, then he shut his eyes and his spirit traveled through the fog of the other realm and jetted pass the living in a blur.

"Dr. Acknid," Vincent's voice echoed.

"Oh! Vincent," a high-pitched voice said. *"It is a pleasure as always to hear from you since you rarely cast keys."*

"Lady Rosemary failed, and I need this matter cleared up immediately."

"Of course. Just let me know who and where."

"I don't have a solid identity, but we are looking for at least four women, two of which have red hair."

"Ooo! Ooo! Ooo! And let me guess you do not know where they're at? Please tell me I get to hunt?"

"I will send you as much information as I can, but as of this moment we do not know the location of the group."

"Excellent! Please leave the matter to me, I have new puppets in development that I would love to show you. Please stop by."

"Very well." Vincent ended the communication spell.

He opened his eyes as his gate faded and looked down at his arms, his coat sleeves and dress shirt were singed and the brand on the back of his neck throbbed. He had used too much power again. He sighed and reached for another cigarette. This was the exact reason he preferred the old fashion way of combat. This key casting stuff was for the birds. This ceremony and all the drama around it could go to hell, but a job was a job and if he wanted to stay alive around here, he needed to keep himself useful.

"Take me back to the Fort'nee's, they'll want an update," Vincent said. Knowing what he knew about Dr. Acknid, it was best not to show up too quickly unless he wanted to have a conversation with him over one of his cut open corpses.

The driver complied and pulled away, heading for The Great Wall. At midday there wasn't much of a line. Not that there was ever a backup, since all the help had to leave their cars and motorbikes outside the wall for check in. Vincent's car was next and the driver stopped at the large wrought iron gate and rolled down the window.

"ID," the gatekeeper said, without sparing them a glance. The driver cut the gatekeeper a look and when the gatekeeper finally looked into the car they jumped. "A-ah, Mr. Vincent, I'm so sorry. Please, please come on in."

The driver rolled up the window as the wrought iron gates opened. Vincent reached for another cigarette as his driver took him back to his employer's house. Jaden was not going to be happy with the news. He leaned back in his seat as he took a long drag as he stared at all the unnaturally blooming trees and plants. The Yield really had their work cut out for them if all they had to do with their blood magic was make a bunch of rich people's flower's bloom. All the manors had beautiful, lush gardens blanketed with sheets of artificial grass. Even at night this place was beautiful. All the rows of gas streetlights lit the way, giving every single bush and tree monstrous shadows. What could hide here with all this light and yet, before him were the darkest shadows.

The driver pulled into the brick loop driveway where two Silers were posted as guards. Vincent grunted. He guessed ol' Jaden wasn't playing around. The Siler guards straightened up when they saw Vincent approach. He gave a short nod as he dipped his ashes into the ashtray located on the porch that wrapped around the entire manor.

Vincent followed the housemaid inside as the doors closed behind him. He walked through the marbled foyer that was decorated from floor to ceiling in art. Most of which displayed the female form in various stages of undress. He lifted his cigarette to his mouth at what he was sure was the latest piece. A stone statue of a nude woman riding a horse. He was sure Lady Nia got a kick out of that.

Housemaids, all female, scurried about the huge house cleaning and tidying up. Vincent blew out a puff of smoke after he entered the elevator. The housemaid hit the button for level three and the door closed. The elevator hummed and the pair stood in silence. When they reached the third floor the elevator chimed, and they exited. Vincent didn't have to guess how Jaden would react, but there was little he could do about his failure. Strike one, two more and they would all be dead.

Vincent walked down the royal purple carpeted halls, past all the humongous oil paintings of family leaders long past. Two housemaids waited for them at the door and promptly opened the heavy wooden doors for them. The housemaid who walked him there bowed as Vincent entered the private study of Jaden Fort'nee. The lord looked up from his desk and smiled as he walked around his polished black wooden desk.

At six foot four, Jaden Fort'nee was an intimidating man, but his height and money were all the bite he had to him. Lounging in one of two black leather chairs was Jaden's eldest son, Evan Fort'nee, who was grinning like a drunk, flashing his mouth full of gold teeth. Evan raised a half empty glass of whisky to Vincent.

"Lord Jaden, Lord Evan," Vincent greeted.

"Vincent." Jaden flashed a fake smile, but didn't allow Vincent to walk any further. "I trust that you have taken care of our little problem?"

"I am working on it," Vincent said nonchalantly.

Jaden's faced twisted into a scowl. "Working on it? You said Lady Rosemary recovered the ring."

"And she has failed me," Vincent said. Jaden clenched his jaw. "She has failed me, and I have disposed of her and placed Dr. Acknid in her charge."

Jaden scoffed and walked over to his liquor cabinet. He poured himself a drink, then took a generous sip. "And how can you assure me that he won't fail too?"

"I have faith that he will deliver the results you seek," Vincent said, but Jaden dismissed him with a wave.

"Need I remind you who you work for? Who owns you. If I wanted your body turned inside out I could do so with no repercussions. You are as replaceable as the body parts you've had pasted on your sloppy excuse of a body."

"I understand sir," Vincent said without emotion.

Jaden tossed back the rest of his drink. The burn of the alcohol caused him to bunch up his face. "Do whatever you see fit, but hear this, Vincent Lorne. If you fail me again, I will never let your corpse die."

"Yes, sir. I understand, sir," Vincent said with the same amount of emotion he spoke with before.

Jaden snapped his fingers and the two housemaids opened the doors to the office, but Evan stood first. He wobbled to his feet and threw back the rest of his drink.

"Let me walk 'em out, Pops," Evan said as he walked towards Vincent and patted him on the shoulder.

Jaden pinched the bridge of his nose, but did not protest. Evan walked him out and the two housemaids closed the door behind them.

"Let's take a walk." Evan grinned from ear to ear.

Vincent walked next to the eldest son, who acted as if he didn't have a care in the world. In a weird way Vincent admired his willful ignorance. The man truly had no idea how deeply fucked he and his family were. Evan swayed down the hall towards the elevators in the east wing. He pressed the button as he laughed at a joke he must have been replaying in his head. Vincent withdrew another cigarette and plopped it into his mouth. He pulled his lighter from his pocket and lit it. Of course, Vincent knew a lot more than the Five Families thought. He didn't claw his way to the top and not pick up on a few juicy secrets. He knew all about the binding keys the Five Families used to lock in their wealth.

And of course, it all started with the Fort'nee family who descended from a line of monks who were charged with protecting the creature they kept locked away in the lowest level of their basements. Some hundreds of years ago about nine of them hatched a plan to make out rich. The only downside was that the spell they used to control the beast cost the lives of all nine of the greedy monks, so the bastards didn't even get to live long enough to enjoy their wealth.

Now every year the Five Families had to renew the binding keys and to do so, they needed the gear ring and the blood of a three-year-old child. It was nasty stuff. If the public knew they'd probably riot, but no one stood against them with the amount of runners they had under their belt.

Vincent stepped into the elevator with Evan and the man leaned against the wall as if it were an extension of his bed. He smirked at Vincent and dug his hand into his pocket and pulled out a large ao almasi gemstone. Vincent raised an eyebrow. Something like that was worth well over fifty thousand dollars.

"Hey, Vincent buddy," Evan slurred. "Why don't you help a brother out and see if you can find me some honeys that are looking for work."

Vincent wanted to laugh, this guy couldn't be serious, but Vincent knew better. He reached out his hand and Evan plopped the fifty grand stone in his palm like it was nothing.

"That a boy," Evan laughed. "I knew I could count on you, brother." Evan laughed as the elevator door opened to the first floor. "And since you're such a good guy, let me give you a little something extra, you know, so that you know what I'm looking for."

Evan snickered. Vincent said nothing and followed. Vincent was no stranger to Evan's taste, but Evan liked to reserve some of his wilder kinks for highly specialized sex workers. Vincent pocketed the gemstone as he followed Evan to the private baths outside. Evan leaned on the door and put his finger to his mouth. He leaned on it gently and walked out onto the steamy deck where the family had their private hot spring. Evan waved Vincent over and found Evan's sister Dottie bathing nude under the magic enhanced light. Evan burst into laughter, but quickly covered his mouth, trying to be discrete, but it was clear that the woman heard him, and she smirked.

"Check 'er out," Evan slurred.

"That's your sister," Vincent said flatly.

Evan snickered and shook his head. "Nope, nope, nope, Daddy had his cock snipped after having to pay off one too many mistresses and Mommy refused to fuck 'em, so they adopted her to keep up appearances and don't worry, she knows. Nia's got a nasty streak, but you want to know the best part?" Evan hiccupped and started to undress in front of Vincent. "And you wanna know the best part? She's totally into me. Wanna join?"

"No thank you," Vincent said.

"Suit yerself." Evan didn't sound offended as he stripped completely nude and joined her.

Vincent shook his head and took another drag from his cigarette. What a complete fool. Vincent's driver was waiting on him and opened the door for him when he approached the car. Vincent withdrew the gem and closed his eyes to cast a bit of magic to make it glow. The stone warmed in his hand and Vincent opened his eyes. So, Evan Fort'nee really paid him with the real deal. Ao almasi was the brainchild of the Sapphire family and they sure knew how to make a good enhancement stone. This would come in handy indeed.

Vincent returned to the office where he could finally kick up his feet and relax. He reached for a fresh pack of cigarettes and tore open the sealed paper binding before pulling one out and lighting it. This ring mess was an unanticipated pain in his side. The ceremony had gone on without issue since his tenure. In fact, even ol' Jaden didn't make a fuss about security. Though he was disappointed in Lady Rosemary's performance. She was such an accomplished potion master and necromancer, but ultimately useless to him in the end. Vincent heard footsteps coming up the corridor and pulled himself forward, so he could at least feign the idea of giving this person his full attention. The footsteps stopped and Vincent raised an eyebrow. He wasn't expecting to see Yrwen.

"Vincent," the thin man greeted him as he walked in wearing his usual too tight body contouring suit. It was missing the string tie, but today he wore his thin black hair slicked back into a high ponytail.

"Yrwen, what a surprise," Vincent said as he plucked the cigarette from his mouth and beat the ash off with his thumb into the ashtray. "I can only imagine how busy you are. The wine orders must be through the roof," Vincent joked.

"It is nothing I cannot manage," Yrwen said without a blink of emotion. "I am however very concerned about your tenure here."

"Is that so?" Vincent leaned back, hoping his friend would take a seat and join him.

"As you know, if the ceremony fails to come to fruition..."

Vincent held up his hand to cough, then let his cigarette twirl loosely in his fingers. "Yada yada."

Yrwen tightened his gaze and walked closer to his desk where he elegantly lowered himself to the seat. He was stiffer than the last time he saw him. In the dim light Vincent saw the speaker implants that were installed to enhance Yrwen's telepathy, which were another *optional* improvement provided by the Siler Gang. Vincent flashed a half smile before putting the bud back into his mouth. Sometimes when he stared at Yrwen's double implants it made him think of his own, which were crudely installed in what was left of his mangled left ear.

"I do believe you should be taking this more seriously," Yrwen said.

"Don't think so lowly of me, my friend. Arrogance doesn't suit me, but I have faith in Dr. Acknid."

"And if he should fail?" Yrwen raised an eyebrow, but Vincent only shrugged. Yrwen frowned. "In that case, then I believe you should think about yourself."

Vincent met Yrwen's eyes. They were so dark and intense and focused on him. "You're being serious right now." This actually made Vincent laugh, but Yrwen did not look away. Vincent calmed down and relaxed his shoulders. He wasn't ignorant of Yrwen's feelings, he just didn't believe in outs. "Of course, you would have a crush on the one asexual aromantic guy in the gang, but thank you," Vincent paused to let the ash fall from his cigarette, well aware of the anxious look in his friend's eyes. "Thank you for caring, I mean it, but I have confidence that everything will fall in place."

Yrwen sucked his teeth and straightened his neatly buttoned suit jacket. "Of course, but you best believe your employers are making contingency plans. I just believe you should be doing the same."

Vincent grunted.

"I am serious. Vincent, your life is worth something. You do not have to go down with this organization."

Vincent sighed, but let a smile rise on his lips, which seemed to only make his friend appear more annoyed.

"There are rumblings, you know," Yrwen said. "Mama Roach senses trouble in the air."

"The cook?" Vincent leaned back in his chair. "Is she not generally suspicious?"

"The Black Gate has fallen, too." Yrwen met Vincent's eyes again. Vincent knew this already. Dr. Granite had acted quite brashly after his son died. It was very shortsighted of him, but necromancers could be replaced. "Only five of the original members stand, and if we were being honest, that number has actually been reduced to three."

"Hmm, that would be worrying, but you know as well as I that The Yield always has members ready to rise and take their place. Try not to worry so much, it'll make you frail."

Vincent's eyes met Yrwen's gaze again, then Yrwen's head jerked to the side as he listened to the telepathic message probably blaring in his ear.

"Understood, well if you would excuse me," Yrwen said, then promptly stood and walked to the door. Then he stopped, with his back to Vincent. "Please, consider my words."

Vincent watched his friend walk out the door. So Yrwen wanted him to run? Vincent stared up at the ceiling. Vincent had given ten years of his life to this gang and none of those years were worth the blood it cost him. At nineteen he was an arrogant fool and the Silers knew it. He signed his death warrant the day he joined and every mission they sent him on had to be completed unless he wanted his body chopped up for parts and sold. It was a shit deal, but the idea of running away did cross his mind once.

When he was just a few years in, after a particularly brutal robbery, Vincent found himself huddled in a small room, post back-alley surgery, begging for a solution. He didn't want to die, but he couldn't take it anymore. Turns out he wasn't the only one. Four of his buddies shared the same sentiment. In fact, his friend Chase had found a girl. He wanted to run away with her out of the country to start a family. So, Chase pitched the idea one day and the four of them jumped on it like flies on shit. What they didn't know at the time was that many of the tunnel routes leading out of the city were marked by The Black Gate. Sure, common folk could come and go as they pleased, but property wasn't allowed to do so. It was the same scheme debt collectors used to keep sewer folk trapped in Sewer Town, but with one twisted difference. It wasn't just the metal armbands that identified someone as a member of the Siler Gang, all gang members were magically branded. So, if one wandered too far off hunters in The Black Gate would be lying and waiting.

So, Chase hatched a plan, and everyone agreed to meet at the west tunnel, that lead out of the city. One of the guys got cold feet and stayed behind, while Vincent and his other buddy made their way to the tunnel via the ceiling vents. Chase got there first, but before Vincent and his friend could reach him, already The Yield were on him. They had opened his bag and saw his clothes and a wad of cash and knew that he was about to run.

Vincent watched from the vent above and cursed, but he was dumb back then, so he swallowed his fear and jumped down to help his friend. Between the three of them they beat down about four of the six necromancers, but then fire erupted through the tunnel. There was a hidden member of The Black Gate in the shadows. Vincent and his buddies fled, but Chase wasn't so lucky.

A big meeting was called the very next morning. Vincent could still remember the feeling of nausea and diarrhea he felt, after just having one of what would be many surgeries on his broken body. The bosses summoned the entire east wing of the gang and made them stand in a crowded warehouse around a stack of crates that formed a stage. He was scared shitless and sure that they would call his name at any moment. Instead, they hauled Chase's beaten, naked body out in front of them. The boss' sneered, their face filled with sadistic delight.

"Looks like we got a sprinter." the man pulled Chase to his knees and jerked his head around by his hair. Two other men appeared and hung Chase by his bound hands in the air. Then the man turned his attention back to Chase. A wicked smile etched across his face. "And you went through all this trouble because of a girl, aye? You wanted a future outside of the gang, aye?" The man slapped Chase's face playfully before he pulled out a pair of shears. "Look here. There are no outs in the Siler Gang. Any future you want starts and ends here. So let this be a warning to all of you. Anyone who even thinks about a future outside of this gang, will share this poor bastard's fate, because we are the only legacy you will ever leave behind."

Vincent clenched and unclenched his fist. He could still vividly remember all the blood that gushed from his friend's groin as he was castrated in front of the entire crowd. The screams haunted him to this day. So no, there was no out for him. He, who was nothing more than a glorified slave. If the gang fell, then so would he.

25 Mia

Mia stirred as the sound of voices became louder and louder. She didn't want to open her eyes, but there was also a building pain in her right arm and stomach. She turned her head and opened her eyes as her vision started to clear up. In front of her was a sloppily put together brick wall. She struggled to move her arms and legs, which felt heavy and sore, but she felt the roughness of the bed she was laying on. She was not at home. Panicked, Mia's heart raced. Her attention was pulled to the voices she heard. She looked up and saw two women with bright red hair. They fussed, but the words weren't clear enough for her to understand, then the two of them left. Mia tried to move, but her joints were sluggish. She rolled over to her side and a sharp pain shot up her chest and she collapsed on her back again.

Her head jerked to her right where she saw Billie sleeping next to her. Mia looked down at the dirty bed. Where was she? As the panic set in, the adrenaline started to pump through her veins which helped clear her mind. She had been kidnapped, no tortured. The pain in her arm, she remembered. Some woman—no, a necromancer—was after her blood. Tears wet Mia's eyes, but she needed to move. She leaned up, her head swirled, making the room spin. She shook her head and reached over to try and wake Billie.

"Billie." Her voice rang in her head like someone was shouting through a loudspeaker. "Billie," she said again, then grabbed her hand. She felt a headache coming on and winced. She opened her eyes again as Billie came around. Her eyes were glossy. Mia shook her again, but it was hard to maintain balance.

"Oh good, you're awake," a voice echoed from somewhere behind Mia.

Mia turned, it felt like everything was in slow motion. A dark-skinned woman with bright red hair braided into two long braids approached her, and Mia put up her hands to defend herself.

"Wo, calm down," the woman said in a calm voice. She held out a cup. "Here, drink this, it's water."

Mia squinted, even though the light was dull. She felt herself tilt backwards, but the woman caught her. Mia's eyes wandered to the woman's side, and she noticed her braids close up. They really were long and probably went down her back.

"Take your time," she said.

The woman offered the cup again. Mia looked down at it. It looked clear, but her mind was spinning. She looked into the woman's eyes, surprised to find that the irises were blood red.

"Here." The woman held the cup to Mia's lips.

The taste of the water was bitter at first but then the flavor of water registered and the more she drunk the more her brain fog began to clear, only to be replaced by a deep hunger. Mia placed both hands on the cup and gulped down the rest.

"Wow, someone was thirsty," the woman chuckled. "My name is Aries, by the way. You and your friend are safe now."

Mia blinked a few times and swallowed. Her mouth was so dry. She looked at Aries. Who was this woman? Where were they? "Um, how did I get here?" Mia asked.

Aries stood. "That's a long story, but I'll try to explain everything once my sister Karina gets back. For now, take it easy. I'll be back with more water."

Mia sort of nodded as she watched the woman leave. She grabbed her aching, growling stomach. She was so hungry, but the outside of her stomach felt sore and bruised. She looked down at her bandaged right arm wrapped in a torn piece of dirty cloth around the elbow. She hovered her left hand over it, before she got the idea to check her stomach. She shuddered at what she might find, but she had to know. So, she gently pulled the low-cut collar of her white body suit open and gasped at the edges of black and purple that peeked through. She let the collar go. It was bad and she didn't need to see the rest to know that.

She looked over at Billie, whose eyes were barely open. Mia shook her again. Billie blinked a few times then Mia shook her harder. Billie groaned and Mia allowed her to roll over and stretch. Billie turned onto her stomach and buried her face in the mattress. She groaned again, then jerked back her head.

"Ewww," Billie said with a sour face. She spit out dust as she looked around. "What the?"

"Billie, Billie can you hear me?" Mia said. Billie looked over at her friend. Her eyes were barely open as if she found it hard to see. "Hold on, Aries will be back soon with water. It'll make you feel better."

"A-Aries, who-who's that?" Billie's head slowly fell back down to the dirty mattress as she groaned again.

Aries came back with two filled cups of water this time. "Is your friend awake?"

Mia nodded, then Aries smiled and handed Mia the cup and sat the other one on the floor next to the mattress. Mia forced a smile as waves of panic rolled in like a patch of storm clouds. Answers, she needed them, but her mind was still foggy. She turned to Billie and poked her.

"Here, drink this," Mia said.

Billie resisted at first, but with the help of Aries, they got Billie upright. Mia helped Billie drink and slowly she came around.

"Yuck." Billie made a face.

Aries looked puzzled. "Hmm, I thought the water up here tasted pretty good."

"You think so?" Mia said, trying to remain calm, as she eyed her water. "It's really bitter."

"Is that not normal?" Aries said.

Mia shrugged, not wanting to sound rude. "It's about the same." She took another sip even though she didn't want to.

Aries nodded and Mia studied her face. She couldn't get over the stunning dark red eyes. She'd never seen anyone with red eyes before and she wondered if they were fake. Mia's eyes wandered from Aries' face to her thick, long, crimson hair that was separated into two long braids. Mia followed each braid to their ends on the ground where they circled Aries like a rope. She'd never seen someone with hair that long either. Was this woman a foreigner? Mia checked both of her biceps, no armbands, so she wasn't a runner. Then suddenly Mia remembered the ring. She reached up but couldn't feel it. Where could it have gone? Mia looked up and caught Aries looking at her. Mia put her hand down and looked away.

"I'll be right back." Aries stood and left the room.

"Okay," Mia squeaked, then deflated.

She looked around the room. It looked like a basement of sorts. The walls were brick, and the ceiling and floors were concrete. Trash lined the floor and behind her nothing but wall. It was about the size of her bedroom. She looked over at Billie. She looked absolutely miserable, but the real question was, who were these women, and could she trust them?

"You gotta finish your water," Mia said.

"This nasty stuff?" Billie turned her head away. "What did they do, soak dirty socks in this?" Billie held to water away from her, but Mia pushed it back.

"It's not that bad." Mia said as Billie made a face. "Come on, drink up, it'll make you feel better." Billie resisted, but Mia stood her ground.

Billie gave in, then stopped. "Wait a minute, where the fuck are we?"

"I'm not sure," Mia said.

Billie looked at her with worry. "Who was that chick?"

"No idea," Mia said.

"Oh, shit, Mia, I think we've been kidnapped," Billie said.

"I think you're right, but maybe only half right."

"Half? What the fuck?"

"I think someone did kidnap us and I think it was the lady from the spice shop," Mia said as she unconsciously covered her right arm.

"The green haired bitch?"

Mia nodded. "I think she was a necromancer, but Aries said she rescued us."

"That fucking bitch, wait till we get back to the brothel," Billie growled. "Come on, we need to get out of here."

"W-what? Billie, wait."

"We don't know these people, Mia, they could be just as worse. We need to get out of here and tell Lady Valkyrie what happened."

Billie was right. Even though Aries hasn't hurt them, they could be traffickers or recruiters. The two of them crawled off the mattress onto the floor. Mia helped Billie regain her balance when they heard two voices from outside the door. Mia looked at Billie, who looked worried. Billie pushed a little for Mia to move, but right as they took their first step Aries and another girl with bright red hair appeared. Mia froze, but Billie stepped in front of her.

"Who the fuck are you?" Billie pointed at the two women, she struggled a bit with her balance, but her tone was unmistakable.

Aries looked at the two women. "I can explain."

Billie sucked her teeth and folded her arms. "Bitch, you better get up outta my way, ion finna listen to two musty ass bitches that are trying to kidnap us."

"Kidnap?" the younger girl with the bushy puffs gasped.

Aries took a tight breath. "Please, just listen to us."

Billie sucked her teeth again, but Mia pressed a hand to her shoulder. "Mia."

"I want to know," Mia said. Billie searched her friend's eyes, giving her the 'I can take these two' look.

"Fucking shit, get on with it then," Billie snapped.

"Thank you, but you might want to sit down for this," Aries said. Billie and Mia looked at each other.

"I'm good, make it short," Billie said as she rolled her eyes up and down Aries' body.

"Very well, my name is Aries, and this is my little sister Karina."

"Hiya," Karina waved.

"We were sent by my granny to find you, because of this," Aries reached into her pocket and pulled out the rose gold ring.

Mia and Billie gasped. Billie looked towards Mia. She could almost tell what she was going to say. Mia should have known that ring was trouble.

"It's not mine," Mia said. "We were trying to return it, we swear."

"Return it?" Aries said. "To whom?"

"The guy, Howard Earl something. He left it at the brothel we work at."

"Mia." Billie elbowed her in the side.

Aries and Karina looked at each other, then Aries spoke. "Well, we believe you regardless, but I don't think the ring should be delivered to this Howard Earl person."

"Wait, why do you care?" Billie asked. "Are you runners?"

"Runners!" Karina said. "No way, we're here to help fulfil the prophecy."

"Karina," Aries hissed.

"Sorry." Karina looked down.

"Oh, hell naw," Billie said. "These people are on some cult shit."

Mia stepped back. Prophecy, what were they talking about? She was just trying to return a lost ring, nothing more. If they wanted it, they could have it. "Well, it's your problem now," Mia said as she rubbed her injured right arm. "You can have it. Billie and I have to get to work." Mia and Billie started towards the door, but Aries and Karina blocked them.

"I wish it were that easy," Aries said, "but I'm afraid your lives are in grave danger."

"From whom?" Billie retorted.

"The owners of this ring," Aries said. "With the help of some friends, we were able to rescue you from a powerful key master."

"A what?" Billie asked.

"A necromancer," Aries said. "She, along with some runners, kidnapped you to get the ring."

Mia looked at Billie. She could not have meant to say necromancer. What the hell would a necromancer want with her and a piece of costume jewelry? What had Mia stumbled into? "And these people want to hurt us?" Mia asked.

"You're buying this, Mia?" Billie asked.

"I just want to know the truth, please," Mia asked.

"Mia, we can't trust a word they're saying," Billie said, but Mia found it hard to think over the sound of her beating heart. She needed to sit down. No, she needed to run away. "Mia, hey, it's okay." Billie calmed her. Mia hadn't even realized she was hyperventilating.

"I'm sorry to have to bring you this news," Aries said, "but the people after this ring have all the gangs looking for you."

Billie folded her arms and sucked her teeth.

"I know this doesn't make much sense, but trust us, they have runners crawling above looking for us," Aries said.

"Wait wait wait," Billie said. "Above? Where are we?"

"We're in the sewers, but just the first level," Aries said.

Mia felt a pang of pain in her chest. They were in the sewers? This wasn't happening, it must be a sick joke. She circled the room; her mind was spinning. She was only trying to return the ring for Zetti. She didn't have anything to do with some cult or necromancer shit.

"It's going to be okay," Aries said. "We just need to figure out the key to this ring."

"We're not figuring out shit," Billie said. "We're leaving. Our boss has high connections with powerful gangs. If there's a mess, she can handle it."

"I'm afraid it's not that simple," Aries said a little louder.

Billie stepped into Aries' face, and the two women locked eyes with each other. "It is that simple. You're just trying to play us and rope us into your little game, but we're not stupid. Come on, Mia."

Billie waved for Mia to come. Mia looked over at Aries and Karina. She really didn't want anything to do with this. She just wanted to head back to work and forget about this entire thing. Mia ran to Billie and grabbed her hand and Billie pushed past Aries.

"If you leave you will be killed," Aries said with her back facing them. "All the runner factions are looking for you and even if your so-called boss has connections, how would her boss' boss feel when they find out that she is hiding the most wanted pair in the city? What would your friends think when you lead the danger right to them?"

Billie gripped tightly to Mia's hand. "Come on, Mia, Lady Valkyrie will know what to do."

Mia looked back at Karina, then at Aries. They were just kidnapped by some woman, if what those two women said was true the last thing she wanted was this mess to follow her back home. The people there were like her family. Mia put on the brakes.

"Mia." Billie turned around.

"Wh-what if they're right?" Panic laced Mia's voice.

"It doesn't matter, Mia. Lady Valkyrie knows powerful people, too. If we're in a bind, the rule is to always go to her. Trust me," Billie said.

Mia started to nod. Billie was right. Lady Valkyrie was a lot tougher than she seemed and she always had their back.

"Let's go," Billie said.

Mia felt Aries' eyes on her as she left. This wasn't her problem. The two of them had the ring, isn't that what the runners wanted?

"Are we really going to let them go?" Karina's voice echoed as Mia hurried away, concerned laced through her voice.

Mia followed behind Billie through a maze of halls. She'd never been in the sewers before. It was dim and dusty, and the pathways seemed to continue forever. Billie ran quickly from corridor to corridor. She seemed like she knew where she was going, after all, Billie partied down here a lot. Mia stayed close, jumping every time she ran into a cobweb or rat. She just wanted to be in her nice warm bed far away from this madness. Billie kept moving, but Mia struggled to keep up. Her body was so sore.

"You okay?" Billie turned.

Mia was breathing hard, and she hadn't even realized it. "I-I'm fine."

"No, Mia, you look pretty banged up." Billie's eyes looked her over. "And what happened to your arm."

Mia didn't want to talk about it, the memory was still fresh.

Billie sighed. "It's okay, let's keep moving. Things will get better when we get back to Valkyrie House, I promise."

Mia half-smiled and forced herself to keep going. They heard voices from up ahead. Billie ran to the end of the tunnel, which was much nicer than the tunnels they had been running down before. Off white tile lined the walls and Mia began to relax the more voices she heard. Billie turned back and smiled; they must be almost there. Mia inched up closer on Billie as they walked up a few steps, then around a tiled wall up a few more steps.

"I think we're on the lower end of the city, probably ten or sixteen blocks from the brothel," Billie said.

Mia nodded. They reached the next level. It was open space with street people lined on the walls talking, hanging out, and playing cards. Mia breathed a sigh of relief as Billie took Mia's hand and walked towards the exit. They headed to one of the short corridors leading up to the above ground. It was dark, but they could see the light at the end of the tunnel. A pair walked up behind them. Mia couldn't see their faces in the darkness, but they weren't following too close.

"Ja, I can't believe we got this all-call shit again," one man said.

"Don't worry yourself, I'm sure one of the other gangs will find them," a woman said.

"I mean didn't they just catch those bitches?" the man said. "How hard is it to find and capture four chicks?"

"I can't speak for no one but myself, but the big boss said it's all-call. Rumor has it that the witch Lady Rosemary is dead."

"No shit?" the man said.

Mia started to tremble. They were talking about them. Billie cursed and pulled Mia towards the wall. They both played it cool as the pair passed, but Mia couldn't stop shaking. Those runners were talking about them. This was unreal. How could an entire city be looking for them? Mia heard Billie curse again and looked to her face but couldn't make out her expression in the darkness. They held their position until the runners were far away. Then Billie let out a big sigh.

"Billie..." Mia reached out to her friend. Billie's hands were shaking, too.

Billie didn't say a word then grabbed Mia's hand and headed back down the tunnels. Mia struggled to control her breathing as she was pulled along. What were they going to do? Those girls were right, everyone was looking for them and all over a ring she didn't even have. Why would anyone turn the city inside out over a piece of jewelry? Was it really worth that much? Mia doubted, now they were in real trouble and Mia felt even worse, because she got Billie wrapped up in this, too. Billie turned around the tiled corridor down the steps and nearly ran into someone. Mia yelped but saw that it was Aries and sighed with relief.

"Okay," Billie said. "How the fuck do we fix this?"

They went back to the room with the mattresses. Where Karina was waiting for them. Mia forced a smile, but dread built in the back of her throat. Aries offered them more water and it was Billie who reluctantly took the offer this time, while Mia stood there frozen.

"Hey, come on, have a seat." Billie gently nudged her.

Mia shifted her gaze to her friend and slowly moved. She found a spot and Karina offered them food, but Mia wasn't hungry and how could she? The entire city was after them. This seemed so terribly unlikely, it was only yesterday that she was fucking clients and dancing on the stage as some nobody. Now everyone knew about her. Billie nudged her, but Mia turned her head away, tucking her knees to her chest.

"Hey, shit sucks, but it'll suck even more if you don't eat." Billie rubbed Mia's back.

"I-I'm fine, really," Mia said.

"Okay," Billie said with a comforting smile. Mia was so grateful Billie didn't push, she knew her so well. Billie saved Mia's piece of bread and put it on the cloth. She took a bite of her bread and stretched out, then pointed it at Aries. "So, why's everyone so up in arms about this fugly ass ring?" Billie said bluntly.

Aries looked away, as if she were holding something back, then took a sip of water. "Unfortunately, my guess may not be any better than yours," Aries said. "I was sent on a mission by my granny to find the Crimson Mouse. She is the one who will lead our people out of the darkness."

"The what?" Billie stopped eating.

"The Crimson Mouse!" Karina said with a little too much enthusiasm and reached into her knapsack and pulled out a book. The book looked old. The cover was wrinkly, and the pages were dark brown. "It's a part of our clan's prophecy. The Crimson Mouse will lead the Darkness to the light. My sister Aries is the Darkness, and she needs to find the Crimson Mouse to led our people out of the darkness."

Billie blinked, then leaned back. "Great, it's a cult. Thanks, I hate it."

Mia groaned. This was sounding worse the more they explained.

"It's not a cult," Karina pouted.

"Karina it's okay," Aries said. "Let me explain better. My people believe that the world is unbalanced. We worship a great mountain spirit by the name of Acome, they are the keeper of balance for our region. They are the arbitrator of the trio of balance; death, birth, and life; past, present, and future; black, gray, and white. They control it all. I know this sounds weird, but our people believe that they are being blocked somehow."

"I'm sure they do," Billie said under her breath. "So, let me get this straight, your magic granny said go find my best friend?"

"More or less," Aries said. "Our granny has the gift of sight; she can see things that might come to past."

"And a magic ring is the key to what exactly?" Billie asked.

Aries pulled out the ring and she winced as if it was hurting her to touch it. "I'm not sure. I can only go on what my granny saw in her visions."

"A-and what did she see exactly?" Mia looked at the two women.

"She said she saw a woman running, and she saw some kind of cage. But most vividly of all she saw a gold ring tainted by blood. A rose gold ring and this looks exactly how she described it."

Billie reached out for the ring, Aries hesitated at first, but she handed it to Billie. "This thing can't be that special," Billie said, holding it up. "Is it magic?"

"I'm not sure..." Aries trailed off, "but when I hold it, I feel...overwhelmed." Karina looked at her sister. "That's why I believe the keeper should be the Crimson Mouse, just like how my granny described it in her dreams."

Billie held the ring in her hand. Then she looked at Mia and nudged her with her elbow. "You want this?"

"No way." Mia pushed the thing away. "I don't want anything to do with that weird ring."

"I understand, but I believe that you are the Crimson Mouse," Aries said.

"Me?" Mia said. "What about you guys? What about your sister?"

"Yeah!" Karina said.

"Karina," Aries warned, and her sister slumped.

Mia looked to Billie.

"Hell no, it ain't me," Billie said. "You found the ring."

"Bullshit, it was right after I found it you came in," Mia said.

"I don't got nothing to do with this little mission of yours." Billie put the ring down. "Besides, it's ugly anyways."

Mia eyed the ring. To her, it now looked like a cursed object. She wanted to throw it far, far away and forget about the whole thing and yet she couldn't stop looking at it. Something beyond its beauty drew her in and she hated herself for it. This was just supposed to be a fun little side trip, an excuse for her best friend and her to go shopping. Nothing more. Something was seriously wrong if runners and necromancers were after them because of it. And what if what Aries and Karina were talking about was true? What if there was some God thing? No, Mia couldn't bring herself to think about it. This was crazy, nothing but foolish talk. There were no such thing as powerful spirits.

"I-I'm not the Crimson Mouse," Mia said. "I work at a brothel, I'm just a regular girl."

"I can't imagine how you must feel," Aries said, "but I promise to stay by your side and protect you."

"What about your granny?" Billie said. "Do you think she may know more about this ring?"

Aries stayed silent.

"That's right," Karina said. "We could go to Granny's. I'm sure she'd be excited to see the ring and the Crimson Mouse. Oh, she'd be thrilled!" Karina clapped her hands together, but when she turned to her sister her expression dampened. "What? What's wrong?"

Aries took a deep breath. "I don't think Granny can help us anymore."

"W-what do you mean?" Karina said.

"Karina, I think Granny passed away." Aries looked into her sister's eyes.

"What?" Karina shook her head. "Don't play like that, don't say stuff like that, Aries, it's not funny." Karina started to pout. "Aries, I mean it." When Aries stayed quiet Karina's faced melted into anger. "Aries!" Karina shouted.

"She came to me in a vision that time after we left the bar." Aries' eyes filled with tears that she quickly wiped away.

"No, no, no!" Karina stood, "No! Granny is still alive." Karina got up and ran out of the room.

"Karina!" Aries got up after her, she looked at Billie and Mia, both girls nodded to her, and then she ran off. "Karina!"

"Damn that's rough." Billie leaned back, and Mia sighed.

"We're screwed, aren't we?" Mia played with her fingers. Nothing about this ring or situation looked like it was going to pan out for them in a good way, but Billie shrugged. "Billie, I'm serious."

"I'm not downplaying it. I fucking hate magic. It causes nothing but trouble, but we're tagged girls. You heard those runners, and they didn't even look like they were from a big gang. And that witch bitch? Who the fuck calls a hit over a fucking ring? The people after this must be seriously fucked up."

Mia frowned. "So, we're going to die, that's it."

"Wo, wo, wo, I didn't say anything about that, but I'll be damned if I'm going to let anyone back us into a corner. If there's a way in, then there's a way out and we're going to find it, okay?"

Mia slowly nodded. She cursed the moment she found the damn thing. Its tainted beauty ruined everything it touched, and Mia hated it for it. But worse of all she got Billie involved in this. There had to be a way out, and she hoped Aries and Karina had a plan, because if not they might as while jump into the river.

26
Karina

Karina ran down the dusty corridors with Tink on her shoulder, barely holding on. Aries shouted after her, but Karina ignored her. Aries sprinted behind her and reached out one arm to try and catch her sister, but she missed several times. Aries finally clasped her hand around Karina's arm and grabbed her sister and pulled her close. Karina fought and kicked and pushed her sister away. How could Aries keep such an important detail from her? Even if Karina refused to believe that her granny was dead, did she not have a right to even speculate on it?

The fight caused both women to fall to the ground. Karina wiggled out of Aries grip and started to her feet. She didn't even want to look at her sister right now. Aries tripped Karina with her leg and Karina fell to the ground.

"Karina," Aries said.

"Fuck you." Karina looked over her shoulder as she tried to get up, but she stumbled. Her body was weak from lack of food and sleep, and it was showing. Karina sniffled, then cursed as she started to cry.

"Karina," Aries inched over to her sister and sat down beside her. "I'm so sorry."

"But how do you know? How do you know?" Karina said in between sobs. "A-and why didn't you tell me?"

"I-I can't say for certain, but it felt so real when she appeared to me."

"By why you, though?" Karina said as the tears mixed with the dirt on her face turning it into a muddy mess. "Why you?"

Aries didn't say anything at first, then she sighed. "I don't know, but she said she used the last of her strength to tell me to finish this mission."

Karina looked up at her sister, her anger growing. "What a fucking joke."

"What?"

"What a fucking joke! Why do you get to have everything just because you're older! You don't even believe in the prophecy. I studied every day of my life to be ready and all you do is dismiss me like Mom and Dad. And now, and now Granny is dead, and she spent her dying moments coming to you." Karina balled her fist as the tears ran down her cheeks. Aries looked hurt, but she didn't care.

"Karina..." Aries reached out.

"No, I don't want to hear it. You treat me like a fucking child, but I'm mature I can handle it."

"A child? Are you hearing yourself? This isn't a game."

"Fuck you!"

"Fuck you." Aries threw her hands up and stood. She started to storm away, but she turned around. "No, I'm not going to fucking argue with you." Aries turned her heated gaze to her sister.

Karina balled her fist as the pain of loss filled her chest. It wasn't fair that Aries got everything when Karina wanted so badly to help. When she wanted so badly to see Granny's vision come true.

Aries glared at her sister, but then she sucked in a breath and exhaled. "You're-you're right," Aries finally said and looked her sister square in the eyes. "I-I don't deserve to be the Darkness. I don't even want to be the Darkness. I'm tired of this miserable life. Tired of all the suffering. I only went on this mission to escape the pain of Zopi and Nyekundu's murder. It was so gruesome, b-but I had to swallow it. Swallow everything for the sake of Bluu and Mom and Dad and you. They needed me to be strong, but I-I'm broken."

Karina felt a tinge of guilt in her chest. She hadn't realized her sister was carrying so much. She didn't even stop to consider if Aries even wanted this. Karina got up and hugged her sister. Aries tensed, but then melted into the hug.

"I'm so sorry, sis," Karina said.

"No, I'm sorry," Aries said. "I should have told you right away. You're not a child and I know you've been working hard learning summoning keys and trying to cast."

Karina pulled away and smiled. She reached up to wipe her tears away and took a deep breath. Crying time was over. "How are we going to do this?"

27
Vincent

Vincent fought the urge to yawn as he trailed behind his number two, Dr. Jaystof Acknid. He was the mastermind behind all the *improvements* made to the gang and he was not shy about talking about it. He stroked his gray, braided beard as he talked circles around Vincent. Vincent responded with a nod as he watched the mechanical lenses of Dr. Acknid's eyes constrict and expand. They walked the dark steamy corridors to his laboratory with great haste, because Dr. Acknid insisted that he show Vincent his latest advancement in medical necromancy.

"Have I mentioned what a glorious day it is to be alive?" Dr. Acknid said as he flung his mechanical arms outward.

Vincent only smiled, because this was the third time in this conversation Dr. Acknid had said this. They made a sharp turn and hurried down the short flight of steps onto a metal grate. That clanked as they walked pass various pipes and exposed wires.

"I will admit that I am sorry to hear what happened to Lady Rosemary. She was a great scientist and an extreme beauty. It was no surprise that she was labeled with the word 'witch'. There are always those who confuse science for magic, especially if such great mind belongs to a woman."

Dr. Acknid reached the metal door of his laboratory and stuck his fist into the lock. Like clockwork, pins shot forward and impaled him in all the right places, then rotated the hand around the wrist a few times. The door unlocked and he pulled out his fist and rubbed the warm metal of his wrist joint.

"I suppose nothing can be done about it," Dr. Acknid said. "Blood magic comes at a great cost, hence why Lady Rosemary turned to ash, but for me, I am a man of pure science. I don't have to worry about such cost, I can replace anything. And I mean anything." Dr. Acknid rubbed his mechanical boney fingers together, then adjusted the round lenses embedded in his eye sockets. Vincent flashed a thin smile, which seemed to make Dr. Acknid even more thrilled.

His laboratory was packed wall to wall with gadgets and body parts made from machinery. Vincent was careful not to stray too close to anything because Dr. Acknid's little experiments had the habit of coming to life. Dr. Acknid stopped and faced Vincent.

"Now, I have not brought you all this way for nothing. I've been working on something new! I've been experimenting with a different form of necromancy."

"Is that so," Vincent said.

"Yes, it is. You know I tire over fiddling with the organics of breast and butt implants. Who needs flat stomachs and chiseled chins when you can have lobster claws for arms! Of course there are drawbacks, I'm well aware that lobsters are many times smaller than the average human, but the aesthetic can be replicated with ease. Just a little metal work. But that is child's play, I'm taking it to another level. Here, allow me to show you."

Dr. Acknid sat at his desk and buried his face in his notes. He jotted down the date and time, then pushed himself from his desk and swirled around the room. Vincent made himself a wallflower to stay out of his way as he hoped this experiment wouldn't turn into a lecture. Vincent knew how magic worked. It was simple if one didn't ask too many questions and just accepted the mark from the spirits, but necromancy worked a bit different. Necromancy was purely the art of reanimation. Simple things like prosthetics and organs were easy to transplant, because all it required was a living soul to power an equivalent transplant. This was the bulk of medical necromancy, however the energy required to raise a corpse was much more dangerous for the caster. The energy required to perform such a task used the unrenewable power of the caster's soul. The latter, understandably, was not used frequently.

"Of course, this test is not without its drawbacks. It will take a considerable amount of energy, and it might have an effect on my dashing good looks, but nothing ventured, nothing gained." Dr. Acknid laughed as he stopped next to a hanging mirror and tugged at his wrinkled brown skin and stroked his gray ponytail braided beard as he dilated the laser orange lights in his lenses.

Dr. Acknid stood and rubbed the circular port on the back of his neck. Then opened the door to his testing room. Vincent walked to the viewing window and eyed the circular room that was lined with shelves that reached the ceiling filled with hundreds and hundreds of tiny, dead, black spiders. This was new. Vincent stood with his hands behind his back.

In the middle of the room was a chair at a control table with several panels with dials and gauges. Dr. Acknid smiled wildly as he inspected what looked like key sigils on the projector at his desk. Each key on the screen matched one of the key sigils written in a circle on the floor. He stopped and took a peek at some of the dead spiders on the shelve before he settled in his chair.

"Soon, lovelies, you will live again, but this time as my puppets." Dr. Acknid grinned as he moved wildly around his control panel, flipping on switches and pushing up dials. Then reached down and unhooked a plug with dozens of thin black cords bound together with rope. Then he fingered the back of his neck for the port and delicately inserted the plug into the back of his head. His body jerked, but then he snapped back and relaxed again.

"Oh! That never gets old," Dr. Acknid chuckled.

He turned up a dial on the control board and everything lit up. All the gauge readings read zero as he pulled out sticky tabs with wires and placed them on his body in varies places, even opening his lab coat and dress shirt and placing tabs one his chest. He opened his hands and started to cast his summoning keys into his palms and his key gate appeared next to his head. His black metal hands glowed a faint orange, then his eyes lit up. He kept casting the key sigil as the gate glowed, then it slowly opened for him. A bright orange tendril slithered out and split into two then wormed itself into his ears. Dr. Acknid's head flung backwards and started to glow bright orange. The orange intensified as it moved up his arms and over his shoulders, and down his back towards his legs. Everything grew brighter as he continued casting his keys, which now lit up all the sigils painted on the floor, making them glow an intense orange.

All the gauges on the control panel flicked into the red, but he continued his casting. Vincent squinted so he could see as the room vibrated with energy. Then a flash of orange lightening burst from Dr. Acknid's body, gushing outward like a stormwater pipe. It swirled around the room and flowed into every spider on the shelf. The black spiders shook in their exoskeletons. Their legs jerked and popped open, their eyes glowed bright orange and they came to life swirling around the room in a well-coordinated pattern.

"For all the glory," Vincent uttered. He had never seen anything like this before.

Dr. Acknid cackled, holding out his arms. "It worked! It worked! It worked!" The spiders surrounded Dr. Acknid like a herd of dogs, then the doctor turned to Vincent. "Impressive, huh?"

Vincent nodded to show his admiration.

"Of course, I have not brought you here just to wow you with my experiments. I have been working on this for a while, but I have never performed this key chain at full power, but this is the future. No more lobotomized replacements, now we'll be able to have real, live, independent puppets! Organic creatures that can be raised from the dead and completely under our control. The drawback is the cost, but the body of an insect is small, which drastically decreases the cost and at this scale I am unstoppable!"

Vincent resisted the urge to clap. This was impressive indeed, but also forbidden magic. Medical necromancy had its limits and reanimating the dead was one of them. Vincent had seen plenty of necromancers burn up when they casted too much of themselves to bring back the dead. This and other things, were one of the many reasons Vincent didn't like magic. Why would you risk spending your own precious life force for power? Especially, if life force was not renewable, but leave it to Dr. Acknid to find a loophole. The doctor returned to his lab and scurried over to Vincent.

"Impressive work, Dr. Acknid," Vincent said. "You give The Black Gate a run for their money."

"Thank you." Dr. Acknid beamed.

"But surely something like this isn't sustainable?" Vincent didn't want to crush the good doctor's hope, but Dr. Acknid only grinned.

"This is where size matters, look for yourself." Dr. Acknid pulled down his collar to show the black veins on his chest.

"You used your soul to cast those keys, but it barely had an effect." Vincent eyed him curiously.

"Exactly," Dr. Acknid pulled his hand away and waved Vincent over to his desk. "No blood or slaves required and if you're concerned about the cost, insects are much smaller than human corpses and they have many uses. Here let me show you."

Dr. Acknid plopped on his rolling stool and rolled over to his desk. There was a device connected to a large ao almasi gem with a large sheet of crystal in the middle. Dr. Acknid flipped a switch, the device buzzed, and the crystal came to life. Vincent stood behind him. It was some kind of physical telepathic picture, much like the magic Lady Rosemary used. In the crystal the image turned from a cloudy fuzz to something more recognizable. Vincent leaned in and scanned the live image that looked like a small kitchen that looked to be in a house or burrow. There were three people sitting at a table, two with bright red hair, the other a small child. Then many more feeds popped up, all of people with bright red hair. Vincent eyed them all, until his eyes laid on a feed with four girls. Two with bright red hair, another one who was blonde, and one with purple braids. Dr. Acknid turned around and grinned.

"Impressive?"

"Are these?" Vincent asked with curiosity.

"My spiders?" Dr. Acknid cackled. "I would say the early experiments went well, wouldn't you? As for your ring problem, I shouldn't have any trouble retrieving it for you."

Vincent smiled. Results, that's what Vincent liked to see. There was no point in employing individuals who could not get the job done. Vincent reached into his coat pocket, withdrew a cigarette, and lit it.

"I leave this matter in your hands then," Vincent said as he blew out a thick cloud of gray smoke.

28 Mia

Mia rested for a bit on the old mattress in the room. She hadn't realized how much time had passed; it was actually quite late in the afternoon. She was sure the hostesses were furious, though it wasn't against the rules to take time off, but just skipping out without notice could be grounds for dismissal. She really wished she had a way to contact everyone, but telephones were not universal, even in a huge city like Laurasia. The brothel only had a few and who knew where there was a telephone box around here. Mia rolled over and stared at the wall.

Billie went with Aries to take a leak, and Karina was napping on the other side of the room. Aries left the ring for her in a pouch on the bed, but it wasn't like she wanted it. Mia was a little upset the chain was gone, it was Billie's, and she doubted Billie cared, but the fact that the witch stole it upset her. She could have just taken the ring and let them go. It didn't matter though, she was dead, and good riddance.

Mia closed her eyes. She was so tired, but she couldn't sleep here, not with everything going on. Hunger also played tricks on her mind, but at least her stomach and right arm were feeling a little better. Mia ignored her growling stomach. The bread Aries and Karina shared with them was a nice snack, but hardly a meal. She wished she could pay them back, but her purse and all her money were gone, too. What a complete waste, all that money and new clothes she busted her ass for, gone.

Her thoughts didn't linger on money for long as she found herself looking at the ring again. Aries wouldn't carry it, she said it made her feel strange. Billie didn't want the thing either. Why couldn't Karina carry it? She seemed the most eager? And why wasn't she the Crimson Mouse or whatever that was? She had a literal rat sleeping on her shoulder. This just didn't make any sense.

Billie was right, they would have been better off pawning the thing. Mia glared at the sack. She didn't care if she looked stupid. A piece of jewelry should never cause this much trouble. Mia sat up and snatched the small sack off the floor. She tugged on the draw strings and opened the sack. The rose gold ring gleamed at the bottom, and it made her sick. She rolled the ring from side to side, before letting it slip out. It went right through her fingers and bounced on her chest.

"Oops," Mia grabbed it, then looked over at Karina.

She was still sleeping, good. She could take the ring and throw it out somewhere, but then what would happen if they were caught, and the ring wasn't on them? And how long would they search for them anyways? Mia would probably have to flee the city, maybe even the country at this rate. Mia squeezed the thing, trying to punish it for all the grief it caused her. But it was pointless, it only left the embedded shape of its crown shaped sides on her palm. Useless, she thought.

She rolled the ring around through her fingertips. It was oddly warm and worn, but not dull. She looked closely at it again. Perhaps she could ask one of them what these patterns meant? That would be at least one mystery solved. Mia stretched out her left hand allowing her fingers to spread as far apart as they could. It was hers now she guessed. She hovered the opening over her left ring finger and slipped it on.

Mia fell through the mattress. She screamed and flailed through dense gray and white clouds, twirling downward at impossible speeds. There was no ground, no up or down. Only the terror of falling. She shut her eyes, and the sensation ended as quickly as it started.

Her heart pounded as she laid curled up in a tight ball, too scared to move. Mia took deep breaths, but something wasn't right. There was no cloth beneath her. She reached out a shaky hand and something prickly and soft grazed her palm. She yanked her hand back as a strange feeling of warmth heated her sides.

Mia opened her eyes and gasped. Green, miles of green plants covered everything. Thousands of blades of grass? It couldn't be, Mia slowly looked around. She breathed in the strong smell of dirt, like real dirt, not sour like trash or pungent like sewage. She gazed up and saw blue. That couldn't be the sky. She followed it around, until she spotted a fireball in the sky. It burned her eyes to look at and Mia screamed. It was coming right for her, she was sure of it. Mia kicked and stumbled backwards for a good ten minutes, before she realized it was just hovering there, like a cloud. Mia stole glances at it, but it hurt so much to stare directly at it. It couldn't be...could it be the sun? She had heard about it, but never seen it before in her life.

"Hello there, Crimson Mouse," a voice rolled across the plain on the wind.

Mia jerked around, who was speaking to her?

"I do not mean to frighten you, but I am short on time and short on energy. I am using all that I have to speak with you, so please, hear me out."

Mia tried to pen down the echo of their voice as wind blew strongly through her short blonde coiled hair. She looked ahead, blocking the extreme light from her eyes, when she thought she saw a tall blue glowing tree. Mia gasped. It's leaves were soft blue and they glistened in the wind, contrasted against the dark brown bark. Was that a real tree? Mia blinked. What was this place?

"Come to me, Crimson Mouse."

Mia's body lifted from the ground, and she yelped and found herself being pulled towards the tree. Mia screamed and shut her eyes, and when she opened them, she was before the tree, and it was even more beautiful up close. Light gleamed through its blue veiny leaves and the dark brown bark shimmered as if it had been painted with glitter.

"Let me show you how the world should be."

Light blue tendrils rose from the tree like steam and circled around her. Mia's eyes shot open, and she gasped. "W-wait, n-no—"

The light around her intensified and suddenly she was somewhere else. Goosebumps appeared on her brown skin from the feeling of cold, clear, blue water as she sat atop a bed of sand.

"What's...?" Her fingers touched the water, so clear she could see tiny fish swimming below its surface. "F-fish?" But then there was another pull.

Her consciousness left her body and transported her to a golden field where birds with beautiful feathers and long legs stretched their wings. Beautiful, winged insects she had never seen before rode the winds. One of the great birds took flight, soaring above her. Then the sensation of cold blew through her clothes. She closed her eyes as something fell on her eyelashes and nose.

"S-snow?" She held out her hand to catch a snowflake so big and pure that when it melted, it melted into a beautiful pattern.

White snow covered everything now. An animal with thick, brown fur and hoofed feet appeared next to her and rubbed its long snout on her arms. She jumped and jerked away and when all the creature did was stare calmly back at her she reached out a shaky hand to pet it, mesmerized by its deep brown eyes.

"H-hello." Its fur was so soft and warm. She felt its heartbeat that pulsated through her and all around her. Such beauty, it was incomprehensible. Then Mia found herself above it all. On the winds, traveling towards a great mountain range. White birds with long wings squawked beside her as she sailed towards a rising sun.

Suddenly Mia was back in her body with tears streaming down her cheeks. What world was that? That could not be her world. Had she crossed into the land of the dead? A warmth wrapped itself around her and she held up her hands as gold dust floated behind a dozen gilded butterflies. Mia coughed out a smile as one of them landed on her fingertips before it fluttered away.

"Where, where is this place?"

"This is Laurasia. As it should be."

"Laurasia? That can't be." Mia looked at the tree. "Laurasia has no blue sky or grass."

"That is because Laurasia does not have me."

"W-who are you?"

"I am Acome, the spirit of these lands. My domain resides over the mountains to the west and covers the valleys to the east stretching until the land meets the sea. I maintain the balance of light and life. I am the water, the grass, and the spirit and soul of all creatures who reside here. I am the caretaker of this place."

Mia's mouth opened and closed. "I-I don't understand."

"That's okay, my Crimson Mouse. There is little I can do to help you in my current state. That is why I have appeared before you today. That ring, it is a part of me. My very flesh was forged in its making."

Mia looked at the strange pinkish tint. The ring pulsated and for the first time she could feel it beat. It was alive.

"I need that which was stolen from me, so that I might return and be free."

"Return? Free?" Mia uttered and Acome replied with a hum.

A strong wind blew through the valley, but this wind was heavy. It blew through Mia right into her bones and pierced her heart with thousands of images of dying lands, tortured people, and death. She trembled as the pressure sat atop her very soul. Hundreds of years of pain drowned out all light and made her curl up into a ball.

"Make it stop! Make it stop!" Mia screamed.

"I am sorry. I am very weak, so nothing but pain travels on my winds and in my words"

Something reached out to Mia and touched the top of her back. She looked up and saw the face of an animal attached to the body of a person. She gasped, but when she looked into its dark starry eyes, she felt a sense of familiarity, like they had met before. She felt safe. She didn't understand this, but somewhere deep inside of her she believed them.

"H-how can I help you?"

"I am in a golden cage, deep below the surface in the great city."

"I-I don't know where that is."

Acome reached out and touched the ring. Mia tensed as it pulsed. It glowed a pinkish gold, which tinkled like glitter raining from the sky.

"I will lead you to me. Do not fear the darkness, for good also thrives there."

Mia nodded as she cupped the hand that wore the ring. The wind picked up and on the horizon she saw what looked like the shadows of hundreds of rats and mice. They scurried past her towards a storm way off in the distance. Mia looked back at the tree, but Acome's form was fading. She didn't want them to go. She had so many questions, but Acome didn't look sad. A smile bloomed across their canine like face.

"I will lead you to me."

A gust of wind blew through Mia's hair and clothes as the army of rodents increased. Mia covered her eyes with her forearm, when her eyes caught a flicker of red. She squinted and abruptly the hoard of rodents turned toward her. Mia inched back.

"Oh no...oh no..."

She didn't want to get attacked by rats, but she spotted that flash of red again and followed it. It danced in the distance, moving more like an insect than a beam of light. It drew closer and Mia gasped. It wasn't a flash at all, but a small animal. It was a mouse, and it ran on the backs of hundreds of rodents.

The rats and mice were upon Mia at once. She put up her hands to protect her face, but they all ran around her. She lowered her arms and watched them run by in a hoard easily over a thousand. She turned back to the tree and spotted the red mouse again. It was coming right for her. She didn't know what to do, so she held out her hand. The red mouse sprinted faster and leapt towards her.

Mia made a bowl with her hands to catch it, and it landed perfectly in her palm. It looked up at her with its tiny black eyes, then looked towards the ring and Mia understood. The red mouse looked off into the distance, before it transformed into a beam of bright red light and struck itself into the ring. Mia gasped as she flipped her hand over repeatedly.

"Lead us," a chorus echoed. "Lead us."

The winds picked up and intensified as Mia felt herself being pushed backward. She gasped as the chorus repeated over and over again, "*Lead us. Lead us. Lead us.*" Mia was swept away, but she still had so many questions. Her legs left the ground and suddenly she found herself in a hurricane of rodents. "*Lead us. Lead us,*" their chorus echoed as she was swept away into the darkness.

Mia gasped and found herself back in the same sewage smelling brick room again. She shot up and looked around the room and saw her best friend.

"Look who's up," Billie said.

"Wh-what?" Billie looked at Mia confused, but before Mia could say another word she jumped when a shadow of a black rat ran towards Aries and disappeared into Aries' leg.

"The-the Darkness," Mia muttered as she drew her hand back.

"What?" Billie looked at Mia.

"N-nothing," Mia said.

Suddenly everyone in the room was looking at her. How could she explain what she just saw? Aries looked over at Mia suspiciously, but Mia looked away.

"So, what's the plan?" Billie asked. "We have this magic ring. What the heck do we do with it?"

Both Aries and Karina were silent, but Mia bit her lip. Should she say something? Would they even believe her? She looked at Billie. What would she think? Mia looked down at her finger. The ring felt warm. She touched it with her other hand, and it pulsated like a beating heart. *Acome.*

"I think I know where some texts are stored," Aries said, then looked at her sister. "Have you hid away any books?"

Karina nodded.

"I-I know what to do," Mia blurted out. Everyone looked at her, with Billie giving her the strangest look. Mia didn't know how to word it, but she had to say something. "I-I had a vision."

Both Aries and Karina gasped, but Billie rolled her eyes.

"Bullshit," Billie said.

"Really?" Karina said with her hands clasped together. "Tell us, tell us, what did you see?"

Mia looked between the girls and her best friend, feeling nervous under the spotlight. Then Billie sighed and waved Mia on.

"Come on, spill it. I promise we won't judge you." Billie's reassuring smile steeled Mia's nerves.

"Okay." Mia took a deep breath. "I-I saw the sun I think, and I think I saw Acome." The minute that word fell from her mouth she saw a flicker of something in Aries' eyes.

"You are the Crimson Mouse," Aries said.

"No, I mean." Mia waved her hands in front of her as if she could make the words she just spoke disappear. "I..." Mia sighed as Karina clapped with glee, finally giving in. "They appeared before me, but I'm not sure what it means."

"It's okay. We don't exactly know either. This is the first time the prophecy has revealed itself true," Aries said, "but it's the Crimson Mouse's job to lead the Darkness to victory. What did Acome instruct you to do?"

"Um," Mia said. "To find them and free them."

"They're trapped?" Karina's eyes widened and Mia nodded.

"In a cage," Mia said.

"The cage, Aries!" Karina said. "Remember what Granny said about the cage?"

"Wait, wait, wait," Billie said. "You're really eating this shit up?" Billie looked between Aries and Karina.

Aries sighed. "We don't talk about this with outsiders, but the prophecy has been passed on from seer to seer in my clan for generations. It is our mission to see this through."

Billie turned to Mia, but this time she wasn't smiling. "And you're buying this shit? Truthfully?"

Mia looked into Billie's eyes. She was asking her if what she was saying was something she truly believed in. All jokes aside, but truly Mia could not say for sure if what she saw was real or some side effect of the witch's potions. Mia wasn't special. She wasn't a caster or necromancer. She didn't have a family. She didn't even have enough money to rent a place on her own. The Crimson Mouse or red mouse should be someone special, like Karina or someone from their clan and yet, even as the doubt grew in her chest, she felt the heartbeat around her finger. Mia could not deny that. Mia clenched the hand that held the ring.

"Yes," Mia said.

Billie sighed and a smirk found its way to her lips. "A sex worker who was rescued from a dirty alley is going to be a magical hero. Lady Valkyrie would close the brothel in your honor girl, you're a fucking badass. Alright, I'm in then."

"You haven't much choice really," Aries joked.

"Oh, I got choices, but I choose to stand by my best friend," Billie said and turned to Mia. "Even if this cult stuff is full of shit."

"Alright then." Aries turned to Mia. "Did they tell you a location? Anything that would allude to where the cage is?"

"Um, they said they were somewhere in The Great City," Mia said. "And that this ring is a part of them, and it will lead me to them."

"The Great City?" Aries looked at her sister. "That could be anywhere."

"No," Billie said. "That's Uptown."

"Why do you say that?" Aries asked.

"Some of the folks from Uptown call it The Great City, I've done some work up there," Billie said.

"That's right," Mia said, "but how are all of us going to get past the runners at the great wall?"

"You know," Billie said as she flashed one of her devilish smirks.

"You can't be serious." Mia frowned. "We have to go through Sewer Town?"

Billie rubbed her best friend's leg. "The wall may wrap around the entire city, but it doesn't go down to the sewers."

"Yay! Adventure time!" Karina declared.

"But we better get moving, nightfall is the best time to enter the city," Billie said.

"Alright," Aries said. "Let's go."

29
Mia

Mia walked quickly to keep up with the group. She didn't have a clue that the sewers went a full eight levels down and they were only on level one. All she knew about the sewers were that people lived down there for work. She saw the labor contracts advertised for the recycling plant nailed to walls and taped to light post all the time. It always looked shady to her, because they promised things like free housing and guaranteed work, but the fine print always required some form of buy back and she was very wary of pre-investment jobs. Lots of pimps ran their business like that. They would pay for new sex worker's rent, and clothes, even beauty upgrades, but the sex worker would always have to pay them back, sometimes with terribly high interest.

She walked down a curved ramp as Karina and Billie led the way. Billie and Karina seemed to be the ones who knew where they were going. Karina had an idea of how to get to a section called Core, but apparently that was on the other side of the city. Of course, it made sense, the sewers ran all over the city. Now they were trying a way Billie knew.

"Fuck," Billie said, and the group stopped. "Runners."

Aries looked. There had to be at least fifteen of them. "I thought there weren't many runners up here."

"Their numbers are different in different places," Karina said.

Billie sighed. Mia didn't have anything to add, she had no clue where they even were. She rubbed her ring, wishing she could teleport there somehow.

"I-I do know of another way," Karina said.

"Where?" Aries asked.

"Don't hate me when I tell you this." Karina shied away.

"I don't care about being mad right now," Aries said. "Now, where is the path?"

"Okay, but it's a little dangerous," Karina said as the group looked around at each other.

Karina led the way back up the ramp and back into the lobby area. Karina glanced around, and Mia noted there were mostly street people on this level. Aries did mention something about folks sleeping here at night, but Karina waved them on, and everyone walked without a word towards a dimly lit hall. They walked around a tiled wall and immediately saw what Karina was talking about. This hallway had collapsed. Concrete, dirt, and bricks lay in a mound that led to the ceiling. Aries jerked up when the sound of voices came from above.

"There's people up there?" Aries asked.

"Mostly street people, but they don't bother anybody," Karina said.

"Karina." Aries pinched the bridge of her nose.

"Sorry, I've only been this way once," Karina said as she started up the mound. "It's pretty dark up here, but light filters in from the manholes. Stay close, we'll be heading to an area that is just above the machine room on the second floor."

Aries eyed her sister.

"And don't worry, no one is over there," Karina said, "because half of the hallway collapsed there, too."

"Shit," Billie said.

"You never been this way either, Billie?" Mia asked.

"No, I always go straight down each level," Billie said.

"With all those runners?" Karina asked.

"Well, I never go cashless," Billie said.

"Billie," Mia said.

"I don't go that way all the time, but it's the easiest you know," Billie said.

"Okay, let's move out," Aries said.

Karina climbed up first followed by Aries, Mia, then Billie. The ground on the mound was so uneven that Mia had to look down to dodge trash or anything else that could cause scrapes or bruises.

"Ow!" Billie said.

"You okay?" Mia looked back.

"I'm fine," Billie said as she wiped her hand on her shirt.

Mia breathed a sigh of relief then crawled into the hole. It was nothing more than a crawl space. Though the smell of mildew and sour sewage was a little overwhelming. She looked up and could somewhat make out Karina out in front, but it was pretty dark, and her eyes hadn't adjusted yet. Crawling forward, Mia heard voices and saw shadows in the distance. Every once in a while, someone would light a cigarette, and she would see a face with deep shadows around the nose and eyes. Mia looked away.

Laughter radiated from her left and she looked and found a group of people but couldn't make out their faces. She crawled on as her hands landed in puddles of liquid and through dirt and cobwebs. Her knees waded through the puddles getting soaked through the fabric of her tights. She coughed as the dust tickled the back of her throat and nose. She wanted to wipe her face, but it was so dusty in there she was sure it would only make it worse.

"Wanna hit?" a man popped out of nowhere and Mia screamed.

His hot breath was so close she felt his presence. A hand jerked her back and pulled her into an embrace.

"You okay?" Aries asked.

"Y-yeah," Mia said as her heart raced. She would be glad when they got out of here.

"You guys okay?" Karina checked in on them.

"We're fine," Aries said.

"Okay, we don't have long, just a few more feet to the first manhole," Karina said.

Mia nodded as Billie crawled beside her. "Hang in there," Billie said.

When they reached their first manhole, Mia looked up at the dim light. She could barely make out anything it was so dark. The only bit of light came from the streetlight above, but Mia continued on, earning herself a few scrapes and cuts on the palms of her hands and knees.

"Guys, up ahead," Karina said.

Mia looked around Aries, she could see a bit of light coming from a square hole in the floor. Finally, Mia sighed. The group crossed the final four yards and made it to their next stop. Mia could see Karina's face dip into the hole and come back up.

"All clear," Karina said.

Karina and Aries went first, then Mia came up to the hole. She looked down. It was a small closed off tiled room that reeked of piss. Mia held back her head.

"It's okay," Aries said. "Jump down, the crate is stable."

Mia peeked her head over the edge again. It wasn't that far down and in the center of the opening was an old wooden crate. It looked sturdy enough and she had jumped down from higher. Mia drew her legs closer to her when she felt something crawl on her ankle. She ignored it, but then she felt something crawl on her neck. She ran her fingers through her hair to shake it out, then it bit her.

"Ow!" Mia shouted and lost her grip on the edge of the hole and fell through.

"Mia!" Billie shouted.

A blur of red flashed into Mia's vision and Mia shut her eyes as two strong arms stopped her descent.

"You okay?" Aries said as Mia opened her eyes.

"I-I'm fine," Mia said as Aries placed her on her feet. "T-thank you for catching me."

"Don't mention it." Aries smiled.

Billie hopped down next, "Damn it fucking stinks."

Mia looked back at Aries. Her arms were rock solid, she must really have an intense job. Though Mia wasn't sure she even asked. A hand rubbed her shoulder and Mia jumped.

"You good?" Billie asked.

"I-I'm good," Mia said as she rubbed her neck.

She was not a fan of spiders, but she'd been bit before, and it wasn't that big of a deal. She rubbed her neck and looked at Billie in the dim light. She looked so dusty. Mia attempted to wipe her knees, but it was pointless. The dirt had dyed her thick winter tights brown, and the stain would probably never come out. She would probably have to sew an entirely new pair.

Mia glanced around the room; it was small and rectangular shaped. There were skeletons of wooden frames where she was sure stales use to be and small boarded up holes in the middle of each of the stalls. Graffiti tags painted the walls of gangs and symbols she had never seen before. On the opposite side of the room was a door that hung sideways off the top hinge. Mia felt a rumble in the ground and yelped as she used the wall to brace herself.

"I-Is that a collapse?" Mia started to panic.

"No," Aries said. "It's the trains."

"So, my guess is that we ain't getting out of here through that door," Billie said.

Karina shyly looked away and stepped aside to reveal a thin piece of plywood that leaned against the side of the wall. Everyone walked over, then looked at Karina. She couldn't be serious. Aries removed the plywood with ease and sat it on the side next to the square hole. It looked like there use to be a grate here, this must have been a vent. Mia walked closer to it and already she felt the heat.

"This the machine room?" Aries asked her sister, and her sister nodded. The vent was about three feet around and it was pitch black.

"Is this safe?" Billie asked.

"Um," Karina said. "Well, it's really not that bad. It's a mini shoot actually. It goes down, well, you'll see."

Aries glared at her as Karina went first again. Mia winced as she looked down the thing. It looked menacing. Karina put her feet through first and hit something right away with a thud, then she inched down slowly.

"Come on, but be careful, okay," Karina said as she disappeared into the darkness.

Aries followed next, she too went feet first, then slowly bent down. "Karina!" Aries shouted.

"Sorry, I said don't be mad." Karina's voice echoed from the vent.

Mia looked at Billie. That didn't sound good, but what other choice did they have? Mia sighed and went next. Her heart pounded against her chest. What horrors awaited her now? She looked down the vent and didn't see much. It couldn't be that deep because it sounded like both Karina and Aries could stand on it without falling. Mia took a deep breath and went in, feet first.

Her right leg floated in the air until it reached something solid. Mia exhaled, moving her left leg next. This wasn't bad. She bent down slowly, feeling the heat on her legs and lower back. She was standing on a metal grate. There was a slight tinge of red below her feet, but she heard the low hum of machinery below. She pulled her head all the way down, to get out from under the vent. Aries helped her maintain her balance as she inched Mia forward out of the vent and into another room. Mia was in the clear when she stood up but was greeted by the fast-moving parts of some kind of machine. A metal arm rotated on gears just inches away from her face. Mia yelped as steam shot out from one of the pipes above her.

"Mia, you okay?" Billie called out.

"She's fine," Aries said. "Come on down."

Mia looked down to see through the grate, but she wished she hadn't. She was at least five stories from the ground, maybe more and standing on the flimsiest stairwell she had ever been on. Karina pulled her carefully out of the way so Billie could have room to get onto the small platform. There was a light rumble in the ground that shook the entire stairwell. Everyone grabbed the rail as everything rattled. Mia shut her eyes wishing she was anywhere but here as the train passed, but she didn't dare take her hand off the rail.

Aries peeked down the steep steps. "Where's the way out?" she asked her sister.

Karina looked down. "It's that door down there with the light, see."

Mia strained to see in the dim red light, from here it looked like a speck. How were they going to make it down there on these raggedy stairs? Not to mention, the train tracks.

"Okay," Aries said unfazed. "Everyone be careful."

"You can't be serious," Billie said.

"We don't have any other choice," Aries said.

"But it's so close to the tracks," Billie said.

"It'll be okay," Karina said, "but be careful."

Aries placed a hand on Mia's shoulder and Mia forced a smiled. Her stomach was doing flips. It wasn't like she was afraid of heights, but usually when she was roof jumping, she was landing on stable surfaces. Karina started down first. She grabbed the rusty rail and slowly started her descent. Aries motioned for Mia to go next, but Mia wanted to stay close to Billie and told Aries to go on. Aries went without a problem, as Mia looked over then stepped back.

"Shit, Mia." Billie looked over too.

"It's going to be okay," Mia tried to reassure herself. "It's going to be okay."

Mia took a deep breath and stepped onto the first stair. She tensed when her foot touched the metal, but nothing happened. She exhaled and nervously smiled as she tried to focus on Karina and Aries up ahead. She stepped onto the next one, and felt the stairs vibrate under Aries' weight and she paused but forced herself to take the next step. It was holding, and Mia smiled and looked back at Billie and gave her the thumbs up. *Okay Mia, you can do this,* Mia focused on each step.

She tried not to look down, but they were so far up, and the creaking stairs eroded her confidence. Seriously, these steps looked like they could collapse at any moment. She watched Aries walk with ease and tried to tell herself everything was going to be okay. Mia stepped onto the next step, and it creaked. The noise made her jump, but she continued on and put her foot on the next step and the metal screeched as her foot dipped suddenly. Mia screamed as part of the stair started to bend, which caused Mia to slip forward.

"There's too much weight!" Aries shouted.

She was going to fall. She was going to die here. Panic ripped through Mia's body as her heart beat heavy in her chest. Then a strong hand yanked her back by the arm, onto the platform.

"I got you." Billie wrapped her arms around her.

"Is everyone okay?" Aries shouted from below.

"F-Fine," Billie said. "You guys go on."

"Okay...." Aries hesitated, "but we'll wait for you on the next platform."

Mia trembled in Billie's arms. She wasn't getting back on that thing, but Billie started to release her embrace.

"Wait, wait, wait." Mia reached out and grabbed Billie's sleeve.

"I'm not going to leave you," Billie said before she checked on the others below.

Mia slumped to her knees. This was a mistake, but then a hand found its way to her shoulder.

"We can do this," Billie said.

"Okay!" Aries shouted. "It's clear!"

"Come on," Billie said. "It'll hold our weight." Mia shook her head, but Billie rubbed her shoulder. "It will, we just need to go slow."

Mia didn't like this, this was too much. Mia looked up and Billie smiled softly at her. Billie reached down to help Mia up. Billie was so brave to her. She must look so embarrassing right now, but it was hard for her to gather up her emotions, with so many terrible things happening back-to-back. Mia trembled as Billie took her hand.

"Hey, remember what Lady Valkyrie use to say," Billie said. "A girl must always be quick on her feet, so that she can get out of any situation. Lady Valkyrie didn't spend all that time teaching us parkour for us to be afraid of some stank ass stairs. This is nothing, we've been through worse. Come on."

Billie pulled Mia's hand and took the first step, and the stairs screeched. Mia yelped, but Billie's grip was strong, even if Billie's hands were shaky as well.

"Okay," Mia said after taking a deep breath. Billie was right, she could do this. She took her first step, then another and then another.

"Good job, keep at it," Billie said as she led.

Mia followed carefully as puffs of hot steam blasted from the pipes above her. She kept taking it step by step, trying to focus on reaching the ground as the stairs groaned under their weight. The ground shook as a train passed. Its lights lit the entire tunnel, exposing the black soot-stained bricks and the extensive body of the caged machinery. Mia shrieked as the stairwell rocked and held onto the wobbly rail. She was so close to pissing herself, but Billie never let go of her hand.

"It's okay, we're almost there," Billie said.

Mia shut her eyes but continued to let Billie lead. She kept them closed through the entire thing until she made it to the platform Aries and Karina stood on.

"Great job," Aries said. "The rest of the way looks pretty stable."

Mia trembled but nodded and they continued down the stairwell and made it to the door. The tunnel started to shake again. Another train approaching and the fact that the tracks were so close freaked her out. Aries went for the doorknob and opened it, she held her hand out, then waved everyone along. They were in a dimly lit brick tunnel. It smelled musty and the smell of sewage was stronger. Mia made a face, even Billie looked uncomfortable. Aries and Karina looked at each other.

"We're near Central," Karina said.

"Great," Billie said, "That's not far from the main stairs, we can get to Gomi City from there."

"Wait," Mia said. "Do we have to go through the city?"

"Pretty much," Billie said.

"There's not another way? Aries asked. "Someplace more discrete?"

"I'm afraid not," Billie said, "Unless you wanna walk the perimeter of the wall."

Karina shook her head wildly. "That'll take forever."

"It doesn't matter. Runners are looking for us, we need to be discrete," Aries said.

"Don't worry about it," Billie said.

"Why?" Aries said.

"Gas mask," Billie said. "Everyone in the city wears gas mask and they're super easy to get."

"I barely have any cash on me," Aries said.

"It's okay," Billie said as she reached into her bra and pulled out cash. "Emergency funds and don't worry they're super cheap, I swear, and if this is Central, I know a shop that sells 'em for cheap."

Aries thought for a second. "Okay, let's head to Central and get the gas mask. I'd feel better if we had something to cover our faces."

"What about your hair?" Mia said, pointing to Aries long red braids and Karina's big puff balls.

"I'll take care of it," Aries said.

Aries wrapped her long red hair up in a low bun, then she walked ahead to a broken pipe that dripped water. She bent down to sniff it, then nodded. Karina walked over and her sister wet her hands and pulled the two puff balls out from their ties and detangled her hair enough to braid two large braids on each side of her head. When she was done, Karina reached into her bag and grabbed two cloth scarfs.

Billie looked impressed. "Ya'll came prepared."

Karina handed one to her sister. "It's for spider nests. They breed all year round down here cause it's warm."

Mia recoiled, as Billie's lips turned up into a sour smile.

"Right," Billie said.

"Let's keep moving," Aries said.

Karina led the way to Central, but Mia still had no idea where they were. They left the tracks and walked down a tunnel that led out into a path with more people on it, most of which wore mask and coveralls. Mia spotted a few runners, but she did her best to keep her head down. Laughter and shouts made her jump as she tried not to look around frantically. She wished her nerves would let her be, because she normally wasn't like this. Then again, on a normal day her life wasn't in this much danger. Sure, people got handsy from time to time, but as far as she was concerned, they were playing in her domain, so she always knew how to find an out. Down here, she felt completely lost.

"How you holding up?" Aries whispered, as she slowed to walk next to her.

Mia flinched away from a group of people walking next to her. "I'm okay. Where are we?"

"Third floor, right above Central."

"Only the third?" Mia asked.

Aries nodded. "It won't take long to get to Gomi. The distance between floors is short."

Mia nodded. She felt too keenly aware of people. She usually didn't mind crowds, but things were different when you had a target on your back. "I forgot to ask, but what do you do for a living?" Mia tried to make small talk to calm her nerves.

"My family and I are pickers. We work at the recycling plant," Aries said.

"Oh yeah, I heard a lot of people work in the plant," Mia said.

"Yup, but it's not a huge operation like the mines. Mainly we sort out the metal and send the rest to the incinerator," Aries said.

"You're burning down here, too? That can't be good for your lungs," Mia said, but Aries only shrugged.

"Not much anyone can do about it. No one can move up, because surface landlords don't rent to sewer folks like talkin' about it," Aries said.

"W-why not?" Mia asked.

"They claim it's because we're basically glorified squatters, even though we have homes, but it's really the gangs. They don't wanna mince business down here. Debt is how most people get trapped here. The gangs demand so much to live in the sewers, who can save even if they wanted to move? And if by some glorious chance you manage to save up enough to move up, if the runners catch wind of it, they just shake you up. They need the bodies down here, so leaving is almost impossible," Aries said bitterly.

"That sucks," Mia said. "To be fair, I live at my job. There's no way I could afford a place in the city, when most apartments are shared by one or two families."

Aries looked at her with a bit of surprise. "Wow, I thought it would be better up top. I mean, a little better at least."

Mia smiled. "You and I both, but really, it's only good for the folks in Uptown."

"I see." Aries nodded, but it was the lingering gentleness in her eyes that helped calm Mia. She hoped her family could make it out of here one day.

Mia heard creaking above her and spotted a line of rats walking over the pipes and shrieked away. She was used to rats, but somehow any creepy crawlies down here seemed, dirtier and more frightening. Maybe it was the lack of skylight and fresh air that was getting to her. She knew the folks down here were good people, it just sucked that they were forced to live here. This was a terrible place to live, even if people did what they could to make it better.

"Um, so this Acome spirit, are there any more spirits like them?" Mia asked.

"Oh yes!" Karina said from the front.

Billie turned to Karina. “Where their asses at? And why they ain’t doing anything about this?”

“It’s not that simple,” Karina said. “Spirits work in strange and mysterious ways. I read in the old books that the world is full of them, but Acome happens to be one of the strongest, so it’s not likely that many of the smaller ones can do much to help.”

Billie rolled back her neck. “And we are the better option?”

Mia had to agree. She didn’t know any magic and nor did she want to learn.

“We’re not alone,” Aries said. “We do have help. The Rat King is on our side.”

Karina smiled and nodded. “Yes! He is and he is the one who gifted Aries and I our power.”

Mia perked up. “You have magic powers?”

Karina grimaced. “N-no, not really.”

Aries chuckled. “No magic powers, but we have been trained to fight like hell if we need to. Fate is guiding us.”

“I see,” Mia said. “I just wish we could call on some other powerful spirit to help.”

Karina nodded. “I know what you mean, but most super powerful spirits are bound to their domains. Like for example the Moonbay Mountain Spirit is bound to her mountain range farther north and the Great River Spirit Megami Ua is bound to her river farther west. I’ve read that they’re super strong, but they can’t move.”

“Bummer,” Billie said.

“We can still help,” Aries said. “We just need to stay the course.”

Mia touched the ring on her finger. There was so much about her world she didn’t know it was making her head spin. It was probably best to focus on one thing at a time, but she would be glad when she got out of here.

They arrived at Central, which was a hub of activity. It was much busier on this side compared to where they left. People flooded in from everywhere. Billie waved them on and pointed to a few vendors that had set up shop along the road to the main city. Mia was surprised to see so many surface people down here. She guessed Billie was right when she said the city was popping at night. Billie led them to a vendor, whose shop was nothing more than a metal cart on wheels. It looked like he sold a variety of gas mask, mouth mask, and goggles.

“Four fulls, please.” Billie put on her best smile with her money out.

The short man eyed the girls, then grinned. “Heading down to party, I see?”

“Yes sir, girls like us can’t be contained.” Billie leaned in, working him with her eyes.

The man grinned exposing his yellowed teeth. "For a kiss I'll throw one in for free?"

Billie leaned in closer and stopped just inches away from the man's face. "I'll give it some tongue if you make it two?"

The man visibly shivered then puckered up. Billie smirked, leaned in, and tongue kissed him like she was trying to suck his soul from his body. The man completely fell into the kiss and when Billie pulled back the man jumped with excitement.

"Take your pick!" the man said with glee.

Billie smiled as she tucked the money in his shirt collar, then picked up four dark green full-face gas mask with two filter chambers on each side. "Thanks, hun."

They left and Mia caught Aries looking back over her shoulder. "You do that all the time?"

Billie chuckled. "If it works. I'm a working girl, I don't waste my money on what I can get for free."

Both Aries and Karina looked at each other and Mia laughed. This was sometimes people's reaction to sex workers, but Billie was right. Anything that can be worked with your body was much cheaper than spending a night's wage. Money just wasn't flowing like that, even at a big brothel like Valkyrie House.

The group gathered in a nook just before the entrance to one of the main ramps leading down to the city. Mia held her gas mask in her hand. It looked a little silly to be wearing this, but then she noticed other people were wearing them up here, too. Billie put on hers; the fit looked tight, displacing her dark purple braids. Mia could barely see her face because the eye shield was tented so dark. It made her look other worldly.

Mia groaned at the idea of wearing hers. She hoped she could breathe in it. She opened the straps and placed the mask on her head. It smelled of cheap rubber and moth balls, but she could handle it. Aries came around behind her to help her tighten the straps.

Aries tugged on the back of the mask and Mia winced. "You okay?"

"Y-yeah," Mia said, then Aries started adjusting her straps again.

"Let me know if it's too tight, but it's important that it is properly fitted." Aries worked quick, but gently. It hurt a little, but the more she adjusted it, the better the air flow seemed. "How's that?"

Mia gave a thumbs up. Her breath felt hot on her nose as she breathed the air that was somehow fresher than out in the sewers. Mia turned around and looked through the tunnel vision windows of her mask. Something reached out and grabbed her hand and Mia jumped. She turned her head to see a blur of purple.

"Billie," Mia said.

"My bad." Billie's voice sounded muffled.

Mia sighed as Aries stepped into her line of sight and gave her a comforting pat on the shoulder. She could barely see out of her mask. She would have to turn her head completely around to see anyone beside her. She was not going to like this, but what other choice did she have? Billie waved them on, and the group started their descent.

Walking down five flights of several different types of stairs was actually the easy part. The further they went, the more the city came alive, and Mia wasn't alone in her choice to wear a gas mask, virtually everyone had one in the city. She was also surprised to see how much it looked like a normal city, granted with different materials, but there were shops and people rolling by on motorbikes. Gas lamps hung on street poles, illuminating the dirt road and store fronts. Most of the city barely rose above the third floor, but the ceiling stretched as high as the sky. There was probably dozens and dozens of blocks of buildings made from train carts and bricks and stones.

People gathered outside of bars and stands drunk or high on drugs and flooded into the streets, no different than back home, but there were a lot of people. Mia flinched when anyone bumped into her because it was impossible to see, and to say it was making her nervous was an understatement. They were so packed tight that there was no place to breathe and as a marked woman, it made things even worse.

Aries and Karina stuck close, with Aries holding on tight to her sister. Billie held Mia's hand as she led them deeper into the city, where the music pulsated so loud Mia felt it beneath her feet. People shouted and danced, and they weren't even in the clubs yet. Billie pulled harder on Mia's hand and turned back and looked at Mia. Billie made eye contact with her and Mia was all too familiar with that look. It was about to get wild.

Through her limited view, Mia saw Billie get Aries and Karina's attention. She pointed further into the crowd, then pointed up to one of the many large circular storm drains protruding through the stone wall. Mia looked up, they needed to get to the one straight ahead. Aries nodded and pulled her sister close. Billie tugged on Mia's hand twice, which was their signal. It was time to go.

Billie pulled her fast into the dense crowd that overflowed from the many clubs and bars on this block of the city. The buildings looked monstrous here, made from crudely welded train carts, and a hodgepodge mix of scrap metal and concrete that towered above them. The crowd danced in waves that threatened to tear the group apart. It was so loud she felt the bass in her chest, and she wondered how such a sound could be produced. Light strobed against the lens of her gas mask, creating a glare that blocked her from seeing. She held onto Billie tighter as she stumbled over debris.

The music picked up and morphed into something utterly chaotic. A clash of metal and electronic sound she had never heard before, throbbed in her ears as the crowd transformed into one solid beast. Bodies ebbed and pounded against one another like arms and legs tangled together in an orgy. The music raged with such bass filled lows and intense highs that it sounded like the last breath of a dying machine.

Mia gasped for air. Her mask fogged around the edges as sweaty bodies knocked into her, testing the grip between her and Billie. Gropey hands found their way to her breast and butt, and she could do nothing about it.

Fog settled on the crowd from the steamy sewer vents below, casting once clear figures into shadows. Mia breathed hard as her eyes were torn every which a way in a sea of black and gray casted by the strobe light. Mia stumbled as she reached up to wipe her foggy lens and saw a shadow that fixed its gaze on her. A shadow that seemed to draw closer in each cycle of the strobe.

Her breath hitched as she blinked and scanned the streets. The party continued, but the shadow was gone. She blinked again as her breath rattled in her ears and the shadow was back only closer. Mia tugged on Billie's hand, hauling her to a stop and Billie looked back, but Mia couldn't read her face through the dense fog. Mia looked behind her, fear gripping her chest. Her heart raced, as the strobe casted black, then white and then the shadow was upon her, inches away from her face. It towered over her like a steel trap.

Mia kicked to get away, losing her grip on Billie's hand. She tripped and all the bodies enclosed around her. They sucked her down like water in a drain and Mia swirled out of control as the light skittered away. She gasped and screamed and reached for anything or anyone. She yanked at clothes, but they only tore away, as she sunk deeper. It was over for her. She was going to be crushed beneath the feet of a hundred people like a spider. Mia clawed helplessly at the air when a hand grabbed her right arm and pulled her up.

Mia yelped at the pain that shot through her injured arm and looked through her foggy gas mask and saw a flash of red. Mia gasped at Aries' deep red eyes glowing an unnatural red through her mask. A tingled flowed up Mia's arm that felt like a bucket of fresh water. Mia leaned into the sensation that seemed to scream *I am here for you. I will always protect you.* Mia gripped Aries' hand tighter as she led the way.

They made it to the other side of the crowd and Mia collapsed as Billie and Karina circled around her.

"Mia! You okay?" Billie asked and all Mia could do was nod.

Mia reached for her gas mask, she wanted to take it off, but a hand stopped her. Mia looked up to see Aries holding her hand.

"Not yet, okay," Aries said, then helped Mia to her feet. "Just a little longer, okay?"

Mia was shaking from exhaustion or fear or both, but in Aries' arms she felt that same safe feeling she had experienced in the crowd. Mia nodded again.

Billie pointed to the storm pipe and lead that way, with Karina not far behind her. Mia groaned but took a look back at the crowd. Usually, big crowds were nothing for her, but her mind had never played tricks like that on her. Was there really something there? Did she even want to know the answer to that question? She could feel the warm metal of the ring on her finger and wished so badly she could be done with all of this.

The group walked towards the storm pipe where there were less people. Mia looked back behind her again, but only her shadow followed. They reached a metal ladder that went three flights up and started their ascent. When they reached the top, they all took off their gas mask and threw them to the ground.

"Fuck that was intense," Billie said as she wiped the sweat from her forehead.

"And this is why I don't like coming into the city at night," Aries said.

"I see what you mean now," Karina said out of breath. "How can anyone dance in all that?"

Mia panted as she tried to catch her breath and stood as she wiped the sweat from her forehead. "And you like this, Billie?"

"It's more fun when you're half naked and high and not on a mission to free a magical spirit," Billie said with a grin.

A shaky smiled appeared on Mia's face. "And what kind of music was that? I've never heard an instrument do that."

"It's called glitch," Billie said. "It's all the rage, it combines electricity and sound. I kind of like it." Mia and everyone looked at each other, but Billie didn't seem embarrassed at all. "We're not far now. We just gotta head down this storm pipe and take the third manhole up."

"Alright, let's go," Aries said.

The group moved together and Aries walked next to Mia. Mia flashed her a smile and was surprised to find Aries looking back at her. Mia quickly looked away as she tried to ignore the flutter in her heart. She wondered what would happen when they finished this? What kind of world would they live in? The things Acome showed her were so unbelievable that it seemed more like visions of the afterlife than the real world.

All her life she had either grew up hungry and poor or living barely above being thrown out on the street. That was still true even in her current position. Sex work paid more on the streets, but without the safety of a brothel it was dangerous. Not that she was complaining about all the things Lady Valkyrie did for her, she just couldn't see the world Karina and Aries were brought up to imagine. Especially given what she knew about the rest of the continent. All the foreigners she came to know, whether they were from the northwestern nation of May-Liliya, Markios or the southern nation of Augtus, said basically the same thing: life was hard. How could anything they did here make a difference? How could a little coastal nation like Julilie change the world? Mia stumbled and tilted forward, she flailed, but a hand caught her.

"You okay?" Aries asked.

"Y-yea, feet hurt, sorry," Mia said, and Aries nodded with a smile.

"Don't mention it, it's really uneven down here," Aries said.

Mia smiled back and watched Aries out of the corner of her eye. She and her sister lived in this miserable sewer picking through trash all day, and if there was a chance that they could live up top in clean air then maybe it was worth all the trouble. They seemed like really nice girls to her. It wasn't fair they didn't get a chance to move. The ring pulsed on Mia's left ring finger as if it agreed and that made Mia smile. She reached over to touch it. It felt warmer, more like a body. So warm she felt the warmth radiating up her arm and into her chest. *Acome,* she uttered as the waves of heat made her heart flutter, *you want this too, don't you*? The ring pulsed again, and Mia balled her fingers into a fist. She did not understand this one bit. It actually shocked her that she was out here at all, but for Aries and Karina and people like her it was worth it to help, even if she wasn't a full believer like them.

"How did you find out about this path?" Aries asked Billie.

"From the other girls at the brothel," Billie said. "They said I could make a lot of money up top."

Karina walked next to her. "And they just let you in? I mean, they just let you go, you know, up top?"

"Pretty much," Billie said. "I think they really only focus on people jumping the wall, but all the runners and workers go this way, and no one says a word. Trust me, those people up top ain't shit. half of them are on drugs anyways. And besides pussy is pussy, people will always open the door for that."

Karina nodded. "S-so you like your job? A-as a sex worker?"

Billie shrugged. "It pays the bills and for me it's easy work."

"I see," Karina said. "Why did you pick it over something more traditional? I've always thought about being a shop clerk, especially at a book shop."

"I wouldn't say I picked it," Billie said. "When I turned eighteen, I got into a little trouble playing dice and realized I could fuck my way out of a lot of my problems. So, I worked the streets a lot before my Madam, Lady Valkyrie, found me and offered me a job at her brothel."

Aries eyed Billie. "And you are a slave there?"

"A slave? Hell no," Billie chuckled. "She's not like that, I'm free to come and go as I please as long as I don't ditch my clients. Speaking of which, Terese and the others are going to be pissed."

Mia laughed. "You are so right."

Aries smiled, too. "What about you, Mia? Why have you chosen to go into sex work?"

Mia scratched the side of her head. "I don't think I really choose it either. I didn't grow up with a home, my parents abandoned me to an orphanage when I was a child. When I turned fifteen, I ran away. I was mostly a pick pocket, then one day I think when I was nineteen or something, a gang approached me with an offer to do sex work for them. I didn't know much about pimps and stuff like that, so I thought it was a good deal at the time, but then Lady Valkyrie appeared with a better deal. She offered me a job, but also a place to stay. She treats us as if we are her daughters."

Karina beamed. "That's really nice. I'm glad you both were able to find a safe place to live."

Billie grinned. "Who you telling and I cannot wait to get back to my Sara. My heart has had enough adventure for one day."

"Is she your girl?" Aries asked.

"Yup, I know she's going to do great things one day," Billie said. "You see, she's a great dancer, she knows how to tell stories with her movements and stuff. I think she could make it up there, in Uptown."

Aries smiled. "I hope she does."

Billie beamed as Mia zoned out of the conversation. Billie was right. This was enough adventure to fill a lifetime. She was so ready to go home. The group passed a few people in the storm drain but not many. Billie said that it only got packed at the start and end of the night, so they were pretty much safe for now. Their biggest threat would be dodging runners. They were sure they would be looking for them up there. So, they kept walking until they were the only people in the storm drain. It was peaceful, but it was also painfully quiet. They were too far away from the city to hear or feel the thud of music, but Mia was sure they should be hearing something. Mia looked over at Aries and Billie. They seemed fine. Even Karina didn't seem to worry.

"Huh," Aries stopped. She looked as though she was listening to her rat. "What did you say?"

"Um," Billie said. "Who are you talking too?"

"I'm not sure," Aries said. "Tink said—" But before Aries could finish her sentence, she was cut off by Karina's screams.

"Ew! Ew! Ew! Spiders!"

Aries sighed. "Karina, it's just spiders."

"I know, but it's a lot of them!" Karina said as she swatted at them in the dark.

Billie chuckled, then her expression changed. "What the?" Mia turned around and Billie was swatting at something ,too. "Where the fuck are all these spiders coming from?" Billie flung one after another off her. "Ow! Ow!" Billie screamed. "What the fuck!"

Mia rushed to her best friend, but then she looked down the tunnel. Hundreds of spiders with eyes that glowed orange stormed towards them. Mia gasped as she stumbled over her feet and fell to the ground. She looked at the ceiling and they were crawling above her, too. Mia screamed as they scaled down the walls right towards them.

"Run!" Aries yelled.

Aries helped Mia up and the girls ran down the storm drain. Their footsteps echoed down the pipe when they finally reached the end where the manholes were.

"Wait a minute." Billie looked up. "They're all—they're all closed!"

"What?" Aries gasped as she ran to a bar ladder and rushed up. She banged on the top and tried to push it open, but it wouldn't budge.

Mia gasped. "What? Is there another way out?"

Billie looked down the storm drain, "I-I don't know, but come on."

The group ran down the storm drain, but there was nothing for yards. Mia tried not to panic as she stumbled down the tunnels. She looked over her shoulders and could see the faint glow of hundreds of beady orange eyes crawling after them.

"Guys!" Aries shouted. "What about here?" Aries pointed to a connecting pipe large enough for people to go down. "Where does this lead?"

"I'm not sure," Billie said, "but we'll figure it out later."

They rushed to the pipe and started down the slow incline one by one. It was pitch black inside, but it would seem the spiders hadn't caught up with them yet. The deeper they went the quieter it got. Only the sounds of their panting echoed around them. They continued and didn't stop until they felt a low rumble coming from behind them.

"Guys!" Aries said. "Guys! Stop! Do you feel that?"

Mia looked around in the darkness. She could feel something coming.

"What is that? A train?" Billie said.

The rumble got stronger followed by an intense rushing sound. Mia nearly lost her footing and used her hand to keep herself upright. The rushing sound intensified and was replaced with something more familiar, and much more dangerous.

"Water!" Aries screamed.

The group ran as fast as they could down the pitch-black drainpipe. Mia ran on the balls of her feet to keep up. The water crashed like angry waves on the backs of their heels. Mia could smell it, and she screamed as her lungs burned. It caught them and sucked them up like a vacuum, so violently and powerfully, that it threw them around like rags in a wash bucket. The water spit them out onto a sewer pit that quickly flooded with water. Mia hit the water, and everything sounded muffled as she kicked up to the surface. She gasped for air, but she had no control over her body in the fast current of the water.

"Mia!" someone screamed her name.

The tunnel was barely lit, and her eyes burned from the sewage. Mia's head dipped under the surface, and she kicked to keep herself above water. When she resurfaced, she saw Billie in a glimmer of light that poured in from above. Mia smiled with relief and swam towards her, but her smile quickly faded, when Billie's head dipped below the surface.

"Billie!" Mia reached out. Billie resurfaced. Her screams filled the tunnel. "Billie, I'm coming!" Mia kicked her tired legs towards her, but another hand grabbed her first.

"We gotta go," shouted Aries in a hoarse voice as she pulled Mia away.

"N-no! Billie! Billie!" Mia screamed over the gasp and sputters of her friend. The current was too strong and yanked them backwards. Mia thrashed over the waves until she saw Billie's head disappear. "Billie! Billie!"

The water carried them backwards, but Aries did not let go. She pulled Mia into the darkness as Mia screamed for her best friend.

30
Karina

Droplets of water dripped on metal around Karina. She stirred, but her body felt too heavy to move. The pitter patter of feet and squeaks echoed through her mind like the muffled sound of talking interrupting a dream. Something nipped at her hair and clothes. Karina groaned as she shook her head to and fro. The nipping stopped but started up again. Karina laid her head to her right as the sound of squeaking began to get louder and louder. Water dripped around her, splashing on her cheeks and arms, but then she felt something warm on her nose. Something soft, that licked her. She used her hand to swat it away, but the message was not received so she wiggled her nose instead.

What was that? A question appeared in her mind and with it she slowly opened her eyes. It was dark but she could see red light coming from somewhere. Something squeaked close to her face, a shadow, then the figure came into focus and not just one figure, but dozens.

"R-rats?" Karina uttered as the animals jumped back. There were so many around her. Then she saw a familiar face. "T-Tink?" Her voice was so soft and weak, but her friend danced around regardless.

Karina tried to move her body, but a sharp pain shot up her back. Everything was sore, but she could feel her arms and legs so that was a start. She slowly stretched, despite the pain, and felt the need to get up. She moved one leg and the rats around her backed up. She shifted her weight until she was completely on her back, her eyes shut tight in an effort to stop the throbbing in her head. What happened? She could barely remember. Then the image of orange eyes shot out from the recesses of her mind. Karina screamed and shot up, then cried out from the sudden movement. She swiped her hands up and down her arms and legs, but there were no spiders, but it looked like she scared her new friends. At least two dozen rats stared back at her cautiously.

"Well, hello," she said softly. Tink ran into her lap and placed his paws on her stomach.

She lifted her arms slowly to pet him and he curled up into a little ball. She smiled, then she remembered that she had been running with her sister and her new friends. She looked around and there was nothing but damp metal grates. How on Earth did she wind up here? She looked up. The storm drain was so high, surely a fall like that should have killed her. Then she realized where she was. She was in an overflow channel. She couldn't stay here, this area was bound to flood again. She looked up and saw a few manholes, but where was everyone else? Should they not have washed up here, too? Maybe they washed up elsewhere. Regardless, they could not have gone far.

She looked down at Tink and moved her hands. He looked at her, got up, and ran down her legs, back onto the grate. It looked like he was ready to go, too, so Karina reached to her side for her knapsack and didn't feel it. She was caring her spell books when they started. She had written all her favorite summoning keys down, along with her notes on Ratalia history. She looked around everywhere but didn't see her knapsack. Where could it be? Did it get lost in the flood?

As if it were a six sense, she saw a shadow move in the distance. She squinted, then started to move her achy legs into a standing position. She looked ahead towards a drain low to the floor and saw about ten rats or so dragging what looked like her knapsack. Karina limped over to them and bent down.

"Oh my gosh, where did you guys find this?" Karina clasped her hands together as she inspected the soggy mess.

"It took a great amount of time indeed," a voice said.

Karina froze and looked around. There was no one here but her and the rats. "Who said that?" Karina asked.

"I said that." The voice was closer now, as if it were right next to her.

Karina looked down and saw Tink standing on his hind legs. "T-Tink?"

The rat nodded and Karina gasped as she clasped her hands to her mouth. She could hear him now, just like her sister. She started hyperventilating. Only members of her clan that had a strong connection to Acome could commune with rats.

"I can't believe this is happening!" Karina said. "D-does this mean I have become stronger?"

Tink only tilted his head and twitched his whiskers.

"Wait! I think I understand. We must be close to Acome, that's why I've been feeling so weird. Their power, it must be making me stronger!" Karina was so excited. She wondered what else she could do. She rushed to open her knapsack and grab her books only to feel it squish in her hands. "Oh no! Oh no!" She panicked.

She pulled out her books and everything was completely soaked, every book, every page. She tried to open one, but the pages melted away. All the ink melted to the bottom of the pages into a black goopy mess. It was completely unreadable.

"Oh no! Oh no!" she wailed. "My summoning keys!"

She picked up her knapsack and cried out again. Every one of her summoning keys she had spent years tirelessly gathering were gone. Summoning keys that weren't even in her grandmother's books, some from relatives long past, from books long lost. All were lost. She squeezed the knapsack tight, then pushed it away from herself. Maybe she could still save some, maybe they could be dried. She reached in and pulled out another book, but the pages felt like slime. She cried again. Cheap paper was not meant to last, but she'd always been careful to never let them get wet. Tears ran down her cheeks like the dripping sewage that oozed from the drainpipes around her, taking all the dirt and sweat with it. How could she have let this happen?

"Too sad, why cry?"

"H-huh?" she said between sniffles.

"Too sad, why cry?" Tink asked again.

"Tink, I lost my summoning keys." She wiped her snotty nose with her damp arm. "I lost everything."

Tink lowered his head. If she wasn't so sad, she might have enjoyed the simple fact that she could talk to her best friend, but now she was utterly useless. She'd couldn't cast keys without her summoning books that had all the translations for the keys. She didn't even know if she could cast keys at all, even if she knew the words, and worst of all, she was alone.

"Oh ,Tink, what am I going to do? I don't know where anyone is or where I even am. I'm completely lost." Karina buried her head in her hands.

"Up low, where the clean people go."

"W-what?" Karina said. Tink pointed at the storm drain in front of her. "D-do you know where we are, Tink?"

Tink nodded, coming from behind him a dozen rats gathered. That's right, Tink was a rat, and he could ask the others where they were and how to get out.

"Tink, have you seen my sister or Mia or Billie?" Karina asked.

Tink lowered his head and Karina groaned. What was she going to do now? She wasn't the Darkness or the Crimson Mouse. She felt like a tag along. And worse off, she didn't have a single special quality. She slumped.

"What am I going to do?" She felt the tears coming again.

Tink lowered his head again and placed a paw on Karina's leg. He was so sweet, but somehow it felt like everything was lost. She had been preparing for this moment all her life and now it was completely hopeless.

"Damn it, Karina," she said in between sobs. "Pull it together."

She balled her fist. There had to be another way, a reason why she was still alive, a reason why she was now able to understand Tink. When Aries was chosen to be the Darkness, shortly after, Granny appeared to her, and she was able to understand Tink. This must be some kind of sign. Karina looked down at her hands. Maybe she didn't need her summoning books, after all she use to spend hours writing them on her arms and legs when she didn't have paper. So, she knew a few by heart. Maybe she was stronger now, maybe this was her sign that the Darkness had called her, too. She had to try.

She cupped her hands together and thought of the most basic summoning key she knew, a light key. With shaky hands she closed her eyes and whispered the key into her palms. She waited, then shut her eyes even tighter and waited some more. How was casting supposed to feel? She had no idea, but it was worth a try. She opened her eyes and to her disappointment there were only her dirty hands. She let her hands fall by her side.

"Oh well, Tink, I tried." Karina looked down at him through watery eyes.

"Try, good try."

"Thanks," Karina sniffled.

"Try more?"

"Huh? Oh no, Tink, I'm not a caster." Karina wiped her face. "But I am done crying. I think I'm going to find my sister and the others." Karina stood and Tink ran around her feet like he always did. She didn't know where to start, but there had to be something familiar she could use as a landmark. "Tink, do you or any of your friends know a way out? A way to other people perhaps?"

Tink stood on his hind legs, then turned to the other rats. They chatted amongst themselves, then one thin brown rat scurried to a storm drain a few feet away. Then scurried back.

"People."

"People Tink?" Karina asked.

Tink nodded. It wasn't the news she wanted, but it was a start. She knew of a few paths near the storm drains around Sewer City, if she could make it back, she could probably retrace her steps, and maybe her sister and the others were already looking for her. Karina stood and started to walk away but stopped. She looked back at her soggy knapsack. Those books were her entire world. Karina felt so horrible about leaving them there to rot.

"I-I'm sorry." A tear ran down her face as she adjusted her damp clothes best she could. "Tink, lead the way."

Tink nodded. He turned to his friends, and they chattered, then the thin brown rat scurried to the drainpipe. Tink looked back and Karina nodded. She walked over and bent down, the drainpipe was small, just wide enough to crawl through.

"Here?" she asked and Tink nodded. "Okay."

If there ever was a creature to trust in a sewer, than surely it must be a rat. She got down and looked inside, it was pitch black, but she was sure Tink would not lead her astray. She crawled in on her hands and knees, the pipe was still damp from the flood water. So much for staying dry. Karina sighed, then crawled on all fours as she followed Tink's squeaks. Straight here, wet there, Tink chatted to her the entire way.

She crawled for a long while until she saw a dim light. She squinted, it wasn't bright like the surface, but it did smell strongly of sewage. Tink and his friends made it to the rim and stood on their hind legs when she got closer. They looked out and it was another grated platform. Looking down, she saw a wide river of dark water, above she saw drainpipes midway from the floor to the seemingly endless ceiling, but the oddest thing was the large, sealed flood door. Why was it placed here? There was a grate for people to walk on presumably, which wouldn't be necessary if this were a place designed to capture flood waters. Not to mention, that this door had weird looking locks—and she knew her locks when it came to flood gates. Karina gazed up again.

"Wow, that's high."

"People, up up up."

Karina looked up. There was a bar ladder on the wall next to her. It stretched far up into the darkness. "Yikes," Karina said as she stood.

This looked even higher than the stairs in the train tunnels. Both Tink and his friends climbed up Karina's pantleg and unto her shoulder. She nodded. Up it was, she said to herself as she walked towards the ladder. She placed one hand on the metal bar. It was cold, but sturdy. The grip was worn but looked pretty safe to climb. She rolled up her sleeves and started her ascent, step by step.

"I wonder how high this goes up?" She looked at Tink, who also seemed to be staring into the abyss.

Karina continued to climb. This was a lot higher up than she thought and the further she climbed the darker it got. Her eyes adjusted slowly, but all the light flooded in from below. What an odd cylindrical tunnel, like most tunnels in the sewers it seemed to be constructed with no efficiency in mind. This one especially seemed too big for its intended purpose. Why would anyone need a vertical tunnel this big to move water? But Karina continued on.

She controlled her breathing the further she ascended. She must be at least ten stories up by now, which seemed impossible in an eight-level sewer. The light below looked faded now. Karina reached for the next step when the bar below her collapsed beneath her feet.

She screamed as she dropped, but her hand managed to grab hold of a bar. Her arms popped, sending pain up her shoulders as she stopped her fall. Tink and his friends squeaked in terror as her heart thudded in her chest. Her arms shook, but she froze to control her breathing. The pain in her arm was intense, but she felt her fingers starting to slip.

"Oh no, oh no." Karina pulled up her legs to the next step up.

Her shoe slipped on the moist bars, but she finally worked her foot in to it enough to get a better grip. She hung there in silence, even the rats stopped squeaking. She didn't want to look down or up. This was so stupid. She should have been more cautious, but the fear of falling didn't allow her to properly reflect on that. So, she slowly removed one of her callused hands to the next bar. Both Tink and his friends watched, closing their eyes when she made contact with the bar. She held her breath and tugged. *Sturdy*, her brain registered.

"Okay," she whispered to herself. "You can do this."

She moved her body up slowly. *Sturdy,* she pulled herself up. Her mind had still not forgotten what happened a moment before, so fear still gripped her heart, but she didn't want to be stuck up here either. Her hand reached out for another bar, *sturdy,* she breathed a sigh of relief. *Almost there,* she continued until she heard the sounds of rat chatter. She looked to her left and right, then up. There was chatter coming from what looked like another drainpipe next to the bar ladder.

"Friends!" Tink squeaked. Karina looked to Tink. *"Up! Up!"*

Karina continued to climb and bit by bit her head arose to the entrance of the drainpipe. It was narrow like the one she used to enter the tunnel, but way more safer looking than the bar ladder she was on.

"Oh, hi there," Karina said to a trio of rats who cautiously scooted back at first, but then Tink and his friends jumped from Karina's shoulder onto the drainpipe and chatted.

"Friends." Tink turned to her.

"Yes, I see." Karina smiled.

"People this way."

"Right." Karina nodded as she slowly pulled herself into the drainpipe.

It was dry in there, but the further she crawled the more intense the smell of body odor and pee became. She wanted to cover her nose. What was back here, live animals? It couldn't be, even animals didn't smell this rank. Karina continued then froze when she thought she heard the sounds of people. Tink stopped and tilted his head.

"People," Karina whispered.

She crawled faster and noticed a bright light. She must have hit a main tunnel. The smell didn't get any better though, but she didn't care. Finally, she would be able to orient herself. Up ahead she saw a wire screen, beyond that the makings of what looked like a gray wall. She crawled faster. Tink and his friends stopped at the screen as Karina inched up to it. She looked down and to her shock it wasn't a main tunnel at all, but a small room with eight cages full of mainly women.

The people looked frail, dirty, and sullen. Was this some kind of a prison? The people were dressed more or less in the same outfit, dingy off-white short sleeve shirts and loose-fitting soiled shorts. She scanned the faces to see if there was anyone she knew, but there wasn't. She looked down at Tink. Why did his friends bring her here? A thin brown rat pushed at the screen, it barely budged, but they kept on pushing, and soon the other three rats joined in. Why were they so eager to get in there? Karina looked at the people, when she noticed that there were rats inside of the room, too.

They scurried across the floor, close to the cages, disappearing beyond Karina's view. The door rattled and everyone in the room stood up. Karina watched the handle turn, and the door dragged open. The people immediately started shouting.

"Shut up!" a runner with a metal armband and black worn suit shouted, as another man peeked in behind him.

"Eww!" The other man kicked a rat. "All these fucking tunnels are infested with rats."

"Well, you better get used to it, cause it's no better above." The man looked at each of the caged people. "Clear!" he shouted to his friend.

"Please!" a woman shouted and reached out her hand.

The man smirked. "You ain't got nothing to worry about, breeder. The bosses will find many uses for you," the man teased before leaving the room.

The sound of a lock clicked, and the woman collapsed on the floor of her cell. Karina furrowed her brow. She looked at Tink who was now helping his friends push the screen open. Breeder? These runners were traffickers, Karina glared. She had to do something. She turned to Tink and his friends. The rats did lead her to people, even though this wasn't what she expected.

Now she needed to come up with a plan to help them. She wasn't very good at picking locks, but she could try. She pressed her hand against the screen, and it was surprisingly weak. She pressed harder and heard the top pop and creak. She froze as all eyes were on her. The rats joined her and threw their bodies at the screen. The screen croaked and came undone from its rusted nails, tossing Tink and the others to the ground as the metal screen crashed to the floor behind them. Karina winced at the loud rattling sound it made, as the rats scattered.

"Shit." Karina's eyes darted to the door, but thankfully it remained locked.

She really didn't think that through, but her cover was up now. She peeked down and everyone was looking up at the pipe. She inched back and took a deep breath, *Okay, Karina, you got this.* She took another deep breath and rushed forward.

She stuck her head out and the people gasped. It wasn't too far down to jump, but as soon as she started to climb down everyone started wailing and throwing their hands out to her. So many people were talking over each other it was overwhelming. Tink found her and crawled up her pant leg onto her shoulder. She walked into the middle of the room as she scanned the terrified faces.

"I-I'm here to help," she proclaimed. Some of the people stopped shouting and looked at her, but then they started up again. "Please," Karina said. "I-I can't understand all of you all at once. First, how did you get here?" The voices overlapped each other again, and it was so loud that she had to cover her ears. "One at a time! Please!"

"We were captured!" a woman to her left said. She hushed the voices around her, and slowly the room fell silent. "We were kidnapped by runners, please help us."

Karina nodded and moved towards the cage. It was locked with a key, but the lock was very basic. Karina bit her lip. She didn't know how to pick locks.

"Please," the woman begged.

"I-I can't pick the lock," Karina said, and the voices started to get loud again. "I-I..." Then hands started to reach out to her. Karina stepped back, nearly tripping over a rat.

"Try." Karina heard a voice in her ear and looked at Tink. *"Try."*

"What?" Karina said to Tink.

A man in one of the cages groaned. "She's crazy, look she's talking to a rat."

"Damn it," another said.

"Shut it up," the same woman from before said. "She's all the hope we got."

Karina ignored them. "Try what, Tink?" People in the room groaned.

"Try!" Tink held out his paws as if he were trying to cast a key.

"Tink, I can't." Karina frowned.

Tink did the motion again, and the woman in the cage watched the rat intently. "What's he saying?" the woman asked.

Karina looked up, "U-um, it's nothing."

The woman pressed herself against the bars. "Now some may call me crazy, but I ain't never seen rats act as friendly as they do around here." She eyed Tink. "I don't know what he's saying, b-but I believe it's something important."

Another person groaned. "Now she's crazy, too."

More people groaned and slumped over, while some took a seat back on the dirty cell floors. Tink squeaked again. What was he trying to get at? She wasn't a caster. She already tried that. Tink held out his paws, in a cup, then put them out in front of him. This was impossible. It wasn't like she even knew any lock picking keys. The most she could do was pull out the screws on the cage or something, but even that sounded foolish. Aries was the Darkness, the chosen one. Her older sister was the one with all the power, but the woman from before never stopped looking at her.

In her eyes Karina saw something familiar. She saw the very spark she used to see in her own reflection. What would her granny say? Would she allow her to give up so easily? The people in the room started shouting again. Some yelled that she should go through the doors, while others begged for death. Karina took a deep breath and nodded at the woman who encouraged her. The woman's expression brightened.

"Okay," Karina said as some sucked their teeth and waved her off.

Karina spread her feet wide, planting them firmly on the ground. She had read about casting, so she knew all the mind calming stances. She could do this, magic was not something that could be taken and recklessly used. It was a gift from the spirits and she had The Rat King on her side. She formed a cup with her hands and closed her eyes. She blocked out the voices best she could and started to cast, but this time with all her heart. She wanted to believe that everything her granny said was true and that every member of their clan served a purpose as long as they had the desire to do so. Her granny had passed on but her memory, her words, and her spirit lived on inside of her.

She started to chant, and a warmth built up in her chest and soon all the voices faded out. She finished casting the key and closed her hands tight. She held her breath and focused only on the beating of her heart, which drummed like the march of feet. She heard a gasp from somewhere around her and opened her eyes. Everyone stared at her. Their eyes wide and mouths open. Karina was confused as some backed up, towards the wall. Karina furrowed her brow, then looked down at her hands, her palms glowed bright red as sparks shot off around them. Karina jumped back.

"Wo!"

Tink squeaked beside her, then stood on his hind legs again. *"Try!"*

Feeling a strong surge of power, Karina took a deep breath and put her hands out in front of her. "Move!" she commanded and the people did as they were told.

Karina reached for the summoning key in her mind, and something appeared in her peripheral. Her eyes turned sharply to her right. It was a tiny door, with a small triangle arch above it. On the door was the sigil for the very key she was trying to cast. She gasped. A gate! She had read about these in her books. Gates were the portals from which casters borrowed their magic. The sigil pulsed from black to dark red. It was her key. She stretched her hands out wider, and sigil glowed bright red and the door opened. Karina's jaw dropped, but she quickly pulled her mind back to focus. Dozens of bright red tendrils flooded from the door and shifted into the key she needed.

She focused on the words of the summoning key, to hone it into the action she needed. Her body heated up, sweat built under her underarms, just like she had felt before during her fight with Lady Rosemary. The heat rose into a tight pressure that searched for a way out. Karina held in a grunt and finished forming the key, then she opened her palms. Red lightening exploded into the screws and pulled them from the cage door one by one. The cage door creaked then fell from its place onto the ground. The sound got the attention of everyone in the room. All stood in shock, as Karina breathed heavily. She did it. The woman stepped out first, looking at the place the door once stood.

"Didn't I tell ya'll!" she said to the others, her face bursting with relief.

Karina beamed. "Go now. That vent leads somewhere, not sure, but it's better than here."

The woman and the others in the cage nodded and headed towards the vent. Others in the room reached out for Karina and rubbed her shoulders with gracious smiles on their faces. She looked at her hands, she felt so powerful. She nodded and moved onto the next cage. She attempted to cast the key again, but this time she noticed light brown markings on her skin.

She gasped as the markings became clearer, shifting from blurry light brown markings on her brown skin into words. Her words, the language of the spirits, the very words she wrote on her skin when she did not have paper to do so. The markings glowed. Her summoning keys were literally coming to life. Karina could cry from joy, but she refocused on freeing the rest of the people. She pulled out all the screws with her magic and the people ran free as she took a break on the ground.

A shadow stood next to her, and Karina looked up at the man who doubted her before. "Thank you, thank you so much, and I'm sorry I doubted you before."

"It's okay, now go," Karina said between breaths.

The man nodded, all that remained was a single woman. The woman the runner called a breeder. She ran towards the door, but it was locked from the outside.

"Hey, it's probably safer if you go through the vent that leads to the drainpipe," Karina said.

"I-I can't leave." The woman's shoulders slumped as she turned towards Karina. "I can't leave without my baby."

"You have a child?" Karina asked. "Where?"

"They took him, they took him to the ceremony." The woman started to cry.

"The ceremony?" Karina reached out to the trembling woman.

"They're going to sacrifice him to some god," the woman sobbed. "I-I tried to escape before, but t-the runners, they caught me."

Karina froze. What kind of God required a child sacrifice? It couldn't be Acome? They would never require such a thing. There must be something more sinister going on here and Karina was sure it had something to do with the prophecy. Karina balled her fist and reached out to the woman." I don't know what they're planning, but it's wrong. Let me take care of this."

The woman blinked away her tears. "You-you would do that? For me?"

"Yes, I'm here to help make this world better." Karina mustered up a smile.

"Thank you, thank you," the woman sobbed.

"Now go," Karina said.

The woman hesitated at first, but Karina softened her body language, and the woman left her with one final smile before disappearing into the vent. Karina let out a sigh. She wasn't sure what she was getting herself into. A child sacrifice sounded so grizzly. Tink ran to her and circled around her legs.

"Alright, Tink, I'm trusting you, okay."

Tink squeaked. If Acome was truly trapped, that meant evil was afoot and likely a great evil at that. Karina closed her eyes again and tried to reach for a summoning key. She felt a tingle on her arms, like a blanket being pulled over her body. It felt natural, like she wore a cape made of magic. She clasped her hands together, feeling grateful that she never gave up on her studies.

If Aries was the Darkness, then she would be her shadow, working behind her. It was destiny, because her granny said that everyone in their clan had a purpose if they believed and she would not fail them all now.

31
Aries

Aries waded through the murky water of the overflow pool as she dragged Mia's unconscious body over to the concrete walkway. She gasped as she struggled to keep Mia's head above the water. She kicked her legs and reached out for the ledge and grabbed it as she brought Mia's body to the edge. She had to take a break to catch her breath, because she was completely exhausted, but she knew she couldn't stay in this stagnant water any longer.

The smell of it was horrible, but it wasn't pure sewage. It was probably more like stormwater. Runoff from the streets above. Aries put her hands around Mia's waist and heaved her up by her skirt and rolled her over the ledge. Aries followed and pulled herself up and onto the concrete, where she collapsed on her back. Her chest, arms, and legs burned, but she made it. She closed her eyes under the dim maintenance lights that dotted the walls.

Then she thought of Mia and jumped up. She wasn't exactly sure how long she had been unconscious. They had been ripped every which a way down the storm drains. It happened so fast she could barely keep up. *Karina,* Aries gasped and looked around. Her little sister was nowhere to be found.

Aries cursed as she checked Mia for a pulse. Mia's heart was beating, but it was still too early to tell if she had been injured. Aries checked the water for her sister and saw nothing in the choppy current. The last thing she remembered was seeing her sister's head bob in the water and then she was gone.

"Fuck!" Aries shouted.

Her sister was a strong swimmer, but Aries barely made it out of the currents alive. Not to mention Karina had that heavy knapsack. What if she drowned? What if her sister's body was floating down a sewer tunnel right now? Or worse, what if she was injured somewhere dying. Aries clasped her hand over her mouth to stop the sobs and tears that she didn't even realize were coming. What had she done in involving her sister in this mess? If her sister died, it would be too much for her to bear. How would she face her mother and father? She wouldn't be able to. Aries cried fully now. She was sick to death of losing the people she loved. Had she not paid enough? This cost for freedom was just too much to bear.

She looked at Mia next to her. She hadn't asked for any of this either, and what about her best friend? Billie was gone, too. Aries looked away. What was the point of this? She was so tired and yet fate must have spared her for a reason. It would seem in some cruel twist of fate that she, the most undeserving, would have to complete this mission. Even if she had to do it without her sister.

Aries took a deep breath and patted her waist. Her retracting pole was still there. She still had the Crimson Mouse, and she knew the way. Aries went to stand and was surprised at how easy it was. She was a little stiff, but the soreness was fading. She took a step and felt a wave of dizziness overtake her. She used the wall to brace herself, but even that sensation came and went quickly. This was odd. She didn't want to bring it up while they were traveling, but she'd been feeling this strange buildup of pressure throughout her body. It only seemed to subside when she was moving, as if the sensation was fuel that begged to be burned. It was something she had never experienced before.

Aries stretched her arms, legs, and back before she dragged Mia's body over to the wall and gently sat her up. She then bent down, with her back facing Mia and reached back to pull Mia's chest onto her back so she could carry her. She hoisted her up and adjusted the weight a few times before she looked out at the flowing water. If she followed the water, she was bound to reach some kind of landmark. So, she set off.

Aries carried on down the tunnel in what felt like forever. The weight on her back was heavy, but nothing could compare to what she felt on her heart. She tried not to think of her sister, but her brain haunted her with images of her dead body, bloated, somewhere downstream. What if this was all for nothing? What if she found her too late, just like she did her cousin? No, she couldn't let her mind take her down that road, even if her heart ached. Grief, whatever blight it promised for her, would have to wait until this was over. She just needed to hold out a little longer

The flow decreased as she went, but there were no doors or manholes she could reach to get out. Sometimes she hated the design of the sewers. There were sometimes doors that led to nowhere or no doors at all. Some with paths, but others with dead ends. One could easily get lost and starve to death down here. It wasn't like she hadn't come across her share of dead bodies that had proven so.

When Aries rounded the fourth bend, she knew she needed a break. She gently lowered Mia's body to the ground away from the water, in case she woke up and rolled in. She tried to wake her by tapping her cheeks and shaking her shoulders, but Mia didn't stir. She hoped she hadn't fallen into night sleep. No one she knew ever came back from night sleep. Aries eyed the rose gold ring on Mia's finger. She felt it's heartbeat without even touching it. This was another weird thing she didn't want to share with the group. Acome must still be guiding them, but she wished they would leave a message on the wall or something or open a magical door to help them. Aries scooted her back against the wall and leaned her head back. She felt the burn now and could probably sleep for days at this point.

She looked at the dry, curved ceiling. If she had to guess she believed she was in the main sewer system near Uptown, given the lights and how clean it looked around here. She couldn't be far from something now. Aries closed her eyes as she started to nod off to the sound of flowing water.

"Hello?"

Aries' eyes shout open to the sound of a woman's voice.

"Hello?" it said again.

"Hello?" Aries responded. "Karina? Billie?"

"Hello, is that you?"

Aries shot up. "It's Aries. Karina? Billie?"

Aries wanted to run, but she didn't want to leave Mia. She paced and then cursed. The voice sounded close. She glanced at Mia one last time. "Stay here," Aries said as she ran towards the voice. "Hello? Karina? Billie?"

When Aries didn't hear anything, she ran faster. She ran around another bend and there was no one. She looked up towards the ceiling, then down at the walls for vents or open pipes. Who was calling her?

"Hello?" Aries repeated as she headed towards a fork.

"Hey!" a voice said to the left.

"I'm coming." Aries jetted over a grate that was installed over the channel. Then jumped from that and ran until she reached another bend. She spotted a flash of red hair that was hunched over and sighed with relief. "Karina, I was so worried about you," Aries said. She hoped her sister was okay. "Karina?"

Aries approached and suddenly the head twisted all the way around and it wasn't her sister at all, but her cousin Jasmany.

"Jas?" Aries said in horror at the sight of her cousin's mangled face, which looked like it had been broken and sewn back together.

Jasmany rose to her full height and the brown blanket that covered her body fell to the floor, revealing her cousin's naked body. Except something was seriously wrong. Her cousin was missing her hips and legs. Instead, she looked like a medical necromancy experiment gone horribly wrong. Her abdomen was crudely fused with the metal body of a round bulb shaped thing, with four thin metal spikes for legs.

"Aries! What have you done? What have you done?" Jasmany stumbled forward on her flimsy legs. Her breast shook from side to side as her arms struggled to get at Aries.

"Jas—I-I don't know what's going on. What happened to you?" Aries panicked as she stumbled back.

"You! You led the monsters to us!" Jasmany wailed. "You led the monster to us! You killed our clan!"

Jasmany charged towards Aries and tackled her to the ground. Aries screamed as she blocked her cousin's blows.

"Jasmany, stop! Stop! We can get help for you!" Aries cried out, but her cousin continued to beat down on her.

Aries took blow after blow, but she couldn't fight back. Jasmany was her cousin. She was only twenty years old. Last time she saw her, she was making art to sell in the markets. No, no, this wasn't right.

Jasmany raised one of her flimsy legs and Aries rolled out of the way to stop from being impaled. Jasmany's body turned around. "You killed us! You killed us all!" Jasmany hollered and charged again.

Aries ran. She couldn't fight her cousin, she couldn't. The metal feet clacked after her and Aries ran faster, but she slipped on some green sludge that leaked from the wall and slid hands first across the concrete. Aries hissed, but her cousin was upon her, and she grabbed Aries by her long, red braid and slammed her head against the wall. Aries saw spots in her vision as her cousin yanked her by her hair again towards her.

Aries screamed but Jasmany had a good grip on her braid. Aries stumbled forward, when she looked up and saw a bunch of crudely fused tubes attached to her cousin's abdomen. Aries ripped them from her cousin's flesh and the tubes gushed out blood and bile and other nasty smelling body fluids. Jasmany wailed as she choked and stumbled back towards the water. She still had Aries' braid in her hand as she yanked Aries' head towards the concrete edge. Aries screamed as her face drew closer to the ground, then there was nothing.

32
Mia

Mia coughed and spat out foul tasting phlegm. With her eyes still closed, she fingered around the ground expecting to feel the soft woven fabric of her bedsheets, but instead her fingers slid across rough concrete. She opened her eyes immediately and realized that her nightmares had come to life. She was trapped in a sewer. To her right a cruelly put together red brick wall with dim lights hanging from rusted nails and to her left was a canal of slow-moving, stale smelling water. In front and behind her the tunnel seemed to go on for forever.

She stood and shivered. Her clothes were damp, and she was alone. She pulled her soiled jacket around her. For all the glory, what was going on? She swore she was having food poison dreams, because her brain refused to believe that anything she had gone through over these past twenty-four hours was real. Untucking her folded arms, Mia gazed down at her hand. There on her left ring finger, the item that solidified this frightening reality. The rose gold ring shined unnaturally in its dirty surroundings as if something evil kept it alive.

Mia pulled off the ring and held it high in the air. She should just get rid of it. This wasn't her problem. She wanted nothing to do with this. Mia squeezed her hand tight and pulled her arm back, but she felt it pulse. The heaviness of its grief was undeniable and so strong that she couldn't do it. Acome didn't deserve this hate; they were trapped, too.

She collapsed onto her knees and cried out. She remembered the feeling of the soft wet grass, like a damp shag carpet. The smell of dirt and plants that seemed so unreal it terrorized her senses. It was beautiful, but she still struggled to see the possibility of it all. This had to be a nightmare. She wasn't a Crimson Mouse. She was a twenty-two-year-old woman who worked at a brothel and had a peaceful life. She should have never taken this task from Zetti.

Mia buried her head in her arms. What did it matter if she had the ring. She wasn't trained to fight evil. Terrible people were after her and she saw firsthand what they were capable of. Mia squeezed the ring tight and cursed it.

"Mia," a familiar voice echoed down the tunnel.

Mia stood and looked in the direction she heard her name. Who was that? She looked straight forward, trying to see in the dim light.

"Mia, where are you?"

Mia gasped. That sounded like Billie. Mia clinched the ring. She knew the others couldn't be far. Mia put the ring on her left ring finger and ran towards the direction she heard her name.

"Billie!" Mia shouted. "Billie, I'm coming, hold on."

Mia ran at full speed down the damp concrete sidewalk. She ran around a bend into another long tunnel but saw no one. She furrowed her brow. Where could she be? She sounded so close. Mia cursed the acoustics. She hated being in the sewers. Mia heard her name again, but it sounded far away this time. There was no other path for her to take, so she booked it down the tunnel. *Billie I'm coming*. She picked up the pace as she ran alongside the dark stagnant water. She passed under bits of light as her shadow appeared and disappeared on the walls and on the walkway. She came to a three-way path. Each looked exactly the same.

"Mia!"

Mia turned to her left; the sound was louder now. Billie couldn't be much farther. Mia ran down the tunnel to the left. Above her metal barred manholes allowed more light to pass through. The water was nothing but a trickle the further she ran. From a storm drain, water dripped slowly into the canal as Mia ran past. It smelled a bit better over here, too, like a strange mix of fresh air and plastic.

"Billie?" Mia slowed when she approached some metal stairs.

She walked up the short seven steps into an open area with a few tunnels and doorways. Dim light came from them all, but it was hard to tell what was beyond the tunnels, for all she could see were the walls. She looked up, the lights looked to be in better condition here. She must be closer to civilization. Mia headed to one of the tunnels and peeked in. It looked like there were some steps circling down, but there was no noise coming from it. She tried the other three door frames next. There were two to her right and one to her left. She walked to her right, when something clanked loudly behind her.

"I-Is anyone there?" Mia called out.

"Mia? Mia is that you?" she heard Billie say, more clearly now.

"Yes! Billie, hold on."

Mia ran through the door frame on the right side of the room into a small dimly lit hall. There were a few doorways, and she heard a faint ticking noise coming from down the hall. She peeked in a few of the rooms. There were nothing but boxes and crates in some and cots in others. Maybe Billie had found shelter or something. She hoped she wasn't injured.

"Billie?" Mia ran up to a room that was almost completely dark. There was a faint ticking sound. She looked in and the room reeked of road tar and dirt.

It was hard to see, but she could make out the shape of tall metal bars. She reached out and touched one, it was cold and stiff. She moved her hands around it and there were more bars, as if this was some kind of cage.

"Billie?" Mia called out.

"M-Mia?" Billie said.

"Yes, Billie, it's me. Are you trapped?" Mia asked.

"Mia, I'm so glad you found me. I've been captured," Billie said.

Mia squinted inside the cage. She couldn't see Billie, but then a figure started to approach. She couldn't see her face, but she could make out the thin frame of her friend's body. She recognized the beautiful dark skin of her legs, while the rest was cast in shadow.

"Mia." Billie reached out her hand.

"Oh my gosh, Billie." Mia teared up. "If you're trapped, I'll get you out."

Mia reached out to grab her and Billie stretched out her hand to meet hers. Mia reached in as far as she could and grabbed Billie's arm but gasped at how cold it felt. Mia pulled back, but Billie's other hand reached out and grabbed Mia's arm and yanked her body towards the cage. Mia slammed into the bars, and she screamed as Billie stepped into the light.

Her face was sunken and dozens of little bumps crawled under her skin as if something was moving under her flesh. Her lips were puffy, swollen, and bruised and her mouth hung open as if the jaw was no longer connected to her skull. Terror ripped through Mia's mind as she tried to pull her arm back through the bars, but Billie's grip only tightened. Mia cried out. The pain was so intense that it felt like the bone could break.

"Billie, stop! Billie!" Mia screamed.

Billie's body flung itself at the cage and tore the skin of the forehead as it pressed harshly against the bars. Billie's eyes bulged and split open as dozens of tiny black spiders crawled from her sockets and down her face. Mia screamed as she yanked her arm back violently and used her free arm to push against the bars. Billie's jaw hung open and hundreds of black spiders crawled from her throat and ran over her tongue and lips and down her neck towards Mia. Tears poured down from Mia's eyes as the spiders crawled up her arm and towards her neck. Mia spit and gasped as they ran into her ears, her nose, and over her eyes.

"Thank you, my dear, for bringing the ring directly to me," an eerie voice said from somewhere above.

Mia gasped for air, desperately looking around for where the muffled voice was coming from, but soon her world darkened to black leaving only the clicking sound of hundreds of spiders crawling on her skin.

33

Aries

Something nibbled at Aries' arms and thighs. It pulled and tugged on her pantleg and shirtsleeve. She groaned as she pulled her hands towards her body. Her left arm was cramped, and her right arm was completely soaked, which should have set off alarm bells in her head, but her brain was fuzzy. A pain pulsed on the left side of her forehead and she reached up to touch it and felt something wet. The nibbles on her skin didn't stop, but the stimulation lulled her awake.

"Jasmany!" Aries shot awake.

She looked up and down the tunnel but only saw the stagnant slow-moving water in the channel. She pushed herself up and her left hand fell into something wet. It was blood. Where did this come from? Was it from the fight? Then she felt something crusted on the side of her head. She reached up and winced when her fingers grazed an open wound. She frowned, but it looked like the bleeding had stopped for the most part. When she turned around, she was surprised to see a few dozen rats and mice around her. They tilted their heads and flicked their ears. They must have woken her.

"Thank you," Aries said.

Then she heard a scream. It echoed off the tunnel walls and the pressure in her chest suddenly inflated. The Crimson Mouse was in danger. She ran down the concrete walkway to the location she left Mia only to find that she was gone.

"Mia!" Aries shouted.

Aries continued to run down the tunnel, but she heard nothing else. She rounded a bend, but still found nothing. She stopped and listened for any sound, anything at all, but there was nothing but silence. Aries clinched her fist and cursed. Of course, how could she be so stupid. She looked forward again. Now she was truly alone with no hope of finding her. Aries sucked up her nerves and continued on. She couldn't give up now, after she had come so far, sacrificed so much. She came to a corridor with three pathways and stopped. She cursed under her breath as she looked at each one. Which way was the right way? She winced as the pressure continued to build in her chest.

"Mia!" she called out again, but only her echo returned. "Damnit."

Aries dug her fingers into her palms so hard she was sure it would leave a mark, but she didn't care. She needed to find Mia. Aries took a deep breath and carefully pulled her long red braids into a bun. *Think, Aries, think.* She shut her eyes tight. It was hard to concentrate with all the blood rushing through her ears. She opened her eyes and caught the glint of something small and black. She moved her hands out of the way and saw a rat so dark it could have been mistaken for a shadow. The rat's black eyes glimmered as it sat up on its hind legs. Aries watched it as a pressured boiled up inside of her, so powerful that it brought her to her knees. She reached a hand to her chest and gasped. What was wrong with her? What was this pressure? The pained flared up again and felt like something was trying to claw its way out of her.

She saw a shimmer of light and looked up to see the steel-black rat looking at her. It's eyes shimmered and for a second Aries thought she heard it whimper. She turned her head to the left and more clearly now, she heard something letting out quiet sobs and it pained her. It actually made the pit of her stomach churn. She saw a flash of a tear rolling down a cheek and instantly knew who it was.

"Mia!" Aries followed the sound until she came to a small set of stairs and found herself in a room with three tunnels and open door frames.

She immediately started her search down one of the tunnels. Light was scarce but she was used to wandering around in the dark. She heard a clanking sound in the distance and flinched. What if there were more creatures like her cousin out there? Aries couldn't think about that now, she didn't want to think about that now.

Aries hovered her hand over her retracting pole and continued cautiously until she reached the end of the tunnel that broke off into a caged walking area that had a grated metal platform where a circular storm drain dumped off. Aries backed close to the wall and looked to the bottom. Thirty feet below, it looked to be a wide river of slow-moving water. It must be what all those canals fed into. Looking up through the cage, on the ceiling, were dozens of large metal cages hung from the ceiling. What kind of place was this?

"I see that you've found yourself here all on your own. What a treat."

A voice echoed somewhere above her. Aries looked around, but then a flood of light blinded her. She covered her face with her arm. When her eyes adjusted, she saw the circular dome shape of the room more clearly. From behind her a large metal door shut with a slam over the tunnel she had just came from, then all around her metal doors closed over the other tunnels, *thud, thud, thud,* one by one. Aries hovered her hand over her retracting pole.

"Aries!"

Aries looked up and gasped, in the sea of floating cages not only did she see Mia, but she also saw a few of her family members including her mother and father.

"Mom! Dad! Mia!" Aries cried out at the cages that swung slowly on thick black chains.

"Aries!" her mother shouted.

"I see you two have reunited," the voice spoke again. "Good for you, but you probably would have been better off leaving your little friend behind."

Aries couldn't tell where the voice came from. She searched the walls and ceiling until she saw a rectangular slab of dark glass. She glared at it and then the light turned on and revealed a bald-headed man with brown skin and large circular lenses for eyes. He cackled over the intercom as he held his metal arms over his sleeveless white coat.

"Who are you?" Aries demanded.

The man smirked. "I am Dr. Jaystof Acknid, scientist and master necromancer. Welcome to my lair."

Aries growled as she looked between her family and the Crimson Mouse.

"I am so very excited to be in the company of two pretty girls, though I think you both could benefit from some improvements." He tapped his thin mechanical fingers together.

"Not a chance. Let them go!" Aries spat. She ran towards the cage wall and looked for some way to get access to him.

"Now now, there's no need to rush. My mission is complete, and I am assuming yours is too, but I do tire of studying your red headed lineage. See, I am very familiar with the ancient bloodline your family descends from. It is said that your ancestors were once very strong, though that is a claim yet to been proven. So, I shall make you a deal. I will release you and your family if you agree to leave me the pretty girl." Dr. Acknid turned to Mia. "I'm not one to lust, but I could definitely benefit from the company of that beauty. I've already come up with new designs for her face."

"Not a chance!" Aries shouted.

"Aries!" her father shouted out. He pressed his hands against the cage. "Please! Take the deal, Aries! Please!"

"D-Dad—" But he wasn't the only one shouting at her. So many of her relatives begged for their lives, shouting over one another. Aries took a step back, her mind went immediately back to her cousin Jasmany.

"Do we have a deal?" Dr. Acknid asked.

Aries looked between her father and Mia and everyone else in the room. How could she make such an impossible decision? Her family was everything to her. What was the point of continuing if they wouldn't be there to see the future? Shouts from other family members filled her ears. Their panic and fear nearly brought Aries to her knees as images of what happened to Jasmany flashed in her mind.

"You did this!" Jasmany cried out. "You did this to us!"

Jasmany's words repeated in her mind like a broken radio. What was she going to do? Mia was the Crimson Mouse, but her family was her world. She didn't want them to be tortured beyond recognition, abused, and played with like a toy. Aries pulled at her hair.

"Don't do it!" Aries' mother's voice cut through the chaos. "I have seen the light! Acome's light! Mother was right!"

Aries eye's shot up to her mother's.

"We can't let this opportunity pass. There is a future out there for us, so don't worry about us, please, Aries. You are the Darkness!"

Aries gasped. "M-mom..." Tears escaped her eyes.

"Please, Aries! There is still time! The rats! The rats have said so!" her mom shouted.

Dr. Acknid growled. "So annoying. All of you red-haired mistakes are. So weak and useless. None of you are key masters and yet you crown yourselves as some kind of blessed protectors. Now you're clouding the girl's decision. I already have the ring."

Aries furrowed her brow, noticing the glint of gold on his ring finger. Aries looked to Mia and looked at her hands. The ring was gone.

"You see, I've already won," Dr. Acknid said. "Though I'm not sure how the blonde and purple haired woman got involved, but you red haired people, Ratalia or some nonsense, I suspect this was exactly something your people would do. Now make your decision, girl."

"Aries, don't! Please don't!" Aries' mom shouted.

"Sasha! Please!" Aries' dad pleaded. "Aries, let's just go home. Think of Bluu!"

Aries inched back as her eyes shifted from Mom and Dad, then back to Mia, who's eye's welled with tears.

"How annoying. I guess I will make the decision for you. Your people have always been the weakest, and I've studied every key casting subgroup there is. And of course, you Ratalia people have never been smart or discrete in your pursuits." Dr. Acknid moved in his booth. "Time to die."

"No!" Aries shouted as the cage that held her mother lowered to a train cart sized cage below.

The top of the larger cage opened first, then the bottom of the cage her mother was in opened from the bottom and dropped her mother into the larger cage below.

"Mom!" Aries screamed as the top closed again.

Her mother ran to the cage bars as the cage slowly rose and moved towards the other side of the room.

"Mom!" Aries shouted again, as her mother's cage connected with a closed metal tunnel and locked into place.

"Remember what I said! Don't stop fighting! Acome needs you!" her mother shouted just as the tunnel door opened behind her.

"Mom!" Aries screamed, then she saw a shadow move behind her. "Mom, look out!"

A multi-armed creature slithered out and stabbed its tail through her mother's abdomen. Aries screamed as her mother spurted blood from her mouth, but the creature's tail continued to slice her mother in two. It ripped her flesh apart like a piece of fruit and blood gushed everywhere. Then it chittered like a bug and ate her innards. Aries dropped to her knees as her father's screams rung in her ears. The pressure in her chest choked her. She wanted to die. She wanted to vomit. She wanted to explode.

"Now before you lose focus on the pointless task of rescuing your friend, I would like to see the true extent of you rat people one last time. You've managed to make it this far, so perhaps you are special. Prove your worth and maybe I'll upgrade you, too."

Aries breathing was out of control. She couldn't focus or move her body. She was going to die here, and she had no hope of rescuing Mia, or her family, let alone herself. A loud screech of metal pierced her ears, and her head shot up. Three of the closed-off pipes connected to the caged walkway began to open. Slowly the doors pulled apart, sounding like old train wheels on metal tracks. Aries froze. She was next. They were going to tear her apart.

"Aries!" Mia screamed. "Aries! Please don't give up! You're not weak! Aries please!"

The pressure in Aries chest throbbed now. Aries looked up. Her vision was doubled from fear, but she saw Mia with a strange red aura around her. It was faint, but it radiated rage. Was Mia mad at her? No, that wasn't Mia. It was something else, someone else. *Acome.* Aries gasped at the thought of their name, because that pressure in her chest wasn't weakness. It was rage. She felt Acome's rage.

"Aries, please!" Mia begged.

Aries inhaled, reached for her retracting pole, and pulled it out. The tip smacked the floor.

That fucker was toying with her. Toying with her family. Hatred coursed through her veins as dozens of little black spiders flooded into the cage. Aries glared. She wasn't afraid of a few spiders. They circled her, then turned and looked at her with their beady orange eyes. They settled in place like voyeuristic audience members. So, this doctor fucker wanted to watch. Well, she would give him a show.

From the darkness of the three pipes, a stomping sound echoed louder and louder *boom, boom, boom.* Aries backed up. Something roared and she flinched as she gripped her pole tighter. She looked to Dr. Acknid, who grinned. She loosened and tightened her grip around her pole. She wasn't finished yet.

The growling grew louder, and the stomping rocked the cage. Aries saw shadows at first, then she saw the faces and gasped. From the three pipes about a dozen humanoids stepped out. They growled and groaned like a bunch of animals, but they looked more like necromancy experiments gone wrong than people. Some had mechanical pinchers for arms, while others had knives for hands. Their faces were sewn together to fit over lenses and other mechanical fixtures. Their ears and hair were completely cut off and their skin a ghoulish brown. Their humanity had been completely wiped away. That bastard toyed with people's lives. It was so wrong, but Aries didn't have time to dwell on that as the first round of beast charged.

Their movements were sluggish and slow from the poor fitting attachments they had for legs, but she did not underestimate them. She struck them on their weak spots just as she had done before. She hit tubes that pumped blood to their brains, and severed connections easily, as she spilt their thick, oil-like blood all over the cage floor. Dr. Acknid didn't seem bothered one bit that his creatures lay groaning and dying before him. In fact, he almost seemed delighted.

Aries ignored his wicked grin as she used the bodies of the fallen to jump into air attacks at the others. With swift movements she struck more and more down, but not without taking damage. Their numbers were many and their skin thick. A monster with a large metal mallet for hands swung at Aries. She barely dodged as she leapt into the arms of a creature who had eight metal tentacles for limps. The creature wrapped his appendages around Aries, squeezing her tight as the others charged.

She flailed her legs wildly, then kicked the thing in the leg where an exposed gear turned. The creature wailed and loosened its grip enough for Aries to wiggle through. Another creature, with its mouth sewed open, hurled acid at her face. Aries screamed and dodged, but some of the acid spilt on her arms. She hissed as she tried to fling it off and it ate through her jacket. She ripped off her jacket and threw it to the ground. The creature choked out a ghoulish laugh. More creatures circled around her.

"You're very strong, I'll give you that," Dr. Acknid said. "I think I will make good use of you after all, especially those beautiful long legs."

Aries growled and charged at a creature with axe hands. She wasn't going to be anyone's puppet. She leapt into the air and swatted them across the neck, which severed another tube. Blood stained the gray grate beneath her, but more came still. They flooded in from the pipes even more ghoulish and grotesque than the last batch. Aries kicked some in their faces and knocked out knee joints of others. She swatted ruthlessly at any loose part, but the mass kept coming.

Her heart beat in her chest as her arms and legs grew tired from dodging every blow, but also from the ones she could not. Her movements slowed and she was struck in the back. She cried out and hit the grate and scraped the skin of her knees as more surrounded her. She bounced back and swatted at another creature, but she misjudged the distance and they caught her by the arm and flung her into the wall. She bounced off it and her metal pole fell to the ground, retracting as she hit the floor. She struggled to get up and crawl to her retracting pole, when another monster with large metal elephant feet nearly crushed her hand.

"Shit!" She pulled away just in time, then reached up and yanked out the tube connected to its gut, spilling bile all over the place.

How many more did this monster make? She grunted as she rolled out of the way and grabbed her retracting pole, but the monsters had already cornered her and were closing in. One creature shot an arrow into her right thigh, and she cried out as it dragged her by its chain into the closing pit of creatures. They grabbed her hair and her arms as they closed in. She gasped as she held tightly onto her retracting pole. The beast yanked her around by her clothes, stretching the seams. There were too many of them. She looked up and saw the shock and horror on Mia's face. It said it all, Aries was going to die here. Pain coursed through her body as two creatures with giant metal clamps for hands twisted her ankles as another creature used its knee to bare down on her chest.

"Get-get off!" Aries tried to buck them, but their combined weight was too much. More creatures piled on, some that pinched her sides and thighs, while others took swipes at her face. Suddenly a clamp latched onto her breast and pulled. Aries screamed, this was too much. She couldn't go on like this. The pain overwhelmed her, and she dipped in and out of consciousness.

"Remember to breathe," her uncle said to her.

"Okay." She nodded as she practiced her arm movements.

"That's it, feel the power course through your body."

"I-I don't feel anything," Aries said as she moved her arms outward and slowly brought them in, in slow meditative movements.

"That's okay," he said. "Your body needs to learn how to control the power before it comes in. You need to train your body and mind in the proper movements. Now, when your ready retreat inside, pull from the summoning keys you've studied and release."

Aries pulled back her arms and pushed them forward. "Like this?"

"Yes." Her uncle clapped. "Pull them back and release."

Aries practiced the motion over and over again.

"Pull them back and release!" The voice faded.

The monsters enclosed her, and Aries withdrew inside herself. The pressure was so unbearable that she could barely breathe. The monsters pinned her to the ground, breathing their hot rancid breath onto her. Aries trembled. *Pull them back and release!* Her uncle's voice echoed. Her vision faded as blood mixed with pain. This was the end, and her resolve was crumbling, but not in fear, but in anger. Anger over her failure to protect her sister and her mother. Anger over her failure to protect the Crimson Mouse. Her anger ran through her veins like hot oil until it filled every inch of her body and she slipped into the darkness again.

"One day," her uncle said as he rubbed Aries' soft, thick, red hair. "One day, you'll encounter an unmovable target. An obstacle so great you may not think you can pass. On that day you'll have to make a decision: accept defeat or accept the true power Acome and The Rat King has given you and push forward."

Hot tears ran down Aries face as the pressure in her chest took shape. Something formed inside of her mind. Something square, like a door. A triangle arch appeared and underneath, a paper-thin door with a glowing black sigil. A key and it burned red. Aries gasped for breath as she tried to reach it, she only needed to say the words. She choked out a cough and chanted the summoning combination and the sigil burned like fire in the darkness into the shape of a flaming star.

A light burst over her head and tendrils of energy flowed into her more powerful than any key spell she had ever heard of. It was so much pressure, looking for a way out and there was only one thing to do with it. Aries pulled back her hands as the monster roared around her and released.

Bolts of red lightening erupted from the pile and struck the walls, casting the room in neon red. The power surged from the middle and rumbled the pit of creatures that lay atop her until it boiled over and exploded. Blood and guts rained from her cage as Aries emerged from the middle. Her eyes were blood red and glowing and bolts hit the walls like fire beams, burning a hole through the caged walkway and leaving deep burn marks on the walls.

Both Dr. Acknid and Mia covered their eyes. The creatures who were not as injured charged, never flinching in their pursuits, and were met by the fiery glare of a new enemy. Aries wasted no time and charged for her pole. She reached down and grabbed it, and her power dripped down her pole, turning it hot red.

She charged with the same vigor, but this time she severed arms and heads from bodies, not just tubes. Aries flashed a glare at Dr. Acknid who gasped as he watched her put down his creatures one by one. Aries hollered and from her a surge of energy swarmed the walls around her, killing spiders and creatures alike as it blasted a hole completely through the cage holding her.

She turned her gaze to Dr. Acknid in his room. He turned and disappeared from sight, but not before Aries ran and jumped into the air and shot off a powerful blast at the place where he once stood. The glass shattered and the room was lit ablaze. The lights went out in the tunnel and the creatures scattered. Suddenly fire spread from the small room and up the ropes that were mixed in with the chains. Smoke flooded the room as Aries' body felt weak. She felt her strength leaving her, but she could also hear someone calling her name.

"Aries!" Mia screamed. "Aries!"

Aries, bent down on one knee, looked up. Mia was still trapped and so were the rest of her family. Aries put away her retracting pole. How was she going to rescue Mia and her family now?

"Don't worry about us!" her father said. Aries looked up; fear gripped her heart. She couldn't lose her dad, too. "Go! Get the Crimson Mouse and get out of here!" he shouted.

"N-no," Aries said.

"Go!" another family member shouted.

"Get out of here, Aries!" another said.

"You are our only hope," an aunty said. "You are the Darkness!"

The smoke burned Aries eyes. She couldn't leave them. She wouldn't. Mia screamed as beams fell onto her cage, causing it to swing wildly.

"Please!" her father's plea reached her ears. "I-I'm sorry about before. I was afraid, but I believe you now! I can finally see what my eyes have refused to see for so long."

Tears fell from Aries eyes.

"Please! Don't worry about us," her father said. "We're a strong people, but you, Aries, you are the Darkness, the answer we've been praying for, and I-I just want to let you know how proud I am of you. For being so brave. For taking on this impossible burden."

"D-Dad..." Aries let out a sob as she saw the whites of her father's smile.

"We are with you, Aries," her dad said.

Flames consumed the room as Aries turned her face away from her father and her family. "Thank you, Dad," she muttered. Then Mia screamed, cutting off her thoughts. "Mia!" The pressure built in her body again.

Think, Aries, think. She was underground. There was water everywhere, there had to be. Mia screamed again. She needed to get to her before the smoke choked her out. She spotted amongst the lifeless corpses of experiments, a creature with a rope spool around its waist. She limped over to them and yanked it off. She tied a piece around her injured leg first to slow the bleeding, then drew the rope out and looked to Mia's cage. It looked to be locked with a simple lock. She could probably beat it off with a mallet or something. Aries coughed as she rubbed her burning eyes. She remembered there was a creature with a mallet. She scanned the area and found a creature with a small metal mallet and tucked it into the back of her pants.

"Mia! I'm going to throw this! Try and catch it so I can climb up!" Aries tied something weighted to the end of the rope.

"O-okay!" Mia called out.

Mia was only two stories up. Aries swung back her hand and threw the object towards Mia. Mia reached her hands through the metal bars, but she couldn't reach it, and the rope fell towards the middle of the pit. Aries reeled it in and threw it again, and this time it hit the cage, but it bounced off quicker than Mia could catch it and fell towards the middle of the pit again. The smoke was so heavy she could barely breathe. Aries coughed and limped backwards to reel the rope back in again.

"Forget about me!" Mia said. "They have the ring and Billie's dead."

Aries already knew that, but it didn't matter. "Try to catch it this time." Aries prepared to throw the rope again.

Mia cried. "There's no point."

"Try to catch it!" Aries hollered and threw the weighted rope Mia's way.

The object hit the cage close to Mia's face, but instead of jerking back, Mia reached through the cage to catch it.

"Good, now tie it off," Aries shouted. Mia did as she was told, then Aries started up the rope.

Fire and smoke swirled around the room. It was so dense she could barely see her family who were trapped in the cages around her.

"It's pointless," Mia screamed. "Just leave me!"

"Hold tight!" Aries said. "I'm coming!"

Aries pushed as the burning pain in her hands intensified as she climbed. She was so close. The cage shook and bounced from the extra weight as Mia held onto the sides. The fire choked and spat out smoke, gobbling up all the clean air, but Aries was so close she could almost reach the bottom of the cage. A sharp pain shot through her right thigh as she forced herself upward. Aries cried out but did not stop as the pressure in her chest started to build again. She reached the bottom of the cage, and another hand appeared to grab her.

"Aries! I got you," Mia said as she pulled.

Aries swung her left leg onto the edge of the cage as Mia helped support her weight.

"A-Aries, you came for me," Mia whimpered.

"Of course I did." Aries flashed her a painful smile. "You're the Crimson Mouse and it's my job to protect you."

Mia shook her hand. "I'm no one special. You're the one with all the power."

"You're wrong. In Acome's world there are no ordinary people. Everyone brings something to the table, even if others refuse to believe in or ignore your worth." Mia looked teary-eyed as Aries smiled. "Now stand back."

Aries raised her mallet and attacked the rusted lock. It bounced and popped around, but it eventually crumbled under Aries' blows. Aries popped open the cage door and stepped in.

"Come on," Aries said.

"B-but what about the fire?" Mia coughed.

Mia was right. Shit, even if they made it down, they would likely die before they reached the door, wherever that was. Aries shut her eyes as the pressure in her chest filled her with such intense bloat that it felt like her organs were going to be crushed. Mia's fear was feeding her, and she could barely contain the energy surging into her body.

Think, Aries. They were underground. There had to be water somewhere. She looked around the room. She couldn't see or hear anybody, but as the flames lit the room it exposed dozens of feet of pipes. There was bound to be water in one of them.

Aries grunted as she inched back to close the cage. She wasn't even sure how to control this power, she didn't even know how to use it at full strength, but she had to try.

"Aries!" Mia called to her.

The smoke was getting to her now. Aries felt dizzy and stumbled back. *Weakness,* a voice in her head said. Aries coughed and winced as her legs started to fail her. *Weakness does not suit you,* the voice spoke again. *Rise to your mantle, Darkness, bring light to this world that lacks truth!* Aries eyes shot open. The Rat King's fiery image appeared in her head.

"Aries!" Mia cried out again.

"S-stand back." Aries stood up straight.

So much pressure built in her and she needed to release it. *You can do this,* she said to herself. Aries started to chant and the door appeared again, but this time right beside her head. Aries gasped, overwhelmed by the intense pressure, but concentrated. The door appeared and the black sigil turned a fiery red. She knew what she needed to do.

"Mia, get down!" Aries shouted.

Aries shut her eyes and focused on her enemy: metal, long, on the walls, destroy it all. She pulled back her arms and released. Bolts of bright red lightning exploded from her body and struck the pipes around her. Red hot and bright, the power of it all blinded her. Aries let out a scream as darkness consumed the light until it felt like all of creation had been destroyed.

"Aries!"

Something cool hit her burning hot skin, but she couldn't move, she was tapped out. She floated backwards. The cool air rushed through her clothes and hair as all feeling went numb. A soft red light wrapped itself around her like a blanket. Faint, muffled sounds vibrated around her.

"Aries..." Her name came to her like a whisper. "I've got you..." Then there was nothing.

34 Mary

Relief washed over Mary when she got the news that Dr. Acknid recovered the ring. She had drunk herself unconscious during the final hours of her watch and prayed that she would never wake up, but the following morning, her mother and father stood over the bed with the news. So now she sat at her vanity and looked at herself in the mirror. There were dark circles under her once flawless eyes and her roots were puffy and kinky from lack of care. She didn't even know if she had time to have her brows done. She looked so rough, and she couldn't stop her hands from shaking. Mary took a deep, shaky breath. Regardless of what happened during the last forty-eight hours she needed to get herself together for the ceremony tonight at six.

Mary stood from her vanity and went to her walk-in closet. She had so many dresses to choose from, but she struggled to pick one. Somehow, beautiful things didn't seem as beautiful after all the horrors she had been through. All of this happened under the Fort'nee's watch. They were the ones who controlled the Silers, and they were the ones who cast them aside at the first sign of danger. Mary felt so much rage. She wanted them dead. She wanted them all dead. It was so unfair after everything her father and her family did to keep this country together.

"Jaden Fort'nee, count you days," Mary cursed.

Then there was Vincent Lorne. Oh, how Mary hated him. She would find a way to see to it that he was skinned and burned alive on a stick, impaled through the ass and that wouldn't even be enough. Mary was shaking mad now.

There was a light knock at her door and Mary nearly jumped out of her skin. She walked to her bed and put on her bedroom robe.

"W-who is it?" Mary said as she reached the door.

"Yours truly," a sweet voice said.

Mary's heart fluttered as she opened the door to her lover and Kym strolled in, wearing his best suit and polished shoes. Mary felt so embarrassed at her appearance that she shied away from him. The door closed as Kym looked around.

"My my," Kym said. "Have I arrived at my beloved at a bad time?"

"N-no, never," Mary said as Kym closed the gap between them.

Kym grinned. "If so, please accept my apologies. I just had to see the woman who saved us all." Mary eyes fluttered to his. "I know my fathers can be harsh with their words, but I have always had faith in you ,Mary. Under your watch the ring has been returned. What a praiseworthy feat indeed."

"T-thank, I mean yes, I-I am a capable woman, after all." Mary straightened up, right when another knock came at her door. Confusion flashed across her face, but she quickly shook it off with a smile. "W-who is it?"

"Status report," a young male voice said. "A message from Vincent Lorne, Lady Mary."

Just at the mention of that man's name, Mary shook. Rage turned her vision red. If she had it her way, she would kill every last one of those Siler dogs.

"My lady?" Kym touched her arm, and it was then that Mary felt something wet fall down her cheek. "You're crying."

Mary gasped. "I-I'm sorry, I'm so—"

"Hush, my love." Kym wiped the tear away with his thumb. "Does something upset my lady?"

Mary turned her face from him in embarrassment. "I-I..."

"Just name it, and I can make it go away," Kym said.

Mary was so sick and tired of dealing with this. She deserved to be treated better. She deserved to be in the highest ruling house. "I-I hate them." Mary's voice came out a whisper.

"Who?" Kym pulled her close.

"Those Siler scum." Mary buried her head in his chest.

Kym turned to the door, then lifted her chin. "Want to make them pay?"

Mary's eyes went wide, but not a single cell in her body wanted to go the civil route. Mary nodded.

Kym smiled and walked to the door. "Come in."

"Thank you—" A young Siler member walked through the door and immediately Kym punched him in the gut.

Mary gasped. The man didn't look a day over twenty, a young man, but Kym dragged him into the room by the hair and kicked the door closed.

"L-Lord Kym," the man begged, but there was no mercy in Kym's eyes.

Kym punched and kicked him in the head and the man knew then that he had to fight. The Siler growled and charged forward, but Kym easily dodged and delivered another deadly punch to the man's face. Mary yelped but could do nothing to hold back her excitement. She wanted to see him beaten and broken. Kym found a fire stoker resting on the rack next to her chimney and turned its sharp end on the runner. Each blow was rewarded with a delicious wail from the man. Kym punctured the man's back, abdomen, and legs, splattering blood on her marble floors and Mary didn't care at all. She instead jumped at every stab, feeling so overwhelmed by how powerful and strong Kym was. Kym kicked the runner in the head a final time, then looked to his love.

"I am so sorry," Kym said. "Look at this mess I've created."

Mary tried her best not to frown. "It-it's okay. We can have a maid or someone clean it up."

Kym smirked. "Would you like to deliver the final blow?"

Mary froze. Was he really asking her to do *that?* Mary inched back. Once she crossed this line, she could never go back. Kym handed her the stoker and smiled. Mary looked at it warily, but then all the events from before flashed before her eyes.

"Siler scum," Mary growled. She took the stoker and stormed towards him. The young Siler opened their eyes and begged for mercy. "Don't you dare look at me," Mary hissed, then walked past Kym towards the cowering runner. "I hate you!" Mary raised the stoker and gouged out his eye. The man screamed so loud, but it only fed Mary's rage. She grabbed the stoker with both hands and stabbed him uncontrollably in the chest, spearing nothing, not even his groin. There was an agonizing scream, then Mary drove the stoker through his neck.

The man choked and gasped as Kym pulled her off of him. Mary was breathing hard as Kym pulled her in for a kiss. "He deserved it, they all do, my beautiful future bride."

Mary's heart did a flip on that last word. His love was true, Kym still thought of her more highly than any of those other vixens, even after watching her do this. "Y-you mean that, Kym?"

Kym moved into her space again. He cupped her bloody chin and caressed her cheek bones. "Of course I do. I need only to associate with people who truly have good business sense. You see, I will be inheriting my father's business and the ao almasi plant cannot run without that demon your family keeps."

Kym let his arms drop past Mary's shoulders and grabbed her hand as he led her to her window. Mary followed with no resistance, her hands streaked in blood. She missed her Kym so much. She would give anything to spend every waking hour in his arms and now that he was practically professing his love for her, she now knew that fate had finally looked kindly upon her.

"You see, Mary, we need that demon to power our alchemy. The key gate must remain open so that we can do our work and without the ceremony that thing would simply die and what use would that serve us?" Kym turned to her. "That is why if I should take a wife, I would rather be with someone who has intimate knowledge of the beast. The others in the Five Families are so blinded by their greed that they have become dull and useless but imagine a union between two of the most powerful families."

"Two? I hope you're not talking about that whore Dottie," Mary revolted.

"No, Mary, I mean two of the most powerful families being you and I. Lord Jaden is nothing without his thugs and as you can see, they have no respect for a woman of your caliber. They deserve to be cast out and Lady Gladie practically works for us. And look how Lord Lor'es and Lady Amma handled this ring situation? Were they not the ancestors of the original writers of the key spell? Should they not have had a backup plan?"

A spark of rage flared up in Mary again. Kym was right, those good for nothing Hoo'naes did nothing to help. "Yes, they should have had some kind of contingency plan. It should have been them to handle this."

Kym smiled. "They should have and yet, it was the Granites that put their lives on the line. That is why you, Mary, are the only correct choice. Your family controls the keys and the sacrifices. Think of all the possibilities a union like this could bring. I have great plans for my family's products. Did you know that ao almasi is very sensitive to necromancy, especially when it is infused with blood?"

Mary shook her head. She didn't know what he was getting at, but she didn't care. Kym was going to marry her.

"I've been studying the Hoo'nae's magic. They enhanced their binding key spells with blood, too, and I think I can do the same. Just think, Mary, with my knowledge and your family's breeding of slaves, we could have all the resources we need to expand, even conquer. I have Augtus on my mind, the little shit stain of a country, who dare not trade with us even if we would pay good money for their ore. They would crumble under our might and once they fall, soon the other ten nations will as well. We could raise an army with our necromancers," Kym said with such a fiery passion.

"Oh, Kym, you're such a dreamer." Mary fell into his arms.

"Always." Kym leaned down to kiss her.

Mary giggled as he swept her away towards her bed. Their bloodied bodies both fell into the sheets. He landed on top of her and reached for her breast, giving it a playful squeeze. Mary moaned. She wanted this, no, she needed this. Fuck anyone who stood in their way. Kym moaned into her neck as he kissed her above her collar.

"My Mary, please allow me to show you what I can truly do," Kym whispered.

"Anything for you, my love." Mary's eyes fluttered close as she lifted her neck to give him more access.

"Then shall we try something different?"

Mary nodded as she opened her eyes. Kym grinned and reached for his box of toys that he'd left under Mary's bed for such visits. He opened the box and pulled out a small case and laid it on the bed. Mary watched as he opened it, and inside were a row of syringes.

"Do not be frightened. I just need a bit of blood." Kym gazed hungrily into his lover's eyes.

Mary gasped. "My blood?"

"Of course. Only the very best," Kym moaned into her ear.

"Anything for you, my love." Mary melted into the bed and Kym smiled as he prepared his kit.

He tore away her bloodied robe and lifted her silk nightgown, revealing her naked body. Mary shivered from the cold, but her body ached for his touch. She wanted him, needed him to breathe his life into her. Kym tied her to her bed frame, then ran his strong hands down her chest towards the nook of her hips and stopped.

"Do you want me, Mary?" Kym said as he sat on top of her.

"Yes," Mary moaned.

"I don't think I believe you," Kym leaned down to her ear. "I'm going to need you to beg for it."

"I need you, Kym! I can't think or breathe without you, Kym!" Mary begged.

"That's a good girl." Kym grinned as he tied a cloth around her arm.

He took out his needle, pierced her skin, and watched with delight as he collected her precious blood. Mary's heart raced. She wanted more. She wanted him to fuck her into a bloody wet mess.

"Eager, are we?" Kym smiled as he pulled out another box of large, phallic-shaped stones. Kym reached for a particularly girthy one. "Shall I show you what my blood magic can really do?"

Mary bucked and squirmed for his touch. "P-please..."

Kym grinned as he chanted and his key door appeared beside him. It opened, and out slithered his tendrils that wormed their way over Mary's body. Mary moaned as they moved towards the stone, making it glow. Her eyes closed, then opened again to the sight of the man she just killed bleeding out on the floor. A burst of excitement rippled through her body. She would make them pay.

Kym bent and devoured her with a kiss. Mary moaned with anticipation as she begged Kym for his touch, and he did not hold back, fucking her in the sheets, filling every opening with his presence.

35 Vincent

A cigarette hung from Vincent's lips as he walked through the ceremony hall. All this stress and headache over a ring had put him quite far behind on his paperwork. This was not how he wanted to start the year. Servants hurried around the room making sure everything was in place. White chairs sat atop red carpet that covered most of the concrete floor. Tables for hors d'oeuvres lined the walls as if this were a normal cocktail party and not a ritual sacrifice. It made Vincent smirk.

Vincent took a long drag from his cigarette and blew the smoke out into the stuffy room. He eyed the dull concrete walls that the servants fruitlessly tried to liven up with wreaths and drapes.

"You know, you should really cut back."

Vincent pulled the cigarette from his lips and let his hands fall to his waist as he turned around. "Yrwen? Here to count the inventory?" Vincent put out his cigarette with his finger and tucked it in his coat pocket.

"More or less," Yrwen said as his gaze flickered upward. There was an edge to it. Looks like Yrwen was still worried.

Vincent smirked as he shook his head. He turned and walked towards the grand altar where the ceremony would take place and Yrwen followed. Thanks to the Hoo'naes everything was completely automated. None of his bosses had to lift a finger. At the altar sat a golden crank that only activated when the ring was inserted. All it needed was the blood, completely drained, of a three-year-old child, some magic words, and of course, the gear ring. The past, the present, and the future, and once again the beast would be sealed. A servant walked up behind Vincent and bowed their head.

"Should we bring up the beast?" they asked.

Vincent shrugged. "Do as you please."

The servant nodded, then dashed away. Vincent and Yrwen stepped back as the floor rumbled. Metal screeched and clanked as the gears in the ground moved the concrete. Two large half circle concrete slabs opened to reveal a deep, dark, circular pit. Immediately the room was flooded with the smell of death. Vincent didn't flinch, but servants were ready with hoses and buckets of incense to freshen up things. Candles were lit to mask most of it, it was a real spectacle.

The gears turned and cranked up the large concrete platform below and soon the top of a gold cage slowly made its appearance. Inside was the sickly matted fur of a beast taken right out of someone's nightmares. It was sealed by its arms, body, and legs and it groaned as its poor eyesight adjusted to its surroundings. Above it was the key gate the Five Families used to harness its never-ending flow of magic. Dozens of mosquito like tendrils fed on its life force, even now.

Servants who couldn't bear the smell coughed and gagged at the sight as rats scurried from its body across the floor, dashing quickly to the vents on the side of the room. Above the cage was a black metal grated platform where armed runners inspected the living corpse, with their guns at their waist just in case someone tried to pull something. The ceremony would take place at six this afternoon and the Five Families were expecting everything to go perfectly as planned.

The eyelids of the beast rolled under its crusted skin and slowly it opened its eyes. It gazed up at Vincent, then closed its eyes as the servants got to work hosing it down with water and refreshing it up as if this were its living wake. Vincent pulled the rose gold ring from his coat pocket. All this trouble to appease this creature, this relic from the past? Vincent eyed the ring. The rich cowards clung to their wealth as life preservers.

A servant appeared by his side. It was time to set the items in place. He turned and walked towards the altar, placed the ring on a plush red pillow, and secured it in a locked golden cage.

"Shall I send out a few runners for Mary?" Yrwen asked. "Technically, she did not complete her task by midnight."

Vincent held up his hand, withdrawing his cigarettes from his coat pocket. "Don't bother. Doctor Acknid did an excellent job as expected, so I'll let this slide. We'll call it a New Year's miracle."

Yrwen nodded. "I also have news pertaining Doctor Acknid."

"Hmm?" Vincent hummed as he took a long hit from his cigarette.

"It would appear a woman connected to the ring thieves is a powerful caster. Her power far surpassed what Doctor Acknid was able to defend against. He is alive, but gravely injured, but warns not to underestimate this threat."

Vincent inhaled and exhaled the smoke slowly. "Hmm, alright. Prepare my suit."

Yrwen stared Vincent in the eyes, "Are you sure?"

Vincent shrugged, "My job is to see to it that this goes on without interruption. If a problem arises this time, I'll take care of it myself." Yrwen paused, long enough for Vincent to raise an eyebrow. "Something wrong?"

"No," Yrwen finally said, but even Vincent could tell he was distracted by what he saw in the cage. "I'll prepare your suit at once." Yrwen turned to leave but stopped. He faced Vincent, and opened his mouth to say something, but stopped.

"You clearly have something on your mind," Vincent said. "Come on, spill it."

Yrwen maintained eye contact, but it was clear his thoughts were elsewhere. "I just have a feeling that something is...off..."

Vincent chuckled. "I'm the Siler's number one guy and I never fail."

"Of course," Yrwen promptly nodded, but his gaze lingered on Vincent. "You know...if this is becoming too tiresome, it's not too late..."

"You worry too much, dear friend," Vincent said as he led the way.

"You're right." Yrwen followed.

Vincent took one last look at the creature that sat pitifully in its cage, conquered and defeated. He guessed this was one thing in common he shared with the beast and that was he would always be permanently forced to serve his bosses until the bloody end, but the difference between he and it, was that he carved out a good life for himself. And he never settled for being a mindless mule.

36
Karina

Karina felt a powerful rumble in the ground and gripped the wall for balance. She had been crawling through tunnels and this tremor was the latest in a series of quakes she had been feeling all night. She hid in the shadows in one of the many ground tunnels where slaves were being held. She had created quite the bit of chaos on her mission to find the ceremony child and set a lot of people free, but now runners flooded the place. Something serious must be going on because runners hurried towards the lower levels in increasing numbers.

Another tremor shook the tunnel she had been crawling in. This was starting to become unsafe, but it wasn't like she could walk in the open. Unless she could find a way to blend in.

"Hey, you think you can find me a room that's empty? I have an idea." Karina turned to Tink.

Tink nodded and raced ahead. He returned and placed his paws on her legs. *"This way."*

"Thanks," Karina said.

It was risky, but she would be able to cover more ground if she didn't have to back track every time she ran into a dead end. Tink led her to a vent that fed air into what looked like a storage closet. There was just one runner in there, sitting on a crate taking a smoke. Karina eyed the shelf next to them that looked like it had a lot of heavy boxes on it.

"Perfect." Karina closed her eyes and reached for the summoning key in her mind. If she could use her key to grip the box, she could pull it forward and let it fall on their head.

Karina started to chant, and the key gate appeared in the air. "Unlock."

The door opened and out slithered the tendrils of red light that floated towards the box and hooked on to the sides. Karina beamed with excitement as she called for the tendrils to pull. The lines tightened and slowly the box inched further to the edge until it tipped over and fell. It made a loud thud and Karina winced, but it got the job done. She unscrewed the vent and hopped down.

"Sorry, buddy," she said as she took their uniform and metal armband and put them on.

She tucked her bright red hair into a cloth scarf she found in a basket on a shelf filled with cleaning supplies. Now she would be able to walk around more freely and if she was questioned, she knew enough runner lingo to at least state she was lost.

With Tink tucked away in one of the large pockets of her pants, Karina was able to cover more ground. She easily blended in and out of task and when she got lost most runners rolled their eyes and pointed her in the right direction. Apparently, she wasn't the only greenhorn. The leaders had announced an all call and summoned nearly all the members of the gang from every corner of the city to where they were in Uptown. So quite a few of them got lost, not to mention all the new faces. So, she was able to become quite familiar with the place without raising too much suspicion.

According to what she overheard, she was just below the main estates of the Five Families and boy were they involved with a lot of shady stuff. She kept her head low as she passed a pair of slavers. They trafficked a lot of people, from their own who fell into debt to street people. Why they needed so much manpower, she couldn't say, but she also noticed a lot of people with strange modifications on their bodies. Surely it was the result of large-scale medical necromancy, but to what end?

Karina hurried along as she tried to ignore how sweaty she was. Her body was constantly hot, and it didn't help that it was so warm down here. She needed to hurry and find this ceremonial child before it was too late. So she could at least buy her sister and the others some time and interrupt the ceremony. That was if they were still alive. She couldn't quite confirm it, but she felt they were. Like a small flame in a furnace, she had hope.

Karina heard the sound of footsteps behind her and moved closer to the wall. At least twenty runners ran by with guns in hand. It looked like everyone was on high alert. Karina followed the concrete halls for a bit until she reached two large swinging doors. A few runners exited without sparing her a glance. She peeked through the closing door and noticed this area was better lit. She glanced behind her and pushed on the door and found a long damp corridor that smelled somewhat fresher. She walked a few feet and saw a few doors then a fork that split two ways. One way was a dead end, but the other was far busier.

This corridor was mostly staffed by what looked like servants. Karina leaned against the wall and fidgeted with the gun she stole, pretending to fix it, so she could watch. The servants looked like normal people, but their expressions were blank, almost lifeless. None of them even bothered to make eye contact with her as they moved in and out of different rooms. They all had pale, milky-gray eyes which creeped Karina out. There were also strangely big runners walking around, though they kind of lumbered about like giant dolls instead of the normal gait of a person. None of them seemed to pay any attention to her as if they were too focused on their task. Then she heard quick footsteps drawing closer. That couldn't be a servant. With little place to hide, she pretended to stand guard on the wall, when she felt Tink roll around in her pocket.

"Down, down." Tink squeaked and nodded towards the floor

There was a vent. Karina looked both ways before she kicked it in with her foot. It made a loud sound, but none of the servants flinched. She slipped inside and replaced the screen best she could and listened.

"I do not give a rat's ass about any additional accommodations they need," a man said. "They can all die of green lung for all I care."

"But, sir," another man's voice pleaded. "You are needed at the ceremony."

"Screw the ceremony! My son is dead! My daughter and wife are distraught! I will perform the ritual myself, but nothing more. I am through with this mess. If they want doctors, tell them to hire someone else!"

Karina watched the men walk further down the hall towards a door where servants came in and out of. She saw the heads of the large guards she saw earlier. They, too, appeared to have the same vacant look on their face, but no words were spoken to them when the two men walked by. Karina laid in the vent and pondered. This man had something to do with the ceremony, but this area didn't look like someplace she could walk right into.

She could try and jump a servant, but they all looked so plain in their black uniforms, and none had caps to hide bright red hair. She would have to think of a different way to get in. Tink crawled down her leg and she looked down. He sniffed the air, then looked down the vent.

"You sense something?" Karina whispered.

"People, this way," Tink said.

Karina squinted, maybe she wouldn't have to walk in the open. Tink led the way down the vents as Karina crawled quietly. She inched through thick layers of dust and spider webs, until she was in a part of the tunnel that looked a lot nicer than the area she was in before. The walls were a crisp white instead of concrete. There were more servants here than runners, but none shared the same urgency as the others in the previous corridor, even though they still seemed mindless.

"Where is Veronica?"

Karina heard further down the vent the voice of the same man who had talked about the ceremony. She crawled towards it, and she passed a few dark rooms until she reached one that was well lit.

"My goodness, is there not a single person competent enough to understand me around here?"

Karina saw the man's shoes as he stormed out of the room. From her point of view on the floor she couldn't see much, but the room smelled like strong cleaning bleach and that yucky formaldehyde liquid that sometimes leaked into the sewers. She saw the legs of silver metal trays and a few counters as Tink inched up beside her. He sniffed at the screen, as his ears rose and dropped.

"What do you think is going on in here?" she whispered. Tink only stared at her, but then she heard the door open again.

"Set him here," the man said.

"Doctor Granite, please allow me to help you," a woman said.

"Not now, Veronica," Dr. Granite said. "We have little time to drain the boy, so I will need to hook up the suction device. Not to mention I have to start prepping the altar."

"Please," Veronica pleaded. "Go prep the altar and leave the rest to me. You've been working so hard lately and after everything that's happened. Please, sir, I beg of you, let me serve you."

Dr. Granite sighed. "Very well, but we're not going to have time to drain the body organically, so use the machine."

Dr. Granite's feet walk by and the door closed behind him. Karina's heart pounded in her chest. She didn't want to think about what they meant by *draining the body*. Karina heard the woman walk around the room and stop at a counter where she heard a child cry.

"Now now, no need to pout. It'll be over soon."

The child made some inaudible noises as the woman walked to another counter on the other side of the room. The woman pulled a pole on wheels over to where she was, followed by a chair.

"It's sleepy time now," the woman said softly.

Karina clinched her fist. They were going to kill that child. She needed to do something quick. Karina pushed on the screen, but it was nailed in tight. She cursed under her breath, as she inhaled to control her breathing. *It's okay. Karina, its only nails. You can do this.* She reached for her key again. It came more easily now. She started to chant, and the key door appeared beside her. She continued and the key sigil burned bright red.

"Unlock," she uttered. Her eyes and the words on her arms glowed as the key door opened.

The tendrils seeped out of the vent and formed into a flathead near the screws. The nails made scraping sounds as they slowly began to unscrew, one by one. The nails clicked against the floor as they fell, and Karina froze. She listened out for the woman, but it sounded like she didn't notice. Karina sighed in relief and caught the screen before it hit the floor.

"Tink, you think you can bite that lady's leg to distract her?" Karina whispered.

Tink nodded, making chopping motions with his teeth. Karina eased the bottom of the screen to the floor and inched it open with enough space for Tink to slide through.

"There there, see, that wasn't so bad," Veronica said.

Tink scurried out and ran across the room. Karina peeked through the screen, she could see Tink as he ran up next to the rolling chair and climbed up the legs.

"Good, good," Veronica said.

Tink jumped on her leg. Veronica jumped from her seat and screamed.

"What the!" Veronica swatted at the rat. "Ewww! You fucking animal." Veronica stomped around after Tink.

Karina slid the screen all the way over and crawled out. The floors were clean, light gray, and cold, made from something that resembled tile but softer. Karina shot up and found herself in what looked like another storage room, but much bigger. Glass cabinets filled with tiny jars and vials lined the entire room. Tables with sharp knives and scalpels laid upon metal trays and sat on the main table in the middle of the room, next to a machine with a long plastic tube, that looked like it drained into a large glass jar with the same strange markings she saw on the ring and in some of the older books.

"Hey!" Veronica shouted and pointed at Karina.

Karina gasped and backed up into the counter. Looks like she'd been caught, not surprisingly, but it was so easy to get distracted by this new and strange environment. In front of her was a child with a gas mask on its face. He was laying still as if he were sleep. *Oh no!* Karina hoped she wasn't too late.

"What are you doing in here!" Veronica ran towards Karina.

Thinking fast, Karina charged for the child and pulled out the tube that was connected to the gas mask.

"Hey! Stop that!" Veronica reached the other end of the room as Karina ran to the other side.

The woman cursed and turned off the machine. Then turned to Karina with a knife in hand. "If you're here to cause trouble, you've come to the wrong place!"

Veronica lunged across the room and swung her knife around. Karina dipped back and dodged. If Karina wasn't careful this lady could kill her. Heat built up in Karina's chest as she jerked and ducked. Veronica swiped the blade close to Karina's head, taking her cap right off. Karina yelped as she ran around the counter and spotted a metal tray to use as a shield, spilling all the knives and scalpels onto the floor.

"Brat!" Veronica hollered.

"Better a brat than a dirty witch." Karina swung and hit the woman's hand with the metal tray, knocking the knife to the floor.

"What did you call me?" Veronica growled.

The woman reached across the counter and knocked over tissues and gauze to grab at Karina. *Oh crap!* Karina scrambled back, but Veronica grabbed Karina by the shirt as she tried to get at her neck. Karina screamed and slapped the woman across the face and chest, but she would not let go. The woman was surprisingly strong for her size. She pulled Karina over the table onto to floor and kicked and punched her relentlessly. Karina put her hands up to block against the blows that landed on her legs, shoulders, and stomach.

"You won't ruin this for me!" Veronica hissed as she pummeled Karina.

Veronica did not let up, but Karina managed to kick her in the upper thigh. Veronica hissed as Karina scooted back and hit the strange machine with the tube, causing it to fall.

A long sharp syringe nearly fell on top of her hand and Karina screamed when she saw it and jerked her hand back. That would have sucked so much if it went into her hand, but Karina's thoughts were cut off by a swift kick to her face. The pain was so sharp and intense it knocked Karina's mind blank. *Shit, ow, ow, ow,* Karina winced as blood dripped from her busted lip as she scurried away.

"Gotcha, you little brat!" Veronica hissed.

Karina crawled back as Veronica approached fast. On the floor Karina fingered around for something to defend herself with. Her fingers grazed something cold and metal, and Karina picked it up and threw it at Veronica, impaling her in the thigh. Veronica screamed as she grasped her leg.

"You little bitch!" Veronica growled, even more enraged.

What were they feeding this lady? This woman was not going to go down easily. Karina pushed herself up and launched herself at the woman's legs to trip her.

Veronica swooped down to grab Karina, but Karina made contact with her legs first and pulled her to the ground. Karina slid onto the floor where her finger poked the long sharp metal point of the syringe, drawing blood.

"Ow! Fuck!" Karina pulled her hand back as Veronica fumbled to get herself upright.

She hated syringes so much, but Veronica was already up. "Damnit, lady! Stay down!"

Karina reached for the syringe and swung it wildly at Veronica when she lunged at her. Karina closed her eyes when the needle connected with flesh and let go. She crawled to the other end of the counter and turned back only to find that she had stabbed the woman in the throat. Karina gasped right as the machine turned on, almost as if it were magic and began to suck the woman's blood. Veronica clawed at her neck, but the needle likely impaled her trachea, and she was choking on her own blood as crimson liquid poured from her mouth. Karina winced as the woman gagged and flopped over to the floor and twitched, in a small pool of her own blood.

"Oops." Karina inched back, watching the gruesome machine do its work and fill the glass jar with rich, red blood.

That's when Karina remembered the child. She got up and ran over to the back counter. Tink was there licking the child's face. Karina removed the gas mask and swatted away the fumes. She checked for a heartbeat. He was still breathing, so she opened his mouth and filled his lungs with clean air. She blew on his nose, too, and repeated the process.

"Come on, come on." Karina gently shook him. She lightly pinched his little feet and fingers. "Come on."

Tink helped by nibbling on his cheeks. The child stirred, then with a choked cry, he slowly came back to life. Karina looked at Tink and smiled. She grabbed the child and cuddled him. She was so glad he was okay, but they needed to get out of here. She turned around and saw the machine that pumped the blood. *Blood*, that's what they wanted. She cuddled the child in her arms as she looked around the room for a place to set him. She found a large sink basin and ran over and put the sleepy boy inside so he wouldn't roll onto the floor.

"I'll be right back. Tink, can you watch him?" Karina asked.

"I watch, you work!"

"Thanks!" Karina said. If she could trick them into thinking this woman's blood was the right blood, maybe she could stall the ceremony and give herself more time to find the others.

37 Mia

Mia crouched down when she heard people run by. She sat still in the dark room and hoped no one would peek in. When the footsteps passed, she let out a sigh and looked down at Aries, who was still unconscious next to her. She readjusted her legs and crisscrossed them as she rested against the wall. She didn't know how long she had been hiding here, but it felt like hours had gone by since they escaped. Mia fidgeted with her naked ring finger as she sat in the dark. She lost the ring, and all this crap and sacrifice she went through was for nothing. She wanted to cry, but she was too emotionally numb to summon the anger and pain she felt about it.

She closed her eyes and still felt the flames biting at her arms. The feeling of hopelessness took root in her heart. She couldn't get the sight of Billie's decaying body out of her mind, and yet in her lowest moments Aries was still there to protect her, even if her own family was at risk. She balled her fist. Even without the ring, Aries still believed they had a chance. And after Aries gave everything to save her, she felt she owed it to Aries to continue this fight. But how was she going to do that? Mia sighed as she leaned her head to the side. Aries stirred and groaned as she moved her head from one side to the other.

"Aries," Mia whispered.

Mia was grateful she found them a room that had first aid supplies, because they both were bruised from their escape. She was lucky they even survived. When her cage came crashing down onto the metal walkway below, she thought she was a goner, but somehow, she found the strength to drag Aries and herself out of there. She found this place completely by accident when she escaped down a hall she saw the monsters run in. She didn't want to go at first, but she had little choice. Her legs ached at the memory of her running. She checked so many areas until she reached one with open doors and that was how she found this room.

It was down this long hall that had a lot of white walled clean rooms with tables in the middle or long chairs. In the cabinets were gloves, jars of knives and other medical supplies and powerful potions. After seeing all those monsters, she didn't have to guess what kind of work they were doing here.

Mia heard the sound of voices again and lowered her head. It wouldn't be long until they found them, but she didn't want to wake Aries. The voices faded and Mia sighed again as she leaned against the cabinet. She was so tired, and everything felt so hopeless. She rested her head back for just a second as her eyes slowly began to close, and the familiar comfort of darkness crept in.

"What are you doing?" Billie laughed and pointed at her with one hand, while the other covered her mouth.

"I-I'm working it," Mia said as she struggled to walk in her seven-inch heels.

"You're working something all right. You're working your ankles into an early grave." Billie stood and walked towards her. "Here, watch my feet." Billie eloquently walked to the end of the hall in her six-inch heels and made a perfect turn and walked back. "See, take it slow, don't try to force it."

Mia nodded and gave it another try. She nearly tripped, but Billie was there to catch her.

"Easy now, take it slow." Billie placed a gentle hand on Mia's shoulder.

A tear tickled her cheek and she reached up to wipe it away. When she opened her eyes, she saw that her fingers were wet. Was she crying? Mia stared at her hand.

"For all the glory, Billie." Mia choked on her tears and felt a firm tug on her leg. Her head shot to the side, and she found herself startled by a pair of red eyes staring back at her.

"It's okay, Mia," Aries said. "It's just me."

"How are you feeling?"

"Much better, thank you." Aries rubbed her thigh where she was injured. "Where are we? H-how did we get here?"

"I'm not sure where we are," Mia said. "I followed the monsters and found this room and we've been hiding in here ever since."

"W-what about the fire? What about the others?"

Mia frowned. "I'm not sure what happened to the others, but you put out the fire. Your magic power blasted a million holes in the pipes above us, raining water everywhere. It was pretty cool, actually." She hoped that made Aries feel better, because there was no way Mia could have saved her family as well.

"I see. How much time has gone by?" Aries asked.

"Not sure," Mia said.

"It's okay." Aries rested her hand on Mia's shoulder and started to get up.

"Hold on. Go slow." Mia stood up beside her.

"I'll be fine." Aries winced.

"No, you won't. Please take your time," Mia fretted and was met with a gentle smile.

Aries looked around as she squinted in the darkness. Mia held onto her so she wouldn't fall. "What is this room?"

"I'm not sure. I just found the first room that looked safe to hide in."

"Are we even in the sewers?"

"Yeah, I think so. I followed some of the monsters, but I ran the other way into this hallway," Mia said. "There's runners for sure around here, but they seemed more concerned with the fire."

"I see. Well, I think we may be close to something, I mean this looks like a completely different area."

"It does." Though Mia had a pretty good idea what these rooms were used for, but she kept that to herself so it wouldn't ruin the mood.

"Hey! Aaron!" a loud voice shouted from the hallway.

Both Mia and Aries crouched down as they listened to the footsteps draw closer.

"Yeah, bro?" another man said.

"You strapped for the event? Or are you off?"

"Off? Yeah right, they got this place locked down, Vincent's orders. They want everyone upstairs."

"Alright."

Mia looked at Aries. She felt like she had heard the name Vincent before. Then she gasped, the doctor guy had said it while he was talking to someone through magic when he captured her. And what was this event they were talking about? Aries squatted down beside her. This must have something to do with Acome, at the very least, this may be the perfect time to look for the ring if everyone was busy at some event, But who was Mia kidding? They probably had the ring on lockdown, and without the ring she had no connection to Acome. How would she even find it? Why did everything have to feel so hopeless?

"Huh?" Mia heard Aries say. Mia turned around, who was she talking to? "Tink?" Aries bent down. Mia gasped and looked over Aries' shoulders and sure enough it was their little rat friend. "Oh my gosh, Tink," Aries cupped the small brown rat in her hands and held him to her face for a cuddle. "I can't believe you're alive."

Mia clasped her hands together. "Tink? Is that really him?"

"Where did you come from?" Aries asked. "Huh? What?"

"What?" Mia looked at Aries' shocked face.

"Mia," Aries said, her eyes filling with tears. "Mia, Karina's alive."

Mia gasped. "That's great news."

Aries nodded, then placed Tink back down on the ground. "And he knows where to go."

"Okay." Mia stood when Aries stood.

The pair ran across the room towards the wall, where there was a vent big enough to crawl through. The screen was torn. Tink stopped and looked at it and then at Aries. Aries nodded and pulled off the busted screen. The nails were rusted so it came off with ease. Mia resisted the urge to groan, but she really didn't want to stay in the open.

"In there, Tink?" Aries asked. Tink squeaked and ran around in circles. He jumped into the vent first and scurried off into the distance. Aries winced but stopped and looked to Mia. "I know this has been a living nightmare. Neither you nor Billie asked for this, but...but I want to thank you."

"Th-thank me?" Mia made an awkward smile.

"You believed in me back there, even if I know you were scared and you saved my life when you could have run away." Aries caught Mia's eyes and Mia felt hers start to water. "I swear to you, Mia, I will do everything in my power to turn this around. I swear this to you."

Mia didn't know what to say, so she only nodded. Aries was right, Mia never in a million years wanted this. She was just a regular girl, living a relatively stable life, but after everything Acome showed her how could she sleep knowing that there was a better world out there? Tink chirped and Aries turned around.

"Coming," Aries said, then turned back to Mia. "Ready?"

"Ready," Mia said.

"Tink, wait up," Aries whispered as she crawled in after him.

Mia waited for Aries to crawl in and watched the door to see if anyone was coming. When Aries was completely in, Mia followed. The vent had enough room to crawl through, but it was dusty and full of cobwebs and dead bugs. The further they crawled away from the room, the darker it became, and a familiar fear flared up in Mia. What if that creepy doctor was still around with those spiders? Mia would never forget those beady orange eyes. The memory alone almost paralyzed her. She slowed, but a gentle hand reached back and touched her arm, which startled Mia.

"It's okay," Aries said. "You're safe."

Mia made a humming sound, but Aries didn't let go of her arm until Mia started moving again. She helped Mia along as Tink's squeaks echoed off the sides of the vent. They crawled for what felt like forever when Aries started to slow.

"Everything okay?" Mia said as she tried not to panic.

"It's okay, but I think Tink wants us to go up."

"O-okay," Mia said as she tried to control her breathing. She hadn't realized how fast her heart was beating as she fought to keep her mind from wandering into scary places.

"I'm going to take your hand to help you up. Is that okay?"

"Y-yeah," Mia gasped. She was so scared that even Aries' voice made her jump.

Aries grabbed her hand and helped her up through a hole in the ventilation system where Mia finally saw a bit of light, much to her relief. The hole in the ventilation system was tight but led to a crawl space with concrete above and below them. It was dusty, but at least she could see. Mia crawled forward enough for Aries to hop up behind her. Then Tink scurried past her and returned. He squeaked as he ran past Mia to Aries.

"Up ahead?" Aries said from behind and Tink squeaked. "Thanks. Okay, follow Tink."

"Right." Mia crawled after Tink through the dusty tunnel.

Her hands and knees scraped against the gravelly surface. She didn't even want to know what her bare hands were touching, then she saw what Tink was so excited about. There was a hole up ahead that had no screen. The light was brighter, but not by much. Tink scurried forward again and disappeared over the edge of the hole.

"What?" Mia heard a familiar voice. Then a head popped up.

Mia saw the flash of red and stopped. "K-Karina?"

Karina gasped. "Mia!"

Mia crawled until she reached the end and slid out as Aries followed.

"Aries!" Karina squealed.

"Karina!" Aries cried as Karina fell into her sister's arms. The two sisters hugged each other as if it had been decades since they had seen one another.

Karina pulled away and looked around. "Where's Billie?" Aries frowned and Mia's smile lessened too. "N-no...I-I mean, I'm so sorry Mia."

"It's okay," Mia said as the sting of memory buzzed in her mind. Mia looked away when she noticed that there was someone else here, too. She could vaguely make out the shape. "Karina who's that?" Mia pointed in the direction of the shadow.

Karina looked behind her. "Oh, it's the baby. Guys, meet Tiny One." Both Aries and Mia were shocked to see Karina pick up a child, no older than three.

"Um, Karina," Aries said. "Where did you get a child?"

Karina comforted the wiggly child, "Well that's a long story, but I'm so glad you're alive, even though..." Karina trailed off.

"There will be time to honor her later," Aries said to both of them, "but now we must finish our mission."

"Oh-oh-oh," Karina whispered loudly. "There's still time."

"What?" Aries asked.

"I know where the ceremony is taking place," Karina said.

"Ceremony?" Aries asked.

"Yeah, it's what they need the ring for and this child," Karina said. "And I think it has something to do with Acome."

Mia reached out and rubbed the boy's cheeks. "They weren't planning on hurting him, were they?"

Karina frowned, then whispered, "They needed his b-l-o-o-d." She slowly spelled out, "For a s-a-c-r-i-f-i-c-e."

Mia gasped. That couldn't be right? This boy was just a child, and Mia didn't want to think about how they found him.

"Show us," Aries said.

Karina led them to another crawl space. Mia crawled behind Karina as she whispered little details about her journey to them. Apparently, she had been through her own little adventure. Mia was so relieved that Karina was able to save the child. It was terrible to think they were actually going to harm a child. Karina told them about the sacrifice room on the way. She said it was dripping with runners armed with big guns, but she said the ceremony hadn't started yet, and that the room it was in was grand and open. As if some kind of cheerful party was about to take place and not an evil ritual.

The strangest thing she mentioned was the large square object in the back of the room covered in a large red drape. She said just staring at it tugged at her heart. She couldn't even stand to be in its presence, so she left. She figured she had the child, and she made sure the people took the wrong blood. Her hope was that it would delay the ceremony, but she knew the ruse wouldn't last forever.

They crawled deeper into the sewers as they passed over many metal vents where people, including children, walked below them. The people didn't look like they were going to a party. They looked more like hostesses or servants as they scurried past with boxes and carts in hand. They climbed the last bit of inclines and found themselves in a tight crawl space filled with vents. Karina slowed, but Mia saw a light coming from a square hole.

"There," Karina whispered as she pulled her legs close to her so she could hop out.

Mia went next and was surprised to find herself in a very small room of sorts. There was a large vent that looked out into a large room below with dozens of people. In the back, just like Karina said, was a large square object with a red drape over it. Mia stared at it and felt an immense energy from it. It was so intense she couldn't look at it and crawled away.

"Mia?" Aries went to her. "What is it?"

"I-I, there's something not right about that thing." Mia started to shake.

Mia covered her ears as her head filled with the sound of rushing water. She trembled. It washed out all the voices around her and enclosed her like a tsunami.

"Forgive me," a voice so deep said that shook her to her core.

Mia clawed at her ears as she felt hands on her shoulders and back, but even that started to fade, then the darkness enclosed around her.

She gasped at the sensation of falling, when she felt something cool and soft under her legs. She opened her eyes, and she found herself on another plane again.

"W-where am I?" Mia looked around.

Hundreds of transparent rats scurried all around her, like ghosts. A cool breeze hit the back of Mia's neck, and a fog encircled her. A warmth found her and wrapped around her back like a blanket. Mia exhaled.

"Mia, I am grateful to have found you, and I am deeply sorry for the pain you have endured on my behalf."

"A-Acome?" Mia stood.

"Yes."

Mia stepped towards the voice as a flood of bright blue light filled the space, so bright she had to cover her eyes with her forearms. Her finger, the one that once bore the ring, tingled as if their connection was still there. Acome called her again, but she didn't have the ring. There was no way she could be useful to them now.

"I-I don't understand."

"I am here, and you have found me, Crimson Mouse."

"What?"

"Now come to me, Mia the Crimson Mouse. Lead the Darkness to me."

The sensation of falling returned along with a great wind.

"I-I don't understand!" Mia reached out as her body was blown backwards.

"Lead the Darkness to me."

A swirl of translucent bodies flowed around her. Ghostlike rats and mice raced by as a mighty cage formed around Mia. The rodents attacked the cage bars as the metal enclosed around her. Mia fell deeper into the darkness. She grasped for the bars as a burst of bright light blinded her. Mia shot up.

"Mia!" Aries said. "Mia, what happened?"

Mia looked around and saw Aries and Karina looking at her with more than a bit of concern on their faces. "I-I spoke to Acome again." Both Aries and Karina gasped. "They're-they're close." Mia's gaze floated to the large object in the back of the room and the shape was unmistakable. "The cage." Mia pointed.

Aries followed with her finger. "Acome." Aries glared with a glint of something dark flashing inside her deep crimson eyes.

"S-so, that is them?" Karina reached a hand up to her chest and Mia nodded slowly.

Aries balled her fist. Then turned to Mia. "Thank you, Crimson Mouse."

Mia's mouth hung open, then it shifted into a small smile. So, they made it after all, but how were they going to recover the ring and set Acome free?

38
Mary

Mary tapped her face with setting powder as she hurried to finish her look for the ceremony. The stress of the past seventy-two hours had been enough to age her ten years, but despite everything her mother still managed to order her a new dress and have it ready in time for the event. She was so grateful to her mother for doing this. The gown was gorgeous, and the midnight blue looked stunning on her flawless brown skin. Mary was going to be the talk of the ceremony when she walked in with her Kym by her side. She couldn't wait to break the news to her parents when Kym was ready to propose. Mary hoped it would bring great honor to her family since Eddy, the family's heir, was tragically taken from them. Then, once she was finally married, she would wipe out those bastard Silers.

She sighed at the still tender wound that lay upon her heart. She hadn't been groomed to take over the family business. Father had been so sure that it would be passed down to Eddy and Mary had been fine with that. Father and Mother were good to her, she wanted for nothing, but she supposed she would have to step up. And with her strong leadership skills and Kym's vision they would restructure this entire city and finally put those undeserving families below them where they belonged.

Mary heard a knock at the door and reached for her perfume. "Coming," she said as she dotted a bit behind her ears.

"It's me," her brother Alvert said.

"Oh, come in," Mary said as she puffed a bit of fragrance under her chin and rubbed a little on her wrist. Alvert sauntered in with a sleepy grin on his face. "Alvert, don't tell me you're high?" Mary gathered up her dress and walked to her brother. His black bow tie was tilted, so she straightened it.

"I'm not high," Alvert said with a playful tone.

"What are we going to do with you?" Mary said. "Come on."

Mary led the way towards the elevator down to the car. Alvert followed behind her in his best black suit and polished shoes. It was so good to see her younger brother again. She was glad he was spared the worst of it. Mother waited for her in the foyer, in her mulberry long sleeved chiffon dress. Her black hair was hot combed and styled into an elegant bun. She looked so graceful and refined, a true example of an upper-class woman who knew how to endure and overcome.

"Where's Father?" Mary asked.

"He's already at the ceremony," her mother said.

Mary nodded and started for the door but stopped when she heard footsteps on the white marble behind her.

"Leaving without me?" Kym grinned.

Mary gasped. "Kym." She ran to him. He looked absolutely perfect in his white and baby blue tailored suit. "I thought you would be at the ceremony already."

"Now, what kind of gentlemen would I be if I left such beautiful ladies to be escorted to the ball alone?"

Mary melted.

"Hey, I'm not a lady," Alvert corrected.

"You are correct, Lord Alvert, but I will not leave a single member of my beloved Mary's family to go alone to the ceremony."

Mary followed behind Kym as he walked to her mother. "Lady Amber, are you ready?" Kym asked.

"I am," Mary's mother purred.

Kym flashed a smile and led them to the door and opened it for them. Mary's mother followed next, but not before flashing an approving grin to her daughter. Mary felt the butterflies in her stomach. She would not only be in the arms of Kym all night, but she would be walking into the ceremony with him. The driver held open the door for them in one of the Sapphire's new black, sleek, gas-model cars. Mary loved the shine of the eloquently designed automobile. It was a gorgeous import, fit for a woman of her status. Mary's mother and brother rode in the first car, while Mary and Kym rode in the second.

The entire way there Mary rested in Kym's arms. "Does this mean that you will finally ask for my hand?"

Kym leaned over and kissed her on the head. "Only at your father's approval."

Mary giggled. "Then I shall start planning right away."

Kym chuckled as the driver took them to the Fort'nee manor.

Bright lights chased away the darkness of the early winter setting sun as luxury cars lined up at the Fort'nee manor. Kym's driver came to a stop and a valet opened the door for Mary. The cold air chilled her exposed legs, but Mary pulled her shawl over her shoulders and her beautiful, long, off-the-shoulder bouffant dress draped over her legs as she got out. Kym was there waiting for her. She smiled and took his hand as guest paused to look at them.

Kym led her up the brick stairs of the main house and all stopped and watched as they walked into the house together. Gasps and hushed whispers followed Mary as they entered the foyer and headed to the ballroom and Mary ate each and every one up. All eyes were on them, and the spotlight completely washed away the terror she had endured the days before. Mary caught sight of Faith and Gloria, and both women were looking at her as if their greatest nightmare had come true. Mary flashed the biggest grin in their direction. Those whores, especially that filthy slut Faith. Mary knew she didn't have to worry about her anymore. Kym could make Faith do anything and Mary had always wanted a pet.

The first to approach them were Kym's fathers. Lord Henry did not look pleased, and neither did Lord Porter. Mary squeezed Kym's hand and pulled her closer as the men slowed to a stop.

"Father," Kym addressed them both. "I hope that you will be civil tonight, especially in the presence of such a beautiful lady."

Lord Porter eyed Mary. "Dear son, I hope you have not forgotten these past seventy-two hours?"

"I have not," Kym calmly said. "I have also not forgotten under who's watch this nightmare has come to an end." Kym turned to Mary and squeezed her hand tight. "She is surely not a woman to be trifled with."

Lord Henry grunted. "I suppose not, and I guess I must thank you, Lady Mary, for coming through when your father could not."

Lord Porter snickered and never has Mary wanted to punch someone so hard in her entire life.

She clenched her teeth at the jab but refreshed her smile. "You can always count on me, Lord Henry. I also have my eye on what is most important and that includes my future. And I hold the Ao Almasi Company in great esteem. I only wish to see it prosper."

Lord Porter laughed out loud this time. "Is that so, child? And what does a dull girl know about business?"

Kym tugged on her hand, but she knew how to hold her own. "My father, though not perfect, is a very accomplished necromancer and key master and a prominent member of the very demographic for your precious gems. Would it not be a blessing to have such a network married into your family?"

Lord Porter raised an eyebrow, then smirked. He turned to his son. "Seems like you've bagged a smart one."

Lord Henry let out a chuckle. "Well, my son, you have surely selected someone with a clear vision."

Kym bowed. "I always have my family's interest at heart, even when I devolve into domestic matters. Let us continue this conversation at a later time."

"Of course," Lord Henry said, then turn to Mary. "Enjoy your evening, my lady."

"Thank you, Lord Henry," Mary nodded to them both. They would see soon enough what an asset she would be.

Kym walked Mary away as the other heads of the Five Family's watched them. She enjoyed every bit of anger on Lord Lor'es and Lady Amma's faces. Had they not raised a bunch of self-righteous whores, perhaps they would be in Mary's place. Lady Gladie spotted them, and she raised her glass right as Mary passed Lord Jaden and his wife Lady Nia on their way to their seats. Mary relished in every bit of attention they got. No one would be here without Mary's hard work and they knew it.

"Lord Kym," a woman's voice called from behind them.

Mary turned and flashed a glare in Joy's direction. She must think she's the talk of the town in that gaudy pink gown she wore.

"Lady Joy," Kym greeted the eldest Hoo'nae sister.

"It is a pleasure to see you, Lord Kym, though I am puzzled at your choice of accessory." Joy's eyes flickered to Mary.

Mary tensed, ready with a comeback, but Kym squeezed her hand and looked down at the small red bow and arrow pin he wore of his collar. "This? Ah yes, I believe it was a gift from your Aunt Loursha. Is she still teaching those young alchemist at the academy?"

Joy's face went sour.

"I've been to the college a few times. Such a rowdy bunch and talkative, too," Kym said. "If I recall correctly, doesn't Professor Kamich work in the transformative arts? I've heard he really likes to get hands on in his class, but you would already know that since you were his top pupil."

Joy's face flushed with embarrassment as she looked between Kym and Mary. "A-well, if you would excuse me."

Joy turned around and walked away and it took everything inside of Mary not to laugh. She was such a whore, just like her sisters. All of them were truly below them, but not without use. Though maybe she could have some fun with Faith. She seemed to like it when Kym had her on the ground. It would be entertainment enough, at least until she could devise a plan to torture and kill Vincent Lorne. That was a man she would love to see his balls crushed, body impaled on a spear, and lit on fire, but Mary took a deep breath and composed herself. Now was not the time to worry about such lowly trash.

Mary didn't see her father anywhere, but she was sure he was downstairs working hard. The clock struck five twenty-three and everyone migrated towards the elevators. Mary hated going down to the ceremony hall, but at least she wouldn't have to do it alone.

As everyone filtered down to the ceremony hall, Mary and Kym made light conversations with distant relatives and family acquaintances. Kym left a few times to gather Mary food and wine, and Mary found she was actually enjoying herself despite the dreary setting.

A light tapping on a glass rung through the room as everyone looked to the front. Lord Jaden beamed in his fitted light blue suit as he raised his glass. The room quieted as some moved towards the front, while others took seats in the middle of the room. A servant girl walked in from one of the side doors rolling in a gold cart with a large jar of the ceremonial blood in it.

"Good evening, everyone," Lord Jaden boomed with a grand smile on his face, "and welcome to our annual renewal ceremony." He held out his hands in a big flashy manner as the servant girl placed the jar on a small table next to the key gear. The servant then opened the top and began to pour the thick blood inside. Lord Jaden watched with glee, then faced the crowd again. "Excellent. We will be starting the ceremony soon, but first may I unveil our generous guest. For without them, we would be a little less rich." Lord Jaden laughed along with the rest of the room.

He stepped to the side as the floor started to rumble. Mary watched with disinterest as the concrete platform that housed the golden cage rose a full two stories. People looked on with smiles on their faces, in anticipation. Even Kym seemed intrigued.

"Please welcome, Acome, Spirit of Julilie!" Lord Jaden lifted one hand.

Servants walked to each side of the raised platform and drew the ropes to lift away the red drape. The room clapped and held up their glasses. Mary looked at the ugly creature in the cage. The thing looked like a corpse dressed for a wake. It rested on a bed of ugly dried flowers and incense, with its rotted body that had the head of a disfigured dog and the body of an emaciated bear.

It was bound at its arms, torso, and legs, even its muzzle was caged. Its eyelids looked black and puffy as if someone had attempted to scrub them clean, but it only left them more bruised. Its matted fur was a dingy light blue, and frankly the creature looked half dead. It was so hideous. Mary didn't see the point of revealing it at all.

"Such a shame to see such a powerful creature in a state like that," Kym said.

Mary scoffed. "You can't be serious?"

Kym chuckled. "Come now, I can have a little compassion for it. If it were up to me, I would have it lobotomized so it could be optimized for its power."

Mary chuckled. Kym never stopped dreaming. He was truly a visionary. Lord Jaden mixed back into the crowd as the guest resumed their conversation. Mary followed Kym around as she counted down the minutes until she could have her beloved once more in the sheets of her warm bed.

39
Karina

Karina wiped tears from her face as she sobbed quietly next to her sister. How could anyone treat another living creature like this? There was so much pain that radiated from Acome's body. Could those people not feel it? Could they not see how much Acome suffered? And yet, they all carried on at the party as if it were nothing.

"We need to get the ring," Karina said.

"But how?" Mia said as she wiped her teary eyes. "We're outnumbered."

Aries didn't say a word, but Karina saw the anger that surged behind her sister's eyes. Karina sat down and thought. The ring was locked away in a cage. Even if they found out the blood was useless Karina knew they had other children waiting. Karina sighed.

"I hate to be a downer, but even if we get the ring, how do we rescue Acome?" Karina said. "They look super heavy to carry."

"They need the ring," Mia said. She gazed out at Acome. "I-I don't know how, but Acome said that the ring was a part of them. It's the key to freeing them."

"That's good enough for me," Aries said.

"Alright, plan get the ring is on," Karina said, but they needed a distraction, something to draw everyone away. "I've got it."

"What's the plan?" Aries looked at her with such intensity and commitment, like she really trusted her and valued her opinion.

"I can unlock the cage using my keys," Karina said.

"Keys?" Mia tilted her head. "As in magic?"

Karina nodded.

"You can cast keys?" Aries said.

"I can now," Karina said. "I'm not sure how, but I think it has something to do with Acome. The closer I get to them, the stronger I get."

Aries hummed. "I-I think I've been experiencing a similar thing."

"Really?" Karina beamed, and Aries nodded. "Right, so, I'll open the cage first, then I'll blow out the lights. That should give us enough cover to grab the ring and try to get it to Acome."

Aries nodded. "Alright."

Just an alright? Karina could get use to this, but now it was time to show her big sister and everyone what she was capable of. Karina took a deep breath and reached for her key. It was easy to find after she spent half the evening using it. She started to chant and all the key spells she tirelessly wrote on her skin started to appear and glow. She heard both Aries and Mia gasp as her key gate appeared in the air next to her. *Okay, Karina, you've done this a dozen times. You got this.* Karina focused on the cage where the ring lay.

"Open," Karina said and her key gate burst open and a faint glimmering red tendril shot through the air vents towards the ceiling and broke apart into the size of a mouse.

Karina focused on it, shaping it down to the size of a coin as she pushed it towards the small cage where the ring sat. Karina held her breath and hoped no one would notice. A glimmer of red connected with the lock and forced its way inside. The lock jiggled and Karina quickly reeled her power back to work the orb of energy more slowly. The lock twitched slightly, then fell open. Karina let out a breath as Mia scooted forward to scan the room.

"The lock! It looks open," Mia turned to Karina.

Karina beamed, then turned to her sister who stared at her with eyes wide open.

Aries' expression softened. "You did it."

"I-um, well I've been practicing all day and I—"

Aries reached out and touched Karina's arm. "Granny was right. You are something special."

Karina's mouth fell open, and her eyes started to water. She quickly wiped her face.

Aries smile lingered, then looked back at the front. "The ring cage is unlocked now."

"Now for the lights," Karina said. "I'll try to burn them out in one burst."

"Be careful," Aries said.

"I will," Karina said, though she was a little nervous. So far she had only focused on little things like nails and hinges. The lights in this room were massive and there were nearly two dozen of them. This might use up all her energy, but she had to try. They were running out of time. "There's another floor vent you can use to get down without breaking your legs from jumping from this height. Tink told me about it."

"Okay," Aries said, then turned to Mia. "I'm not sure how long we'll have in the dark, but if you can get the ring that's a start."

"M-me?" Mia looked between the two of them.

"Don't worry, I'll cover you," Aries said. "If I go alone and die, then the ring will never make it to Acome."

"I can help," Karina butted in.

"No, Karina stay up here with the child," Aries said.

"Aww," Karina pouted.

"No whining," Aries said.

"Fine," Karina said.

"Can you do that for us?" Aries turned to Mia.

Mia looked to Karina and Aries, then down at her hand that once bore the ring. She made a fist, then looked back at them. "I'll do it."

"Thank you," Aries said. "Are you ready, Karina?"

"Ready!" Karina said.

Karina rested her hands in her lap and focused all her energy on her key gate. It blazed bright red and ready to go next to her. She looked at the ceiling and visualized all the lights and tried to ignore the careless chatter from the guest below. She closed her eyes and started to chant as the warmth and pressure swirled in her chest. She concentrated on the lights. She couldn't see them at first, but then in the shadows of her mind dozens of dim lights glowed far away.

She moved her consciousness towards the light, and her focus became clearer. So clear she could hear them buzzing. Karina opened her eyes and held out her hands.

"Brighten," she uttered.

The key door opened and a swoosh of air fluctuated around her. She felt the heat on her skin as the bright red tendrils slithered through the vent once more, but this time they burned bright red and swarm upward. The tendrils attached themselves to the lights like the sticky silk of a spiderweb and transferred their energy into the giant white bulbs. The lights buzzed in response and it rang in her ears. Karina winced, but felt a hand reach out to her. It was her sister, she felt her worry, but Karina shook her head. She could do this. The energy flowed out of her like a sewer flooded with stormwater.

"G-go," Karina hissed through the pain.

Karina heard Aries and Mia shuffle away. She also heard Tink squeak with concern, but she couldn't stop now. She had a job to do. Her heart raced as the tendrils fed the lights its power. She grunted as she took a deep breath and gave the key a final push.

"Brighten!"

Another intense wave surged out of her. All her energy was being sucked away as if someone held a powerful magnet above her. It sucked her dry, but she had to hold on. *Aries, Mia, I got you.*

The bulbs shattered and everything went dark. Karina gasped as she collapsed to the floor. She panted with her eyes shut, but she pried them open so she could find her sister and Mia. Screams erupted around the room as Karina crawled to the vent. She pulled herself up, but she couldn't see anything. Then dim red lights came on around the room.

"Damnit," Karina panted.

It was the emergency lights. Guest scattered to the exits and walls, but still Karina couldn't make out where Aries or Mia were, then she saw a flash of blonde cut through the crowd. Mia ran towards the center. Gunfire rained from the rail above Acome's cage. Karina gasped. It looked like the guards had spotted her as well.

Karina caught a glimpse of red and saw her sister, but the runners on the ground had already spotted her. Aries pulled out her retracting pole and swatted down the runners like flies, but now more poured into the large space. They were going to get caught. Karina started to panic. This was a stupid plan, a stupid, stupid plan. She pulled at her hair. She needed to come up with something fast but what could she do all by herself? She was all alone.

"I go!" Tink squeaked.

"Wait, Tink, no." Karina reached out her hand, but Tink slipped away.

Now she was going to lose him, too. Gunfire rattled in her ears as tears dropped from her eyes and Tiny One started to cry. Karina turned around. The boy was so scared.

"There, there." She opened her arms and walked over to him. She rubbed his soft black hair as she held back a sniffle. They were so close, this was their only chance, and they completely blew it.

"You are never alone."

A deep voice spoke to her and Karina's eyes immediately shifted to Acome. Their eyes were cracked open, but there was a slither of blue light that glinted there. Karina felt the heat raise in her body once more. It filled her up like a rubber glove and continued to fill her until she thought she would explode. What was she going to do up here? She looked below and saw Mia doing her best not to get caught and then she saw her sister who was fighting with everything she had. Even Tink had left.

If only there was a way to call in reinforcements, but her clan was so small. Then in that moment a spell popped into her mind, like a flash in a hot pan. There was a spell, one that she saw in an old book she got from her granny.

"I-I am never alone," Karina recalled the summoning key.

This spell would be much greater than any key she had ever cast, even stronger than the one she used on the lights, but she had to try. The little boy tugged on her shirt and she looked down at him. This was it. She rubbed his head again.

"Wait here, okay?" Karina said. "Can you do that for me?"

The little boy nodded and sat quietly beside her. Karina lowered her head and tried to block out the sounds of screams and gunfire. She stretched her arms out wide and splayed her fingers. The energy surged behind her key gate so intense she felt it. It swirled as it refilled and turned her body hot. The heat rocked her in waves so intense she felt like she would pass out, but she straightened her stance.

"Ancestors long since passed," Karina spoke in the spirit's tongue. *"Walk with me once more in the land of the living. Lead me your eternal strength, come forth, swarm once more in the name of Acome, spirit and keeper of balance, in the name of your great king, Nezumi'Mfalme, lend me your strength!"*

Karina's body bucked forward as sparks of red light lit up the entire crawl space. Her body glowed a bright red and every key she wrote on her arms and legs became as visible as the sigils on the key gate doors. The ancient words covered her body from head to toe as the energy burned through her veins. Karina screamed as light burst from her gate and tunneled into the walls and into the ground.

The ground rumbled. Everywhere the intense energy grew, building up all around her, in the walls, under the floors, and above the ceiling. The chatter and noise of thousands of voices filled her mind and echoed through the vents.

"Come to me!" Karina screamed.

Karina completed the key and every nerve ending on her body caught fire in a bright red blaze so powerful that it kicked off every vent screen in the room. The wave burned through Karina's body, and took her last ounce of strength as she toppled over, but not before she got to see the fruit of her labor.

Rats and mice poured in from every vent in the room. Their eyes flashed a fierce bright red as they screeched. Guns rattled and screams joined their chorus. Granny was right, their clan was the Darkness, and this was the army that was going to follow the light to victory. Karina's body hit the floor and everything went silent.

40 Mary

Mary walked next to Kym as he worked the room. As much as she loved listening to his ideas, she was bored of this party. She hadn't seen her brother Alvert around or any of his friends, so he was likely hiding somewhere getting high. Mary's gaze wandered around the room where she finally saw her father. He looked so terribly tired, and he probably was. He had to put all this together, and yet it was Lord Jaden who addressed the room as if he had lifted a single finger. A figure passed behind her father and Mary caught sight of Vincent Lorne.

Mary tightened her grip around Kym's hand so tight that he turned to her, but she ignored him. How was he allowed to show his grimy face around here? Kym tugged on her hand and led her away from the group of Ruby-Gyme Metal Works supervisors.

"Tense, are we?" Kym teased.

Mary felt embarrassed to have her temper flare like that. "It's nothing, my love."

Kym stopped and cupped Mary's chin. He stared deeply into her eyes with such hunger and wanting. "If anything is causing my love such stress, I will gladly squash it."

Mary fell into his arms. How had she got so lucky in finding this perfect man? Kym leaned in for a kiss when suddenly all the lights in the room burst. Shards of glass peppered the crowd and Mary screamed as Kym brought her closer to him to shield her. Darkness cloaked everything as screams and the sounds of chairs falling to the ground filled the air. Panic ripped through Mary's chest and all the fear she desperately tried to bury floated to the surface like a coffin buried in shallow ground.

"What's happening?" Mary cried out as the red emergency lights turned on.

"I'm not sure." Kym pulled Mary closer.

Gunshots rang out and Kym covered Mary's head as he led her to one of the exits. Guests pushed and shoved to get out of the way as Mary stumbled in her heavy midnight blue gown. Her shawl fell off as she ran and when she tore a look behind her, she saw a blur of blonde running towards the front of the room. They were heading to the ring, and this time Mary wanted no part of it. The doors quickly filled with bodies as guests trampled servants and runners forced their way in.

More gunshots echoed around the room. It was pure madness. Mary saw her mother trying to force herself through an exit door, when a man reached out and ripped her out of the way. Mary gasped as she watched Lord Lor'es tear her mother down so that he and his wife could escape.

"Mother!" Mary cried out, but Kym never loosened his grip on Mary's hand.

Then Mary felt a rumble in the ground. She looked at the floors as guests bumped and pushed her out of the way. Kym yanked her forward right as a rush of filthy sewer rats and mice flooded the room. The wave of animals poured in from the vents above them and through the vents that lined the floor and attacked anyone within their reach. The fearful guests went feral. Husbands abandoned wives, parents trampled children, elderly were knocked off their feet as the rodents attacked anyone unlucky enough to find themselves on the ground.

Kym dragged Mary along, but a man tore through their grip and Mary stumbled to the floor. Feet trampled her body as they stepped on her legs, back, and hands. Heels crushed her fingers and Mary yanked her hand back as it poured with blood. Then the rodents sat upon her. They flew into her dress and tore up her calves and bit her thighs. Mary screamed as they bit her exposed arms and neck and pulled at her hair with their sharp, tiny jaws. One bit her on the lip and another bit her on her nose as she thrashed about. She yanked the one off her lips, which left a gaping bloody hole as another rat sank its pointed teeth into her right eyeball. Mary hollered in agony as the rat burst the eyeball and chewed towards her brain.

"Mary!" Kym hollered as he ripped away the rodents.

He dragged her to her feet as blood poured from her face. Mary cried as the rats continued to attack her and Kym dragged her towards the door. She stumbled again, dragging Kym down with her, but he reached out a hand for her, when a stray bullet blasted through his temple, spraying Mary's chest and face with his blood. Mary screamed as a rat jumped over his corpse and bit her right on the tongue.

41
Aries

Aries jumped back in shock as rats and mice with red glowing eyes flooded the room. She put her hands up to block them, but they all ran around her. She looked behind her. They attacked the runners and the guests, but not her or Mia. Aries furrowed her brow, then looked up at the vent where they were hiding. A faint red light started to fade. *Karina,* Aries clenched her fist, then she quickly scanned the room for Mia. She found her, but she was on the ground as the rodents ran around her.

"Mia!" Aries ran to her. Mia looked up and Aries pointed to the front. "Get the ring!"

Mia scrambled to her feet as Aries turned to cover her. *Thank you,* Aries whispered to her sister above. All she had to do is cover Mia now. She weaved in and out of the crowd as gunshots fired around her. No one had good aim because of the attacking rats and mice, but that didn't mean it was safe to run around. Aries took cover behind a table as another guest dropped dead on the floor, their back bleeding from gunshot wounds. Aries looked up and saw Mia push her way through as torrents of guest and runners that ran into her.

Aries jetted from behind the table, withdrew her retracting pole, and swatted and tripped anyone who got too close to Mia. The ground started to rumble again as a loud scraping sound came from her right. Aries looked around and noticed a large door in the front of the room. It was next to Acome's cage, just off to the side below the rails where the runners were shooting from. Giant, two-story doors crawled open as concrete scraped against concrete, until they were fully open. Dust floated from the pitch-black opening, followed by the sound of metal clinging against metal. Aries froze as she faced the door. Whatever was coming sounded big.

She tore her gaze from the door to find Mia as the sound of metal clinking against metal grew louder and louder. Mia was at the small cage that housed the ring. Aries inched closer to her as Mia grabbed the lock and threw it to the ground. The thud of the metal grew louder, this time it sounded like it hit stone. It was walking towards them. Mia reached in and grabbed the ring and Aries wanted to sigh with relief but Mia was too close to the opening.

"Mia!" Aries screamed as a shadow shifted in the darkness and then the form of a giant metal creature stepped into the room.

Aries stumbled back at the eighteen-foot-tall creature with eight large black mechanical legs. Its two black claws clamped in the air and embedded in between them, on the torso, was a man. Under the man's hip was a gleaming blue stone that shimmered as he walked further into the room, revealing the rest of his body along with a long black segmented tail with a stinger on the end. Aries gasped as the creature turned its attention to Mia. It lunged forward faster than Aries could track and swung its large black claw at Mia and knocked her away from the altar.

"Mia!" Aries screamed.

The creature's eight legs clanked to the middle of the room. Its all-black body looked like a demon in the red light. Its sharp, serrated claws opened and closed as if it were stretching as an animal would do when it awoke from a deep sleep.

"So, this is the troublesome pair I've heard so much about," a man with short wavy hair on one side of his head and a metal plate embedded in the other side said as he turned his full attention to Aries, moving his large body in her direction. "Hardly looks like a challenge, but I'll be happy to relieve you of your duty regardless."

The creature clattered toward Aries at untraceable speed and swung its giant claws at Aries. All she could do was dodge as she raced to the back of the room. This thing was so much bigger than the monsters back in Dr. Acknid's lair. The creature put themselves between her and Acome as Mia lay lifelessly on the other side of the room.

"Fuck you!" Aries cursed.

The man only tilted his head in mild interest before he shifted forward with his claws open. Aries flipped out of the way as the right claw snapped beside her face. Aries ducked and slipped on the carpet, which saved her from the jaws of the left claw. The man pulled back and from behind him his long-segmented tail with a sharp stinger at the end followed and spewed green liquid at her.

She jumped out of the way just in time, but the burning smell of acid was unmistakable. She looked at the spot the liquid touched and there was only a soupy mess of melted chairs and rodent carcasses. Aries cursed, but the swarm of rodents surged forward refocusing their rage. They tried to climb the beast, but the metal was too slick. The man grunted as he showered the small animals with acid once more and smashed others under his eight legs.

Aries couldn't bear to watch. All those rats and mice who had risk their lives to help them didn't deserve this. It filled her chest with so much rage and grief to watch them die. Aries growled as she clenched tightly to her retracting pole. She would not let this monster stand in her way.

"Oh?" the man said. "You still have some fight in you?"

"I will not fall to the likes of you!" Aries pointed the pole at the man.

"Vincent! Hurry up!" an angry man in a blue suit shouted from the exit. "We need to finish the ceremony!"

Vincent sighed and looked as if he were dealing with a tantrum-throwing child. "Very well." Vincent turned his full attention back towards Aries. "It's not too late to run, child. If you leave now, you might make it to the tunnels at the edge of the city."

"I'm not going anywhere!" Aries barked.

"Your funeral, but don't say I didn't give you a chance when you find yourself getting ripped apart by my claws."

Vincent charged and used his claws to grab at her. Aries barely dodged as she ran towards the back of the room. Beast or not, it was a man that controlled it and any man could be cut down. Aries focused on all the pressure building up in her chest. It was so intense it felt like she was going to explode. It must be because of her proximity to Acome, but it was at a level that surely would bring anyone else to their knees.

She tapped into the power raging inside of her, holding nothing back. If it killed her so be it. She was the Darkness. She would carve a hole through this nightmare and release the light.

Her two braids danced in the air as Aries reached for her key gate. "Open!" She released her power with one word.

Sparks of bright red electricity flowed into her body from her key gate and down her retracting pole as she flipped into the air and twirled between Vincent's two giant black claws. Her pole hit one of the claws and the power that surged from it tore through the joint and the claw clattered to the ground. Vincent rushed backwards, but there wasn't an ounce of fear on his face. His expression was deadly blank as his segmented tail spewed acid around the room.

Aries dodged and jumped in the air as she danced between Vincent's working right claw and his stinging tail. She moved faster each time he attacked as if Acome funneled all their energy into her. The power, it felt so painfully good she wanted to rip apart this man's body piece by piece.

Vincent shifted from left to right, his eight legs crashing through tables and bodies like a mallet did through the hard shells of melons. Aries flipped in the air, out of the way, but slipped on a pool of blood. Vincent brought his claw down as she rolled away, only to be caught by one of her long red braids. Aries screamed as her momentum was stopped by a strong yank on her scalp. She rolled to all fours, but both her braids were caught under Vincent's claw.

Their eyes met and there was nothing behind his dark eyes. He looked down on her like one would do a cockroach they were about to squash. Aries stumbled back as Vincent's segmented tail snaked around him. She braced herself for contact, but it never came.

Her eyes shot up and found him swatting at a small group of rats, one of which looked very familiar.

"Tink!" Aries cried out.

Vincent swatted and punched the rats from his body. He grabbed one and Aries gasp as she tried to pull her hair free and watched him crush its body with his hand. Aries hissed with pain as she drew her power from her gate into her hands and suddenly, they ignited. Aries cried out, but the flames did not burn her, instead, they torched the ends where her fingers wrapped around her hair. She quickly drew more power and singed the two braids in half and freed herself.

"Tink!" Aries searched for her friend and saw Vincent swat him away with his arm.

"Flames?" Vincent clinched his fist tight. "Now that's interesting."

The blue stone embedded below his hip where his body was attached to the machine started to glow. Hot, light gray bolts of lightning erupted from the stone and rolled down his body. Aries growled as she picked up her retracting pole and ran towards him with all the power she had. She jumped high in the air to attack Vincent, but he used his claw to block her and blasted her back. Aries flew towards the wall, but shifted her body so that her feet would connect with the wall instead. She then shot towards Vincent as nothing but pure rage coursed through her body. All she could smell was blood. All that she wanted was blood.

Vincent used his good claw to block her. His lightning struck her like a metal rod, but her bright red flames protected her. She shot a blow of hot red energy down her retracting pole as she rolled off his claw and connected with his left arm, slicing the limb clean off at the shoulders.

Vincent stumbled back as his severed left arm hit the floor. Blood gushed from his shoulder as Aries spun around.

"I'm going to kill you!" Aries hissed as the flames crawled up her retracting pole, up her arms and torso, engulfing her face and body in bright red flames that flared outward like the hair of a rat.

Vincent shifted around with his tail aimed at her, pain and anger laced through his face plain and clear to read. "Bring it on! Cause I ain't met a single enemy I couldn't cut down!" Vincent scuttled towards her with his claw open and segmented stinger pointed at her.

42
Mia

A wave of heat blew through Mia's short blonde hair as the muffled sounds of screams reached her ears. Where was she? And what was that terrible smell? Mia couldn't focus. All she wanted to do was go back to sleep in her comfy bed. Mia's stared mindlessly through half open eyes. Everything was a blur of dark red and brown and her eyelids were so heavy. She could easily slip back into the darkness, back into her dreams.

"Mia!" A familiar voice echoed in her head. *"Mia! Mia, get up!"*

"B-Billie..." Mia opened her eyes a little as she watched the floor move.

"Mia! Get up!"

Mia half-smiled, until the image of Billie's gaping mouth and broken jaw flashed in her mind. Mia's eyes shot open, and she slowly leaned up. There was no way Billie was here. Billie was dead. Her head was spinning as her nose twitched from a rancid burning smell. Something crashed behind her, and she jerked her head around. Mia muffled a scream when she saw what looked like a giant metallic insect skittering around the room and Aries was fighting it. Only, it couldn't be Aries, because she was completely on fire. She didn't look human at all as the flames wrapped around her like fur.

Mia watched in horror as the monster's claws knocked Aries into the wall. Aries rebounded quick and exploded towards them in a furious ball of fire so hot Mia could feel it. Rodents swarmed the room feasting on people and swirling below Acome's cage. This was utter madness. Mia winced when she tried to move her right arm. A piece of wooden chair impaled her. She cried out as the smell of fire and acid choked the room. This was too much. She couldn't possibly hope to do anything.

"Aries!"

Mia heard someone scream and looked to the back of the room. A man with bandages over his head held a knife to Karina's throat. Aries turned and looked at her sister.

"Karina!" Aries screamed.

"Give up, girl!" the man shouted and Mia recognized that voice. It was the evil doctor.

Dr. Acknid's orange-eyed spiders joined the swarm and flooded the room. Aries clinched her pole as her gaze focused on Dr. Acknid. She looked completely feral. The monster man moved his giant metal body back as he snapped his remaining working claw.

"Aries!" Karina winced. "Don't worry about me!"

Dr. Acknid pressed the knife harder against Karina's throat. "Shut up, girl! Vincent! Finish them!" Mia closed her eyes. She couldn't watch another one of her friends be killed.

Karina screamed and Mia opened her eyes. The swarm of rodents now circled Dr. Acknid. They attacked his spiders, tearing them apart.

"Impossible!" Dr. Acknid wailed. "Impossible! How can you control that many puppets! Your kind are substandard casters! Impossible!"

Vincent snapped his claw as his segmented tail snaked around him. "Caster or not, they will die today!"

Vincent charged for Karina and Aries dashed out in front of her and blocked him with a glowing ball of fire. Mia crawled away as the flame licked at her back and feet. All she wanted was for this to be over. She was so afraid. She closed her eyes when she felt something touch her arm. When she opened her eyes, she gasped.

"Tink." Mia watched the little rat squeak as he held something. "T-the ring."

He held it up towards her and looked back towards Acome. Mia shook her head. She couldn't. But looking into Tink's eyes she realized this was the only way to end this nightmare.

With a shaky hand she took the ring. Her right arm ached. She couldn't run with this stick in her arm. She put the fabric of her shirt into her mouth and bit down as she pulled out the stick of wood. She muffled a cry by biting harder onto her shirt. It started to bleed, and Mia looked around for something to stop the bleeding. She saw a corpse with a leather purse around the chest. Mia crawled over to it and ripped the purse from the body. She undid the straps and used it as a tourniquet, then found some dining cloths to wrap the wound.

She took a deep breath. It was now or never. Mia turned to Acome's cage. It was at least two stories above the ground and there was no ladder, but she had to try somehow. She crawled to her feet and ran to the front of the room.

A fireball erupted in the middle of the room as hot metal crushed tables and chairs around her. She breathed hard as she stumbled over the half-eaten bodies the rodents had left to rot. Tink ran alongside her, squeaking loudly and suddenly all the rodents swarmed around her. They gathered at the foot of the wall and made a ramp with their swarming bodies. Mia held her breath as she balled the ring up tight in her fist and started to climb.

Behind her she heard the terrifying sounds of the monster's claws, followed by another ear shattering scream from one of her friends. She flinched but she continued to climb over the warm squeaking chattering bodies of the rodents. Crawling forward, slipping constantly, she reached out towards the edge of the concrete. Her fingers gripped it and she swung her injured arm over the side as she kicked herself up from her foundation of warm bodies.

She made it to the top and gasped for fresh air, but there was only smoke. She crawled forward and stood as she used the wall for balance. She looked to Acome, at their puffy swollen eyes that still glowed with a glimmer of hope. She held the ring in hand and sprinted for the cage, but from the darkness a hand reached out and grabbed her by her left arm and threw her into the wall. Mia gasped as flames danced around her.

"You stupid bitch!" a bloodied man shouted at her. "I have worked too hard to get this ceremony up and running! Sacrificed too much to let a dirty street person like you interfere!"

The man charged Mia and she rolled out of the way. She was so out of breath, but she tightened her grip on the ring and crawled towards the wall. The man reached out and grabbed her ankle and pulled her towards him.

"Do you have any idea who I am! I am the only person keeping this shit show running. I swear I'll die before I let a whore stop me, the great Doctor Moore Granite, from fulfilling my duty!"

The man glared wildly at Mia. His eyes filled with rage. He jumped on her chest and wrapped his hands around her neck to choke her. Mia gasped and clawed at his fingers as she tried to buck him off. She tried to scream but her throat was being crushed. Suddenly from the corner of her eye a brown blur attacked Dr. Granite's face, biting him on the eyebrow. It was Tink. The little brown rat chomped down and wouldn't let go.

"Tink!" Mia reached out as Dr. Granite grabbed ahold of his body.

Tink screeched as he bit down on Dr. Granite's hand. The man hollered and threw the rat on the floor and began to stomp on him. Mia cried out as she crawled towards him, but Tink looked directly at her.

"Go!" she swore she heard him say as Dr. Granite stomped him to death. Tears ran down Mia's cheeks as she tore her eyes away from the grizzly sight. She still had a job to do. Mia kicked herself off the ground and stumbled into a run. She was above the cage as her feet pounded the metal walkway. Flames and smoked polluted the air as the last of the living scattered to the exits. Mia reached the edge of the platform and jumped several feet down to the cage below. A sting of pain shot up her legs, but she crawled towards the edge and climbed down the side to reach Acome's mouth.

The spirit opened its eyes and watched her. Mia pushed herself forward as she reached her hand into the cage towards Acome's mouth. She inched the ring towards its black infected jaw and lifted the skin and wedged the ring inside. Mia winced as she pushed it further into its mouth, when suddenly the metal grew too hot to hold and Mia let go. She ignored the pain from her burning fingertips and looked up at their mouth.

"I hope this helps," Mia said as her vision blurred. When her eyes refocused, she watched as hot liquid gold dripped from its lips, then a light started to glow.

"No!" Dr. Granite growled.

Acome's eyes shot open and burned a fiery light blue. They exploded from their cage in a fire ball of blue flames as their body grew and grew until they broke through the ceiling and out into the open air. The blue flames fell from Acome's body like a wave and ate up everything that they deemed unworthy.

Vincent held his claws up in defense but the flames reduced his body to ash. Concrete and stone rained on everyone and everything below as Acome took form. Mia was thrust backwards from Acome's raw power and flew through the air. This was it. Mia shut her eyes, only to be caught by something warm and soft. Mia opened her eyes and found herself on a carpet of light blue fur, only it wasn't. It was Acome's ginormous paw.

A blinding bright light shot from Acome's body and pierced the sky, clearing the clouds away. Mia looked above her and for the first time in her life she saw the vast beautiful star filled sky. It was breathtaking.

"Thank you," a voice said on the breeze as Mia sat hundreds of feet in the air and watched a blue wave of flames flood the city below. The tsunami of power washed through the streets from Uptown, but only crushed the things inside the wall. On her shoulder she felt something tap her, she turned around and saw the transparent shadow of her best friend. Mia gasped and crawled towards her.

"Billie," Mia cried out as tears wet her cheeks.

Billie smirked, as she started to fade away. "Damn girl, you did it."

Mia choked. "I couldn't've done it without you. I-I... heck, I don't know if I can live without you."

"You'll survive. You're a strong girl. Lady Valkyrie made sure of that."

"Oh, Billie." Mia fell into her best friend's arms one last time. Mia held onto her for as long as she could, crying out as Billie slowly drifted away. "Billie."

Mia cried and collapsed to her knees as the last bit of her best friend drifted away. The essence of her swirled from blue to a soft purple, then morphed into a small purple mouse. The mouse ran to Mia's cheeks and gave her a final kiss before it drifted upwards towards the sky. Mia held out her hand to follow it and noticed all the soft bright lights that floated upward around her. It was beautiful.

"Mia!"

Mia turned and saw her friends Karina and Aries in Acome's other paw. Tears filled her eyes. The exhaustion finally took her as the warmth of Acome's spirit purified the city.

Epilogue

One Year Later

Mia walked through the soft green grass of the garden as the warm sun beat down on her back. Her hands gently touched the shell of a home that once belonged to a member of the Five Families. Her long, soft, lavender dressed dragged across the ground as she looked at all the marigolds and snapdragons she planted herself from the seed trade. She stepped into a grand foyer whose walls were crumbled and covered in green leafy vines. She walked over the cracked marble floors and stepped out of the manor into the backyard so she could look down at the glistening river below.

Rats gathered around her feet before scurrying into the tall grass as a soft breeze carried the smell of freshly tilled Earth past her nose. Gone was the smell of sour sewage and smog and the cloudy days that poured rain rank with rot. The city of Laurasia had a lot of healing to do, but at least all could enjoy the feeling of the sun on their backs once again. Mia turned her head when she heard the sound of footsteps crunching through the grass.

"Why am I not surprised to find you here?" a familiar voice said.

Mia smiled as she turned around. "It's a lovely day."

Aries smirked. "It is also lunchtime," Aries said as a small boy peeked from around her legs.

Mia smiled and bent down. "Hi, Bluu," Mia said to the shy child who hid behind his cousin's leg.

"Don't be rude." Aries stepped aside.

"H-Hi," Bluu said softly.

Aries chuckled as she stepped back closer to him so he could grab hold of her leg. "Thank you for being brave and saying hi, Bluu."

Bluu buried his head in Aries' leg and Mia smiled. He was only five and already he was getting so big. Mia faced the river again and watched people carry buckets of fresh water back to their homes. Once, people lived below in the filth of the rich, but now everyone lived above ground happily, without restraint.

"Are the runners fighting again?" Mia asked.

"No." Aries walked up beside her. "Though I won't be surprised if some want to start a turf war by the fall."

Mia swiped her hands over the tall, long grass and sighed. "I suppose we should do something about it," Mia said with no bite behind it.

"I suppose," Aries said as the wind started to pick up.

"I will never tire of looking at the sky," Mia said as she lost herself in the spring breeze.

"Hey, slow down!" a voice pierced the quietness.

Mia and Aries turned and watched three children from the Academy of Key Smithing run up the hill. The academy was Karina's project, and she was very serious about it. The children weaved through the tall grass as a blur of red appeared behind them.

"Wait, guys! I said wait!" Karina said out of breath.

The kids ignored her, but Aries turned her gaze on them, and all three kids froze. Karina caught up and leaned over to catch her breath.

"I hope you are not disobeying the Keymaster?" Aries said to the kids.

"We're sorry," said a young girl in a bright yellow robe.

"We were just so excited," said another young girl in a blue robe.

"Don't apologize to me." Aries nodded to her sister and all three children turned around and bowed.

"We're sorry, Keymaster Karina," a young boy in a purple robe said.

"It's okay," Karina said as she looked out at the field. "We came all this way to tell you that you have visitors, Mia."

"Oh?" Mia turned around.

The little girl in the yellow robe jumped around and pointed towards the huts. "A really tall woman is here!" She said as the beads on her box braids rattled.

"And she has a metal arm!" the little boy in the purple robe added.

"Thank you," Mia said.

Mia and Aries walked down the hill as they watched Karina and the children run ahead. The lawns of the super-rich, once fertilized with stolen magic, now were replaced by fields of corn and soy and native grasses. Their city no longer exported ao almasi, instead they used their magic to export fresh produce to their neighbors, along with the practice of their medical potions and treatments. And not just for the rich. No one was turned away here, and all were allowed to pay what they could.

Mia walked down the stone steps towards the great wall that once separated the cities. It now had many large open archways for people to come and go as they pleased. She headed to her small stone hut where there was a large group of people waiting for her. She locked eyes with a young woman who ran to meet her.

"Mia!" Sara ran and hugged her.

"Sara." Mia hugged her tight. "How are you? I've missed you so much."

"I'm fine, we're just passing through and thought you could use some more help in the fields."

Mia looked past Sara at the others she knew, and then at the new faces she didn't, both young and old. Some had children with them, while others leaned on and used canes and crutches. Mia's eyes flickered over to Lady Valkyrie who stared downhill. Mia smiled and nodded to Sara before joining the madam.

"You know, in all my life I have never seen an inch of natural grass," Lady Valkyrie said. "It's duller and weaker looking than the grass rich folks used their magic to grow, but it's much lovelier in its multi shades of green and yellow. As if it were saying to the gods that I have every right to be here in all my imperfections. You and your friends have done a beautiful thing, Mia."

"It wasn't my idea." Mia chuckled as her eyes shifted to Aries and Karina.

Lady Valkyrie turned to Mia. "No one is born special, but if we are called, we just need to be brave enough to see whatever challenge lay before us through." Mia half-smiled as

Lady Valkyrie rubbed her shoulder. “I hope you don’t mind a few ex-runners in your field?”

“No, not at all. Anyone who wants to help is welcome,” Mia said. “Are you guys on a mini vacation?”

“Hardly,” Lady Valkyrie laughed. “The brothel never closes; however, we have adjusted our programming just a bit. We now have a travailing dance troop.”

“Really?” Mia said.

“Yes, Sara really put her foot down and raised up this idea, and you know what, I’m really enjoying it. We’re even adding playful skits. And can you imagine me writing ballads? Ridiculous, right?” Lady Valkyrie chuckled.

“It’s not ridiculous,” Mia said.

“You’re so sweet. Well, you’ll always have a home with us. All the girls miss you so much.”

“Thank you. I miss them too—even the clients.” Mia laughed. “So, I might take you up on that.” She wouldn’t mind throwing caution to the wind and spending the night in the company of warm bodies. “If you’re up to it, please stop on your way back. I’d love to see the show.”

“Will do,” Lady Valkyrie said.

Mia stood next to Lady Valkyrie and watched the children ask the performers questions. Aries and Karina joined them as they enjoyed the fresh breeze that rolled through the hills. Though they still had a long way to go, Laurasia was thriving, and she was grateful that Acome still called this area their home. She would see to it for as long as she lived that none would go unfed and with Aries, Karina, and their clan by her side they would squash any wickedness that dared grow on this precious land.

Perched on the smallest tree, Acome stretched their delicate wings in the warm early spring sun. So much energy was needed to appear in their full form and after being trapped for decades they rather liked taking the form of a butterfly. Humans passed below and Acome listened to them chat and carry on as they walked by with their goods on their back as the spring breeze rustled their hair. Settled in, Acome watched silently from a branch that still had buds to bloom.

A bush below them rustled and Acome's antennae fluttered in the wind as a large fire red rat appeared at the base of the tree.

"So, you're still sticking by the humans?" the creature grunted.

Acome's wings fluttered, then rested against the tree branch. "King Nezumi'Mfalme."

"In the flesh," King Nezumi'Mfalme said as his crooked whiskers danced in the breeze.

"This is my land, and these are my people," Acome said.

King Nezumi'Mfalme scoffed. "And that's why all the other spirits call you a fool." Acome only chuckled at that. "But regardless, I'm happy to see ya back."

"I am grateful for your help, King Nezumi'Mfalme."

"Don't mention it," King Nezumi'Mfalme said. "I mean it."

"Will you be staying long?" Acome raised their wings, slowly batting them up and down."

"Nope, can't stand being around all these humans," King Nezumi'Mfalme said. "But it's about time I deliver Megami Ua the news. The goddess of the Bustani River will be pleased to hear of your release."

Acome hummed. "Thank you."

King Nezumi'Mfalme grunted again as a comfortable silence grew between them. Acome missed so very much the smell of the fresh air and the feeling of the warm radiant sun. Be it wicked humans or wicked spirits, evil did not have a species. Good, however, always lurked in the darkness, always waiting for its chance to reclaim the light. And that was the gleam of hope Acome knew above all else was true.

THE
BLACK
GATE

1

Ark walked briskly down the stone stairs leading to the practicing room. The narrow stairwell was lit by the fire in their sconces. He was nearly to the bottom, but his mind was clouded, being pulled in a multitude of directions. A late-night summons for a dangerous key spell was not how he wanted to end his year. Ark stepped through the arched threshold into the chaos. Yield members parted for him as he crossed the massive stone-chambered room. Its domed ceiling lit by the flames of half a dozen chandeliers revealed the work his underlings had put in. The once smoothed stone floors were now scarred with the crudely etched sigils of the key spell. Surely done in haste but would do for their purposes.

A metal forge burned in the center of the six-ringed maze of channels he would have to pour his magic into to create the binding ring his master desired. So much work had been poured into this, and this fact alone should have invited him to be more cautious, but he ignored his gut as he walked towards the back of the room.

No preparation had been spared. Tables filled with precious enhancement stones and potions lined the walls, where most of his fellows gathered in their regal dark purple robes. Ark once again felt that tug. He should be more concerned about this binding. Being summoned in the dead of night should have set off alarm bells in his head, but he dismissed it again, chalking it up to his nerves. Of course, it would only be natural to be a tad bit on edge when performing a spell he hadn't personally done before, especially given the results of his predecessors.

Ark brushed away those thoughts as he joined his peers. All the members of The Black Gate were here. Some talked in hush tones, while others tried to hide their clear annoyance. Ark locked eyes with Shadowstone, one of their strongest members, and there was an edge to his gaze. Ark held it until the clatter of a fallen candle holder startled him. He cursed and cast a scowl towards the useless Yield member. They all scurried around the room in a rush to set everything in place. Ark said nothing as he downed two enhancement potions and calmly exhaled as the warm liquid coursed through his body. A spell of this magnitude had only been performed once, and Ark was no stranger to the consequences of such a spell. After all, it had claimed the lives of all nine of its original casters.

A loud clattering from the side of the room drew everyone's attention as Master Granite burst into the space, eyes wild, shouting at the Yield members. Ark straightened as anxious voices disseminated his master's commands. He had never seen his master so flustered as he watched the final preparations fall in place. Master Granite swept his eyes over his Black Gate, sweat pouring from his brow as if he had run here. Two frantic Yield members crossed the room, their dark purple robes fluttering behind them as they carried one jar of the beast's blood.

"Everyone! Everyone, step in place!" Master Granite shouted, and each member of The Black Gate found their place.

Ten of the most elite necromancers in the whole of Julilie found their spot inside the outer ring of the forging circle, each standing in their own individual smaller circles. Bands of sigils, along with a maze of channels, filled the space leading to the great forge where hot gold cooked, ready to be turned into the great gear ring that would be used to bind the beast they kept in the depths of their city. Ark caught nervous eyes from some of the lesser Yield members, their gazes stuck to him like glue. They were weaker than him and had every right to cower in their fear, but why were such feelings sticking to him as well? Master Granite had assured them that they would not fail. The Black Gate were the masters of modern magic and the perfecters of all summoning keys for the spells of the old magic. So perfect in their craft that they were eons greater than their predecessors, and this was a fact that Ark believed above all else. And yet, there was no denying the fate of the originators of the binding key. They had all died during the casting, but those simple monks had not mastered the craft like he and his peers had. That was their mistake; the chasm that separated Ark and his peers from them. Ark and his fellows were not apprentices; they were the very best of The Yield, the strongest necromancers in the city.

"Step in place!" Master Granite shouted, and every Yield member scurried to their post. "Everything must be absolutely perfect!"

Ark straightened and prepared himself. He moved his hands outward, and so did the others. He could feel the immense magic gathering in the room as their key gates appeared behind each of them. Ark closed his eyes and started to chant in the old language. All ten of them spoke perfectly in sync. Ark's magic gathered behind his gate as the brand on the back of his neck that granted him his magic started to tingle, then burn the more he chanted. He opened his eyes, and every key gate bearing the name of its master started to glow. Ark's power flowed in like the tide, calm but eager to do its work.

"*Am goo da rah,*" Ark repeated, and slowly, the door to each key gate creeped open. "*Am goo da rah.*"

Tendrils of hot, burning magic slithered out and drifted right until they circled together. Ark winced at the sudden connection to his peers. He felt their energy, their power, for the very first time.

"*Am goo da rah,*" Ark steadied himself and prepared for the next part. He eased his tendrils into the Earth to be captured by the channels below. "*Fah goo da rah.*"

The surge of power connected with the ground and lit the outer circle in an ethereal blue. Ark felt a strong pull forward.

"Steady!" Master Granite shouted from somewhere; he suddenly sounded far away. "Steady!"

Ark pulled his magic back so that he wouldn't be drained. "*Fah goo da rah.*" And the magic of his fellows raced through the channels towards the next inner circle, lighting every sigil in its path.

The surge of energy reached the next circle; they were nearly there. The hungry second circle ate and ate, weaving their magic through the channels as it spiraled towards the forge in the center. Ark had to take a step back inside his smaller circle to brace himself. The more energy he let out of his gate, the more the spell ate. It was so hungry and showed no signs of stopping. He pulled and pulled, and the brand on the back of his neck burned in resistance as if his skin were under the hot brand again. The pain was intense but nothing Ark couldn't handle as a necromancer who often performed reanimation spells on himself.

"*Fah goo da rah.*" The hot woven tendrils of magic raced to the center, lighting the room up brighter than Ark could even imagine.

Suddenly, he felt he couldn't possibly have enough magic to feed this spell. There were ten master-level necromancers here, all giving this key their everything. It took only nine monks to cast the original, but it had cost them their lives. Ark would not make the same foolish mistake; he pressed on, ignoring the impulse to run that coursed through his body.

"*Fah goo da rah,*" Ark chanted through gritted teeth as the electrifying energy neared the inner third circle.

This final large inner circle contained three inner rings and the hot burning forge of liquid metal. These three inner rings would be the toughest. Ark knew that and braced himself further. He leaned back to use his own body weight to steady himself as he fed the spell more and more of his magic. Now, they were just inches away from the three inner circles. They were nearly there.

"Steady!" a voice that sounded familiar said, but Ark's ears were so full of the swirling rush of magic pouring into the room that he could not with clarity decipher who had said it.

"*Fah goo da rah!*" Ark shouted.

Their collective braid of magic touched the inner rings, and in a flash Ark felt a pull like nothing he had ever experienced. It yanked him forward, and he had to use all his might to reel in his magic, but too much magic poured from the gates now—no, not pouring. Consumed. The magic in their gates was being sucked out like the flesh of a steamed sea crab. Suddenly, Ark's entire body felt like it was on fire. Ark let out a shrill cry that was drowned out by all the chaos in the room. He flashed a look to one of his fellows, Shadowstone, and when he saw the skin of his face cooking from the heat, he knew that they had made a terrible mistake.

Complete panic hit him then, followed by the heat, and then there was nothing as Ark's soul was torn from him through every pore on his body.

Yrwen

2

"...please report to—work stations..."

Yrwen groaned as the chatter blasting through his embedded earpieces woke him from his sleep. He could only turn them down so low, and no matter how many upgrades he put himself through, it never felt like he could get the volume low enough to enjoy some peace. And today would be no different. Apparently, all the higher-ups were still talking about their precious gear ring. Looks like Edward Granite must have failed—a fatal mistake on his part. Now, it was up to his sister Mary to take care of things unless she wanted to share the fate of her brother, but that was none of Yrwen's concern. As an official accountant for The Siler Gang, his business only concerned the books.

Yrwen yawned and stretched one last time before crawling out of bed. He slept as good as he could through his night sweats—hence the reason why he always slept naked. He caught his slender body in the mirror; his gorgeous dark brown skin looked beautiful, but he wished he could change the near-anorexic appearance of his body. He didn't like the way his collarbone stood out or how prominent his hip bones jutted outward. He rubbed the joints of his elbows as he looked at his bony arms and legs. He hated it all, but due to the precarious nature of his birth, he could never keep on the weight. And that was intentional. As a member of The Cogs, a subclass, his people were purposely bred to be fragile. Yrwen hated that, but still, he tried to find ways to love his body.

He freshened up with a shower and laid out his clothes. He brushed his thin, jet-black, wavy hair that touched his shoulders and put on his tight pinstriped suit and string tie.

He may have been thin, but he loved to show off his body. He was ready for the day now and left his room to get breakfast in the cafeteria.

"Be on the lookout—all runners report to your supervisors. This is an all call..."

Yrwen walked the dimly lit corridor down the slow incline of the ramp, joining the others. He wasn't quite sure what he was in the mood to eat. He usually only ate twice a day. Maybe a bit of bread and bacon, or maybe a cup of oats. Yrwen lost himself in deep thought, but a hand jerked him back to reality. Yrwen let out a yelp and turned to find Cook, his best friend, giving him a pointy-toothed grin.

"Mornin'," Cook said.

"Good morning," Yrwen said. "Fancy seeing you on this side of town."

Cook shrugged, which made her slightly thicker hair shift around her face. He was always jealous of the fact that she had thicker hair. "What can I say? I get the job done quick."

"I cannot argue with that." Cook was a debt collector, which could be a pretty taxing job, but she had the body for it. The *healthier* ones were the only ones who got to leave the confines of their cage. "How long will I be graced with your presence today?"

Cook looked up, then reached her fingers into her mouth to pull out her pointed silver grill to inspect it. She was missing a lot of teeth, but if it bothered her, she never let on. "Don't know." She popped it back in. "But if I have to hear one more bitch whine about the money they owe us, I'm going to start shooting people in their dicks."

"You're leaving people intact?" Yrwen raised an eyebrow.

Cook laughed. "I'm not a monster, Yrwen. I go for the big meaty parts—legs, arms, asses. Besides, runners should know better when borrowing money from the treasury. You'd be better off tricking in the streets."

"But then you would be out of a job and stuck in the office blocks checking numbers and filing receipts like me."

"That would be your wet dream, lover boy." Cook laughed.

The pair walked together into the large cafeteria full of Cogs, runners, and a few Yield members. This was primarily their eating space, but any member of The Silers could be found here. They stepped into Mama Roach's line. She had the best oats. She knew just what every Cog needed and made the best nutrient-rich food found anywhere in the sewers.

"Yrwen, Cook," Mama Roach hacked out their names in her raspy voice. She hunched over a large pot of cinnamon nutmeg spiced oatmeal that had bits of dried fruit in it, but she wasn't smiling.

"Mornin'," Cook said without concern.

Mama Roach grunted as she picked up a bowl and served Cook her fill. "Something ain't right around here." Cook brushed it off as she took her bowl, but Yrwen paused.

"Are you talking about the gear ring?" Yrwen asked. Every Cog knew about the ring; they had no choice in the matter as updates were constantly being blasted in their ears.

Mama Roach hacked out a cough. "Bigger. I can feel it. Something in the walls got the roaches and rats moving like a trimmer. A great darkness is approaching; I'd bet my good lung on that."

Yrwen took his bowl of oats. "It's all the talk of the gear ring. Try not to let it stress you out, okay?"

Mama Roach scoffed. "Imma be alright, but you watch your ass. You too, Cook."

Yrwen flashed a look to Cook, expecting her to be wearing one of her shit-eating grins, but her light brown eyes were suddenly very serious. Yrwen said nothing more and followed Cook to a table. He had to admit they had never encountered a problem like this before—and so close to the ceremony, too. Sure, there had been little things here and there, like a ceremonial child dying before their time or a runner or two trying to make off with some money while their bosses were away, but Dr. Granite's family bred lots of ceremonial children as back up and The Black Gate took care of any and all detractors in the gang. After all, they were the internal police of sorts. But to awake and find that the gear ring had been stolen... Well, that was big news.

Cook found them a seat close to the stone wall in the back of the room. Yrwen sat down after fetching them some water, actually feeling quite hungry today.

"You heard what happened, right?" Cook said in a low voice.

"Latest updates say they still haven't found it."

"Not that." Cook scanned the room before speaking again. "Yrwen...The Black Gate is dead."

Yrwen stopped mid-bite and let out a laugh. "That's preposterous."

"Hush, it's true. Last night, they tried to forge another gear ring, but shit went south."

"I...I..." Yrwen opened and closed his mouth. He was having trouble processing this, and it was killing his appetite.

"Believe it—I've seen the morgue. A couple dozen Yield members bit the dust, too. There are rumblings in the group now; folks are talkin' weird. It's like everyone can feel something is...not right."

Yrwen pulled back and searched his thoughts. It was hard to think with all the chatter between his ears. He wished he could just shut off the darn thing. "The spell... It failed, I presume," he said mostly to himself. "And The Black Gate?"

"Dead," Cook said bluntly. "Shit's been obliterated."

Yrwen breathed harder. If all the members of The Black Gate were dead, then that meant that his Ark... No, it couldn't be. Yrwen reached for his spoon and shoved oats into his mouth. Cook, reading him like a pro, gave him the space he needed to process, and he was grateful. He forced down each spoonful, trying hard not to think about Ark's confident smile, those beautiful light brown eyes. Was it not just the other day that Yrwen helped him take the braids out from his wavy copper-orange hair? No, Cook must be mistaken.

She could be dramatic like that. They were likely a little injured, maybe a few of their lesser had perished, that was all. His Ark would be fine, just like his beloved Vincent would be fine, because Yrwen only fell in love with good, strong men who fate could not drive its greedy hands into and take. After work today, he would check up on Ark and find that he was okay, maybe a little bruised, and that would be the end of that.

Ark

3

Ark awoke with a start. Pain seared through his body in new and excruciating ways, leaving him unable to utter a word. Where was this unbearable agony coming from? Where was he? And why did his nostrils fill with the scent of burning magic and cooked flesh?

Ark looked around the room. He was surrounded by bloodied cots. Yield members scurried around him in their dark purple robes. Something was wrong. Something was oh so terribly wrong here.

Another spike of pain shot up his left side, and he reached over to grab his left arm, only to find nothing. He craned his neck to see his hand, but all that was there was a bloodied mess of bandages around a nub that didn't even include an elbow. And then everything came back to him.

The gate... The power of the hungry forge eating their magic... The pull. Never in his life had he experienced pain like that. Then there was the sight of Shadowstone's face cooking right before him. The flesh bubbling up and melting off. The intense look in Shadowstone's eyes, as if the pain had already been conquered. What in all of Ozama's hells had they just put themselves through?

Ark tried to get up, but the blasted pain was too much. He cursed and reached for his magic; relief found him when he discovered it was still there. He chanted through gritted teeth, and his gate appeared, despite the worried cries from The Yield members now surrounding him.

"Get away," Ark hissed.

He was fine. The gate door opened, and he turned his bright orange tendrils onto himself and had them seek out and fix anything broken within his body. The healing process was extremely painful but burns and cuts quickly scabbed and scarred over. Broken bones regrew and snapped back in place. Sweat poured from Ark's body as he pushed himself harder. He could handle it; healing magic was one of his specialties—or rather, medical necromancy was one of his specialties. He knew how to get in and out of a body. He was a master organ harvester, after all.

Ark gasped out a breath. His healing was complete, reducing all his wounds to nothing more than nasty bruises and scars. He steadied his breathing and placed a hand over his missing left arm. It would need to be replaced, but he didn't have time for that now. A Yield member brought him a booster, a special healing potion enhanced with blood that helped heal the spirit after great uses of power. Ark chugged it, and it helped reduce the throbbing in the back of his neck where the brand that gave him unlimited access to magic lay.

He got up slowly, put on the black tunic and dark purple robes laid out for him, and sought out the junior commander, the head Yield member in charge of this operation. "You there! What has happened here?" Ark demanded.

"Gate Master Ark," The junior commander bowed. "I-I regret to inform you that there have been many casualties after Master Granite's forging attempt."

Attempt? That would mean that they weren't successful, leaving Ark to wonder if he should be grateful or not, given the high mortality of such a key. "Casualties? Be specific," Ark commanded.

"Yes, Gate Master. I regret to inform you of the fall of Gate Master Que."

Ark sucked in a breath. All other words floated away as a face appeared in his mind. A grinning man with eyes as dark as the night with a curled beard dyed a vibrant teal. Que was not only his best friend but also his mentor. He helped perfect everything Ark knew. He couldn't be dead. Ark demanded the junior commander show him the bodies.

"Y-yes, Gate Master Ark." The junior commander led him to the remains.

Ark followed behind him. He could smell the death in the air and felt the heat from the spell that still lingered here, but he didn't care about any of it. He needed to see with his own eyes. When they came to a back room where many bodies lay, a wave of prickling pain shot through his body. The junior commander bowed in respect and then showed Ark the terrible things he was unprepared to see.

His fellows Windwatcher, Echo, and Rosethorn were all dead. Only identified by the black gold threaded sash bearing their sigils that lay over the black cloth covering their bodies at the foot of the bed. All extremely talented necromancers. It stunned him to silence. The junior commander politely excused himself, leaving Ark alone.

His eyes settled on one corpse in particular. He walked to it and stopped. The sash bore the sigil of his mentor. Ark reached down and pulled away the black sheet. Que's once rich dark brown skin was a mangled mess of burnt flesh. Half of his face was burned off, and there was nothing left of his once vibrant teal beard. A new pain stung through him. The sudden pang of loss rocked him in nauseating waves. Ark's eyes drifted downward. There was little below the waist. He was torn apart as if his body was nothing. Ark cursed.

This was only four—what about the others? Ark turned and headed to the door where The junior commander who had not been properly dismissed waited for him.

"Take me to the others who are alive," Ark commanded.

"Yes, Gate Master," the junior commander said.

He took Ark to another room, but each step created cracks in Ark's resolve. Questions boiled up to the surface that he did not want to face. Excluding himself, there were still five other Black Gate members; he had to see if they were okay. The junior commander leading him made way for Ark, cutting through the mess of people running around. Ark made no attempt to meet their eyes. His anger and growing uncertainty made his emotional state as fragile as glass. When they entered another large room, Ark spotted Duke first and rushed to his bedside.

"Duke," Ark said, but upon walking closer to him, he saw that Duke had slipped into deep sleep. Likely placed there by a Yield member to heal. The old man's eyes were bandaged, likely unusable.

Ark balled his fists. He could probably heal him, but he knew he was nearly spent after healing himself.

"A-Ark?" a shrill voice called out to him.

Ark turned around and saw Iron sitting up in bed. He rushed to her side. "Iron."

"A-Ark," Iron said through sobs. Ark had never seen her this distressed. Her long black hair was pinned to her head by bandages, and dark circles lay below her eyes. "A-Ark, I-I...I don't know where to begin. I-I-I..."

Horror lay behind her brown eyes. A nightmare Ark was uncertain any of them would escape. He looked down at her legs; everything was missing below the knee. That could be fixed, but the emotionally broken person before him... That was what hurt him the most. For all the glory, what had they done?

"A-Ark, please...please listen to me." Iron reached out and grabbed his robe.

"I'm here," Ark said, cradling her shaky hands.

"A-Ark, it's-it's Hollow. It's Hollow, he-he's... There's something wrong with him. He's out of control," Iron repeated over and over again. "He's out of control."

"Hollow?" But Ark couldn't get anything else out of her.

She just kept circling around that idea, tugging on him like a dying animal. Eyes wild with fear. Something might have been wrong with Hollow, but it was clear Iron was the one who needed to be put to rest. Ark held her as he started to chant. He could ease her pain and put her in deep sleep; that way, The Yield members could do their work and prep her for new legs once they found a suitable donor. It would be easier that way. Iron consented, but she never stopped trying to warn him about Hollow. Something was seriously wrong with him.

Ark found himself a quiet place to gather his shattered thoughts. He still didn't know what happened to Shadowstone or Cinder, some of the strongest members in The Black Gate. And did he want to know? He didn't dare look under the cloths of his other deceased fellows. Gazing at Que was enough, but he needed to check in with them. Then find Hollow. Ark started for the door, but his body suddenly felt exhausted. He stammered back and found himself a chair. He was in an interrogation room, one of many used by the Yield for The Siler's whims.

Once his body folded into the chair, he found he couldn't budge. The weight of the day was too heavy. What had happened to them? Why had this been allowed to happen? Master Granite assured them over and over again that they were more than enough to complete the key for the forging. But thinking back, had Ark ignored the signs? His master looked like a madman last night, rambling on and on about his son and his daughter. Why was that? Ark knew how important the gear ring was, but surely they could forge one simple magic ring?

A tremble rocked through Ark's body; the booster was doing its job, but healing his body so quickly still took a lot out of him. Ark buried his head in his hand. He had nearly died. It could have easily been him lying with the corpses of his fellows. He had given his all to be a part of this organization. He removed his own kidney to save the life of Master Granite's niece, and his master thought highly of him, rewarding him with a place amongst the elite for his work. Had Ark not shown how irreplaceable he was? He was a master necromancer, a studied mage who commanded the currents of electricity, as well as the vessels of the human body. He was so loyal to this organization, and yet, this had been allowed to happen. He was so loyal, but where had that led him?

Ark gathered himself and continued his search, hoping to ease his troubled mind, but accomplished little more than walking around aimlessly trying to find his remaining fellows. In the shadows, Ark picked up on hush talk of fleeing, a crime punishable by torture or death in The Silers. It was his main job in The Black Gate to deliver said punishments, but he ignored all of it. There weren't even any orders coming from The Yield command; it was as if the entire organization had been shattered, and he was alone to pick up the pieces. Ark used the wall to steady himself. He was so exhausted, but his soul would not allow his body to rest. Allow him to sit in the fresh horror of all that he had seen. Footsteps echoed from ahead, and Ark looked up.

"Yr-Yrwen?" Ark blinked twice to push away the idea that his eyes deceived him. "Yrwen." Ark staggered towards him.

"Ark? What's happened?" Concern laced through his beautiful Yrwen's voice.

Ark wanted to fall into his arms and cry. His heart raced when their bodies finally touched, and Ark could smell the cologne and hair mousse Yrwen used every day. He wanted to bury himself into his chest, have Yrwen wrap his legs around his naked body, and kiss him until all the pain went away, like a wounded child before their mother. Such childishness, but Ark could not reel in the brokenness of his body, of his spirit. Ark was so in love with Yrwen. A love others would look down on with Ark being a prominent member of The Black Gate and Yrwen being a Cog, but they didn't know Yrwen like he did. Yrwen's stunning beauty and sharp tongue. His calculating mind and ability to see two steps ahead in every situation, but he bitterly knew Yrwen's heart belonged to another.

"Come, we shouldn't rest here." Yrwen did his best to haul Ark away and escort him to a proper room.

On The Yield side of The Siler complex were many study and meditation rooms. Large libraries filled to the ceiling with books and practicing courts available to all members. Yrwen found Ark a quiet room with a pitted couch for lounging, a bookshelf full of books, and a red carpet covering the stone floor. Yrwen helped him to the couch and quickly lit the kerosene lamps, soaking the room in warm soft light. Ark watched, feeling helpless as his composure further unraveled. All he wanted was for Yrwen to come to him.

Yrwen turned, his gray eyes soft. "Ark." Yrwen walked to him. Ark's name sounded so good on Yrwen's tongue. His body ached for him, so when Yrwen fell into his arms, Ark pulled him closer. "Please, tell me what's wrong? What's happened?"

“Madness, absolute madness,” Ark began as Yrwen made room for them on the couch, allowing Ark to rest his head on his chest.

Yrwen

4

Yrwen didn't intend to spend the rest of his evening in the arms of his Ark, but he was truly alarmed at what Ark told him. Ark was usually so composed and cool-headed. He was a curious but friendly fellow, certainly one of the easiest Black Gate members to get along with. And even if Yrwen knew what Ark had to go through to get into The Black Gate, he never allowed the public to see his scars. That was one of the things Yrwen loved most about Ark, his resilience.

How had things ended up this wrong? Did Vincent know about this? But why would Vincent care? He always regarded Dr. Granite and his Yield as lesser in comparison to his own fleet of necromancers. Not that Yrwen shared the same sentiment; when thinking straight, Dr. Granite's work was quite impressive, but clearly, the man wasn't thinking straight. First, his treacherous brother steals the gear ring; now, the old fool had gone and decimated his Black Gate over the death of his eldest son. Maybe the man wasn't as brilliant as everyone gave him credit for. But now, Yrwen could see all the pieces in play. With The Black Gate shattered beyond repair, who was going to stop those who wanted to flee?

"Report...check in...report...check in...clear."

The chatter was choppy now, with so many orders going through. So much movement the day before the ceremony, all of it made more chaotic with the gear ring missing. Yrwen looked down at his Ark and wished his heart would let him give it away to this lovely man, but all he could worry about was Vincent. What if things spiraled even beyond Vincent's control, the Siler's number one guy.

Yrwen heard thunderous footsteps, and suddenly, the door burst open. Raging mad, Hollow, who was usually calm and collected, scowled down at them both. Ark started awake, but Hollow was already above them, brown eyes a storm of rage. The necromancer ripped Yrwen away by the arm and tossed him to the floor.

"Traitors!" But Hollow was addressing Yrwen and not Ark.

Yrwen quickly gathered his emotions and hid them deep inside of himself. One sudden movement could cost him his life. Hollow walked towards Yrwen. A sickly aura rolled off the man as he looked down at him.

"Gate Master Hollow, please forgive me," Yrwen bowed until his head touched the floor, submitting himself fully.

"Silence!" Hollow barked.

"Fellow Hollow," Ark was on his feet, alarm in his voice. "What is the meaning of this?

Hollow growled and yanked Yrwen up by the hair. The pain stung, but Yrwen knew better than to fight back. He muffled a whimper as Ark looked between the two of them, shock and horror painting his face.

"Fellow Hollow!" Ark said again.

"Traitor! You were trying to flee with this slut Cog." Hollow pulled Yrwen around and held him there like a rat.

"Flee?" Ark let out a confused laugh. "Preposterous. I was simply resting, and Yrwen joined me. Can you not see I am missing an arm?"

Hollow's grip eased, and he released Yrwen, but Yrwen remained where he was placed. "I...I see." Hollow cut a glare to Yrwen but looked back to Ark. "I have killed five people with my bear hands, four of which were filthy Cogs trying to flee. I can hear their whispers in the halls. They mean to betray us, but I will not allow it."

"T-then good work, Fellow. You are keeping the balance," Ark said.

"I am going to make The Black Gate even stronger! We will not be defeated in this our darkest hour," Hollow barked, his eyes wild with a burning rage and something else. "I-I will..."

"Thank you, Fellow. You are the light we need," Ark walked to Hollow and rubbed his shoulder.

"Scum and that bitch Iron," Hollow was shaking with every word. "Had it not been for her weakness, my Cinder would still be here."

Yrwen's eyes flickered to Ark.

"Fellow Cinder is..." Ark nearly choked.

"Dead." Hollow slowly turned to Ark, who was stunned to silence. "She stood right next to Iron, and I watched Iron turn and run as the tendrils broke apart and ripped my Cinder to shreds. It should have been Iron."

"Hollow, Iron, she wouldn't—" Ark tried to get out.

"Lies! But that is in the past. I will rebuild The Black Gate and make us ten times stronger! Come, we have work to do." Hollow turned and left the room, and Ark followed without hesitation, but not before exchanging an apologetic look with Yrwen.

Yrwen remained silent. He was already gathering himself up from this little event. He was used to this type of violence from The Silers and The Yield, but he was shocked to hear of Cinder's death. She was a powerful necromancer, one of the few who had mastered talking to the dead. Using her sound magic, she could broadcast the last words spoken on the vocal cords of the deceased. It was quite interesting to see. This was a great loss indeed. Yrwen stood, brushed the dirt and dust from his black pinstriped suit, and took a shaky breath before heading back to his workstation.

All this action troubled him. So much grief and rage were behind Hollow's eyes; the man was shattered and in no condition to lead anyone. Only more would die if he wasn't stopped, but what was a Cog like him to do? His people were nothing but glorified slaves, born and bred to serve in exchange for cushy jobs. All Cogs were either forcibly bred through strict coercive breeding rules that demanded every uterus bearer to have one child or cursed with birth defects that made them physically weak. They were like spiders, prized for their diligence and organization but not strong enough to stand up to the boot that crushed their backs.

Now he worried about Shadowstone, the only member of The Black Gate Ark didn't talk about. Was someone as powerful as him dead too? Hollow and Shadowstone were both amongst the strongest, usually calculating and calm. Yrwen sighed; he guessed Cook was right. Everything was shattered, and even if the gear ring was found and returned, they would all have to deal with the destruction of The Black Gate and all the turmoil that would cause.

Yrwen made his way to his station and passed a Cog's corpse, clearly beaten to death. The runners who were left to clean them up complained because they knew nothing on the body could be harvested. Yrwen walked past them; he knew the woman—her name was Mayfly. She had a passion for language and word games. "*Blessed life, you will be remembered. Wishing you everlasting peace,*" Yrwen uttered as he continued. He entered the busy office and made his way to his little block with his typewriter.

"Yrwen," someone hissed.

Yrwen turned and saw Cook standing over him, looking dead serious. She nodded to the door, and Yrwen followed her into the hall. She moved quick down the tunnel toward one of the runner's wings. She exited their section and walked out into the sewers. It was more humid and danker here, which made Yrwen sweat, but he followed her without a word, without displaying any emotion.

They passed runners and other Cogs going back in. Cook remained silent as she turned left down a narrow tunnel barely lit by the yellow lights of the dirty bulbs above them. Cook stopped at a door and opened it, and Yrwen went inside. It was a service closet full of cleaning supplies.

"We need to get out of here." Her voice was barely audible to a normal person, but Yrwen could hear her clearly. "I'm serious. Shit ain't right. Mama Roach has fled."

"Successfully?" Yrwen said with sharp surprise.

"With her two daughters," Cook said. "We need to be next."

"But..." Yrwen thought of the blood on Hollow's hands.

"I know a way; it's safe," Cook said. "We can flee to Septland New Nation, but we must not delay. Are you with me?"

Yrwen resisted the urge to scoff—she couldn't be serious. But had Yrwen not seen for himself a taste of what's to come? Cogs were low on the pole, easy to kill when tempers flared. Then his mind wandered to his Vincent. He could not flee without passing the warning off to his love. If Mama Roach thought it was too dangerous to stick around, it was certainly too dangerous for Vincent. "Cook—"

"Think about it," Cook said quickly, then she opened the door and left without another word.

Yrwen followed and walked back to his station but stopped at the entrance to the office area. He could fake a lot of things, but he couldn't fool himself. Something was seriously wrong, but he couldn't leave without talking to Vincent. They were close like that. Even if he knew the man could never return his love, Yrwen still loved him. He always had. He needed to talk to Vincent before doing anything else.

Ark

5

Ark hurried to follow Hollow. It was clear as day Hollow was completely unhinged. He had led them on a rampage all day, killing anyone who so much as mentioned the word 'flee.' Ark watched him beat to death one Siler runner and two Yield members he caught in the back halls. When Ark did have a chance to speak openly with other members of The Yield, it was clear a schism was growing. Half of The Yield did want to flee, while others wanted to remain loyal. Master Granite was no longer paying them any attention; his focus was on protecting his daughter and finding the gear ring.

Ark had no idea where he stood. His body was tired, and his heart hurt with the loss of his fellows.

He wished Hollow could be made to hear reason. They needed to slow down, regroup. Show their strength through compassion to the junior commanders below them so that they would be in better shape to usher The Yield back to some form of normality. But of course, Hollow was hearing none of this.

In one of the mansions above ground, on the Granite Manor, was The Black Gate's keep. They were the only ones allowed to take office above ground in Uptown. Their keep was modest, full of grand libraries and rooms for studying. Their private quarters still resided below, in the basements, but they were fully furnished with the finest furniture and art. On the top floor was the grand meeting room. Around a large mahogany table sat ten chairs. There, Hollow called a meeting for the remaining Black Gate members.

Duke was there, but not with his new eyes. Luckily for Duke, he was a master of visual and auditory telepathy. Ark was also relieved to see Shadowstone was there, though he was wrapped nearly head to toe in bandages. Ark met his eye but said nothing as Iron was the last to be wheeled in. She had her new legs, but she clearly looked distressed. Everything moved so fast. What they really needed was rest.

Hollow stood then.

"Fellows, members of The Black Gate, we have suffered a great loss, but let that not deter us from our mission," he barked. "We still have much work to do."

"W-work," Iron said. "We've lost half of our members. We should just cut our losses."

Hollow slammed his fist on the table, making both Ark and Duke jump. The look he gave Iron was murderous.

Ark cleared his throat. "Hollow, might I suggest—"

"Silence!" Hollow spat, then retrained his glare back onto Iron. "You spineless bottom-feeding bitch."

"Fellow Hollow," Duke tried to interject.

"I said silence!" Hollow's voice rose to a new level. He pointed directly at Iron. "You... It was you who destabilized the entire spell."

"M-me?" Iron shrieked. "Did you not feel the power it was pulling from us? There would have been no way to stop it even if we could. It nearly killed us all."

Hollow growled, and in an instant, he shot across the table towards Iron. Iron shrieked and leapt out of her wheelchair to run away, but Hollow grabbed her by the robe and threw her into the wall. Ark didn't move an inch. It was clear from the very beginning that this was going to be the only outcome. Iron screamed for her life as Hollow grabbed her by the head and smashed her face into the stone over and over again. She could do little to defend herself in her state as she tried to beg for her life.

None of them moved a muscle to help her, all knowing full well the violence Hollow was capable of. After all, Hollow's special ability required him to rip open the skulls of his enemy and eat their brains. Ark averted his eyes and saw the sweat gathered on Duke's face, and Shadowstone remained cool and still. Iron begged and screamed as Hollow turned to beating her with his fist, then his foot. Each blow created something unfixable in Ark's heart. He was too afraid to save Iron, and he knew this act of cowardice would haunt him for the rest of his life. There was a final crunch that made Ark flinch. He wanted to throw up. Duke turned away; Shadowstone remained silent.

The meeting ended with commands being sent to The Yield. All followed Hollow. He was on the war path to rebuild The Black Gate and to purge The Yield and their ranks of detractors.

Why had everything gone so utterly and explosively wrong? Were they not the strongest in the land? Or was their arrogance the true villain? Ark only knew, deep in his heart, that he needed to get far away from this place.

Ark walked to his study, hoping to ease some of his pain with one more booster and maybe perform some extra healing magic on his aching body when he saw Shadowstone up ahead.

His fellow made eye contact with him before turning around the corner. Ark followed, and the two quietly walked into a study room. Ark closed the door behind them, and up close in the clear daylight, he better saw the awful condition of Shadowstone's body. Blood pooled in the joints around his fingers and elbows. His locs looked thinner, some clearly singed, and there was no sign that he ever had a beard.

"Fellow Shadowstone," Ark said.

"Don't worry about me." Shadowstone grunted, clearly in pain.

Ark ignored him and waved for him to sit as he started to chant. He would give credit to the junior commanders for their work, but their skills were nowhere near his own.

"I said—" And Shadowstone let out a pained gasp, clearly trying to take control of the situation and failing.

"Remove your tunic and pants, and lay down," Ark ordered.

Shadowstone glared at him, but this was going to happen one way or another, so he did as he was told. Ark pulled the tendrils of magic from his gate and fed them into Shadowstone's body. Small grunts escaped Shadowstone's lips, but there was always an ease to healing other people's bodies; in an injured state, they were always hungry for his magic. Finally, Shadowstone relaxed and allowed Ark to do his work. This would not perfectly heal him, but it would heal most of the more serious burns, leaving him with only minor bruising and scarring.

"Can I...can I tell you a story?" Shadowstone shut his eyes as he let out raspy breaths.

"Go on." Ark knew he should order him to remain quiet and rest, but it seemed that whatever Shadowstone struggled to get out crowned on his lips.

"Magic... There is so much more to it..." Shadowstone said with his eyes closed tight. "Do...do you know of the story of the fall of the Gylvian Empire?"

Ark was familiar with the name but not the history. The Gylvians were the land-conquering tyrants from across the seas who nearly claimed this land but lost their control over the great continent during the civil war hundreds of years ago. "Afraid not."

Shadowstone smirked. "I...I know. I was told by my Junsuxian grandfather when I was a boy...during our migration here."

Ark nodded, having forgotten that Shadowstone was only half Tyrazi, which was pretty uncommon in their country Julilie.

"The spirits... The spirits, they are alive, and their power..." Shadowstone muffled a chuckle. "Unfathomable." He let out a strained cough.

"Easy now." Ark shifted the tendrils of his magic to Shadowstone's respiratory system.

Shadowstone forced out another cough but opened his eyes to meet Ark's. "Whispers from the sea spirits told of a great fiery titan that rained from the sky like a fireball. It totaled an entire empire."

Ark furrowed his brow but said nothing.

"Completely wiped them out." Shadowstone coughed again. "Abisai, Abisai, the gift." Shadowstone raised a hand to the ceiling; there was a reverence in his voice. "That kind of power...that kind of destruction...laid waste to an entire empire."

Ark found that hard to believe, but then again, they bonded a powerful spirit deep below the city. A spirit so powerful that its harnessed magic powered the city.

"And that type of power can be wielded," Shadowstone turned his fingers into a fist. "Imagine what could be accomplished if we could harness that power. That's...that's why we should flee," Shadowstone said between grunts—and that caught Ark so off guard, he almost stopped his healing. "Listen," Shadowstone said through the obvious pain. "We are too strong to die here. I...I can sense something is different with the beast. It knows too that it will be free soon. It can feel it, and so can I."

Ark continued to heal him, letting him finish.

"If...if Acoma is freed, they...they will kill every single one of us." Shadowstone gasped when Ark reached the worst of the wounds on his legs and back.

"Steady." Ark concentrated, shoving his emotions into organized pockets in his mind, allowing his brain to think clearly.

Ever since he joined The Silers at the age of fifteen, his life had been hell. He only started practicing magic at nineteen because he was sick of selling his body in exchange for higher positions in the gang. There were only so many higher-ups who offered cushy jobs, and Ark was lucky his mother taught him to read. So he studied magic, but even in The Yield, it wasn't safe.

Lesser casters often went mad when the brand didn't take, or they openly killed their peers either by accident or on purpose. When Master Granite's niece fell ill, and she needed a kidney, Ark leapt at the chance to offer his because he had found a way to use magic to make organ transfers safer. He'd proved himself by cutting out his own kidney right in front of Master Granite. He'd thought that would be enough to keep him safe for the rest of his life, but clearly, he was just as expendable as everyone else.

Then there was Hollow. The aftermath of the failed forging would likely haunt him for the rest of his life, and who was to say that they wouldn't be used up and thrown away again? He wasn't safe here; he never was.

Ark took a deep breath. "Very well. What do you propose? Hollow is on the warpath."

"Let's...let's talk tomorrow," Shadowstone struggled to get out, clearly too weak to carry on this conversation. "Close...closer to ceremony time, when things have calmed down."

After Ark finished healing Shadowstone, he was completely drained. He downed two boosters and used his Ao Almasi stone to further enhance his healing. He would need to be as close to full strength as he could muster if he was going to pull anything off.

It was very late at night, but he needed to talk to Yrwen. He could not stand the thought of leaving him behind. If something went terribly wrong and the beast did get out, Yrwen would surely be killed.

Ark sent a summons to Yrwen telepathically, and within the hour, Yrwen was knocking on the door to his private study in the main Yield area. Ark got up to open the door. As soon as their eyes met, Ark went in for a kiss, and Yrwen let him. Ark pulled them further into the study and kicked the door close behind him. Ark deepened the kiss, but he couldn't ravish him right now.

"Yrwen, run away with me," Ark said through breathy pants.

"Ah...run away?" Yrwen started to pull away, but Ark would not allow it.

"Run away with me," Ark said again and hoped Yrwen could hear the pleading in his voice.

"Ark, I..." Yrwen went stiff in his arms, and Ark pulled back to meet his eye.

Yrwen's gray eyes were conflicted. There was something there, or rather *someone*, and it angered Ark. "This is about Vincent." Ark did nothing to hide his disgust. Yrwen averted his gaze, and Ark pulled away.

"Ark—" Yrwen reached out.

"I knew it," Ark said angrily. "If you want to stay and die, so be it, but don't risk your life for a man who can never give you what you want."

"Ark..." Yrwen's voice came out in a whimper this time, and it hurt Ark, but he had to say what he had to say, or he feared it would never come out.

Ark turned to him, locking eyes with him. He walked over and took Yrwen's hand into his. "Yrwen, I can give you everything you want and so much more. I have nothing against the aromantic, but the only thing Vincent wants from you is your friendship, nothing more. I am gay, and I am alloromantic. I can give you the love you so deeply desire. I can give you the life you yearn for."

Ark felt Yrwen's hand tremble in his grip. He knew how much Yrwen loved Vincent, they had been friends for longer than Ark at known him, but it broke his heart to see his love in a one-sided relationship. He needed to move on.

"Ark, I..." Yrwen's voice cracked, and Ark's posture softened.

"I'm sorry. I should not have raised my voice like that," Ark said, but he was surprised when Yrwen fell into his arms.

"Please." Yrwen's voice was so small. "Please, Ark, protect me."

Ark had never seen Yrwen so vulnerable. "I can do better than that."

Ark leaned in for a kiss that opened into more. As the two of them wiggled out of their clothes and Ark made a passionate thrust into Yrwen's beautiful body, he promised Yrwen that he would give him a good life. Even if it killed him, Ark would protect Yrwen always.

Yrwen

6

It was Triday, the morning for the ceremony, and even if the gear ring had been found and returned to its place, Yrwen worked to get himself ready to flee. Everything was still in turmoil. So many Siler runners and Yield members had fled, and the leadership wasn't the least bit concerned at the moment. Everyone was much more focused on the ceremony tonight, for which the security had been extremely heightened. But this morning, Yrwen would perform his duties like normal...after he talked to Cook.

She wasn't hard to track down because she came directly to his living area before he could leave. When they locked eyes, they shared a moment of relief that the other was still okay. Cook followed Yrwen into his room and closed the door.

Cook cut to the chase, speaking in hush tones. "You thought about what I said?"

"I have," Yrwen said, then nodded to the door.

"Good. Then let's get the fuck out of here."

"Wait, we need to meet up with the others."

Cook cut him a look. "Who'd you tell?"

"No one," Yrwen said as he filled his wallet with as much cash as it could hold and stuffed his pockets with rations. "It was Shadowstone's idea."

"Gate Master Shadowstone?" Cook said with a brow up.

"Yes. He recruited Ark, who recruited me, and now, I'm recruiting you," Yrwen said, careful to keep his voice low.

"Shit," Cook said. "Well, we're fucking straight then. When and where?"

"Before the ceremony. I'll give you the exacts when I know—be ready," Yrwen said.

Cook grinned. "You don't have to tell me twice." She patted her gun at her side, then left Yrwen to make her own final arrangements.

Yrwen could feel his heartbeat. He had never even considered doing something like this. As a Cog, he could risk punishment, but he could feel it too—Mama Roach was right. There was something in the air, the stench of hunger and the lust for blood. It buzzed all around him; he could feel it on his skin.

Yrwen strategically hid the rations he'd stuffed on his person. He couldn't take a bag and risk looking like he was going to flee, so he could only take what he could hide in his suit jacket or pants.

He set off to work like normal. The day would be busy, with many orders coming in and out. Practically each member of the Five Families went all out during this event, and it cost The Silers millions. Yrwen made his way towards the cafeteria for breakfast when he saw a few Cogs walking briskly in the opposite direction. All played it cool, but Yrwen could clearly read the fear behind their eyes.

Yrwen had just turned his stare back toward the cafeteria when Hollow burst through the doors. He flashed one glaring look at Yrwen and raised his hands to attack. Yrwen froze, and a green tendril of light burst past him and struck something behind him.

"Got you!" Hollow growled and pushed his way past Yrwen.

Duke followed, along with some other Yield loyalist. Yrwen turned calmly around to look at who it was and found two Siler runners on the ground writhing in pain. Bags of fruit and bread spilled from their clothes and pockets onto the stone floor. Hollow smashed it all with his feet as the two runners screamed, their eyes turning blue and light erupting from every orifice as their souls exploded and died. Then their bodies began to rapidly rot. Hollow's specialty.

"Treacherous scum," Hollow spat before walking off down the tunnel.

Other Yield members started shaking up Cogs in the immediate area, harassing them with questions and threats. Yrwen simply turned toward the cafeteria because that's what you were supposed to do. Appearing shocked or appalled often made you look guilty or like a sympathizer. That was a lot of runner's problems—they thought their fellow Silers respected their humanity. The Cogs knew better.

Yrwen scarfed down as many nutrient-rich oats as his tiny stomach could hold and left for work as normal. In the shadows, he noticed Cogs who were discreetly not following the script. Cogs were fleeing, and they were much better at it than the runners. All Yrwen needed to do was play the part, and he would have his turn later today.

That evening, Yrwen received a bit of important information he had to tell Vincent. Maybe he could change his mind this time.

Vincent never really cared about defectors. He only looked down on them if they got caught. But Yrwen made his way to the ceremony hall one last time, hoping and praying that his friend would listen to him just this once.

Yrwen found Vincent in the ceremony hall three stories below ground. In this exact spot, four stories below, the Five Families kept the beast. Vincent had a cigarette pressed to his dark brown lips and took a long drag. Yrwen detested smoking, but the ease it washed over Vincent's face made Yrwen glad for it.

"You know, you should really cut back," Yrwen said as the servants around them fruitlessly tried to liven up the dull concrete room with wreaths and drapes.

Vincent pulled the cigarette from his lips and turned his deep brown eyes onto Yrwen. Yrwen couldn't help but study Vincent's face, committing it to memory like a painting. He loved the way his short, dark, wavy hair fell around his face, blemished only by the metal plate embedded into the side of his skull. He loved this man, and it burned him up inside to know that he may never get a chance to be around him again.

"Yrwen. Here to count the inventory?" Vincent put out his cigarette with his finger and tucked it into his coat pocket.

"More or less," Yrwen said as his gaze flickered upward to where the cage would be. Yrwen could feel the beast from all the way up here; he couldn't explain it, but his skin tingled with unease.

Vincent smirked as he shook his head. He turned and walked toward the grand altar where the ceremony would take place, and Yrwen followed. The entire ceremony was completely automated. No one from the Five Families had to lift a finger, thanks to Dr. Granite and his family. At the altar sat a golden crank that only activated when the gear ring was inserted. All it needed was the blood, completely drained, of a three-year-old child, and once again, the beast would be sealed.

A servant walked up behind Vincent and bowed their head. "Should we bring up the beast?" they asked.

Vincent shrugged. "Do as you please."

The servant nodded, then dashed away. Vincent and Yrwen stepped back as the floor started to rumble. Metal screeched and clanked as the gears in the ground moved the concrete. Two large half-circle concrete slabs opened to reveal a deep, dark, circular pit. Immediately, the room was flooded with the smell of death. Neither of them flinched, but servants were ready with hoses and buckets of incense to freshen the thing up.

The gears turned and cranked up the large concrete platform, and soon, the top of a gold cage slowly made its appearance. Yrwen struggled not to take a step back. There it was, that feeling of dread and fear, but it wasn't coming from the beast. It was coming from him. Something about just looking at the beast ignited a terror in his heart. Couldn't Vincent feel that, too? Yrwen shot him a look, but of course, his Vincent stared on impassively. Nothing could shake that man, and that's what Yrwen loved about him.

Inside the cage was the sickly matted fur of the beast. It was bound by its arms, body, and legs, and it groaned as its poor eyesight adjusted to the new surroundings. Above it was the key gate the Five Families used to harness its never-ending flow of magic. Dozens of mosquito-like tendrils fed on its life force, even now.

Servants who couldn't bear the smell coughed and gagged as rats scurried from its body across the floor, dashing quickly to the vents on the side of the room. Above the cage was a black metal platform where armed runners inspected the living corpse, their guns at their waist, just in case someone tried to pull something. The ceremony was taking place at six this evening, and the Five Families were expecting everything to go perfectly as planned.

Vincent pulled a crowned-shaped rose gold ring from his coat pocket and eyed it. A servant appeared by his side, but Vincent turned them away. He walked towards the altar, placed the ring on a plush red pillow, and secured it in a locked golden cage.

This one small piece of jewelry was the trigger for all this grief. Sometimes, it was impossible to think such a trivial thing could cause such an uproar, but he hoped for Vincent's sake it would be enough to seal the creature once more.

"Shall I send a few runners out for Mary?" Yrwen asked. "Technically, she did not complete her task by midnight."

Vincent held up his hand, withdrawing his cigarette from his coat pocket. "Don't bother. Doctor Acknid did an excellent job, as expected, so I'll let this slide. We'll call it a New Year's miracle."

Yrwen nodded, but really, he didn't care if Mary lived or died. "I also have news pertaining to Doctor Acknid."

"Hmm?" Vincent hummed as he took a long hit from his cigarette.

"It would appear a woman connected to the ring thieves is a powerful caster. Her power far surpassed what Doctor Acknid was able to defend against. He is alive but gravely injured, and he warns not to underestimate this threat."

Vincent inhaled and exhaled the smoke slowly. "Hmm, alright. Prepare my suit."

Yrwen stared Vincent in the eyes. He wasn't serious, was he? "Are you sure?"

Vincent shrugged. “My job is to see to it that this goes on without interruption. If a problem arises this time, I’ll take care of it myself.” Those words stunned Yrwen, and Vincent noticed, raising an eyebrow. “Something wrong?”

“No,” Yrwen answered in heartbreaking defeat. “I’ll prepare your suit at once.”

Yrwen turned to leave, knowing he should not have been surprised by Vincent’s reaction. What was he expecting? That Vincent was going to give this all up and run away with him? And yet...

Yrwen stopped. The pain in his chest was too much. He turned to face Vincent again and opened his mouth to say something but couldn’t bring himself to utter a word.

“You clearly have something on your mind. Come on, spill it.”

Yrwen tried to maintain eye contact, but his heart was shattering. “I just have a feeling that something is...off.”

Vincent chuckled. “I’m the Siler’s number one guy, and I never fail.”

“Of course.” Yrwen nodded as he breathed in a shaky breath, but his gaze lingered on Vincent. “You know...if this is becoming too tiresome, it’s not too late—”

“You worry too much, dear friend,” Vincent said as he led the way.

“You’re right.” Yrwen followed and watched Vincent’s back with tears building up behind his eyes.

After Yrwen prepared Vincent’s suit, he found himself a quiet place to uncoil his tucked-away emotions. He sobbed in the shadows of a supply room, knowing he would never see his Vincent again, even if everything went right. His best friend, his crush. He’d always been in love with Vincent, ever since they first met those many years ago. *His* Vincent was the type to never give up or give in, no matter how banged up or bruised, but he was also surprisingly gentle when it came to his friends, and they became fast friends as Yrwen was known to be a good nurse.

It was always Yrwen who looked after Vincent when he returned from a mission injured, and Vincent in turned kept the worse of the Silers off Yrwen. That’s how he fell so deeply in love, but Vincent was an aromantic asexual, and Yrwen always knew he needed to respect that. Even when it was hard, so very hard, when he loved Vincent more than life itself.

A memory of a young Vincent flashed in his mind. *“Always, always put yourself first. Make it to the top so that no one can step on you. You hear me?”*

Yrwen remember nodding then but never taking those words to heart. Now, it was time to move on. It was time that Yrwen put himself first.

7

Three hours before the ceremony, Ark and Shadowstone stood patiently in the back tunnels of Gomi City on the eighth level of Sewer Town, waiting for Yrwen. Ark was grateful Shadowstone didn't protest when he said he was bringing two more along. Leadership in The Yield was in shambles, with loyalists and detractors fighting. Most, if not all, the runners were prepping or being stationed around the ceremony above and below ground. As it stood, all orders and all punishments would have to wait until the key renewal was complete, meaning that this was their only chance for a successful escape.

Shadowstone looked better after Ark worked his magic. That rest put him in a far better condition, and if Ark had time to give himself praise, he would feel quite proud of himself. Earlier in the day, Ark managed to pass the location information onto Yrwen, who relayed to him that he would be bringing his debt collector friend along. It didn't matter to Ark as long as he had Yrwen.

He wasn't sure the exact moment he knew that everything he had belonged to Yrwen, but maybe it was the realization that his entire life was built on a house of cards. Now shattered, he could see that the only real part of his life was the man who was always polite and patient with him, and if he lost Yrwen, he would be losing himself.

To avoid suspicion from other Yield members and their command, Ark and Shadowstone wore their full outfits—the black tunics and black pants covered by their floor-length royal purple robes—and stalked around pretending to hunt for detractors. It had worked as most sewer folks knew exactly who they were and stayed away. Runners did the same, and Yield members quickly straightened up, under their orders, to look for detractors, even if they weren't going to do anything to anyone if they found out they were fleeing. It was best to pretend to align with Hollow's orders.

Ark heard footsteps coming down the tunnel and tensed, but when two figures came into view, he immediately jogged to his Yrwen.

"Ark," Yrwen said as Ark embraced him. They shared a kiss, not caring who saw.

Shadowstone stood. "We ready?"

"Yes," Ark said, and Shadowstone led the way.

Ark was grateful Yrwen's friend didn't ask a lot of questions. He knew how Shadowstone could get; he wasn't always a patient man. Heading out of the city through the old tunnels was risky if one didn't know the route. This part of Sewer Town had suffered the most from collapses due to poor infrastructure. Ark himself had caught a few defectors this way, but he trusted Shadowstone.

The group slushed through ankle-deep water, then came to a stop at a small tunnel only big enough to crawl through.

"There." Shadowstone pointed, then got down on all fours and started to make his way in.

Everyone followed without question. The shallow water soaked their clothes and robes, but Ark didn't care. They needed to reach the edge of the city as soon as possible and head to the river to make their escape. It was easier by boat; the runners who worked there could be easily bought off, and Ark had packed a few sacks of ao almasi gems to sweeten the deal.

They came to an end and found themselves in another water-filled tunnel tall enough to walk through. Shadowstone took them up a set of stone steps, and they climbed until they reached the fifth level. Shadowstone suddenly stopped, and Ark leaned in to ask what was up, but Shadowstone cut him off with a look. Above them was the big sorting plant; they would be running into more crowds, and crowds meant unwanted attention. Many Siler runners didn't know The Yield had members in common clothes who could report back. If any Yield member spotted them this far out, it would definitely expose their plan. They needed to avoid the biggest of the crowds and find a path with a large enough outfall out of the city.

Shadowstone started up again and chose a route around the sorting plant on level four and found just what Ark was thinking about: a large culvert that drained into one of the swamps outside of the city. Normally, they didn't check this way because, unless you knew the route, it was impossible to get to. Water didn't even drain here; the lines had all but collapsed. So it was completely dry.

Shadowstone dashed forward, fully stealth. They were nearly in the clear when Shadowstone jumped back as a blaze of fire landed in the spot where he was just standing. Yrwen and Cook backed away from the flames as Ark tore his eyes around.

"You can come out now!"

Fear sparked in Ark's heart, and Shadowstone cursed. "Hollow."

"What do we do?" Ark shoved his fear aside, turning on his strategic brain. If it was Hollow, they could fight him, but Yrwen and his friend Cook could not.

"Fight." Shadowstone walked forward towards the light.

Ark cursed, then turned to the others. "Hang back," he whispered.

"You don't have to tell us twice," Cook said in a low voice.

"Be careful," Yrwen whispered.

"Shadowstone?" Ark could hear the surprise in Hollow's voice, then Ark made his presence known as well. "Ark!"

Hollow's eyes were piercing with anger. Behind him was Duke, his eyes still bandaged, and about five other Yield members. Hollow's fury radiated off him like an old wood stove, and he was directing all of it at Ark.

"Why am I not surprised?" Hollow growled. "Fucking selling out your body to Cogs, your hesitation, all clear signs of your weakness. And you, Shadowstone... You dare align yourself with such worthless trash?"

"I align myself with any who match my goals," Shadowstone said coldly.

Hollow scoffed. "Well, if your goal is to die, then I can grant you both that wish. I'm going to slaughter you both and then rip apart that slut Cog you like to fuck afterward."

Ark growled, but Shadowstone was the one who charged for Hollow first. Both necromancers pulled great tendrils of energy from their key gates as they fought in the dried dirt of the outfall pond. Ark focused on Duke and the other five Yield members.

"You don't have to do this!" Ark said to all of them, but still, the Yield members charged forward.

Ark summoned his key gate, and bright orange tendrils of power shot from the door and into his right arm. Ark readied his spell and fired three fatal bolts of electricity at the Yield members, killing three of them instantly. The other two held back, but that gave Duke enough time to ready his keys. Duke manipulated the shadows, creating claws that tried to pin Ark down, but Ark knew all his tricks. He used his light to keep Duke's shadows at bay.

"Duke! Duke, listen to me!" Ark said. "You don't have to do this."

But all the old man did was grunt and fight harder. Ark could tell, based on his movements, that Duke was fighting in a panic. His control of the shadows was sloppy, but he also needed to maintain focus on his mind awareness so he could see. All this drama with Hollow hadn't even allowed him to have a proper eye transfer.

"Duke! Listen! We can get out of here, put an end to this," Ark pleaded as he jumped and dodged Duke's reckless attacks.

"You must think I'm a fool! I won't be going anywhere with you!" Duke growled.

Ark clenched his teeth. Already, he saw the cracks in Duke's facade. The man may have had the advantage of age, but Ark's younger and better-rested body had the stamina. Sweat built on Duke's brow, attack after attack. He saw the fluctuations in his tendrils. Duke teaming up with Hollow meant that he was using his magic nonstop, not to mention the magic he used in overdrive to be able to see as well. Ark's gate hummed with hunger. It knew what Ark's heart refused to do.

Ark then thought of Yrwen and his friend. If Duke wasn't smart enough to choose himself, then so be it. But it would still break his heart.

I'm so sorry, Iron; I couldn't protect you. And I'm sorry to you, Duke. Please forgive me. Ark closed his eyes for a brief second as Duke recklessly charged at him with another bite less attack. Ark reached for his power, and his hungry tendrils obeyed. He fired a bolt of lightning at Duke's heart, and the muscle exploded in his chest. Duke fell, and Ark cut a look at the other two Yield members, who inched back in fear. *Good*, Ark thought. *No one else should have to die here today.*

Ark turned to Hollow and Shadowstone. Despite the level of exhaustion Duke displayed, Hollow appeared to be the opposite. His rage and grief must have fueled him because he was going toe to toe with Shadowstone. Ark needed to help him.

"Shadowstone!" Hollow growled. "I know you can do better than this!"

Hollow shot balls of light gray energy at the ground, turning it black with rot. He was just as reckless as Duke but only ten times more powerful. Shadowstone dodged and danced around, fending off purple balls of fire where he could. Then Ark heard noise coming from the culvert. Yrwen was climbing down, and Ark gasped. Cook appeared next, gun in hand. She shot two Yield members dead. Someone must have called reinforcements, and it would only be a matter of time before they were surrounded.

Ark cut a look to Yrwen, who was hiding instinctively. Ark needed to end this now.

Ark readied his bolts and fired at Hollow, drawing his rage towards him.

"Slimy bastard!" Hollow shouted. "I'll rip you apart!"

Hollow rushed towards Ark while dodging Shadowstone's flame attacks. Ark blocked him with a wall of electricity, sending him into the ground. Hollow growled as he landed amongst the corpses of his fallen men, but then suddenly Hollow was back on his feet. He sent his light gray tendrils of power into the skulls of Duke and one of the Yield members, cracking open their heads.

"Shit!" Ark rushed to stop him, but Hollow fired a ball of rot his way, and he had to dodge it.

With the brains of his fellows exposed, Hollow ate the flesh of his followers, thus gaining the techniques they mastered. Ark cursed. This wasn't a power Ark wanted to go up against. Hollow roared with rage, now able to control the shadows and shoot fireballs. He tore into them both, and Ark and Shadowstone struggled to hold him back. Usually, this rotten power only lasted for an hour or so, but there was no way Ark and Shadowstone could hold him back for an entire hour.

A fireball singed Ark's leg, catching his robes on fire. Ark quickly tossed them off, not realizing that he left his shadow unprotected. Hollow grabbed him by his shadow's leg and threw him against the stone rim of the culvert. Ark gasped as he felt his ribs break, then cursed when he saw Cook and Yrwen looking at him. One of the remaining Yield members took their chance then to attack Ark when he was down, but Cook shot him between the eyes. Blood colored the ground, and Ark was genuinely surprised. She was a good shot.

"T-thanks," Ark said.

"Don't mention it." Cook grinned. "Now, get your ass up and get us out of here."

Ark smirked and started to stand. He could still fight.

Shadowstone and Hollow exchanged fire attacks, scorching the ground around them. One of Hollow's rot attacks killed the remaining Yield member who got too close. The man's eyes went bright blue as his soul was destroyed and his body melted away, and it didn't even seem like Hollow cared one bit.

Ark needed to end this. He called forth his power and shot a net of electricity at Hollow. It landed, but Hollow broke through it with his flames. He was acting recklessly; it didn't seem like he even wanted to protect his life. He was pushing his magic and himself to the limit.

Shadowstone pulled back and Ark jumped in, hot orange lightning and purple flames combined into one attack, but Hollow captured Shadowstone's shadow and threw him back. Ark cursed, but already, Hollow was upon him.

"I should have killed you along with Iron!" Hollow seethed.

"I would have liked to see you try," Ark bit back.

Suddenly, Hollow was yanked back. "What the?" Hollow cursed.

Ark looked around him and was shocked to see Duke, with his head split open, standing behind him. His arm was outstretched, his power to control shadows fixed on Hollow.

"What the hell!" Hollow growled.

Shadowstone stood some feet away with a dozen lavender-colored orbs floating around him. He shot one of the orbs into the corpse of another fallen Yield member, bringing them back from the dead, too. Ark gasped. Shadowstone used bits of his soul to raise the dead, and it was going to kill him.

Duke's risen corpse tightened its shadow power around Hollow's arms and torso as the other risen Yield member lifted their hand and called forth thorny plants from the ground. Hollow growled and foamed at the mouth as he kicked his legs around.

The thorns grew and became thicker until they found an opening in Hollow's backside and worked themselves in. Hollow screamed in terror as the thorns twisted and shredded his insides before exiting through his mouth. Ark stood there shocked as Hollow's body went limp, and then all three of the corpses dropped. Shadowstone fell to one knee. Ark had to blink himself back to reality, but then he remembered how much power Shadowstone had used.

Ark ran towards him. Shadowstone had just risen two corpses. Raising even one without the protection of an amplifying crystal was dangerous enough.

"Shadowstone!" Ark kneeled at his side.

"I'm fine," Shadowstone said through gritted teeth as the lavender orbs shrunk and found their place around his waist as beads.

"You're not fine," Ark said as he heard two others approach. He looked to Yrwen and Cook.

"I...I said I'm fine." Shadowstone started to stand, and upon further inspection, Ark could not see the black lines of damage often found in the veins of magic users who went too far. It really looked like he was okay. But how?

Ark was just about to ask when suddenly, a blast of electricity hit them all. Everyone flew back and hit the ground. Ark gasped and jerked his head around to see three Yield members coming down from the culvert.

"Shit," Ark cursed but then remembered Yrwen.

He looked for his love and found him a crumpled mess on the ground. Shadowstone, too, seemed stunned. Ark raced to his feet and reached for his tendrils of magic. Hungry, the bright orange bolts of lightning were ready to do his bidding. He fired shots from his right hand, killing two instantly, and then a gunshot rang out. Ark froze but realized it had come from his side. Cook had gotten off another shot—right in the eye.

"Cook," Ark said, and she returned his greeting with a shaky smile.

She was clearly injured. Cogs did not have the best health to begin with, so Ark needed to work fast. He rushed to Yrwen's side first. He was alive but barely. He reached for his magic and poured his tendrils into Yrwen's body, training them to hunt any injury they found. He did this for Yrwen and Cook at the same time, overextending himself to save their lives. Then, through gritted teeth, he noticed the gash on Shadowstone's head from a large stone in the grass. Powerful necromancer or not, a hit to the head was still fatal.

Ark screamed as he demanded more of his power to come forth. He then shot a third beam of magic into Shadowstone, pushing his own body beyond his limit. He felt all his magic being used up, and it started to reach into his soul as a secondary energy source, but Ark couldn't quit. More Yield members would be on the way. Not to mention the overall health of Yrwen and Cook; they were Cogs, and they already needed to be careful about their bodies. Ark pushed and pushed; he felt the heat of damage on his skin. Already, his veins were turning black, but he was almost there.

With one final push, his tendrils pulsed. They had their fill, meaning their work was done. Ark pulled back and collapsed to his knees. His vision was blurry as he slowly fell to the ground.

"Ark..." a voice echoed from far away, and then everything went black.

Yrwen

8

Yrwen rushed to Ark's side and cradled his head in his lap. Ark had given too much—that was plain to see by the black veins on his neck and hand. Yrwen trembled as Cook walked to him, and Shadowstone struggled to get up as well. Ark was knocked out cold, though, and there was no telling when he would wake up.

"We need to get moving," Cook said gently, with a hand extended, but they both knew they couldn't carry Ark like this.

Shadowstone was on his feet and looking down at them all. He didn't make a move or say a word as if he were doing the math in his head. This angered Yrwen.

"Aren't you going to help?" Yrwen snapped.

"Yrwen..." Cook reached out again as if to warn him about his tone.

As Cogs, they were never allowed to be demanding. They were always trained to be calm and friendly, always in the background, ready to serve. Shadowstone cut Yrwen a glare, but Yrwen did not back down.

"He saved your life," Yrwen hissed.

Shadowstone stared at them, then let out an exasperated sigh. "I could very well leave you to die, but if the payment for my life is nothing more than an assist, I suppose I can help."

Yrwen softened, back into his usual compliant self. They really couldn't afford to stop now. Soon, the ceremony would be over, and all Yield members would be sent on a witch hunt for defectors. Cook and Yrwen helped haul Ark onto Shadowstone's back, and they made their way to the docks. The walk was long, but Shadowstone seemed to know the way. And when they ran into others, neither party said a word, even though it worried Yrwen when they encountered other Yield members or Silers. But everyone kept to themselves. Any member this far out of the city only wanted one thing: to escape with their families and their lives.

Shadowstone flagged them down an old steam car, paying the seller three times its value. They drove until they made it to the big river that many merchants used. Yrwen and Cook took care of buying off the runners there, who took their money without fuss. And now they had a small gas-powered dory. Shadowstone and Cook helped place Ark in the boat, and Cook stepped on board as Yrwen paid the runners a little extra for food and water.

"We're heading to Septland New Nation," Cook said. "You wanna come?"

Shadowstone stretched and rubbed his shoulders as he stood on the dock. "This is where we part."

Yrwen eyed him, but it was Cook who seemed the most surprised. "You going by foot or something? Pilar Town really ain't that bad."

"It's okay, Cook," Yrwen said, then turned to Shadowstone. "Thank you for your help."

Shadowstone grunted. "Payment complete."

Cook opened and closed her mouth but said nothing more when, as they parted, a runner walked over to talk to Shadowstone. It would seem he had made some arrangements of his own. Yrwen finished placing their food and water in the dory and got in. Cook looked at him, but Yrwen said nothing more as he started up the engine and pulled off. Yrwen looked back one last time, watching Shadowstone prepare his own boat.

"Do you really think it's okay to part ways like that?" Cook asked.

"Yes," Yrwen said unceremoniously. It was clear Shadowstone was a powerful necromancer. He could look after himself.

"Okay." Cook didn't say another word.

Yrwen let out a sigh and pushed the dory to its max, jetting off into the night. They were out of the city now; all they needed to do was cross the border, and they would be safe. All that remained was waiting for Ark to rest up so that when he awoke, he could remove the tracking spell placed on all Siler members, and then they would be truly free.

A few hours into their journey, the trio found themselves in the dark. Cook found a small kerosine lamp and offered to light it, but Yrwen warned against it until they reached the edge of the country. It was dark but not pitch black. Dotted on the river's edge were little ports and towns where fishing boats or ferries docked. It was dark, so no one could tell whether they were friend or foe, but Yrwen knew they would need new clothes at their next stop. Cook helped steer the dory as Yrwen looked back and saw the magnificent light of the hilltop city of Uptown. It was beautiful, but suddenly, the city erupted into a ball of brilliant blue light.

"For all the glory!" Cook gasped as they watched a huge blue wave roll down the hill into the city. The shockwave of it all seemed to hit the entire area. "Hold on!"

Their boat rocked with the powerful wave that rolled through them. Yrwen looked at the city again and thought he saw a giant beast, but as quickly as it appeared, it disappeared in a cloud of bright blue smoke. Then, there was darkness again.

"What was that?" Cook asked, but Yrwen didn't have an answer.

Mama Roach was right. Something terrible had happened.

"Vincent..." Yrwen uttered.

"Yo, Yrwen, look up!"

Yrwen looked up, and to his shock, the permanent clouds that had covered the sky dissipated into a vast, dark, sparkling sky. Yrwen had never in his entire life seen anything so beautiful.

"Sta-stars..." Ark gasped, and both Yrwen and Cook turned to him. "They-they're called stars...".

"I...I don't..." Yrwen tried to say that he didn't understand, but then he felt Ark's thumb rubbing his leg.

"The-the souls of the spirits," Ark spoke between gasps. "Stars."

Yrwen hummed. He didn't need to ask questions. He just sat back in the boat with his friends and enjoyed it.

9

Epilogue

Summer in Pilar Town Septland New Nation

Yrwen could say without a doubt he would never get used to the radiant power of the sun. Even with his deeply melanated skin, it was exhausting being in the heat. By the time he left his day job as a bookkeeper to an import company, he was ready to crawl into bed with his lover. Cook did good in picking this city. The Silers did a lot of business with the importers here, but no more. Word spread that something big had happened in Julilie. It was all over the papers; the government had collapsed. There were talks of blue titans and vengeful spirits walking the Earth once more. But it was all pure speculation as it related to the people here on the coast, and once the importers stopped getting the business they were used to from Julilie, they moved on. Not that Yrwen cared anymore.

Ark, who now went by his birth name Howard, had taken a job as a dock worker, working in the field office as a medic. He chose not to replace his left arm; he was done harvesting body parts and organs, and he did just fine with one arm. He was now free to do as he pleased, and he wanted to help people instead of slaughtering them.

Yrwen stopped by the tavern Cook worked at to fill his canteen when a man brushed past him."Outta my way, bone man," the burly sailor said, and Yrwen obliged.

Even now, Yrwen never saw the point of getting into fistfights. Whatever someone wanted—as long as it wasn't his money, his body, or his life—they could have. What did Yrwen care?

"Hey! Piss pants," Cook shouted to the man. "Pick back up those manners you dropped at the door, or have your cock blown off. Choice is yours."

Cook had her gun trained on the man, and he tightened up real quick. Yrwen smiled as he walked past the man to the bar. Turns out the tavern had a small problem with unruly sailors, and Cook gladly offered them a solution.

"In for water, Yrwen?" Cook said.

"You know me so well," Yrwen said.

"Star!" A young bar maiden rushed out. "Peary dropped a big crate in the back. Do you know where the soap is?"

Cook turned to the girl, who she had a big crush on, and said, "Daisy, baby, it's in the back closet."

Daisy smiled and rewarded Cook with a kiss. She was the only one who could call Cook by her birth name, a name that seemed to have no origin until they arrived here. Cook filled Yrwen's canteen, and Yrwen promised to return for dinner. That was their routine. Work and then dinner in the tavern, and Yrwen didn't mind at all.

He walked the rest of the way home, wishing that he'd taken his motor bike instead, but Howard said he needed the exercise. Yrwen disagreed, but he couldn't argue with a healer. Yrwen opened the door and found Howard had beaten him home.

"Yrwen," Howard said. "You're home early."

"Me?" Yrwen walked to their dining table and leaned on it. "*You're* home early."

Howard smiled and rescued Yrwen from having to hold himself up. He really was so tired. Howard kissed his neck, awaking something else in Yrwen. Something he was sure he could find the energy for.

"How was work?" Howard asked.

"Easy enough." Yrwen pulled away to look into his man's beautiful light brown eyes. "I still can't believe we made it."

Howard hummed as he leaned in to kiss his neck again.

"I wonder if Shadowstone found his way," Yrwen asked.

"Oh, I'm sure he did," Howard said, pulling back. "He was the only one who mastered the old magic. I can see that now."

"You think so?" Yrwen led him from the kitchen to their bedroom.

"Mmhmm." Howard followed from behind, wrapping his right arm around Yrwen's chest as he kissed on Yrwen's neck. "He's probably the reason any of us survived."

"Oh?" Yrwen turned and faced Howard, who pulled him to the bed. Yrwen fell on top of him.

"Yes, I'm sure of it now." Howard captured his lips for a searing kiss, then looked at Yrwen seriously. "I'm sure he always had a backup plan. He just needed help because he was weakened from the forging. Otherwise, he probably could have killed Hollow at full strength. In fact, I'm certain Shadowstone was the one who saved everyone that night," Howard said as if he were working the idea around in his mind. "We were fools to listen to Master Granite. I'm sure Shadowstone knew that, too."

Yrwen nodded and decided he no longer wanted to worry about that. For the first time in all of his thirty years, he was free.

Howard reached up a hand and ran it through Yrwen's long, thin, jet-black hair, then pulled him closer and captured his mouth once more. This new life, this wonderful life with Howard, was more than Yrwen could have ever asked for. Even though, from time to time, his heart still ached for the man he had to leave behind, he knew that he would heal in his own time. And he would never go back to being a cog to anyone ever again.

Afterword

Thank you so very much for picking up *The Crimson Mouse*. I hope you enjoyed the story. While Mia's story maybe over, there is still more stories to come that take place in this wonderful world I've created. I invite you to check out the two short novellas *The Black Gate* and *The Drum and The Crane;* as well as the novel *The Siren, The Prince, and The Lover* when they become available.

If you enjoyed the story, feel free to leave a review wherever you have purchased the book, and on Goodreads as well. Reviews are one of the biggest ways you can help support an author, and I'd love to hear from you.

Thanks again and take care,

Blair

To keep up with all the latest news, I invite you to join my mailing list.

subscribepage.io/thecrimsonmouse

About the author

Blair Cousins is the author of the science fiction trilogy *Ceapeaya's Awakening* and publisher of *A Day in the Life of Cats* coloring book series. She is a writer of many science fiction, fantasy, and horror stories. In her free time she enjoys traveling and costume making, and is always hungry to write the next exciting story.

www.ingramcontent.com/pod-product-compliance
Lightning Source LLC
Chambersburg PA
CBHW020456310726
48979CB00016B/2676/J
* 9 7 8 1 9 6 2 8 6 6 0 2 6 *